Praise for the novels of
New York Times bestselling author Brenda Novak

"The best romantic thriller I have read.... Novak has a raw talent for bringing her novels to life. Realistic, suspenseful, and an edge of your seat romance that will have readers coming back for more."
—*San Francisco Book Review* on *The Secret Sister*

"One needn't wonder why Novak is a *New York Times* and *USA TODAY* bestselling author. Just read *Come Home to Me*."
—*Examiner.com*

"The past impacts the present with devastating but ultimately salutary results in this engrossing, character-rich story that takes a hard look at responsibility, loyalty, and the results of telling (or concealing) the truth."
—*Library Journal* on *Home to Whiskey Creek*

"It's steamy, it's poignant, it's perfectly paced—it's *When Lightning Strikes* and you don't want to miss it!"
—*USATODAY.com's Happy Ever After* blog

"Gripping, frightening, and intense...a compelling romance as well as a riveting and suspenseful mystery... Novak delivers another winner."
—*Library Journal* on *The Perfect Liar*

"Strong characters bring the escalating suspense to life, and the mystery is skillfully played out. Novak's smooth plotting makes for a great read."
—*Publishers Weekly* on *Dead Right*

"Impressive! This is a sharp-edged, well-plotted story that showcases Novak's superb storytelling skill."
—*RT Book Reviews* on *Dead Giveaway*

Also by Brenda Novak

And look for
BEFORE WE WERE STRANGERS,
coming soon from MIRA Books.

BRENDA NOVAK

THE SECRETS SHE KEPT

mira

mira

ISBN-13: 978-0-7783-3082-0

The Secrets She Kept

Copyright © 2016 by Brenda Novak, Inc.

THE
SECRETS
SHE KEPT

To all families who aren't quite perfect...

1

The call came in the middle of the night. Keith Lazarow was so deeply asleep that he probably wouldn't have heard his phone if not for the attractive brunette who stirred in bed beside him.

"Aren't you going to answer that?" she mumbled.

"No." He was too exhausted. Five years ago, he'd replaced the drugs he'd once used to anesthetize himself against the demons of his past with daily cross-fit training. High-intensity exercise was the only thing that could command his full focus and calm his mind. It forced the anger and resentment back into the shadows so he could be functional instead of destructive. But once he'd left the gym, Dahlia Dooley—someone he'd met at a charity event downtown last week—had called and asked to come over, and after that, he'd put in a completely different sort of workout. After expending *that* much energy, he felt he could sleep for a week, which was nice, since he used to have trouble sleeping at all.

Dahlia rolled onto her other side and, seconds later, his phone stopped making noise.

He'd just begun to sink back into blissful oblivion when the buzzing started again.

Dahlia yawned. "There must be something wrong at work."

No, he didn't have anything to worry about there. He wasn't a policeman or a medical health professional; he was in real estate. Over the last five years, he'd acquired quite a collection of large commercial properties—office buildings, warehouses, shopping malls and strip centers. But he had property managers as well as project managers to take care of his holdings. If there was a problem, *those* were the people who'd be getting disturbed after hours, not him. He handled acquisitions, which was the fun part, and he had nothing particularly important on the horizon—nothing that he might get a panic call about, anyway. Whatever this was, it could wait until he'd had his wheatgrass juice in the morning and was ready to turn on his computer.

Unless…

He shot up in bed and grabbed for his phone. Sure enough, it was his sister Maisey calling from South Carolina. They'd always been close, but these days she had her husband, Rafe, who did such a good job of loving Maisey; his daughter, Laney; and Bryson, the two-year-old boy they'd had together, that Keith never worried about them. He and Maisey spoke on the phone every week, and she'd flown out to visit him three or four times since he left Fairham Island—twice with her family—but she never called in the middle of the night.

Something had to be wrong…

His stomach cramped at the thought.

With a curse, he gazed at the LED screen while trying to collect his faculties.

When he continued to let it ring, Dahlia mumbled, "What is it?"

Suddenly wishing she'd gone home instead of staying over, he looked at her tousled head. "Nothing. Go back to sleep. I'll take it in the study."

Lord knew his house was big enough to provide him with plenty of privacy. Nestled in the Santa Monica Mountains overlooking Malibu, where he had a gorgeous view of the ocean, the ten-bedroom rambler had once belonged to Robert De Niro. The place was way too big for a man who lived alone, and coming here every night meant he added a time-consuming commute to his day. A condo downtown would've been more efficient and would've suited him just as well, since he rarely entertained. But he supposed he was still trying to prove to his megalomaniac mother that he really *didn't* need the fortune she'd held over his head for so long.

Who would've guessed he'd be as adept at making money as his beloved grandfather?

No one. Until he'd walked away from the Coldiron empire and everything he stood to gain by staying, and started making it on his own, even *he* would never have dreamed he had it in him. After winning his first million as a professional poker player, which required no education at all—a good thing, since he hadn't paid attention while he was getting his degree in communications—he'd invested in real estate, where he earned even more money—so much that he eventually quit poker, other than the odd charity tournament now and then.

Before he could pull on a pair of pajama bottoms and move to a room where he felt comfortable speaking to

Maisey, the call transferred to voice mail. He waited to see if she'd leave a message, give him some indication of what was going on, so he'd be prepared when he talked to her. But she didn't.

"Come on, Mais," he muttered and called her back.

"*There* you are," she said, sounding tense, breathless, as if she'd panicked when she couldn't reach him.

He tried to control his own anxiety. "You're surprised I didn't answer right away? Gee, I wonder why I didn't. Could it be that it's *four o'clock in the morning*?"

"I'm sorry."

He regretted his sarcasm when she didn't come back at him with her own smart-ass comment. "Don't worry about it," he said. "I was joking. What's going on?" Holding the phone that much tighter, he lowered his voice. "You okay?"

"I'm...fine, I think." Her voice broke, telling him that she wasn't fine at all.

His heart began to pound so hard his chest hurt. "Is it Rafe? Or the kids?" When Keith left Fairham Island, Maisey had been so in love with the building contractor and his blind little girl that Keith thought he could rely on his sister's happiness indefinitely. The confidence he'd had in Rafe was the only thing that had made it possible for him to turn his back on South Carolina without the guilt that would otherwise have dragged him back.

Well, knowing his sister was with a man she loved wasn't the *only* thing that had allowed him to escape. His life had always revolved around his autocratic mother and what he was supposed to do and be in order to honor his Coldiron heritage. Escaping the jaws of her expectations had required more grit and determination than he could ever have imagined. No way could he have done it without Maisey and Roxanne, his other sister. Their support had been constant and unwavering.

He owed them both a lot…

"They're fine, too—thank God." Maisey sniffed. "So are Roxanne and her family," she said, anticipating his next question.

Their oldest sister lived in Louisiana—and had lived there for most of her life, away from them. That in itself was a long story and should never have happened; it was yet another life-altering event he could blame on his mother. He was just glad they'd managed to find Roxanne when they did, because she'd added so much to his life.

He crossed to the window and stared out at the white, moonlit caps of the waves rolling toward the beach. Even in full daylight, he couldn't see the sand for all the trees and hills. But he wasn't studying his current surroundings. He was recalling another beach—the private beach below Coldiron House, the ostentatious Southern mansion where he'd been raised. "Then it must be Mom," he said with a fatalistic sigh.

"Yes."

Closing his eyes, he pressed his forehead to the cool glass. He'd known he'd have to face what he'd left behind eventually. Was he ready for whatever had happened to Josephine? Had he changed sufficiently to cope with what it might mean? Put enough safety nets in place to make sure he never slipped back into the darkness from which he'd so painstakingly climbed? "What's wrong with her?"

"She's dead, Keith."

The blood began to roar in his ears. *"What'd you say?"*

"It's true. She's gone. I'm so sorry. I know... I know how difficult this is going to be for you, how complicated your feelings about her have always been. Mine aren't any simpler. I hate that I had to wake you in the middle of the night, but I couldn't wait. I wanted you to know before...before you could see it on the news or...or someone else called."

LA could get cold in January. Feeling a sudden chill, Keith straightened and stepped away from the window. Most deaths, even of someone as wealthy and powerful as Josephine Lazarow, weren't reported on the national news—not unless foul play was involved. Was that what his sister was about to tell him?

"What happened?" he asked as he made his way to the desk and perched on the edge of the expensive leather chair his interior designer had claimed he'd love.

"When Pippa arrived an hour ago—"

"Wait," he broke in. "That'd be six your time."

"Yes..."

"Why was she coming so early? Mom's housekeepers have always arrived at eight." Even when his mother was running her flower shop instead of letting Nancy Dellinger do it, she didn't get out of bed until later. The shop didn't open until ten; she generally prepared the night before.

"Mom needed to be at the airport. She was planning a trip to see Hugh Pointer—a new love interest."

Of course. Since their father died, when he was twelve and Maisey was ten, Josephine had been through three marriages (after which she'd always gone back to the Lazarow name), and a long list of other relationships. Considering she could have just about anyone she wanted, there was nothing to stop her. Not only was she rich, she was beautiful.

Had been rich. *Had* been beautiful.

God, could he really be thinking of his strong, determined and often acerbic mother in the past tense?

"Hugh owns a pharmaceutical company, a ranch and a few other assets in Australia," Maisey was saying. "They've been dating, mostly online, for the past few months. She met him in first class the last time she flew to New York and she's been planning to go down under to see him ever since."

They'd been dating for *months*? Keith would know about Hugh if he and his sisters ever discussed his mother, but she was the one subject that was off-limits. They'd grown accustomed to pretending she didn't exist. Keith had insisted on it. She could trigger a relapse quicker than anyone or anything. "So Pippa was supposed to show up at the house before she'd usually appear to drive Mom to the airport."

"That's right." When Maisey paused, overcome by emotion, a lump rose in his own throat. But no tears followed. Something seemed to be jammed up; he *couldn't* cry. Where Josephine was concerned, he'd cut out his emotions almost as precisely as a surgeon might use a scalpel to remove a malignant tumor. He'd had to. Anything less was too painful.

"But…" he prompted when his sister couldn't continue.

He heard her gulp for breath, heard Rafe in the background speaking soft, soothing words.

"Mom wasn't waiting for her in the entry like she'd

said she'd be. And when Pippa went upstairs to see about the hold-up, she…she found her in the tub."

His mother often took long baths. They were part of her beauty regimen. She'd even had a TV installed in the bathroom. But why would she take a bath first thing in the morning, before heading to the airport? Why not use the shower, like she usually did to get ready for work? "She *drowned*?"

Another sniffle. "Apparently. There was a wine bottle and a…a glass that'd been knocked over, as well as s-some candles—"

"Then it must've happened last night," he said. "She wouldn't light candles first thing in the morning. She doesn't like getting up early. She was always in too much of a hurry."

"The coroner hasn't determined the time of death. He…he just arrived a little while ago. But I agree. Seems that way to me, too."

"So…they think it was an accident?"

She sniffed again. "They're not saying, Keith. They won't even let me in the house, won't let me see her. I don't understand what's going on. I only know that she's *dead*."

His sister ended with a sob—and still his eyes remained dry. "I'm sorry, Maisey."

That sounded so mechanical, but he was glad to feel numb. Numb beat the hell out of the devastation he could be feeling. He'd worked hard to overcome anything that made him weak or vulnerable.

"I don't want this to set you back," she said. "You've been doing so well. I—"

"I'll be fine. Don't worry about me." He hoped that was true. He didn't have the best track record…

Maisey continued to cry. "This is terrible. Mom would not have liked going out this way."

She must've been drunk, he thought. But how? She considered it gauche to have more than a single glass of wine in the evening. Unless things had changed more than he realized since he'd been gone, he couldn't see her imbibing too much, even when she was alone.

"Were her bags packed?" he asked.

"How am I supposed to know? I told you. The police won't let me in the house. All I can tell you is what they've told me."

Dropping his head into his free hand, he tried to imagine that the strong-willed, demanding person who'd been their mother was gone. *For good.* That she was completely out of his life, whether or not he wanted her to be.

What did that mean? And did it help or hurt his quest to remain whole and healthy and to keep moving forward with his life?

"Are you all right?" Maisey asked.

"Yeah. I just… I'm trying to come to terms with the news, that's all."

"It's a lot to take in. Don't let it…don't let it throw you, Keith."

Even after five years, she felt she had to worry about him. He was screwed up, had always been screwed up. He suspected that if he ever visited a psychologist he'd be diagnosed as bipolar. That term had been thrown around a great deal back when he was acting out. But he didn't want to hear a professional say those words, didn't want to be pumped full of medication—not as long as he could manage on his own. With cross-fit, his business and his sisters, he'd developed some coping skills. And they were working for him. "Don't worry. I'm not going to backslide." He was still taking it one day at a time, though, and this was a hurdle he hadn't expected—maybe in twenty years, but not this soon.

"Okay," she said. "I—I'd better go. I have to call Roxanne."

How would Roxanne react to the death of their mother? he wondered. She'd been kidnapped and raised by a former nanny. Roxanne had a dim recollection of what a tyrant Josephine could be, but she didn't have the memories and stories he and Maisey did. Since Roxanne had reconnected with Josephine, the two had built some semblance of a relationship. Roxanne probably got along with Josephine best, because she didn't feel the same resentment. Neither did she live close by. Staying a considerable distance away definitely helped.

Considering all of that, would Rocki be heartbroken by the news? Would at least *one* of Josephine's children be able to sincerely mourn her passing?

Or would even Roxanne be left to wonder if she was a horrible person for not experiencing more grief?

"I'll call you back as soon as I can give you more details," Maisey promised.

"Wait," he said. "What about Mom's Yorkie, Athena? Someone needs to take care of her."

"Pippa took her home, which is the best place for her. She doesn't get along with Laney's cat. Max would tear her to shreds. And Pippa pampers that little dog as much as Mom did."

He rubbed the goose bumps from his arms. "Okay."

"Would you like to be on the call with Rocki? I could conference you in…"

"No, I'll let you break the news. I could use a few minutes."

"No problem. I love you," she responded and hung up.

After pushing the end button, Keith set his phone on the desk as if it were a bomb that might explode, rocked back in his chair and stared up at the ceiling. His mother's death had so many implications. What would happen to the Coldiron fortune, which she'd controlled since her father died? Who had she left it to? Roxanne—or Maisey?

Perhaps she'd split it between them. But she couldn't split Coldiron House and would never want to see it sold. So what would become of their ancestral home? Would Maisey move out of the bungalow she shared with Rafe on the other side of the island—from which they managed the eight neighboring vacation cottages for Josephine—and take up residence at Coldiron House?

Keith knew Roxanne wouldn't move. She and her husband ran two businesses in Louisiana. They couldn't leave their livelihood behind. Neither would Rocki uproot her three kids.

A sudden longing sprang up, to walk through the halls of Coldiron House, to see his childhood home through different eyes, to somehow find the peace that had eluded him there. He'd loved visiting his grandfather on Fairham Island, before they moved there, when Grandpa Henry was alive. He used to say that Keith would own it all someday, that *he* would be the one to carry on the Coldiron legacy. Although Keith had never been close to his own father, not like Maisey, and he'd struggled just to get along with his mother, he'd been Grandpa Henry's favorite. Henry had always admired strength and spirit, even when it turned into willfulness—what had gotten Keith in so much trouble. Grandpa Henry had said he was once the same.

Maybe Keith would've put his grandfather's traits to better use if Henry had lived longer. Sadly, he'd died when Keith was only eight and that house hadn't represented the same thing since. They'd moved in after his death and it had been the family home ever since. But going back wouldn't be easy. For one thing, he'd be stepping out of his current routine, which kept him busy and focused on the right things. His schedule, the distance and his refusal to think about the past were what kept him safe from himself.

Still, he *had* to attend his mother's funeral. Had to help lay her body to rest in the family cemetery behind the house, beneath the moss-draped trees. Common decency demanded he attend the service, even if he didn't stay any longer.

After waiting a few minutes, he called Rocki. She'd just hung up with Maisey and was crying.

"You okay?" he asked.

"For the most part. Are you?"

"I don't know." He scrubbed a hand over his face. "Are you planning to attend the funeral?"

"Of course. We'll fly to South Carolina as soon as we know when it is. We can't come before that. With our financial situation, we can't take much time off."

"Things are that bad?"

"They're not *good.*"

She hadn't mentioned this to him before. She'd always said they were getting by.

"Is there something I can do to help? I'll pay for your flights, give you a loan—"

"I appreciate the offer," she broke in before he could list other options. "But we'd rather not accept that kind of help. I'm afraid it would make Landon feel…inept. Just between you and me, he's already been dealing with some kind of midlife crisis. And even if we didn't have the financial pressure, the kids are in school." She sniffed and he pictured her wiping her face. "What about you? Will you go to the funeral?"

"Do I have any choice?"

"Sure you do. Don't go if it'll threaten your sobriety, Keith. Your first obligation is to remain drug-free and healthy. Do what you need to in order to avoid a relapse. That's what the past five years have been about, right? If returning to Fairham could create a problem for you, Maisey and I will handle everything."

He wouldn't rely on his sisters to take care of burying their mother and dealing with the aftermath. What kind of brother would dump it all on them? "No, I'll be there. You and Maisey have enough to worry about," he said and opened the laptop on his desk to purchase a plane ticket to Charleston. He had to attend an important meeting tomorrow afternoon, so the earliest he could reach Fairham Island would be Tuesday.

He wasn't convinced he was ready to gamble on the progress he'd made. But he *had* to go. If he couldn't do his part when his family needed him, what was the point of changing at all?

2

The smell hit him the hardest—that familiar scent of the island, with its briny waves lapping up over the beaches, the soggy wood rotting around the dock and the damp wind sweeping over the fecund marshes to the southwest. As Keith drove his midsize rental car off the ferry, which ran every three hours between eight and eight since they'd added one more crossing at night, he couldn't help taking a deep breath and feeling as nostalgic as he was apprehensive.

From what he could see, not much had changed in the past five years, but he lowered his head to get a better look as he entered Keys Crossing, the island's only town. An elaborate display of exotic flowers adorned the windows of Love's in Bloom, the flower shop that Josephine had purchased with some of the money she'd inherited, along with the house and everything else, from Grandpa Coldiron. The shop, or "shoppe" as she'd had it spelled on the sign, also sported a new coat of pale green paint.

With the sun setting behind the building, only those details could be seen in the dim glow of his headlights, but he assumed that the place looked as appealing as ever. Josephine had always had good taste.

Sitting back, Keith studied the Drift Inn on the other side of the street. Its marquee advertised a "winter special" of $99/night. The vacancy sign below glowed orange and would probably remain lit until the tourists came in spring to swell the ranks of the local population, which stood at about 2,500. There wasn't a lot to do on Fairham during the winter, especially in damp, windy weather such as they were having now. He could see the dark outline of the palm trees up ahead, on the ocean side of the island where he was going, swaying as black clouds blocked what was left of the fading sun.

A storm approached. He felt like one of those black clouds rolling in—and he had no doubt many of Fairham's residents would feel the same. He didn't have a good reputation here. The locals would consider him bad news, the prodigal son returning. But he deserved it; he certainly hadn't done anything to make anyone admire him back when he lived here.

He checked his watch. He'd taken the second-to-last ferry of the day; it was a little after five. He wondered what Maisey was doing. They'd spoken several times since that ominous call that'd disturbed his sleep. He'd spoken to Roxanne in Louisiana more than once, too. And yet he hadn't told either one of his sisters that he was coming to the island today. He'd known Maisey would insist on meeting him the moment he got off the ferry, and he felt reluctant to face her so soon. He needed time to acclimate, to ease into the memories that were rising up and washing over him as if he'd been caught out at high tide.

Ease... He chuckled without mirth. Aside from the connection he felt to his grandfather, which sometimes made him homesick, and a general feeling that he belonged here, coming back was as difficult as he'd expected, especially when he thought about the reason for his visit. His mother was only sixty-three. She'd always been so healthy. At times, she'd seemed darn near indestructible.

What had gone wrong?

When Maisey called him yesterday, she'd said the coroner was expecting to rule their mother's death a suicide. The police had found an empty bottle of sleeping pills on the marble floor of the bathroom, as if she'd tossed them back with a glass of wine.

But Keith couldn't believe she'd do that. Having the police tramp through her house to find her naked in a bathtub would be humiliating to her. If she was going to commit suicide, she'd put on her most flattering dress and arrange herself on the bed.

Except that she wouldn't commit suicide at all. Swallowing a bunch of pills and sinking beneath the water would smack too much of giving up, of admitting that her life wasn't perfect. Josephine was all about appearances. Some of Keith's worst beatings had been triggered by incidents he'd shared with other people that were unflattering to her—usually about the severe punishments she'd doled out to him.

And there was more than her pride to consider. She had spent almost every living moment protecting her beauty and trying to turn back the hands of time. Why would she fight aging so much if she'd had a desire to end it all?

Something else had to have happened. An accident. Or—he hated to acknowledge the possibility—murder wasn't an entirely unreasonable conclusion. His mother had plenty of enemies. She hadn't been the kindest person in the world. Most of the time, she hadn't been kind at all.

But Fairham had almost no crime. Keith couldn't believe that anyone here would harm her. He'd asked Maisey if anything had been stolen or if there was any sign of forced entry, and had been told there wasn't. Even the five-carat, $90,000 diamond ring on Josephine's finger hadn't been removed.

Since Pippa, his mother's housekeeper, typically went home at night—and worked only five days a week—his mother had been alone in the house, taking a bath with her pills and her wine. Barring some injury to her body, which the coroner presumably hadn't found, Keith could see why the police had reached the conclusion they did.

But they didn't truly know her...

He passed The Sugar Shack, the barbershop, the burger stand, The Wild Rose Café and the Fairham Marina. Then the road began to climb. Most of the islands off the coast of South Carolina were flat, but Fairham had a sizable hill on one side, which they called a "cliff." Although it wasn't much of a cliff by most people's standards, it was high enough that someone could be killed by falling onto the rocks below, especially a child. They'd once believed Roxanne had fallen onto those rocks and her body had been dragged out to sea. Coldiron House gripped the top of that hill and peered down on the rest of Fairham Island like an eagle guarding its clutch.

A sudden deluge of rain hit his windshield, hard as rocks, as he rounded the final bend in the road and encountered the tall gates of the fence that circled the property. Through the rhythmic slash of his wipers, he stared at the ornate wrought iron with the elaborate C in the center, wondering if he was going to have to call Maisey for the code.

He assumed he would. But it took only three tries to get the gates to open. The code turned out to be his birthday—ironic considering that he and his mother had been estranged for so long. She'd loved him, in her own twisted way. That was the part that always messed with his head, and his heart.

His phone rang as he parked near one of five garage stalls. Stacia Snider, his assistant, was trying to get hold of him. On the West Coast it was only two thirty. But he silenced his phone instead of answering. He couldn't deal with her now, couldn't deal with anything else. He felt as if his mother had her hands around his throat and was squeezing...

A memory flashed before his mind's eye. She'd choked him once, when she'd gotten worked up and gone too far. After she released him, he'd spit in her face, and then she'd really let him have it. That was the only time he ever remembered his father stepping in. Malcolm had been *so* passive. Whenever Josephine got upset, he'd simply hunker down and wait for her anger to blow itself out. The funny thing was, no one ever wanted him to do anything else. The situation just got *more* volatile if he tried to insert himself. Josephine had to win at everything, which was partly what had caused Keith's problems with her. He was the only one who ever stood up to her, who ever fought her complete domination—at least until Maisey got older and walked out on her. Just like he did later...

The car pinged as he got out, reminding him that he needed to turn off the headlights. His BMW did it automatically; he'd forgotten that most cheaper vehicles didn't.

Although the rain was still falling heavily, soaking his hair, jacket and jeans, he spent a few minutes searching for the groundskeeper, Tyrone, to no avail. The place looked deserted. Since it was after five, Tyrone must've left. Or maybe he hadn't come today. No doubt Josephine's death had thrown the hired help into chaos. If Keith had his guess, they were all at home, fearing they were out of a job, grieving for their own loss if not for the loss of their tyrannical employer.

Flinging his wet hair out of his face, he hurried up the front steps to the wide veranda. The door was locked but, within minutes, he found the key hidden behind the porch light—the same place it had been since he was a teenager. Although he didn't want to think about it, that meant anyone else who knew about the spare could've gotten in without breaking a window or making a fuss...

He swung open the heavy front door and stepped into what he had, for years, sarcastically referred to as his mother's "palace."

The scent of fresh-cut flowers, which were changed regularly, rose to his nostrils. That was when the fact that she was really gone hit him—conjuring up a startling and profound sense of loss. Regardless of what his mother had done over the years, what he struggled to forgive, she'd been a magnificent woman in many ways. He'd never known anyone stronger or more determined to reach whatever goal she had in sight. Everything she did was done well. She had a sharp tongue but a sharp mind, as well—coupled with the face and figure of a femme fatale, a woman who'd looked two decades younger than her true age. *Everyone's* head turned when she walked into a room; he remembered certain moments when he'd taken great pride in being connected to a figure people revered that much.

Maisey had often told him he couldn't get along with her because they were too much alike. He hadn't been able to see it then, but these days he could easily recognize that they both had to be on top, in charge. They were what his father used to diplomatically refer to as "strong" personalities.

His father hadn't admired "strong" personalities quite like Grandpa Coldiron had.

God forbid that Keith made other people's lives as miserable as his mother had made his—although he certainly used to.

Thinking of Grandpa Coldiron, Keith walked into the dining room, where there was a giant portrait of his grandfather looking every bit as somber and austere as the paintings of the old aristocracy hanging in the castles and palaces of Europe. His grandfather had been a "strong" personality, too. And he had accomplished great things. There were benefits to the genes he'd inherited, Keith decided—as long as he could control his temper and his drive.

Before the quiet stillness could press too close, he left the dining room and took the stairs up to the second story. He found no crime scene tape, nothing to bar him from entering certain rooms. Coldiron House was eerily normal, far more normal than he'd thought it would be. When someone as powerful as his mother passed away, shouldn't there be more to mark the event?

Once he reached the double doors of her bedroom, he had to pause, to brace himself for what he might see.

He didn't expect to encounter a bloody mess, or anything like that, but he knew he'd imagine finding her the way he'd been told she was found—and that would be disturbing.

Another expansive flower arrangement confronted him when he went in, only this one hadn't been ordered as part of the household routine. He knew because it included a card.

Keith wasn't in any hurry to reach the bathroom. He was too busy preparing for what the sight of it might do to him. So he took a second to see who the flowers were from.

I can't wait.
H

"Hugh," he said to himself, recalling the name Maisey had given him. His mother and *Hugh* were obviously looking forward to having a good time together.

Her designer luggage was pushed off to one side but appeared to be packed. A quick check confirmed it. That answered the question he'd asked Maisey early Sunday morning, when she'd called to tell him about their mother's death. The bed was turned down, too, another indication that his mother had expected to live longer than she did. Her wrap was tossed across the velvet bench nearby.

Had the police missed all of this? Why would she bother to pack or turn down the bed if she knew she wouldn't need luggage or a place to sleep?

Feeling his muscles tense, he rounded the corner—and entered the bathroom.

3

The water had been let out of the bath, but several wet towels remained on the floor—where her body had obviously been placed after it'd been pulled from the water. Pippa must not have been back since his mother died or she would've cleaned this up...

Had the police told the housekeeper that she couldn't or shouldn't come back? Or was it that she wasn't sure if she'd get paid?

The police must've taken the wine, the glass and the pill bottle, because none of that was in the bathroom, or even in the trash.

Pulling out the chair of his mother's boudoir, Keith sank onto the tiny beige seat. At six foot six, he was much bigger than she'd been at five-eight. His knees came up too high, but at least he had a perch from which he could examine the place where his mother had died.

Why had she drowned? There *had* to be a reason, and it wasn't that she'd decided to end her life right before a trip to meet her new love in Australia.

Her phone. He needed to check her phone. There could be answers there, a text or a call that would give him some clue. She always had it with her. But he went through the whole suite and couldn't come up with it. Her computer wasn't there, either.

He'd just realized the police must've taken both when he received a call himself.

Maisey. If he answered, he'd have to tell her he was in town, and he wasn't ready to do that. He needed answers, some understanding before he could focus on her needs and her grief.

But he understood what she was going through—and that made it impossible to ignore her call.

As he hit the talk button, he happened to turn enough to catch sight of himself in the mirror. So many people had told him he was the spitting image of his mother. Even he could see hints of her in his face. They both had high cheekbones, wide mouths, prominent chins, thick dark hair. They also had the same blue-green eyes, a color so unique he'd had strangers stop him on the street to tell him how arresting his eyes were. Maisey's and Roxanne's eyes were the same color. But his sisters had a calm temperament, like their father. *He* was the only one who'd inherited their mother's tempestuous nature and extreme stubbornness.

"Maisey? What's going on?" he said into the phone.

"They've scheduled the autopsy for first thing in the morning," she replied. "With any luck, we'll know more after they're finished."

He walked out of his mother's room and down the hall, where he felt he could breathe again. "Don't let 'em do it."

"Excuse me?" she said. "*I* have no say over that. It's a state law. They have to perform an autopsy in this situation. So even though the coroner is fairly certain he knows the manner of death, we have to let him do his job."

"I'd rather he didn't handle this, Maisey. I'll take over from here."

There was a long silence. Then she said, "Keith, you can't take over. This isn't up to you."

"I'll get my own pathologist, someone I'm convinced is good and that they trust, too. If I pay for it, I'm sure they'll let me. Why wouldn't they? It'll save the state the money they'd have to pay otherwise."

"Why would you get involved?"

"So I can be certain that whoever does the autopsy isn't just going to confirm what the coroner's already said. I'll hire someone who hasn't been previously conditioned to see Mom's death as a suicide."

"You really think that's necessary?"

"Mom didn't kill herself, Maisey."

"You believe it was an *accident*?"

He poked his head into his old bedroom. This was where his mother used to tie him to the bed to force him to take a nap, not that the room looked the same as it had then. All his toys and sports trophies had been moved to the attic years and years ago, almost before he was old enough to part with them. Josephine had hardly been able to tolerate the childish things her kids had liked when they were young. She'd considered anything with theme-park characters or superheroes "tacky" and got rid of it as soon as possible. So his bedroom had been updated—more than once. But he was looking at the same black wood shutter-style furniture with the expensive yellow and gray bedding and drapes he'd had when he lived here five years ago; nothing had changed since then.

Given the season and the fact that he didn't think anyone had used his room in years, he found it odd that the ceiling fan was on. He watched the blades swoop overhead, stirring the air. The police must've walked through the house and accidentally hit the switch—

"Keith?" Maisey said.

He crossed to the window and opened the drapes and shutters so he could gaze out over the sloping lawn at the turbulent sea beyond, gleaming like crushed diamonds in the moonlight. The view was the one thing he had missed. Even what he saw outside the windows of his house in Santa Monica couldn't compare to the island, especially in the midst of a storm.

"It wasn't an accident," he said above the howl of the wind as it hit the house. "No one takes a bottle of pills by accident." His sister had to know that; she was just reluctant to accept the alternative.

"You're not saying…"

"Mom was murdered."

"That can't be true."

"It's absolutely true," he insisted.

"No. No one on Fairham would hurt her. We know—and love—all the people she associated with."

The people she dealt with on a daily basis were a lot easier to get along with than she was… "Plenty of people on the island have been upset or frustrated by her over the years. Maybe she let Tyrone go, and Tyrone…snapped."

"Are you kidding me?" Maisey cried. "It wasn't Tyrone. For one thing, she *didn't* let Tyrone go. I would've known if that was the case. Mom had Rafe and me and the kids over for dinner Friday night. To say goodbye before her big trip. Tyrone was leaving for the day when we arrived. It couldn't have been Pippa, either. She served us that night. And she was the one who was supposed to drive Mom to the airport."

"Pippa hasn't been here since Mom died," he said, remembering the water on the master bathroom floor. "Do you have any idea why?"

"Here?" Maisey echoed in surprise.

He grimaced at the slip. "I'm at Coldiron House."

"And you didn't tell me you were coming?"

"I'm sorry." He raked his fingers through his hair. "I just got in. Needed some time to myself."

Seconds passed. "I see," she said at length, and rather stiffly.

"Please don't take it personally," he said. "Coming here without calling is about me, not you."

She seemed to soften. "Okay. But it seems strange that you didn't let me know. I'm your sister and I've never done anything except try to love you and watch out for you. You'd think—"

"Maisey, please!" he broke in.

"Fine. I'll let it go," she said. "We're all coping with this the best we can. But…surely we can't be looking at *murder*."

"There's no other alternative that fits," he argued. "I'm surprised the police aren't saying the same thing. Her bags were packed. And there's a flower arrangement from her boyfriend saying he can't wait to see her. No one commits suicide just before a romantic trip to Australia, especially one that's already been paid for. Everything I'm seeing suggests Mom was excited, not depressed."

"Maybe, at the last minute, she and Hugh got into a fight and he asked her not to come. Maybe she was disappointed. Or he told her some of the things *we've* been dying to say."

"Like what? That she's insufferable? *Was* insufferable?"

Maisey sighed heavily. "Basically. That could've pushed her over the edge. Criticism is difficult for everyone, for her most of all. She couldn't tolerate *any* of it."

"I'd consider that a possibility, except that most of the men in her life have been playthings. People who exist purely for her entertainment. *She's* the only one she's ever really loved. So why would she kill herself over something some guy said?"

"*She's the only one she's ever loved?* That's a bit harsh, isn't it?"

He winced. It *was* harsh. Especially now that their mother was gone. And it wasn't strictly true, although Josephine had acted like it sometimes. "You're right. I take that back. But still. I wouldn't expect her to kill herself over losing Hugh or anyone else. Not without some kind of warning." An idea occurred to him. "Is her will current?"

"Her *will*? Don't tell me you're thinking about what we might inherit!"

"No," he said, even though she must have given *some* thought to what would happen to the wealth their grandfather had accumulated. "I'm saying she wouldn't check out of this world unless she'd prepared all of that. If her will hasn't been updated, she wasn't planning on going anywhere."

His sister calmed down. "That's true. But letting it lapse in the first place wouldn't be like her, either. She never let *anything* lapse. Anyway, I can't tell you where she keeps it. I haven't even looked for it. And it's not like she ever took me into her confidence. She was so secretive about her finances, always acted as if what she had, and what she did with it, wasn't any of our business."

Because she didn't think they were as capable of managing wealth as she was. "My point exactly. She would've cared about her father's legacy, if nothing else. Left us a note about where to find the will. Something."

"True. I agree that suicide is unlikely, but I wouldn't say it's *impossible*. She could've acted impulsively. I mean…who would she call if she was upset and needed someone to talk to? You? Me? No. She wouldn't even call Roxanne. No matter how badly she hurt, she was never one to show her pain. She'd suck it up and pretend everything was fine. She never had anyone she could lean on—not since Dad."

Intent on getting his bags from the car, Keith headed back through the house. "She never truly needed anyone, even him. Let's be honest. Dad could barely put up with her, and you'd have to work pretty hard not to get along with Dad." Of course, Keith had enough of Josephine in him that *he'd* managed to upset their father on occasion. "If we *really* looked in to how people felt about Mom, I bet even we'd be surprised by how many didn't like her."

"But everything's been so quiet. For years. Why would this happen now when…"

The way her words fell away, as if an opposing thought had occurred to her, piqued his curiosity. "What is it?"

She hesitated, then said, "Never mind. It—it's nothing."

He stepped out onto the porch, into the nasty weather,

and had to speak louder to make sure she could hear him above the storm. "Tell me what you were thinking."

"I wasn't thinking anything, really. It just hit me that the only person I'm aware of that Mom was having trouble with was Nancy. They haven't been getting along lately. Nancy's changed a lot. She's been standing up for herself, which is good but…it's also made them less compatible."

"Are you talking about a specific incident?"

"I know of at least one. Last week, Mom threw a tantrum in the shop in front of several customers. Yelled at Nancy for not communicating well enough on some order for a big wedding, which embarrassed her—so much that she tried to quit."

Nancy was the nicest person Keith had ever met. He still felt bad about the way his life had collided with hers. He'd been at his worst when he worked with her at the flower shop, had gotten her hopes up about a relationship and then walked out on her—after borrowing a large sum of money, which he'd spent on drugs. He'd tried to make up for what he'd done. Not only had he made several attempts to apologize and repay the money, he'd bought her a car—once he could afford it—to replace the hunk of junk she'd been driving when he left. He'd thought a gift like *that* would compensate for the past.

But she'd sent the car back to the dealership and wouldn't accept his calls or his money. He'd had to leave his apology on her voice mail.

"Nancy would never hurt anyone," he said. "She doesn't have a mean bone in her body."

"See?" Maisey responded. "Tyrone wouldn't do it. Pippa wouldn't do it. Nancy wouldn't do it. Who does that leave? The part-time help? None of them would hurt Mom, either."

"*Someone* hurt her," he insisted. "What about Hugh Whoever-He-Is?"

"We can check, make sure he has an alibi, but I can't imagine he was here on the island. Because of the ferry, someone would've seen him. And what would *he* have to gain by murdering Mom? If they were married, and he was the beneficiary of her life insurance, maybe I could see it, but…they were just getting to know each other."

Keith paced on the porch, taking advantage of the veranda's deep overhang to keep out of the rain. "We have to consider everyone."

"So I should call the coroner and tell him we're going to get our own pathologist?"

"Yes. We'll have to get permission, but we should at least ask him to hold off until then."

"I hope I can catch him. It's after business hours."

"Try, in case. And text me if you can't, okay? If necessary, I'll go over there first thing in the morning."

He was about to hang up when she spoke again.

"Are you planning to stay at the house?"

He turned up his collar. "Yeah."

"Why not come here?"

"You don't have room for me." Maisey lived in one of the vacation bungalows built by their father in the eighties. Her home with Rafe wasn't big or ostentatious, but she said she was happier than she'd ever been.

"We'll make room. Or you could use one of the other units. They're empty during the winter. And you'll like the way I've furnished them."

"I don't doubt that. There's just no need for me to go

to Smuggler's Cove. I'm comfortable here." Although he had his fair share of unpleasant memories, he chose to focus on the times he'd visited Grandpa Coldiron and felt accepted and loved without any criticism.

"I'm not convinced it's good for you to be at Coldiron House, especially right now—and alone."

She was worried about him backsliding. But when he thought of his grandfather, and not his mother, he felt he was exactly where he belonged. "It'll be okay."

"You're sure?"

"Maisey, stop it! Thinking that I'm going to go off on a drug binge at any moment is only making this worse."

"I'm sorry. It's not as if… Well, I don't mean—"

He cut her off as he pulled his car keys from his pocket in preparation for his dash through the rain. "Has Roxanne decided when she's coming?"

Thankfully, she allowed him to change the subject. "Not quite yet. She probably told you she's planning to be here for the funeral, though."

"Yes, although she can't stay long."

"Their tour business falls off during the winter months, but they still have the DVD store."

Which they'd recently turned into more of a new and used video game store that wasn't performing very well. "Makes sense, especially since they have the kids to worry about, too."

"What about *your* business?" she asked. "How long can you be away?"

"I've got plenty of people to fill in for me. I'll have no problem staying for a week or two."

"You're confident we'll learn what happened that soon?"

"*Someone* has to know." Was that person banking

on the fact that the cops would see the pills, label Josephine's death a suicide and leave it at that? That Maisey would be too involved with her own family to do much more than put on the funeral? That the lazy, good-for-nothing Lazarow son wouldn't care enough or be capable enough to challenge those findings?

If so, whoever killed his mother would have a rude awakening.

"So you're really going to dig into this?" Maisey asked. "Even though the coroner and the police—*everyone*—are coming to the same conclusion?"

"They're wrong. And I'll prove it. Mom didn't kill herself. You have to admit she'd hate being remembered that way."

"She'd be embarrassed."

"Mortified," he corrected.

She made a sound of frustration. "God, Keith. Can't anything ever be easy?"

"You did your part when you found Rocki. I'll take care of this."

"I'll do everything I can to help. So will Rafe. But… are you sure it won't…you know, be too unsettling for you? There're a lot of memories in that house…"

They were back to her concern for him. He wished she'd give it a rest. But she had good reason to be worried, good reason to grill him.

"The only thing I'm sure about is that Mom's death isn't going down as a suicide," he said. Maybe he'd never be classified as a model son, but he would do that much for his mother.

4

"Are you okay?"

Maisey looked up to find her husband standing in the doorway of their bedroom. "I'm fine."

He came into the room. "You seemed so worried there for a second."

"I just hung up with Keith."

"And? How's he taking the news about your mother?"

She chewed on her bottom lip. "He's insisting we get our own pathologist to perform the autopsy."

He rested his hands on his lean hips. "Why?"

"He says that Mom would never kill herself, and he doesn't want someone who might be influenced by what the coroner and the police have said about her death."

His dark eyebrows drew together as he sat down next to her on the bed. "Do you agree?"

"Don't *you*?" she asked.

He studied her for several seconds. "Your mother was a difficult person. Maybe something happened that was just…too much for her."

"I've never known her to come up against a challenge she couldn't handle," she said wryly.

"Doesn't mean there wasn't one. She was a proud and private person. We don't have any idea what was going on in her life—beyond the few details she was willing to divulge."

Laney's voice interrupted from the living room, where she was playing with Bryson, their two-year-old son. "Daddy, I think Bry needs to go potty!"

"What makes you say that?" Rafe called back to his daughter.

"He keeps saying, 'Poop.'"

"That would be a good indication," Maisey said with a chuckle.

Rafe got up. "I'm coming!"

"Why can't I help him?" Laney asked. "He'll go for me."

Eleven-year-old Laney was blind and had been since birth, but she navigated their house well. And she loved nothing as much as her little brother. "Sure," Maisey called. "But only give him two M&M's as a reward." Maisey suspected Laney was more generous with the treats they kept on hand for potty training purposes than they were.

"Can I have some, too?" she asked.

"Of course. Just let us know if you need help, okay?"

"I'll let you wipe him," she told them, and Maisey grinned as Rafe sat down again.

"That's probably best," he conceded. "Otherwise, that trip to the bathroom might not end the way we'd like it to."

Maisey imagined the sweet face of her stepdaughter, who had the same dark hair and golden eyes as Rafe. "What would we do without her? I couldn't love her any more if she was my own."

"For all intents and purposes, she *is* yours," he said and leaned forward to peck her lips.

It wasn't as if her real mother had ever taken an interest. She'd essentially abandoned her child as soon as she found out the baby was handicapped.

"Back to your mom," Rafe said. "I'm not convinced the police and the coroner are wrong, but if there's any doubt and getting our own pathologist could relieve that doubt, let's do it. Putting off the funeral for a few days isn't the worst thing in the world."

"True, but getting our own pathologist will mean we have to pay for it."

"Won't be a problem for Keith. He's Midas these days, right?" he said with a chuckle. "And we're doing okay. I say we split it."

"Are you sure?"

"Of course."

She supposed sharing the cost would be fair. Rafe was doing well with his construction and home repair business—had more work than ever before. They were still managing the vacation bungalows, which took care of their mortgage every month. And Maisey had gone back to writing children's books, a passion and vocation that was beginning to pay more handsomely now that she was building a bigger readership than she'd had when she'd been married to her first husband and living in New York City. "But there's more at stake than money."

"Like…"

"What they might find. I could deal with it, no matter what. But I'm worried about Keith."

Rafe fell back on the bed and propped himself up on his elbows. "Keith's come a long way."

"Exactly. I'd hate to see him fall apart. Especially

now that Mom's gone. I want what's left of my family to finally be unified and healthy."

"It's been five years since he was in any trouble. I'm sure he'll be careful not to head back down that road."

"He's had plenty of relapses in the past," she pointed out. Far more than she cared to remember. He was the primary reason she'd come back to the island after her divorce. She'd felt he needed her support.

"But he's never been clean *this* long."

She wanted to believe he'd be able to hang on, but... "Triggers are funny things. He hasn't been home in those five years, hasn't even let me or Rocki talk about Mom. And now, because of what's happened, here he is."

"On Fairham? Really? Already? When did he get in?"

"Not sure. He didn't tell me he was coming. But he was at Coldiron House just now, when I spoke to him. He's staying there and insists on taking charge of everything."

"What can we do to stop him—or make things easier?" Rafe asked.

She curled up against him, resting her head on his broad chest. "Nothing. But it's not the drugs I'm worried about as much as..."

He kissed her forehead. "As?"

"All this talk about suicide. What if Mom really did kill herself? What if he decides the battle he fights every day isn't worth it and he follows her lead? He's tried before. I can't lose my mother *and* my brother."

Rafe sat up, pulling her with him so he could look into her face. "Keith's changed. He can weather this."

She didn't have the chance to argue. Laney called

out, "Mom! He did it! I heard it plop. Come wipe Bry's bum!"

Bryson squealed and clapped, obviously as excited by his accomplishment as Laney was.

"I'll take this one." Rafe laughed as he got up, but Maisey hurried to circumvent him.

"No, I want to be there to praise him."

"Maybe we should all stand in the doorway and clap," Rafe teased.

She paused long enough to slip her arms around his waist and hold him close. "God, I love you."

That night Keith tried to reach Pippa Strong, his mother's housekeeper. He figured if anyone could shed some light on his mother's frame of mind in the days and weeks leading up to her death, Pippa could. The two were fairly close—or as close as an employee could get to Josephine.

She didn't answer, though. When he had to settle for leaving a message on her voice mail, he moved down his list and called Tyrone Coleman, the groundskeeper, instead.

Tyrone was just as trusted and loyal to the family, but he couldn't fill in any of the blanks. He insisted that Josephine hadn't said anything unusual to him before her death. He claimed she hadn't been acting odd, either. And he hadn't noticed any strangers or hostile individuals hanging around the property.

"No, sir," he said to almost every question. "When I lef' work on Friday, she was jus' like she always was. You know'd your mother. If she didn't like somethin' she woulda said—and then she woulda changed it straightaway. That was a woman who knew her own mind fer sure."

He spoke of Josephine with a mixture of awe and affection, the way one might refer to a willful child who was to be indulged.

"Yes, she did," Keith said.

"You're a lot like her—you know that," Tyrone told him next.

"You aren't the first to mention it," he responded.

"That's a good thing, Mr. Lazarow, sir. Your mamma was a strong woman. Once she got somethin' in her head, she was immovable. Like a rock."

As far as Keith was concerned, she'd been more like a sledgehammer. Her iron will could blast through any obstacle. But Tyrone seemed to be the same tolerant and respectful person he'd always been. He seemed truly bewildered by her death and upset that she was gone.

Keith told the groundskeeper he still had a job, that he could report to work whenever he was ready—a proclamation that was greeted with a tremendous amount of gratitude. Afterward, Keith thanked him and hung up. But several hours later, when it was well past the time he could call anyone, he was still going over that conversation and everything else he'd learned since receiving word of his mother's death. How had Josephine died—and why? Had someone strangled her? Drugged her and then drowned her?

The mere possibility enraged him. It made no difference that they'd had so much difficulty getting along. The fact that they'd struggled actually made what had happened worse. Whoever killed her had robbed him of the ability to improve their relationship, to achieve any closure. But anger wasn't all he felt. There was plenty of guilt, too. Would his grandfather have expected him to stay and protect her and the Coldiron legacy?

If he'd been able to cope with his own life, he would've stuck around—and who could say how that might've changed things?

Maybe she'd be alive right now...

Unable to sleep, he pulled his computer out of his bag, opened it and leaned against the headboard while he researched strangulation and asphyxiation and what doctors looked for in determining whether someone had died in that way. From what he read, many of the signs didn't show up within the first twenty-four hours, which was interesting and made him wonder if his mother had been examined the day *after* she was found. He also learned that "petechial hemorrhaging," in which the blood vessels burst behind the eyes, was one red flag. A broken hyoid bone was another.

At nearly three, he set his computer aside and went to his mother's suite. After walking through the empty bedroom and bathroom, he wandered into the retreat set off to one side, which had a balcony with a fabulous view of the beach and ocean below. He stared out at the storm-tossed waves for several minutes. The wind and the rain had gotten stronger. Then he sat down and poked through his mother's writing desk more thoroughly than when he'd been ransacking the place for her phone.

He found nothing that clarified what might have happened, but he did come across a stack of letters tucked inside a big travel book in a deep file drawer. They were addressed to him at his company's address in LA.

Frowning at the discovery, he sat on the velvet-covered bench at the foot of Josephine's bed to see

what they were. Written on perfumed stationery—
his mother couldn't do anything ordinary—they were
sealed, as if she'd planned on mailing them. But he'd
never received any communication from her. She'd
had too much pride to contact him, since *he* was the
one who'd cut *her* off.

He counted them. Ten in all. Tapping them against
his knee, he studied the flowing script. Even her handwriting exhibited an elegance few people could emulate.

So what did she have to tell him? Dare he find out?
There had to be some reason she'd chosen not to mail
them. And he was already feeling troubled and unsettled. Why give her a voice? Would he be able to tolerate what she said?

In case he couldn't, he got up and shoved them back
into the book, which he returned to the drawer. He'd
be smarter to protect his sobriety, he thought. But after
several minutes of pacing, he retrieved them, opened
the top one and skimmed the contents.

It was just a regular letter, like something he might
expect if he'd been stationed overseas in the army or
was away at school. The others followed the same pattern. Some were Christmas cards. Some were birthday
cards. She talked about the flower shop and Coldiron
House and the vacation rentals. She talked about seeing Roxanne and any news about Roxanne's "little family." She talked about Maisey giving birth to Bryson,
noted his size and weight and complained that he wasn't
named after anyone in their family. She also talked
about Pippa taking vacation or getting sick and who
she might get to fill in.

She didn't offer him any apologies, however. She
didn't even acknowledge the fact that they were es-

tranged. She just pretended nothing had happened between them and they were still speaking.

After reading the last one, he stacked the envelopes the way he'd found them.

Maybe he *shouldn't* have read them, after all. They reminded him of how charming his mother could be when she was on her best behavior, made him miss her. They also made him wonder if maybe *he* was the one to blame for their problems. He'd already spent a lifetime wondering. *Is it me or her?* These letters dredged up all of that confusion and uncertainty. But, refusing to succumb to those thoughts, he forced himself to look at the letters more objectively. What did they mean? Was the fact that she'd taken the time to write an apology in itself? Was it her way of expressing her love?

The closings never varied—*Love, Mom.* That was the only thing that might suggest she cared about him, two words that could easily be interpreted as a standard closing. Was there so much wrong between them that she wouldn't risk tackling the issues? Was she hoping to simply go on, to forget the past as if it hadn't existed?

Since she was never one to apologize, that was her favorite approach to making up. He would've been content to let bygones be bygones, too, if he could. He'd tried to come to terms with his mother for thirty-seven years before giving up and forging ahead with a life that didn't include her.

His phone buzzed. He'd received a text from Dahlia.

Should I come over again tonight?

He hadn't told her about his mother, hadn't even mentioned that he was going out of town.

No. I'm not in LA.

Where are you?

On the East Coast.

For what?

Business, he typed because he wasn't willing to divulge the personal nature of his trip.

She sent him a frowny face, to which he didn't respond. Then she wrote, When will you be home? I'm missing you.

He wasn't missing her at all. He barely knew her and was fairly certain he didn't want to see her again. The few times they'd actually had a conversation, he'd been bored stiff.

For some reason, he thought of Nancy—of how real and honest and caring she'd been...

His phone buzzed again. Can't wait to see you.

I'll let you know when I get back, he wrote.

The next morning Nancy Dellinger didn't have to open the flower shop. It was her day off and yet she was still preoccupied with the death of her boss, who'd also been Fairham Island's central figure. She'd been dwelling on Josephine a lot, but not the way she should've been—with shock and grief. Mostly she was relieved to think her boss would no longer be part of her life. She hated feeling like that, hated being unkind. Besides, Josephine Lazarow's death had its drawbacks. Depending on who inherited the business and what that person chose to do with it, she could be out of a job. If it was

Maisey, she'd keep Love's in Bloom. Maisey loved the flower shop as much as Nancy did. But Keith? He'd probably sell it and go back to LA. She'd heard he'd become a big shot out there.

Regardless, Nancy was happier without Josephine. That was how anxious her employer had made her. The minute Keith's mother would glide into the shop, enveloped in a cloud of expensive perfume, Nancy's blood pressure would skyrocket and she'd begin to perspire— even in winter. Because there would be no peace until Josephine left. Josephine would criticize and belittle and nitpick until Nancy was almost in tears.

Attention to detail—that's how a shop stands out, she'd say as if Nancy had never heard that before. Josephine had the power to make Nancy feel inept with a single, imperious glance—never mind that she'd been managing the business efficiently for seven years. Josephine had never even threatened to get rid of her; that, right there, proved she was doing a good job. The "Queen of Fairham" had fired every manager who'd come before her—in a matter of months. And yet Nancy had never received any thanks or gratitude, no kindness or camaraderie. She'd gotten a Christmas bonus each year, but that had more to do with how Josephine wanted to be perceived than recognition for a job well done. Josephine could see only what *hadn't* been accomplished or what could've been handled better.

In short, her boss was—*had been*—the most difficult individual Nancy had ever met, the worst kind of perfectionist. And yet, Nancy couldn't help admiring her. Josephine was everything Nancy would never be— regal, commanding, perfectly put together and never an ounce overweight. Josephine was nearly twice Nancy's age and yet Nancy couldn't compete with her grace or her beauty.

But then…no one could compete with Josephine. Maisey, her own daughter, gorgeous in her own right, felt as inept and unattractive around her mother as Nancy did. Nancy had become close enough to Maisey to understand that.

Climbing out of bed to confront her wall-length mirror, Nancy sucked in her stomach and turned to the side. She gave herself this critical once-over every day, even though her reflection didn't change much. Three years ago, she'd lost thirty pounds and kept them off. So there'd been *some* improvement since she'd last seen Keith. She'd felt a lot better about herself since then. But she still hadn't lost the final twenty pounds.

She wasn't built to be a size 4, she concluded—and that was her one great regret. With thick, dark hair, which fell to her shoulders in a healthy sheen, wide, hazel eyes and smooth, clear skin, she had a pretty face. But she wanted to have more than a pretty face. She wanted to have a body to match. To bring Keith Lazarow to his knees, make him sorry he'd so casually walked away from her.

Maybe she needed to accept the truth. She wasn't going to bring Keith to his knees. How many times had she promised herself she'd be so lean and toned when he returned to Fairham that he wouldn't even recognize her?

Too many times to count. Yes, she'd made some strides in that direction, but he'd stayed away for so long she'd begun to think he'd never come back and her love of food had won out. Now there was no chance to compensate for procrastinating her diet. His mother was dead. He'd return to the island for the funeral, which meant Nancy would see him in a few days, at most a week.

Unless… What if she didn't go to the funeral? Then she might be able to avoid him. If she was lucky…

She considered pretending to be sick. But the thought faded as quickly as it had burst into her mind. No, she couldn't do that. Her conscience dictated that she show up, no matter how much she'd disliked her employer. Even if Josephine hadn't been her boss, Nancy would attend the funeral for Maisey's sake. She wouldn't want Keith to think *he* was the reason she'd stayed away. Besides, it wasn't as if she really wanted him back. There were other men in the world, men who were far less complicated than Keith Lazarow. She'd long since decided she was lucky he'd moved on, because it gave her the opportunity to find someone who was easier to get along with.

A knock sounded at the front door. Simba, her Chow Chow, dashed in from the back through his doggy door and immediately went into a barking frenzy.

Startled by the noise, Nancy stepped away from the mirror and hurried to grab her robe. She wasn't expecting anyone, and had no idea who this could be. But when she pulled Simba back and opened the door, she was pleased to see Maisey Lazarow-Romero. As much as Nancy resented Maisey's mother and brother, she adored Maisey. They'd been friends since Maisey had returned to the island just before Keith left. That was when Maisey had started working at the shop. Once she married Rafe, she'd cut back on her hours to spend time with his daughter, Laney, and then the new baby, Bryson. She was also writing her children's books again. But she still came in and helped Nancy arrange flowers once or twice a week, and those days were always fun. The two of them chatted and laughed like high school girls.

"What are you doing here?" Nancy asked in surprise.

Maisey shook the rain from her umbrella as Nancy stepped back to admit her. "I need to talk to you."

Nancy almost glanced around to find her purse so she could check her phone. If Maisey had tried to call, she hadn't heard the ring. "You okay?"

She nodded. "Just trying to make sense of…of what's happened."

Nancy peered through her front window at Maisey's Audi. Was it running? "Are the kids outside?"

"No. I dropped them off at Rafe's mother's. She's been dying to have them, and I need the time to take care of a few things."

"I'm glad Rafe's mom is so supportive." Especially since Maisey's own mother hadn't been the type to babysit, although she'd liked having Laney over now and then. Nancy had heard a great deal about those visits—because Josephine's interest in Laney had been so unexpected.

"Her arthritis is getting bad enough that she can't take Bryson very often," Maisey was saying. "But Laney's there to help, and I felt I really needed to be free today."

"I can watch them for you, too," Nancy said, "on days like today, when I'm off, or after work. So keep that in mind. I'm sorry about your mother, by the way." They'd talked once, briefly, over the phone, but Nancy didn't feel she'd properly expressed her condolences. She'd been too stunned to hear that Josephine had died.

A sad smile curved Maisey's lips. "I appreciate that. Thanks for the flowers you sent home with Rafe."

"I knew he was working over at the church, and I didn't want to intrude on your grief, in case…in case you needed some time alone." She'd paid for those flowers herself, and hoped Maisey would realize that but didn't mention it.

"You're always welcome at my house, no matter what," Maisey said.

Guilt for feeling relief at Josephine's passing made Nancy cringe. Here she was expressing her sympathy, and yet she was secretly glad Josephine was gone. "So… what'd you stop by to talk to me about?" she asked. "Have you decided on the date of the funeral?"

A shadow passed over Maisey's face. "Not yet. We're getting our own pathologist to do the autopsy, and that'll take more time, which makes it difficult to proceed with…what normally happens when you lose a loved one."

"Why go to the trouble? Of hiring a pathologist, I mean? Haven't they already determined what…you know…caused her death?" Nancy hesitated to use the word *suicide*. That was such a painful thing for surviving family members to face. But even if Maisey hadn't called on Tuesday morning, Nancy would've heard what the police had found—and what they thought. Everyone in Keys Crossing was talking about the fact that Josephine had taken her own life. Not much happened on the island that didn't churn through the gossip mill. Josephine had been an important person, after all.

"Between you and me, Keith feels the coroner has reached the wrong conclusion. He wants someone who's unbiased to take a look," Maisey said.

No one would be keen to accept a suicide ruling. Nancy understood that and felt sorry for Keith and Maisey. But she was more affected by the mention of his name than any other aspect of the conversation, which only made her more disgusted with herself. She should hate him for using her the way he had. And even though she didn't—*couldn't*, for whatever lame reason—she would never be stupid enough to get involved with him again. So why was she still hanging on?

It was pathetic.

"What does Keith think happened?" she asked.

"He's not sure," Maisey replied. "No one is. We just…need more information."

"Because she must've had a heart attack or slipped and hit her head, right? Not because you suspect foul play."

Maisey grimaced. "To be honest, we're not ruling anything out."

"Wow." Nancy shoved her hands in the pockets of her robe.

"It's hard to imagine that anyone would hurt her," Maisey said. "But we should gather all the facts before… before we proceed."

Nancy nodded. She wouldn't bury her mother, either, not until she'd done everything possible to answer any questions that remained—except this could never happen to her, since her mother had passed away years ago. "It's always better to be thorough. If that includes getting someone you feel more comfortable with to do the autopsy, then so be it. That way, if questions arise later, you'll be able to feel you did all you could."

Maisey frowned in apparent uncertainty. "I hope it's the right move."

"How can it be the wrong one?"

"I'm just worried in general. What if the autopsy isn't conclusive? What if it sends us on a wild-goose chase? What if we start to believe my mom was murdered and begin to suspect our *friends*? What if those friends are innocent? Or what if she *was* murdered and we can't find the culprit—or he gets off for some reason? None of that would be easy to deal with."

Nancy slid the clasp of her necklace around to the back. In that case, maybe ignorance *was* bliss. "Was she having trouble with anyone in particular?"

"My mother had trouble with everyone. Well, I guess you couldn't call it *trouble*. It was too one-sided for that. Other people put up with her because they had to, while she did pretty much whatever she pleased. Maybe someone got sick of her throwing her weight around."

Nancy was one of the people who'd had to put up with Josephine and hadn't always liked it. But she would never have done anything to harm her. She *had*, however, imagined—more than once—telling her off. "You mean someone here on Fairham?"

"If we're lucky, it was an outsider."

"We don't get a lot of those this time of year."

"Exactly," Maisey said on a sigh. "An outsider would stand out."

Nancy hadn't noticed anyone around town she didn't recognize. And how would Josephine make someone who didn't even live in the area angry enough to murder her? What would this person's motivation be? "Could it have been a man she was dating?"

"Possibly. Or an old flame. Like Keith, she left quite a few broken hearts in her wake."

Nancy's heart was one of those Keith had broken, but she was glad Maisey didn't acknowledge that.

"I'm trying not to jump to conclusions, though," she went on. "I actually had another reason for stopping by."

"What is it?" Nancy tightened the belt on her robe. "If there's anything I can do, I will."

"There's nothing. Not yet. But thank you. I'll keep that in mind. I just… I wanted to let you know… Keith's back on the island."

Already? Nancy suddenly found it difficult to breathe, although she'd expected him to show up. "I'm glad he was able to make it," she lied. "Considering what's happened, this is where he should be."

Maisey peered at her more closely. "You're okay that he's here? You won't mind if you run into him around town?"

She shook her head as carelessly as possible. "Of course not. We may not even bump into each other."

A skeptical expression claimed Maisey's face. "Keys Crossing isn't that big. And I'm guessing he'll stop by the store. Since you're usually there, you'll probably see him. I know how you used to feel about him, and—"

"Oh, don't worry about that," Nancy interrupted with a dismissive gesture. "That's in the past. I'm dating someone else now—a guy I met online who lives on the Isle of Palms."

"Tom?"

Nancy wished she had another name to offer up, but she couldn't think of one fast enough. She wasn't used to lying, wasn't much good at it. "Yeah. Tom."

"I thought you said there weren't any sparks between you."

She wished she hadn't volunteered quite so much

information. She *wasn't* interested in Tom, but he was still emailing and texting her, hoping to get her to go out with him again. That should count for something. And she had plenty of other men on that same dating site who were showing interest. "I'm trying not to make up my mind too soon."

"Smart."

Nancy almost asked where Keith was staying, if he was at Coldiron House or the rental bungalows on the other side of the island, which Maisey and Rafe managed. The vacation properties at Smuggler's Cove were empty during the winter, so there'd be room. If he stayed there, it'd be a lot easier to avoid him.

But if she really wanted Maisey to believe she wasn't interested in Keith, she couldn't probe for information, regardless of the reason for her interest. "Tom's a nice guy."

"I'm glad to hear that. You deserve the best." Maisey bent to pet Simba. "So how are you doing at the store? You don't mind keeping the business going until we can get my mom's affairs sorted out, do you?"

"Not at all." Nancy enjoyed her work—and would enjoy it even more now that she knew Josephine wouldn't be coming in to lambaste her with one complaint or another. Since learning of her employer's death, she'd been toying with the idea of buying Love's in Bloom. She'd thought that might be a possibility one day, but it had seemed much further off...

"Can you keep up?" Maisey asked. "Or do you need help?"

"Everything's under control," she replied. "I've got Marlene to spell me when I need it. She's there now. So don't worry about Love's in Bloom. With Christmas over, it won't be terribly busy, not until February when we gear up for Valentine's Day. Marlene and I can manage for the next few weeks."

The concern on Maisey's face cleared, which lifted Nancy's spirits. Perhaps she could take some of the pressure off Josephine's daughter during this difficult time. That assuaged her conscience for being so darn relieved that Josephine was out of the picture.

"That's comforting. I appreciate it." Maisey straightened. "You'll call me if anything changes, won't you?"

"Don't worry. I'd never let the business fall apart."

Maisey gave her a quick hug. "Of course you wouldn't. I'd trust you with my life. Somehow that renegade brother of mine has gotten filthy rich, so I'll make sure he pays you until we can get my mother's estate sorted out."

Great. Just what she wanted. Keith paying her salary. But at least he was capable of doing so. He wasn't on drugs anymore; he'd exhibited quite a dramatic turnaround. Not many people could pull that off.

Nancy felt a measure of pride in what he'd done—and tried to quash it. She didn't need anything else to admire. His good looks and sex appeal already created a formidable challenge.

"I've got some savings, so I can wait if you need me to," Nancy said.

"No need for that."

Nancy kept a smile pasted on her face—and waved cheerfully—as she stood at the door and watched Maisey go. But as soon as Keith's sister was gone and she allowed her hand to drop, her smile faded, too. She'd expected Josephine's death to be difficult, had known there'd be a lot to resolve, with the flower shop, all the

Coldiron real estate holdings, which included a good portion of the land outside Keys Crossing, and Josephine's many other assets. Nancy had also known the whole ordeal would start with a funeral and the very real possibility that Keith would return for that reason.

But she'd assumed he'd stay for a few days, maybe a week at most. If Josephine's death turned into a full-fledged murder investigation, who could say how long Keith might remain on Fairham?

"Hopefully, he'll have too much business in California," she muttered and decided to get her grocery shopping done before taking Simba for a walk.

5

A knock on his bedroom door woke Keith. He'd been up so late the sun was about to rise when he'd fallen asleep. His mind had been too busy to let go—and it didn't help that he was still on California time. With the shades drawn, he'd slept late as a result.

"Mr. Lazarow?"

He yawned and adjusted his pillow. "Come in."

Pippa poked her head into the room. "I hate to disturb you, sir, but your sister is here and would like to speak to you."

Keith's first thought was of the letters he'd found in his mother's desk and the odd, haunting sensation that reading those letters had given him. He'd loved his mother; he even missed her, in a way. They'd had *some* good times. But loving someone and being able to get along for more than an occasional day or two were sometimes different things, at least when it came to Josephine.

I had to leave to survive, he reminded himself. But he'd been reminding himself of that ever since he'd received word of her death.

"Sir?"

Rising up on one elbow, Keith blinked at the house-keeper. "I called you last night," he mumbled.

"Yes. By the time I got your message, it was too late to call you back. But...thank you for telling me I can return to work."

Except for the extra gray in her hair, she hadn't changed a bit. She was still wearing her crisp blue and white uniform, as if she'd stepped out of the 1960s South—or as if his mother was around to make a fuss if she didn't. "Just so you know...you don't have to wear that anymore."

"Excuse me?"

He almost repeated himself, then sighed. "Never mind." Perhaps she gained as much comfort from custom and tradition as his mother had. In any case, now wasn't the time to challenge such trivial things.

His bleary eyes sought the fancy perpetual-motion clock on the nightstand. It was nearly eleven. He'd had all of five hours' sleep. "You said Maisey was here?"

"Yes, sir."

"Where?"

"In the drawing room."

"Why didn't she come up?"

"To your *bedroom*?"

He nearly laughed out loud. Pippa had been trained by his mother, all right. "No, of course not. That would be unseemly," he said. "Tell her I'll be down as soon as I get dressed."

"Yes, sir. And... Mr. Lazarow?"

He paused before throwing off the covers. If Pippa was scandalized by the idea of his sister coming straight up to his bedroom, she'd probably faint if she saw him buck naked, the way he liked to sleep. "It's good to have you back, sir. I'm sorry your return is under such dreadful circumstances."

She sounded sincere, so sincere that it took him off guard. "You liked her, didn't you?"

She seemed startled by the question. *"Her?"*

"My mother. You liked her."

"She was a dynamic person," she said as she left.

Keith fell back on his pillows. Even Pippa had admired Josephine but couldn't quite say she'd *liked* her. "Pippa?" he called in an effort to catch her before she could move out of hearing distance.

Now that she'd done her duty by letting him know he had a visitor, his door inched open only as far as necessary. "Yes, sir?"

"I'd like to talk to you after Maisey leaves. Will you be around?"

"I'll be here as long as you need me. With Maisey's permission, I stayed home for the past few days. I was too upset to do much else. But I was grateful you offered to have me back today. I've been coming here for so long. And the place needs looking after."

"I understand. I'd rather you stayed on and continued to do your job. I'll see to it that you get paid. I've told Tyrone the same."

"Yes, I saw Tyrone on my way in, sir. It was a comforting sight. I believe it's a good decision to keep him. We couldn't have the yard here at Coldiron House getting overgrown."

Obviously, she took great pride in where she worked. "No. That would be a *real* tragedy."

She hesitated, as if she could tell he was being facetious, even though his first tongue-in-cheek comment about the impropriety of Maisey's coming to his room had sailed right past her. She seemed to be waiting for some further cue from him, so he said, "That will be all, thanks," and she left without additional comment.

He waited for the sound of her footsteps to fade before he got up. Then he burrowed through his suitcase for a pair of boxers, jeans and a T-shirt. When he retrieved his phone from the nightstand, he could see that he'd missed several calls from Maisey, as well as a few texts, because he'd turned it on Silent.

Coming, he wrote and sent it to her, although he was confident Pippa had already conveyed that information, and went into the bathroom to brush his teeth and hair.

By the time he hurried downstairs and entered the drawing room, Pippa had served Maisey tea and biscuits with honey and jam. He wasn't groggy anymore, but traipsing around Coldiron House without his mother in residence felt odd. She'd always taken complete command of her home, even when his father was alive. She'd been such a dominant presence for so long, it was easy to forget Grandpa Coldiron had lived here first.

At the sound of his approach, his sister swallowed the bite she'd just taken and looked up. "Morning."

"Same to you," he said.

"You sleep okay?"

Her skeptical expression told him he didn't look rested. "Not really. You?"

"Sort of."

"Where's my niece and my nephew? Are the kids with Rafe?"

"They're at his mother's. He's repairing the vestibule of that old church near the marina today."

"Will you bring the family over later?"

"Of course." She lowered her voice. "I'd rather Laney

didn't hear us talking about her grandmother the way we need to this morning. Laney might be one of the few people who's never felt conflicted when it comes to Grandma Josephine. And, oddly enough, Mother *loved* her. Inexplicably. Diligently. Even kindly."

"That's somewhat redeeming." He helped himself to a biscuit without bothering to sit down or get a plate—something his mother would never have tolerated. "Have you heard anything new?"

"I stopped the autopsy."

He'd received her text last night, which was why he hadn't set an alarm to get up early this morning. "I saw that."

"And just a few minutes ago I got permission to call in our own pathologist. I also made an appointment with the new chief of police. I guessed you'd want to talk to her."

"Old Man Reuben finally retired?" Keith was fairly certain Maisey had mentioned it. She'd kept him abreast of the more noteworthy changes on the island. But he'd had no particular reason to remember that. He'd rarely had to deal with Chief Reuben himself. His mother had interceded whenever he got into trouble. She'd exacted her own retribution afterward, which was arguably worse than what he would've received had he been remanded to the police. But she would not allow scandal to befall the Coldiron name—another reason he couldn't accept that she'd kill herself. What could be more scandalous than suicide? That had been her primary complaint when, in desperation, he'd felt it was *his* only escape.

"Yeah. We have a woman now. The city council's showing how progressive they can be."

"A woman, huh? How old is she?"

"Can't be more than forty-one. Attractive, too. *Really* attractive."

"Any good at her job?"

"Seems to be. There was a big write-up in the paper when they hired her. The article made her sound like a solid candidate. She's from Chicago."

"She have a family?"

"No. Her husband was in the military. Died in Afghanistan before they could have kids. They'd grown up two blocks from each other. Gone to high school together. I suspect that was part of the reason she was willing to leave the big city behind. Too many memories."

"I can see wanting to leave, but what brought her here, of all places?"

"A kinder, gentler existence. Lots of sun and sand. Less violence. And there was a job for her, I guess."

"What time do we meet with her?"

She checked her phone. "Yikes! We've only got twenty minutes—barely enough time for you to shower."

"So *that's* why you've been trying to get hold of me!"

"Yes."

He broke off part of his biscuit, popped it in his mouth and slipped the rest onto her plate. "I'll be down in fifteen."

He was halfway up the stairs when Pippa stopped him. "Mr. Lazarow?"

The tone of her voice seemed uncertain, which made him curious. He turned to face her. "Yes?"

She opened her mouth, then seemed to reconsider. "Never mind."

"What is it, Pippa?" he pressed.

"I… I was wondering what you'd like for dinner, that's all."

He could tell that *wasn't* what she'd had on her mind, but Maisey had come out of the drawing room, and Pippa seemed hesitant to speak in front of her. "What're my options?"

"Salmon? Steak? Chicken? Pasta?"

"I'll have salmon."

"Will you be dining alone?"

He looked over at Maisey. "Do you and Rafe and the kids want to join me?"

"That'd be fun," Maisey said.

"Is salmon okay?" Keith asked. "Will Laney eat it?"

"Sure. We all like salmon."

Pippa acknowledged this with a nod. "Then I'll plan for five." She began to scurry off, but Maisey stopped her.

"Are you enjoying Mom's Yorkie, Pippa? Or would you like to bring her to me?"

"I'd be happy to keep her—unless you have other plans."

Maisey smiled. "No, Athena doesn't do well with the cat we rescued. She'll be much better off with you, but I'm happy to cover her expenses."

"No, that's fine. If she's going to be my dog, I'll take care of her." Pippa cast Keith one final glance, reminding him of that moment a few seconds earlier when he'd been positive she had something to say. He was tempted to go after her, to ask what she had on her mind. He had the impression it was important. But he was also fairly certain she didn't want Maisey to hear.

Question was…why?

6

The new chief of police at Keys Crossing was every bit as attractive as Maisey had said. About five foot six, 125 pounds, she didn't look particularly strong, but she had a no-nonsense, direct approach, which Keith liked, and clear, intelligent blue eyes. Once he'd met her, he was glad the old chief had retired. Reuben had had a great deal of experience with minor infractions such as traffic violations, breaking and entering, petty theft and drunk and disorderlies during the summer, when the tourists arrived. But to Keith's knowledge, he'd never investigated a homicide.

Since Chief Underwood—she hadn't offered her first name—hailed from Chicago, he was hoping she'd have more familiarity with violent crime. But once he met her, he didn't feel that was going to be the benefit he'd anticipated. She was fully convinced his mother had committed suicide and nothing he said seemed to sway her.

"There's no reason to assume she'd take her own life," he argued when she refused to change her mind.

"I hear what you're saying," she responded. "I noticed the suitcases myself. But there was no sign of anyone else having been in the house and no indication that she was sexually assaulted, for instance. That'll have to be confirmed when the autopsy is performed, of course—we're not jumping to conclusions there—but so far all signs point away from it."

"There's heart attack, stroke."

"Which will also have to be considered and addressed during the autopsy. But the coroner said she didn't have a flushed face. Her carotid artery wasn't swollen. There was no bluish tinge to her nose, eyes or fingertips—all typical signs of cardiac arrest. I'm afraid the preponderance of evidence, *at this point*, suggests suicide."

"Even with her impending trip?"

"It's possible she didn't decide to…to do what she did until the last moment."

Keith gaped at Maisey, who was sitting next to him in Chief Underwood's small office. "She wouldn't *suddenly* decide to kill herself. That kind of decision takes serious thought." He knew from experience.

"She must've," Chief Underwood insisted.

"Why?" Keith cried. "She had everything. What was there to make her so intent on ending her life?"

Keith hoped the police chief wasn't about to point to their estrangement. The fear that his mother *had* committed suicide and *he* was the cause clawed deeper by the minute.

She formed her slender fingers into a steeple. "You two must be going through hell. There's no need to hash this out. Not right now. Go ahead and grieve, and make whatever plans you'd like to make so you can put her to rest. Then, when that's all over, you can come back and we'll talk, okay?"

A tingle skittered down Keith's spine. "No, that's not okay," he said. "Why can't we talk now?"

Her expression indicated that she was trying to be patient. "I only knew your mother for three years, after I came here. But even three years was enough time for me to figure out that she had a great deal of pride."

"That's not news, Chief." Other than Maisey, who would know Josephine better than him?

She straightened her blotter. "What I'm trying to say is…there may have been certain circumstances in her life—distressing circumstances—she didn't tell you about."

His mother hadn't told him anything in five years. But neither had there been any sign of unhappiness in those letters he'd found. Nothing out of the ordinary, anyway. Wouldn't something have shown up—*some* complaint? "Like…"

Two lines formed on the chief's forehead. "Thanks to an investment she made—a huge resort she and a group of partners were building in Jamaica at a total cost of over a billion dollars—she was losing everything, Mr. Lazarow. All her money. All her holdings. *Everything.*"

"No." Keith stiffened. "That's not possible. My mother would not have risked that much."

"Perhaps the resort seemed like a good idea at the time, but a series of…unfortunate events put the project under water—literally."

"I'm telling you she was more conservative than that."

"I understand why you'd be skeptical."

"She controlled a vast fortune." One his grandfather had built and would've hated to see destroyed…

"I'm sure she expected everything to go well," the

police chief explained, "but, because of a tropical storm, the resort flooded, and the insurance refused to pay because of an exclusion in the fine print that had something to do with the footprint of the hotel portion. Then the other investors pulled out, cutting their losses and leaving your mother holding the bag."

At the news that their mother had been losing everything, Maisey had gripped his arm. Now she surged to her feet. "The situation can't be as dire as you're making it sound," she said. "I've been working at Love's in Bloom since I returned to the island. Business has never been better."

A sympathetic expression pulled at the corners of Underwood's lips before she whirled around in her chair to get a file from the cabinet behind her. "That may be true, but the flower shop was only a small portion of her holdings. The income from that couldn't even cover the expenses of running Coldiron House."

"Then why didn't she cut back?" Maisey asked. "She didn't have to be quite as extravagant as she was."

"Pride could be the answer to that, too," Chief Underwood replied. "She probably feared people would start to guess that she was struggling, thought she could get back on top without giving herself away. And let's face it. I doubt there was ever another time when she encountered this type of setback. She wasn't used to failing."

Could the destruction of the Coldiron empire—the financial pressure—have gotten to her? Keith wondered. She'd admired Grandpa Coldiron even more than he had. In her mind, no one could live up to his example. Perhaps she felt as if she'd let him down, as if she'd had nowhere to turn and couldn't handle the humiliation of losing her status on the island, where she'd always been revered as the richest, most powerful person.

He had to admit it was *possible*, but chances were equally good that she had a plan. Josephine Coldiron-Lazarow would not go down without a fight—even if it meant marrying someone she didn't love in order to obtain the money she needed. Keith could imagine her grooming her new beau, the Australian she'd met in first class, to help her retain her holdings and save face. "How do you know so much about her finances?"

"The second I started digging, I found nothing other than bills and fines and levies and trouble with the IRS," Underwood replied. "The resort is sucking all the money away. You'll probably have to file for bankruptcy."

"No," Keith began, but she talked over him.

"You'll soon find out for yourself, since you're the executor of her estate."

Another surprise. Keith brought a hand to his chest. "*I* am? Is that a recent development?"

She scanned a document inside the file. "Not according to the date I see, which is almost five years ago. That was when the will was modified to include Roxanne. You were to get the flower store and Coldiron House. Maisey was to get Smuggler's Cove. Roxanne was to inherit a chunk of land near the lighthouse. The rest of the estate the three of you were to hold jointly. Your mother's diamond ring was supposed to go to Laney on her eighteenth birthday, by the way."

She threw that aside to Maisey, who gasped a little when she heard it. "She left her ring to Laney? She loved my sweet child. That always came as such a shock to me."

Chief Underwood winced at the pleasure in Maisey's voice. "Only it'll probably have to be sold. That's why I hesitated to go into this today. I didn't see any reason to upset you even more."

"Why didn't she disown me, like she swore she would?" Keith asked Maisey.

"That part doesn't surprise *me*," Maisey murmured. "Even when you two were fighting, she loved you best."

Josephine had a funny way of showing it. Although Keith couldn't say his mother had abused him by burning him with cigarettes, shutting him up in a cage or depriving him of food, she'd always been highly impatient, quick to anger and far too harsh. "I would've preferred to be *Dad's* favorite, like you were," he grumbled but directed his next remark to Chief Underwood. "Where did you find her will?"

"In her desk. I'm sorry if it seems like an invasion of privacy." She pushed the file closer so Maisey could see for herself. "But if she *was* murdered, it could've been a key piece of evidence. I grabbed it, just in case. Besides, once a testator has died, the will becomes public record. I'm not the only one who'll be able to read it, or get a copy, for that matter. Anyone who goes to the trouble of visiting the courthouse to request the probate file can do the same—once probate has been started, of course."

"Who starts probate?" Maisey murmured as she read.

"That'll be Keith, as the executor."

Maisey glanced over at him before returning her gaze to Chief Underwood. "But…how will the businesses and the estate run in the meantime? The flower shop needs to remain open. Nancy and Marlene, not to mention Pippa and Tyrone, rely on their paychecks."

"Keith will have the power to act on your mother's behalf until the court can make the appropriate distributions." Underwood spoke in a smooth, businesslike tone. "But, as I indicated, there won't be much to distribute—maybe a little personal property, which will go to the individuals named. Even then, I'm guessing your mother's debtors will force you to sell her furniture and her jewelry, since it's worth more than an average person's would be."

"Those are keepsakes and family heirlooms!" Maisey said.

"I'm sorry." At least she seemed genuinely sympathetic. "It must come as a blow."

"It's a shock, I'll admit. But this won't change my life. I'll still have what I have now—I just won't be getting any more. Losing everything would've been very difficult for our mother." Maisey nudged him. "Mom must've been distraught. And yet I had no idea."

"None?" Keith asked.

Maisey shook her head. "None."

Keith closed his eyes and rubbed his temples. He hadn't planned on staying on Fairham for long. He'd hoped to get his mother's affairs organized so he could return within a couple of weeks, put some distance between himself and the man he used to be, get back on his regular schedule. But there was so much to try to save here, and it would be far more difficult to manage from across the country.

Almost as if she could read his thoughts, Maisey touched his sleeve. "Keith, this must be beyond upsetting to you. If you'd rather turn everything over to me, I… I'll do what I can."

His sister was a children's book author, and she was married and trying to focus on raising her kids, one of whom was blind and required extra care. She had Rafe's support, of course, but Rafe wouldn't be able to help with this. He had his hands full running his own business.

"No. I've got it." His grandfather would expect more of him than to dump Josephine's death onto Maisey or Roxanne.

"What about *your* company?" she asked.

"It'll be fine." He'd have to stop acquiring for the time being—unless he decided to juggle that with everything else. But there was no need to do that. He could rely on his employees and focus on his own pursuits later.

Maisey turned back to Chief Underwood. "That's it? That's the answer? She was going bankrupt, so she killed herself?"

"Going bankrupt would be no small thing to someone like Josephine," Chief Underwood pointed out. "You said that yourself."

"True," Keith allowed. "But you don't know our mother if you think she'd wimp out that easily."

Underwood tucked several strands of her honey-colored hair behind one ear. "From what I've seen, she's been battling financial problems for at least three years, ever since I got here. That was when she first bought into the resort."

"Still," Keith said.

The police chief scooted her chair closer to the desk. "Look, Mr. Lazarow. I can see how hard this is for you."

She shifted those pretty eyes to Maisey. "For *both* of you. If she were my mother, I'd be just as convinced she'd never take her own life. But…we can't overlook the facts."

"What facts?" Keith asked. "The autopsy hasn't even been done yet."

"At this point, the coroner and I believe the autopsy is merely a formality."

"Which is what makes me uncomfortable," Keith said.

"That's why we're permitting you to select a qualified pathologist from a list of doctors we recognize as having the proper credentials and experience—to compensate for any prejudice you feel we might have. Didn't Maisey tell you? We spoke about it this morning."

"Maisey told me, and I appreciate that you're working with us." He had enough money, and his name carried enough clout, that he could create a fuss if she didn't. Whether that had been a factor or not, he hated to guess. She'd agreed; that was what mattered.

"I'm happy to make the concession," she said.

"That's good. Thank you. But we need more," he responded. "We need an aggressive investigation."

Underwood's chair creaked when she shifted in it, even though she didn't weigh all that much. "O-kay." She stretched out the word as if she was surprised he was still pushing. "Let's look at other possibilities, shall we? Who would've wanted your mother dead?"

Now she was playing along just to show them how ridiculous they were being. Keith resented the fact that she was patronizing him, but at least she was listening.

"Our mother wouldn't end it all without providing for Pippa and Tyrone," Maisey said. "She had other help—

people who assisted whenever she had a party or drove her if she preferred not to drive—but they were only on call and weren't nearly as close to her. She wouldn't have left Pippa and Tyrone high and dry, especially since they're getting on in age."

"Even if she'd lived, she wouldn't have been able to continue paying them," Underwood said.

"You can't say that for sure," Maisey argued. "She was dating a wealthy man from Australia. Maybe they would've married, and that would've solved everything."

"You're talking about Hugh Pointer."

It wasn't a question, more of a confirmation. "Yes."

"I thought so." Underwood clasped her hands in front of her. "He's already married, Maisey."

This news hit Keith like a solid right hook. *"What?"*

"You heard correctly. I called to get a statement from him before he could hear the news from someone else."

"So…what was he doing with our mother?" Keith asked.

She moved some papers onto a pile to her left. "This wouldn't be the first time someone's cheated."

"I'd be willing to bet it was the first time someone cheated on our mother," Maisey said. "Did she *know* he was married?"

Keith answered before Chief Underwood could. "No way. Mom would never tolerate second place."

"I tend to agree," Underwood said. "She didn't strike me as someone who'd accept anything less than total devotion. Although I couldn't say we were friends, I met her on several occasions—at the playhouse one night, at the opening of the new art gallery a block over, at the event we held to raise money to equip our volunteer firefighters. She was…formidable, to say the least. So I'm guessing she didn't know but found out, and that may have precipitated her death. Could be she suspected something was up, hired a private detective to follow Hugh around and…"

Underwood didn't finish, but she didn't need to. If Josephine had suspected, she could've done exactly that. Their mother wouldn't hesitate to protect her interests. From time to time, Keith had even suspected she had people watching *him*.

No longer sure what to say, he sank back into his seat. "What a bastard."

"Well, if she was hoping to marry him for his money…" Underwood raised her hands as if she didn't care to spell out *that* thought, either, and she had a point.

Keith had expected the fact that Josephine had packed her bags and had a fabulous vacation lined up to serve as proof that she'd planned to stick around long enough to enjoy it. But if she'd been battling to save her fortune, her land and her house, and she'd just learned that her only hope of solving these problems wasn't going to pan out…

God, she could've called *him*, Keith thought. He was shocked at how good he was at making money, once he really started to apply himself.

But, as Chief Underwood had mentioned, Josephine had too much pride…

"Wait," he said. "If she was planning to go visit him at his home…what about his wife? How would he keep them from meeting up?"

"Lana Pointer was touring Europe with their daughter, who's eighteen. They have two sons, who're closer to your age, married and on their own, and then this girl, who came as a late surprise when his wife was in her forties."

Les Scott, a uniformed police officer and someone Keith had gone to school with before ninth grade—at which point Josephine had shipped him off to boarding school—stuck his head in the room. "Sorry to interrupt. I'm going to lunch and wondered if you'd like me to bring you a sandwich," he said to his chief.

"That'd be great. I'll have the meatball sub, extra sauce," she told him and the door closed. "So…does that answer your questions?" she asked when they were alone again.

No. In Keith's opinion, what she'd told them only created *more* questions, and he could tell Maisey felt as bewildered as he did. "Our mother would never commit suicide," he replied. "Despite everything you've said."

"It's a long time since you were home." Underwood spoke as if he wouldn't really know. She seemed to think she had it all figured out. But nothing about Josephine was simple. It never had been.

"Her phone's missing," he said. "So's her computer. I take it you have them?"

"Yes. I've got her phone right here." She delved into a drawer and held up his mother's Samsung Galaxy. "Her computer's with an evidence technician in Charleston."

"Because…"

"I'm doing my homework."

"When can I get them back?"

"When I'm done. I'm still tying up loose ends. If I can prove she had a private detective looking for information on her boyfriend, for instance, we'll be able to fit in that piece of the puzzle."

The nervous energy passing through Keith made

him bounce his knee. Thanks to his exercise regimen, he couldn't remember being this tense in quite some time. "You're trying to prove suicide."

"If I prove suicide, I'll disprove murder."

"You'll never prove suicide because she didn't kill herself." He indicated the folder. "Any chance I can get a copy of what you've got in there?"

Underwood returned the file to its drawer. "Not right now. Maybe later."

"Why wait?" he asked. "I only want the truth."

She met his gaze. "Keith, I'm doing all you can reasonably expect of me. I don't need you getting in the way or making my life difficult."

Apparently, his reputation had preceded him. He lifted his hands. "All I asked for is a copy of the file, Chief. That can't be too hard to provide."

With a long-suffering shake of her head, she got out the file again—but set it beyond his reach. "Fine," she conceded. "I'll have Les scan the contents and email them to you. Fair enough?"

Keith wrote his email address on a notepad he found on the desk and handed it to her. "This is where it should go."

"He'll jump right on it."

Keith caught a hint of sarcasm in her response—as if he was being too high-handed—but he ignored it. He wouldn't let anyone stand in the way of the answers he sought. Including her. "I'd also be grateful if you'd call over to the morgue and make arrangements for us to see her today."

Underwood's mouth tightened, suggesting this put her off even more. "The morgue isn't designed for public viewings. You'll be able to see her after they release her body. Once she's at a funeral home, you can go ahead and have a viewing or bury her or whatever you'd like."

"That'll be after the autopsy, which will take another day or two. Maybe more. Chances are she'll no longer resemble the woman I remember, and you know it."

"That's not necessarily true. People have open caskets after autopsies all the time—"

"I haven't seen her in five years, Chief Underwood. Could you show me a little compassion and make it possible to spend ten minutes with my dead mother today?"

"I'd like to see her, too," Maisey piped up. "I don't think any of this will feel real until I do."

Chief Underwood closed her eyes and pinched the bridge of her nose, as if she was digging deep for patience. Keith could tell she thought she was already bending over backward by agreeing to give him a copy of the file. Ultimately, however, she gave in. "I can't believe I'm doing this," she said with a sigh. "I shouldn't. Just keep in mind that they're busy over there and probably won't welcome you. This will force someone to take time out of his or her schedule, so I'd appreciate it if you'd be as brief as possible."

"You have my word," Keith said and waited while she made the call.

"You can head there now if you like," Underwood told him when she hung up and wrote down the address. "The supervising technician, a man by the name of Dean Gillespie, will meet you when you arrive and take you back."

"Thank you." Keith shook her hand before leading Maisey out into the cool, damp weather of another rainy day.

"The morgue?" Maisey said as they climbed into

his rental car. The keys of his mother's Mercedes were where she'd always kept them, but he hadn't been able to bring himself to drive her car quite yet. "We're going to the *morgue*?"

"Would you rather not?" he asked.

She seemed a little shell-shocked. "I'd like to see Mom, as I said. I'm just not sure what else you're hoping to accomplish."

"I want to see the condition of her body."

"You're afraid there might be injuries they're not telling us about?"

"I'd rather not take someone else's word for it. Doesn't hurt to stay involved, right?" He started the car but didn't shift into Drive. "So...are you in? Or should I drop you off at home?"

Although she frowned, she didn't take long to decide. "I'm in. But then what?"

"Then we choose a pathologist we feel we can trust from the list they gave you. Whoever it is will probably need to have her transferred to the hospital where he or she works."

"And after that?"

"I'd like to talk to Hugh."

She buckled her seat belt. "Why? So you can ask him if Mom knew he was married? You'll have no way of knowing whether he's telling the truth."

"I can ask him that and other things. Compare what he tells me with what he told the police. Look for inconsistencies. I can also research his background, find out what's going on in his life and what he might've been after by dating Mom in the first place. That might be more useful."

Maisey rolled her eyes. "Why? Isn't it obvious? Men

adored Mom. I've never seen a woman attract so much attention—except maybe Marilyn Monroe."

That the starlet had also died naked with an empty bottle of pills nearby made the comparison a bit chilling. Was that where their mother's killer had gotten the idea? "So why wasn't he willing to leave his wife for her?"

"Maybe he loves his wife. Or he wasn't willing to break up his family. Chief Underwood mentioned two sons and a youngish daughter."

"His wife *has* to be easier to live with than Mom would've been."

"He wouldn't have realized that yet. No one can resist Mom when she's pouring on the charm."

"Still, I can't buy that she'd ever take her own life."

"Even after what we just heard?"

"Did it change *your* mind?" he asked.

She looked dejected as she stared at the wet, shiny pavement ahead of them. "Honestly?"

"Of course."

"No," she said.

"There you go."

He'd finally shifted and pulled away from the curb when he saw a woman carrying a fluffy Chow Chow— a dog too big for that sort of thing—down the sidewalk ahead of them. "That's Nancy, isn't it? And her dog, Simba?"

Maisey took so long to answer he thought she was going to ignore the question.

"Isn't it?" he prompted, throwing her a sharp glance.

She squinted through the windshield as if she wasn't quite sure. "Maybe," she said.

He *knew* it was Nancy. He'd recognize her anywhere.

Pulling alongside her, he lowered the passenger window. "Hey, climb in," he called out. "We'll give you a ride."

She started at the sound of his voice. She'd obviously been so intent on not dropping her heavy bundle that she hadn't been paying attention to what was going on around her. She was probably also a little surprised to see him. The only interaction they'd had in the five years he'd been gone was a handful of calls, all instigated by him and all of which she'd ignored, and the car he'd tried to give her a few years ago, which she'd forced the driver to return.

"That's okay," she said. "It's not much farther."

If she was still in the same house, and he guessed she was, she lived just down the street in a small cottage she'd inherited from her late aunt. She was right—it wasn't far. But she was already struggling to hang on to her dog. "Simba's got to be getting heavy," he said. "And he doesn't look comfortable. Let us give you a ride," he said again.

"We're wet," she responded.

"Avis will clean the car when I return it," he told her.

"Come on!" Maisey chimed in and, rather than say no to both of them, Nancy slowed to a stop.

7

Nancy couldn't believe it. Maisey had stopped by just this morning to warn her that she might run into Keith and here he was—at the worst possible moment. Her hair was plastered to her head. She wasn't wearing any makeup. She had on a jogging outfit that probably showed every extra pound. And she was breathing heavily from exertion.

She told herself not to even think like that. She didn't care if he admired her. She'd been crazy to believe he could ever give her what she needed. Maybe she wasn't a svelte 120 pounds, like his mother, but she was done hanging on to his every word and feeling grateful for any scrap of attention. She was done starving herself in order to be something she wasn't. She'd find the right companion eventually—or she'd continue to build a fulfilling life alone.

"What happened?" Maisey asked as Nancy situated her dog beside her. "Why were you carrying Simba?"

She held Simba back so he couldn't stick his muzzle between the front seats. "He stepped on a piece of glass while we were on our walk, so I took him to the vet." And here she'd thought she'd been fortunate that the incident had occurred only two doors down from the animal clinic. If she'd taken him home and looked after him herself, she wouldn't have been on the side of the road at that particular moment, and then she might've been able to put off encountering Keith until the funeral. She told herself she didn't care what he thought of her looking so bad, but being around him wasn't exactly comfortable...

"Poor baby. Will he be okay?"

This came from Maisey again. Keith hadn't said anything since she'd climbed in, but she could see his stunning blue-green eyes in the rearview mirror as he eased into traffic. She still dreamed about those eyes...

Only because she hadn't found the guy she was going to fall in love with, she quickly told herself. She was working on that; it was just a matter of time. At least ten new prospects from her online dating site had left her a message over the weekend. And more were coming in every day... "Should be. He cut his front paw, but the vet cleaned and dressed the wound."

Maisey held her seat belt away from her body so she could turn around and pet him. "You were trying not to set him down until you got home?"

"I didn't see any reason to let his bandage get dirty."

"He's too big to carry," Maisey said with a chuckle.

Nancy refused to let her gaze shift back to that rearview mirror and what it revealed of Keith. She could smell his cologne, which was bad enough. "I do it all the time—pick him up and carry him over to the couch so he'll sit with me, or to the tub out back for his bath. He'd never *voluntarily* get in the tub. But I've never tried to haul him several blocks. The distance makes a difference."

"I'll bet," she agreed. "I'm glad we saw you."

"So am I," Nancy lied and turned her face toward the window so Keith wouldn't be able to get a good look at her even if he tried.

"How's business at the flower shop?" he asked.

She cleared her throat. "Better than ever."

"Who's working today?"

"Marlene Fillmore, a new girl. You wouldn't know her. She moved to the island about a year ago. From Charleston."

"Did you train her?"

"Didn't need to—not really. She worked out of her house doing flowers for weddings, so she's had plenty of experience."

"That's good."

Why would he care? He'd left all of this behind...

"I'm sorry about your mother," she said to finally get that out of the way. "I..." She wasn't sure what else to add. She knew how he'd felt about Josephine. She also knew that some of his problems revolved around the fact that he couldn't completely hate her, couldn't completely turn away from the woman who'd raised him.

Or had he come to terms with cutting her off? Maybe that was why he was doing so well. "I was shocked and saddened," she finished.

"Thank you."

His response was polite, nothing that offered any clue as to how deeply he was hurting. But they'd arrived at her house. There was no need to make more conversation.

As soon as he came to a full stop, she reached for her dog, but he spoke before she could take Simba in her arms.

"Did my mom ever say anything to you that sounded like she might be contemplating suicide?"

"No. I got no indication whatsoever."

"Would you say she was acting the same?"

Mrs. Lazarow had been as irritable and caustic as ever. But Nancy couldn't say that. Keith and Maisey had to be mourning, no matter how they'd felt about their mother. "I got the impression she was in good spirits. So I'm as stunned as everyone else."

Simba's collar jingled as she lifted him into her lap.

"Nancy?"

Keith again. She waited while he turned to look directly at her.

So much for avoiding his gaze…

"Have you ever met Hugh Pointer?"

She raised her eyebrows. "Who?"

"Hugh Pointer. My mother was dating him. Did she ever bring him into the flower shop? Mention him to you?"

"She told me she was going to Australia to see someone she was dating. Maybe that was Hugh. She asked me to complete the work schedule at the shop for the next few weeks so she could leave feeling confident that I'd be able to get by without her—having someone to take over on my days off and so on. That's it."

She got the feeling that he would've liked to ask her more, but she didn't give him the chance. She climbed out as gracefully as she could while cradling a sixty-five-pound dog.

"Thanks for the ride," she called and managed to close the door with her hip.

Unfortunately, he got out, too—and hurried around

the car. "Here, I'll take Simba," he said. "You go un-
lock the door."

She wished Simba would growl or refuse to be
touched, but he was the friendliest Chow on the planet.
Even if he hadn't remembered Keith, he wouldn't have
balked. He lowered his ears and wagged his tail in
greeting while Keith took him from her.

Traitor. Cursing herself for ever going out of the
house this morning, Nancy hurried up the walkway
ahead of them—and nearly dropped her keys, she was
in such a hurry to open the door.

Several seconds later, she managed to get the key in
the lock. "Go ahead and set him inside," she said as she
swung the door wide.

As soon as Keith put Simba down, Simba limped off
to curl up in his bed by the couch.

"Thanks again." She thought that was it, that she'd
soon be able to breathe a sigh of relief and congratulate
herself on not melting at the sight of her former lover.
However, Keith put a hand on the door.

"I can tell you're not interested in hearing this, but...
I'm sorry," he said. "I never meant to hurt you. I was...
I was a wrecking ball back then. I destroyed everything
and everyone I came into contact with."

He'd been trying to destroy *himself* more than anything, to escape the pain he was in. She understood. But
it didn't make things any easier that she'd wanted so
much more from him than he'd ever wanted from her.

She pushed the wet hair out of her face. "You have
nothing to worry about," she said. "That was years ago.
I don't think about it anymore."

"Really? Because I still owe you money."

He withdrew his wallet, but she stopped him before

he could open it. Maisey had already reimbursed her for what Keith had borrowed. Keith's sister had made her take the money and asked her not to tell Keith she'd stepped in. They both knew he wouldn't appreciate her getting involved in his business, especially since her actions revealed doubt that he'd ever take care of the debt himself.

The old Keith wouldn't have. He wouldn't have been able to…

"Don't worry about that, either," she said. "I helped out a friend. No big deal."

He blinked at her. "You won't let me pay you back?"

Shit… Considering the situation, and the fact that he now had way more money than she did, pretending wasn't believable, wasn't even *reasonable*. The amount was too great. "To be honest, your sister paid me a long time ago, Keith. So, please, give the money to her."

There went her promise but, short of accepting the money, which she didn't want to do, she felt she had no other choice.

"Oh." He frowned as he put away his wallet.

Eager for a shower so she could begin her day, Nancy nearly shut the door and let it go at that. She planned to forget she'd ever encountered him. But she did feel *some* sympathy for the loss he'd suffered. "I'm sincerely sorry about your mother. If there's anything I can do to help out with the funeral, please let me know. I'm already doing the flowers—for free, of course."

He studied her through the crack she'd left between the door and its frame. "You should get paid for that."

"No. I'm happy to contribute. She was my employer for seven years. I learned a lot from her. I'm a much better designer thanks to…" *her intense criticism* "…her high standards."

"Okay."

"Enjoy your stay on the island." No doubt she'd see him at the funeral, but she didn't plan on speaking to him again. They'd both said all that needed to be said.

After she closed the door, she leaned against it and forced herself to stay put instead of hurrying over to the window so she could watch him return to his car. For five years she'd been telling herself she never wanted to see him again—and yet she craved a better look, a chance to study him without his looking back at her.

He'd changed as much as Maisey had said, she decided, picturing him in her mind instead. He'd filled out that tall, spare frame, packed a lot more muscle onto it, but he was still lean and wiry. He didn't have a weight problem like she did. His face, once so exaggerated, so angular, had softened, as well. He no longer appeared gaunt, which suggested he was eating—something he didn't do enough of when he was on drugs. His eyes were clearer and brighter, too, his whole bearing more confidence.

That he was doing so well made her breathe easier. But that in itself concerned her. If she didn't care about him anymore, why would she feel such relief?

"Damn you," she muttered, but she wasn't sure if she was talking to herself, for still being so susceptible to the attraction she'd always felt, or him, for not feeling any attraction at all.

"Nancy's lost weight," Keith said over a Beatles song that was playing on the radio.

The way Maisey fidgeted with her seat belt gave

Keith the impression she didn't want to discuss Nancy. "A few pounds," she finally said.

"She looks great."

His sister folded her arms as he came to a stop at the light. "She'll never be model-thin."

Her comment struck him as odd. Her weight had never bothered him before; why would it bother him now? "Who says she has to be?"

"No one. I'm just making an observation."

"And that is…"

"She's never been your type."

"I have a *type*?"

"Yes. Skinny, blond and beautiful. More like the police chief. She's pretty, don't you think?"

She *was* pretty, but that was beside the point. "Not everyone I date is blond—or skinny," he said. "I was with Nancy before, wasn't I? And she was heavier than she is now."

"You can't use Nancy as an example."

The light turned green. He made a left, onto the main drag. "Why not?"

"She was a divergence. Even *she* was surprised when you took an interest in her."

"That's ridiculous."

"No, it's not. You're used to getting whoever you want. And when you can have anyone, you typically don't choose someone who's a few pounds overweight."

"She's not that heavy!" *She* thought she was, and had always been self-conscious about it. The first night they'd made love, he'd had a hell of a time getting her to trust him enough to take off her clothes. But it had been worth the battle. She'd given him intimacy and warmth, someone to cling to when he had needed it most. And once she grew comfortable, there'd been plenty of physical attraction and enjoyment. He'd liked the softness of her curves and the fact that she was exactly as nature had made her. Although he wouldn't be vulgar enough to say it, especially to his sister, she had the most beautiful breasts he'd ever seen. Her legs weren't bad, either. She just carried a little extra weight around the waist.

"Name one other woman you've dated who's been overweight," Maisey said.

"Maybe I wasn't *initially* attracted to Nancy, but the more I got to know her, the prettier she became." She just couldn't compete with the cocaine that'd kept him going back then. No one could.

"She's not capable of dealing with someone like you. That's all."

"You remember what I was like back then, Mais. I wasn't capable of having a relationship with *anyone*. Even you. But I'm clean now. Things are different."

"She's still outgunned, doesn't have nearly as much experience with men as those women you've been dating in LA. You need someone more…sophisticated."

He turned down the radio. "You mean someone who can't get hurt because she doesn't know how to care in the first place? Someone more like Mom?"

"Of course not! But what you had with Nancy wasn't a real relationship, either, so don't try to pretend it was."

Keith told himself to relax so this wouldn't explode into an argument. He understood why she might be protective of Nancy, but he didn't need Maisey piling on. He already felt like shit because of what he'd done. "How was it not a real relationship? I liked her. A lot."

He'd never been around anyone less like his mother. She'd been exactly what he needed at the time. He still wasn't sure what he would've done without her friend-ship and support. But she'd definitely given him the cold shoulder a few minutes ago. She hadn't been happy to see him; he could tell.

"You've liked plenty of women," Maisey said as if that was meaningless.

He shot her a scowl. "I'm not going to hurt Nancy. For your information, I just apologized to her."

His sister's attitude seemed to improve. "That was nice of you."

"You don't think I have a conscience?"

"I think you can be devastating, even when you don't mean to be."

He'd never live down his reputation. He'd earned it too honestly. But, in his own defense, he hadn't been ready to settle down—with anyone—and he hadn't pre-sented himself in any other way.

Regardless, there wasn't much point in continuing the conversation. They were driving to the morgue in Charleston to view the body of their dead mother. He didn't need to make this day any worse. "That was five years ago," he said calmly. "I'm not the same person."

"You have the same gorgeous face. The same dis-arming smile. The same appeal to women," she said. "I'd rather you didn't rekindle your relationship with Nancy while you're here. It's not like you need her—or would ever take her seriously even if you *did* start seeing her again. There are too many other women out there who'd suit you better."

He raked his fingers through his hair. The last thing he wanted to do was hurt Nancy again. But it upset him to hear what Maisey had to say. He was used to having his younger sister on *his* side. They'd always banded together. They'd had to—to survive their childhood. "She's an adult. I'm sure she can take care of herself and doesn't need you to run interference for her. Anyway, stop worrying. I won't be here long enough to start seeing anyone."

She sighed. "It's not like I want you to leave. I'm just asking you to stay away from Nancy. As a personal favor to me."

Her earnest expression irritated him even more. "You've gotten *that* close to her?"

"Yes! She's someone I trust and confide in, someone I enjoy working with."

He turned toward the ferry, which would take them to the mainland. "Is that why you paid her the money I owed her?"

The way Maisey fiddled with her purse told him she was suddenly uncomfortable. "I'm sorry if you're mad that I got involved. But she's never had much money. I made sure that what she lent you came back to her sooner rather than later, that's all."

"I tried to pay her myself," he said. "Less than a year after I left."

"I'm glad to hear that."

"She didn't mention it?"

"No."

"So you thought I never tried."

"I wasn't worried. I'd already taken care of it."

"I gave her a car, too—something to make up for how I treated her. But she wouldn't take it."

"You can't be surprised she'd say no. That was an expensive present."

"Wow. You *are* defensive of Nancy."

Maisey reached out to squeeze his forearm. "Not really. I love you, too. It was very generous of you."

He pulled into the line of cars waiting to cross over. "She didn't mention that, either? The car?"

"We don't talk about you. I mean, *I* do sometimes. But if I bring you up, she just listens. She never says anything herself."

He adjusted his windshield wipers to handle a fresh deluge. "She hates me that much?"

"I wouldn't call it *hate*. She's...moved on."

The ferry captain approached the car in front of them. "Who's she dating now?"

"Some guy from Charleston."

"Is it serious?"

When she didn't answer, he looked over and found her glaring at him. "Does it matter?"

"No, it doesn't," he muttered and lowered his window to pay the fare.

Their mother was on a gurney in the back end, where the corpses were weighed and tagged. A sheet covered her from the neck down, but her arms had been taken out from under it and folded beneath her breasts—probably Dean Gillespie's attempt to make her appear "at peace," for their sake.

But there was nothing peaceful or consoling about any of this; Josephine's death felt wrong in so many ways, beginning with the fact that she'd never looked worse. Her hair fell away from her face exactly as it had dried when they'd pulled her from the tub, and dark circles underscored her closed eyes—the eyes that so many people had admired.

As if that weren't disconcerting enough, her skin was

so waxy Keith barely recognized her. He was tempted to check the name on the tag attached to her big toe, just to be sure. *His* mother didn't have age spots or wrinkles. *His* mother didn't have dull, lackluster hair. But this person did.

Her body wasn't the same, either. Although Keith had heard his mother described as a bombshell on more than one occasion, she looked frail and insignificant under that sheet, as if she'd never been a singular beauty.

This was what it took to finally get the better of Josephine Lazarow, Keith decided. Age alone wasn't enough. Age conquered everyone else, but not her. Only *death* could win.

"She would hate that we're seeing her like this," Maisey whispered.

Keith wished he hadn't come. She might have been his greatest stumbling block, his greatest challenge, but she'd also been a constant he could rely on—someone who stood firm in her convictions, commanded respect, lived by her own rules and made damn sure everyone around her did, too. He'd known that if he ever really needed her she might give him hell, but she'd come through in the end.

"We'll hire a good makeup artist for the funeral," he said, but only to comfort his sister. Makeup wouldn't help now. His mother had lost that vital essence that'd made her so magnificent.

Maisey didn't respond.

"Her death feels so…premature," he added.

When Maisey put her hand over his in a show of understanding, he wished he could shrug her off. He didn't want sympathy. He wanted answers. Who had felled their powerful mother? She must not have seen whoever it was. The person who'd killed her *had* to be someone she would never, in a million years, have expected to do her wrong.

"The various funeral homes usually engage someone who specializes in hair and makeup," Dean told them. "All you have to do is bring in a picture, and they'll do their best to make your mother look like you remember."

"I'll ask her regular hairdresser to do her hair," Maisey told him. "And I'll try to manage her makeup myself."

"If that's what you prefer," Dean said. "Just keep in mind that those services are available if you need them."

Keith couldn't imagine being asked to do something like that, but maybe all stylists knew that preparing a client's hair for his or her funeral was a possibility. The last dead person he'd encountered had been his father, and even though they'd never been particularly close, that loss had hit him hard, since Malcolm was the only calm parent of the two...

Trying to shrug off the feelings any memory of his father—or his past, really—evoked, he studied his mother's throat. He thought he could discern a faint tinge of blue, where a strong pair of hands might've cut off her airflow, but he wasn't sure if he was just imagining things. Her whole body looked blue...

"Have you seen enough?" Maisey asked.

Keith didn't answer. "She has no marks on her *any-where*?" he asked Dean.

"Marks?"

"Injuries?"

Dean shook his head. "None that I've seen, but I haven't examined her. They'll do that during the autopsy. Record every bruise or blemish."

But things could change from day to day, couldn't they? Even if she was dead? Keith had learned that the signs of strangulation typically didn't show up during the first twenty-four hours, so it was reasonable to assume that they also might disappear after a certain length of time. "Would you mind removing the sheet and taking a look now?" he asked. He didn't feel *he* could do that. It would be the ultimate invasion of his mother's privacy at a time when she couldn't defend it. But he felt someone should check her corpse before the autopsy was performed. Having more than one person provide an opinion could prove useful later on—although he had no idea how or why. He was just trying to document everything he could before it was too late, trying to use simple logic.

"Um, sure," Dean said. "But...can I ask why?"

"I'd like to know what you see."

The coroner's technician had been quite solicitous. At this, he hesitated, as if it was pretty far outside his expectations. But then he acquiesced. "Of course. If it'll help."

"You look, too," Keith told Maisey and turned away while Dean peeled back the covering.

"Anything?" Keith asked when they indicated that it was safe to turn back.

"She's had breast augmentation surgery," Maisey said drily. "After pretending her figure was God-given, ever since I can remember, that should surprise me, but it doesn't."

That didn't surprise Keith, either. But he wasn't investigating her vanity. "Anything else? Anything suspicious?"

"Nothing," Dean said.

Steeling himself for whatever *he* might find, he lifted his mother's eyelids. "Do her eyes seem bloodshot to you?" he asked Dean.

Dean was startled by the question. "Um… I guess. Yeah, they're bloodshot. But… I wouldn't say that necessarily means anything."

"According to what I've read, bloodshot eyes can indicate strangulation," Keith said.

Dean smoothed the sheet over their mother. "A pathologist would be the one to answer that question. I'd suggest not jumping to any conclusions."

"Because…"

"Because those conclusions could have far-reaching implications," he said. "And they may not be correct."

"Our mother didn't kill herself." Turning to Maisey, he said, "We need to make sure they test the level of carbon dioxide in her blood, too."

Maisey stared at him. "What will that tell us?"

"It's another sign of suffocation."

His sister blanched. "And you know this *how*?"

"Everything's on the internet."

She looked torn. "Keith, I don't want to be rude, but…a little internet research doesn't make your opinion any more relevant than the coroner's."

"It might be relevant to whatever pathologist we choose," he said. "And that's who'll be doing the autopsy."

She reached out to touch their mother's hand—then quickly withdrew. "It's funny. This is the first time I've ever felt as if *I'm* in control while being in the same room with her."

Keith understood what his sister meant. But before he could acknowledge her comment, she said, "Are you sure we aren't in denial, unwilling to see our capable mother succumb to human emotions like depression? Desperation? Maybe she *wasn't* impervious to all the things that get to the rest of us. You have to admit that financial stuff we learned from Chief Underwood would *have* to make an impact on her."

Keith tried to entertain that thought but felt more resolve instead of less. "The mother I knew wouldn't give up."

"When you say stuff like that, I agree," Maisey said. "But I keep coming back to one thing. Who could've killed her? Who would've wanted to?"

"That's what we have to find out."

"Whoa! You think she was *murdered*?" Dean broke in.

"You don't?" Keith replied.

"No. I understand that what you're going through is painful, but the coroner knows what he's doing. You can trust whatever he tells you."

The coroner was an elected official. He had a background in law enforcement; he wasn't even a doctor. "Are you one hundred percent sure of that?" Keith asked.

Dean backed away from the challenge. "He's the coroner," he mumbled.

Keith could barely refrain from rolling his eyes. "Maybe so, but he's as human as you or I."

They thanked Gillespie. Then they went out and sat in the car while they pored over the list of pathologists Chief Underwood had given them. Keith used the internet on his phone to see what he could find out about each one—but they all seemed reputable. So they started going down the list to see who could do it relatively soon.

After three calls and a bit of negotiating—which included the offer of a bonus to get a Dr. Pendergast to rearrange his schedule—they had it booked for early Sunday morning. Maisey contacted the funeral home to arrange for transportation, since the coroner didn't provide that, while Keith started to drive them back to Fairham. After Maisey was done, they called Rocki on his Bluetooth so they could update her.

"It's all set," Maisey told her. "The funeral home will pick up Mom's body from the coroner and take it to the hospital here in Charleston first thing Sunday morning."

"That's soon," Rocki said. "You must be happy about that, Keith."

"I am," he said.

"How much are they going to charge us?" she asked.

"Don't worry about the cost," Keith replied. "I got it."

"Are you sure?" Rocki asked. "Doesn't seem fair."

"We should all split it," Maisey suggested, but he shook his head.

"No, this will be on me."

Maisey loosened her seat belt as if she was having trouble getting comfortable. "There's just one thing."

"What?" He was finally feeling encouraged that they were making progress. So why did *she* sound so concerned and reluctant?

"You're a very passionate person," she responded. "Once you grab hold of something, you don't let go."

She was right about that. Even when he'd been trying to destroy himself, he'd done a damn fine job of it. "So?" He stopped at a traffic light before taking the turn that would bring them to the ferry and then the island.

"Rocki, do you know where she's going with this?"

"I'm pretty sure I can guess," she said.

"As your sisters, we agree with what you're doing," Maisey explained. "But we're also a little worried that Mom's death will consume you, take over your life."

Even though Rocki couldn't see him, he waved their concerns away. "I'm going to catch the bastard who killed her, no matter what."

"We don't even know she *was* killed," Rocki told him.

"*I* do," he said.

8

Nancy sighed as she clicked through the messages she'd received from potential "matches" via the online dating site where she'd put up her profile a couple of months ago. This was where she'd met Tom. Although their relationship hadn't completely ended, it wasn't very promising. There had to be someone else out there for her. But she felt no enthusiasm for flirting, didn't even care to return the messages.

The uncertainty in her life was getting to her, she decided. She refused to believe her disinterest had anything to do with Keith's presence on the island. She knew better than to let the sight of him change anything. She'd lost her employer and could be losing her job. *That* was why she'd lost her zest for dating.

Too bad she hadn't also lost her zest for *eating*. Tempted to drown her anxiety and frustration in a fudge brownie sundae, she glanced at the kitchen. She didn't have any brownies. She'd have to bake.

On the plus side, no one could bake more delicious brownies than she could…

She'd just gotten up from her desk when her phone rang. Her sister was calling; she could see Jade's name and photograph on the screen.

Eager for the distraction, she snatched up her cell. "Hey, what's going on?"

"I just saw him!" Jade exclaimed.

Nancy was on her way to the pantry so she could take stock of her supplies. Although she'd already gotten groceries, she hadn't purchased any powdered cocoa, so she'd have to run over to Smitty's, the island's only grocery store, again. But at this, she forgot about the brownies. "Saw *who*?" She thought she had a good idea but hoped she was wrong...

"Keith Lazarow! He and his sister were on the same ferry I was. They were parked *right* next to me!"

Nancy felt her mood darken. "So?"

"So I thought you'd like to know. He looked good. Better than ever. If I were straight, I would've swooned when he waved at me."

Jade, who'd recently turned twenty-six, was Nancy's only sibling, although they weren't related by blood. Jade's mother had been a free-flowing hippie type who'd floated on to greener pastures before Nancy's mother met Jade's father. But, for the most part, they'd been raised together, since he had custody. She and Jade had grown especially close after Nancy's mother died of bladder cancer. Jade managed the Drift Inn but still lived with her father; she wasn't able to move out. He'd retired from the marina, where he'd worked for more than thirty years, was getting old and needed a little help. Nancy saw them both often, since she went over almost every Saturday to make dinner.

"I have no interest in Keith," she said, purposely using a bored voice.

"Really?" Jade responded. "Then *I'll* go after him. I could be bi—maybe."

Nancy rolled her eyes. "I've never seen you go after a guy. You're definitely a lesbian. And even if you could change your sexual preference, he'd chew you up and spit you out." And Nancy knew just how painful that could be.

"Maybe he could turn me, show me what I've been missing."

Nancy wasn't going to acknowledge his talent between the sheets any more than his good looks. "Remember how much you hated his mother?"

"What's the Queen of Fairham got to do with anything?" Jade asked. "She's gone now. And didn't *everyone* hate her?"

Everyone except the people Josephine had actually tried to win over. She could be irresistible, if she wanted to be. But Nancy wasn't going in to any of that, either. "He's a lot like her."

"How?"

"He's beautiful, but he's also single-minded and determined. When he gets something in his head, there's no getting it out. And I don't believe he knows how to love *anyone*." Nancy could remember moments when he'd been gentle, tender, even vulnerable, but she didn't mention that because she needed to focus on the reasons he wouldn't be good for her *or* her gay sister.

"From what I hear, he's not on drugs anymore. And he owns a multimillion-dollar company. Considering all of that, I could probably put up with a little straight sex, even if he is single-minded and determined."

"Jade, trust me—keep your distance." Veering away from the kitchen, Nancy went into her bedroom instead, where she began looking through her dresses. Did she own anything she could wear to the funeral? She had a simple black dress, but since she'd lost weight it was two sizes too big.

"I'd never make a play for him, even if I *was* straight," Jade said. "I know you still have feelings for him. I was just trying to make you admit it."

"I don't have feelings for him," Nancy argued. "It's been five years since we were together. I'd have to be a glutton for punishment to hang on that long."

"Yeah, yeah. Tough talk."

"I'm over him," she insisted, but she had no doubt her sister could see through her denials. Nancy hadn't been able to sleep with Tom because she couldn't help comparing him with Keith—and finding him lacking. No one she'd met could measure up to the one man she'd truly loved, which was why she hadn't been intimate with anyone since. "What were you doing on the ferry, anyway?"

"I went to Charleston. Had some shopping to do before work tonight."

Her sister worked three days and two nights a week, and Wednesday was one of her late shifts. "For…"

"I was out of blush. I also needed some specialty items I can't get here—those pretzels Dad likes and that one brand of hummus."

"Sounds like fun."

"It got rid of my island fever. How was work?"

Nancy pulled out a sheath dress covered in sequins. It was black but too dated—and too fancy—for a funeral. She needed something classy and subdued, something Josephine herself would have approved of. "I was off today."

"This is Wednesday. Aren't you normally off on Thursday?"

"Marlene had a doctor's appointment tomorrow, so we traded."

"Why didn't you call? I would've asked you to go with me."

"I wish I had. I need a new dress for the funeral." Badly. Until this very moment, she hadn't realized just how inadequate her wardrobe was.

"When's the funeral?"

Nancy thought of Maisey and Keith's suspicions. "They haven't announced it yet."

"Good. That means we've got time. We'll find you a dress that'll make Keith eat his heart out."

"Hello! I doubt he'll be looking at anyone that way at his mother's *funeral*."

"Isn't he a playboy?"

"I wouldn't call him a *playboy* exactly. He was messed up and looking for a safe harbor, which meant he wasn't particularly discriminating. That made him dangerous enough. Anyway, I don't care to talk about Keith."

"Why not? If you're over him, it shouldn't matter."

She shoved more of her clothes to one side and pulled out another dress, one that was even more dated and inappropriate than the last one. "He's ancient history, that's why."

"He doesn't have to be. Maybe he isn't someone you can expect to marry, but…"

Nancy doubted this conversation was going anywhere good, but she couldn't resist taking the bait. *"But?"*

"You told me he was great in bed."

She nearly dropped the dress. *"I did?"*

"Yes, you did," her sister said. "It was your birthday,

and you were drunk—laughing and crying at the same time, remember? It was only last year."

"Obviously, I had no clue what I was saying," Nancy mumbled.

"That doesn't mean it's not true. Lie to yourself if that makes it easier. But consider this. You might as well take a ride—or two or three. Have some fun while he's here. You've been through one hell of a long drought."

"Take a ride?" Nancy said. "My God, you're crude! Anyway, I'm not going near him. And I'm done talking to you. So...go get ready for work. Goodbye." She disconnected. She had no interest in falling back into bed with Keith Lazarow.

But ten minutes later, she started digging through her lingerie drawer. Although she had some pretty things, just like her more fancy dresses, none of them fit.

She hadn't even opened that drawer in the past five years.

Keith liked Maisey's husband. Rafe was a man's man—and yet he knew how to love Maisey and keep her happy. Keith had never been more relieved to have him as part of the family than he was that night when they came for dinner. Without his mother at the table, the fact that Josephine would no longer be the backbone of their family sank in a little deeper. Losing someone like her left a huge hole, and Keith wasn't sure who would fill it. He felt the job naturally fell to him. His grandfather would expect him to carry on the Coldiron legacy. But Keith had a life—for the first time—and it was on the opposite coast.

Besides, as a recovering addict, he wasn't sure he was capable of doing everything his grandfather would expect. How could he follow in such a great man's footsteps? Do him proud?

At least, thanks to Rafe, he could rest assured that Maisey was loved and content, and so were her two children. Laney's real mother had bugged out just after she was born, hadn't been able to face the prospect of raising a blind child. But that woman, whoever she was, didn't know what she was missing. Keith had never met a sweeter, brighter or more endearing child. He wanted to scoop her into his arms the second they arrived, but she'd grown so much since Maisey had brought her to California a year ago. She wasn't a little girl anymore; she was on the verge of puberty. And because Keith didn't see her often, he was afraid she might not remember him.

Hoping to remind her who "Uncle Keith" was, he put her hands to his face to let her feel what he looked like instead of forcing a hug on her. "You're going to be a real beauty one day," he said as her fingertips moved gently and quickly over his features. "Every bit as striking as your Grandma Josephine."

Apparently satisfied, she dropped her hands. "My mom tells me you're not bad yourself."

He grinned at her comeback. "Your mom and I are related, which makes anything she tells you about me less than reliable."

Laney lifted her chin. "I've heard how the women here on the island talk about you."

"And that has some significance?"

"Oh, yeah," she said. "Besides, Grandma told me."

"Told you what?"

"She said you were 'exceptionally' handsome." Her

smile disappeared. "I wish she hadn't died. Did you know she used to have me over for tea every Sunday?"

Keith met Maisey's eyes. "Tea? Really? For an eleven-year-old? That was Mom's idea of showing her a good time?"

Maisey smoothed Laney's hair as she spoke. "Yes. And believe it or not, that was the highlight of Laney's week. She'd always come home with some new piece of jewelry or her hair done up. Mom taught her manners and posture and...basically put Laney through her own brand of finishing school. She even taught her how to crochet. Laney makes all kinds of things now, and she's getting good at it."

Tears filled Laney's eyes, but she made no sound. She just wiped them away when they fell and pulled Bryson, who was threatening to toddle off in the other direction—although Keith had to wonder how she knew that—around to face him. "Did you see my little brother?" she asked. "Isn't he chubby?"

Bryson had a full head of dark hair and big blue eyes, and he was huge for his age. "This kid's a beast," Keith said to Maisey and Rafe. "What're you feeding him? Steroids?"

Rafe shook his head as if he was just as mystified by his son's size. "Not unless there are steroids in breast milk and baby food. He was nursing until a few months ago."

"He must be breaking into the pantry late at night," Keith said as he rubbed the toddler's round cheek.

Laney hauled Bryson into her willowy arms. The baby had backed away, wasn't quite ready to let Keith touch him. Keith had seen him only once before—a year ago—so Bryson had no idea who Keith was. "He can go potty in the toilet now," she announced.

"That's got to be good news to all involved," Keith said. "It'll certainly make it easier to talk *me* into baby-sitting."

Laney laughed as if that was the funniest joke she'd ever heard. "I could help you."

"Perfect. Until he's completely potty trained, you can change him for me."

Her grin spread from ear to ear. "You don't want a blind girl changing a messy diaper, or you might have even more to clean up after."

He loved that she could joke with him. "I bet your keen sense of smell would keep you out of trouble."

"Sometimes, but not always," she admitted.

Maisey seemed so pleased with her daughter that Keith couldn't help winking at her. "She's special."

"I agree," Maisey said and slid her arm around Laney as Keith led them into the dining room.

"I hope you're hungry," he said to Laney.

She let her little brother wiggle down. Then she paused to sniff the air. He expected her to identify what they were having for dinner. But he could tell she wasn't thinking about food. She suddenly looked too sad for that.

"What is it?" he asked. "You don't like salmon?"

"I can still smell her perfume," she said softly.

Keith shot Maisey a look that asked her to let him take over and guided Laney to her seat. "We'll get you a nice keepsake of Grandma's you can take home to remember her by, okay?" He didn't dare promise her the ring Chief Underwood had mentioned. He hoped he could pay off his mother's debts, but he had no way of knowing how extensive they were. With an estate of that size, she could be millions of dollars in debt, and he definitely didn't keep *that* much on hand. Even if he could come up with the money, he couldn't risk everything he'd built by trying to save his mother's holdings.

Careful to avoid his grandfather's eyes, which were staring down at him from that huge canvas on the wall, he told himself he'd look into it and do what he could.

"Can I have her robe?" Laney asked. "I just want to be able to feel it."

"Absolutely," he told her.

Once Laney took her place at the table, she fingered her silverware as if she was checking to make sure everything was where it should be now that her grandmother was gone. "I really wish she'd come back."

"We all do," Keith said, and felt a measure of surprise that he meant it.

Because he and Maisey had agreed they would not discuss the manner of their mother's death in front of Laney, the conversation over dinner revolved around Rafe's work, Maisey's books, Bry's first words and Laney's school. Rafe took the ferry to the mainland and dropped her off four days a week and Maisey picked her up at two o'clock. Keith enjoyed spending time with his family, especially since he'd been without them for the past several years. But no matter how far the conversation drifted from the reason he'd come to Fairham, he couldn't forget what he'd seen at the morgue. The image of his mother lying lifeless on that gurney haunted him, troubled him. And Pippa's silence made him tense. She did everything she normally did, even smiled as she delivered each course, but a sense of pervasive concern hung heavy in the air.

He told himself she was lost without Josephine, but he knew it was more than that. Whatever she'd wanted to speak to him about earlier seemed to be bothering her. He would've approached her about that, given her an opportunity to talk, but by the time he'd returned from Charleston, she'd been in the last stages of making dinner and he'd had several phone calls he needed to make. He had reliable employees, but he couldn't abandon them completely. He'd also been reluctant to have a conversation that might upset one or both of them right before Maisey arrived with the children.

He'd figured waiting until after dinner would be soon enough. But once everyone left, and she finally told him what was worrying her, he wished he'd taken the time to listen sooner.

9

Keith thought he'd be in for another long, wakeful night. He had so much on his mind. But almost as soon as he stretched out on his bed, without even turning off the light or undressing, he fell asleep for a solid four hours.

Then he jolted awake.

Something had disturbed him. A noise.

Lying very still, he listened to see if he could figure out what it was, but all he could hear was the settling noises of the house and the soft patter of rain hitting the roof. Rain had been falling in fits and starts ever since he'd returned to the island, and it didn't show any sign of clearing up.

A moment later, lightning flashed outside. He assumed the weather had to be what woke him. He hadn't closed the shutters, so it was his own fault. But if he got up to close them now, he probably wouldn't get back to sleep.

Squeezing his eyes shut, he tried not to think about the fact that his mother's lover was married and whether or not she knew she was seeing a man who already had a wife. He tried not to think of his grandfather, and the fact that everything Henry had built could soon be gone, including Coldiron House. Most of all, he tried to block out what he'd learned from Pippa. But it was impossible to drift off a second time. Merely opening his eyes seemed to have brought an avalanche of worries down on his head. And the light he'd left on was bothering him.

Still, he was determined not to give up on sleep too soon. Rolling onto his side, he pulled his pillow over his face—and that was when he heard a strange thump followed by a creak.

Pippa had gone home after they'd had their little talk. He was supposed to be alone. And yet…there was movement.

His eyes sought the alarm clock. Nearly one. Who would be in the house in the middle of the night? Had his mother's murderer come back to remove some piece of evidence? Was the perpetrator checking the scene, making sure he hadn't overlooked anything important? Perhaps he was leaving something behind, planting evidence that would further mislead police…

Suddenly glad that he hadn't taken the time to undress, Keith jumped out of bed. He wished he had a weapon in case he needed one, but he had nothing, not even a baseball bat. His mother had insisted that all sporting equipment be kept in the garage. That wasn't a huge imposition, since they had an extra stall with racks and hooks for that sort of thing. But it made dealing with an intruder damned inconvenient.

How did this person get in, anyway?

Keith's mind raced as he struggled to remember if he'd returned the spare key to its rightful place behind the light.

No. He'd put it on the ring with the key to his rental car and had been using it as he came and went.

He wasn't positive he'd locked the front door after Maisey and her family left tonight, however. He'd never felt he was in danger—not from anything other than his own demons—so locking up when he was here on Fairham wasn't a strict habit for him.

Even if he *had* locked the house, there were ways someone could've gotten in without breaking a window. Pippa had a key. So did Tyrone. There were probably other house help who'd had access at one time or another. His mother would've demanded they return their keys when they left her employment, but she felt so safe, so untouchable in her gated mansion that he doubted she'd ever go so far as to have the locks changed.

A disgruntled employee could easily have made a copy. Most if not all former staff could have the code to the gate and could've shared it among themselves— or whoever it was could've just scaled the fence. That wasn't impossible.

Basically, just about *anyone* could be in the house.

After cracking open his bedroom door, Keith peered out into the hallway. He saw nothing but blackness, and didn't turn on another light. He did the opposite. He turned off his bedroom light so he wouldn't reveal his presence.

He could no longer hear movement, but he was sure he'd heard *someone*, despite the rain. Problem was, there were thirty rooms in Coldiron House, many of them closed off since they were so rarely used. That created a lot of places to hide.

Anxiety drew his nerves taut as he crept down the

hallway, calling on his knowledge of the house since he couldn't see.

Lightning flashed at the windows as his feet sank into the plush carpet, giving him a momentary glimpse of the marble foyer below. A long shadow, which looked like that of a man, startled him—until he realized it was his mother's giant flower arrangement and the pedestal that supported it. He saw nothing else. The front door wasn't broken or ajar and, as far as he could tell, no one was creeping around with a bag of the family silver.

Instead of going downstairs, he veered off toward his mother's suite. He wished the noise he'd heard could be her, coming home from a lengthy vacation abroad, as she'd done so many times when he was younger. But he'd seen her corpse in the morgue.

The doors to her room stood open, which made the hair rise on the back of his neck. He'd purposely closed those doors; he hadn't liked the sense of expectation he felt if he left them open.

So why weren't they still closed?

Someone had come inside...

Keith picked up an antique vase that'd likely cost several thousand dollars. A vase wasn't the kind of weapon he would've preferred, but it was the only thing close at hand. He held it above his head and was about to creep inside his mother's room when a bouncing light drew his eye back to the first floor.

Someone was *outside*, moving around the perimeter of the house with a flashlight.

Prepared to chase down whoever it was, he took the stairs two at a time. But he didn't have the chance to dash outside. The moment he threw open the door, he came nose to nose with a wet Chief Underwood.

She eyed the vase he carried. Then she looked down at her gun, which was pointed directly at him. "I think I'd win this fight."

He stared beyond her, into the rain, to make sure she was alone. "I'm just glad you didn't fire the second I appeared." He'd obviously startled her, which made sense, since he hadn't turned on any lights. "What are you doing here?"

She returned her gun to its holster. "Someone called. Said there was an intruder at Coldiron House."

He set the vase on a table. "*Someone* called?"

"Dispatch said he wouldn't leave his name."

"But you have the number. You can track where it came from."

"I can try in the morning when I have more time to look into it," she said. "My mind wasn't on tracking phone calls when dispatch woke me up. I was afraid that if your mother *had* been murdered, there might be some nefarious plot to take your life, too."

He couldn't help grinning at her rain-streaked face. Maybe it was sexist, but he got a kick out of her rushing into the storm to protect him when she was half his size and weight...

"What?" she said.

He shook his head. "Nothing. Thanks for being willing to put your life on the line." She had guts; he had to give her that. And she probably *could* do more than he could—as long as she had that gun.

The way she suddenly glared at him indicated that she'd caught on to his reaction. "You're a chauvinist pig, aren't you? I got out of bed and drove up here to tramp around your house, which is the size of an apartment building—in the rain, I might add—and you think it's funny."

He'd managed to keep a straight face until she said that. Then he had to laugh. Maybe he'd needed the release.

"Okay. I'm leaving." She threw up her hands in disgust. "You're a bastard, by the way. Just in case other people haven't told you."

He grabbed her shoulder before she could start down the porch steps. "I'm sorry," he said, but he was still laughing, which didn't work to his advantage.

"Let go of me," she snapped. "If someone's here, I'm going to let him kill you."

He would've laughed harder—except those sounds *had* been chilling. "I *did* hear something," he said, sobering. "Why do you think I was carrying a damn vase? I'm not rearranging decorations in the middle of the night."

She rolled her eyes. "What you heard was *me*."

"No, these sounds came from inside."

Clearly suspicious that he was mocking her, she hesitated. "Are you serious?"

He rubbed his neck. "Yeah, I am. But it might be nothing." Maybe before Pippa went home, she returned something to his mother's room and left the doors ajar...

Chief Underwood seemed reluctant to forgive him for making light of her efforts, but he could tell she was also a stickler about doing her job. "So now you want me to check out the house?"

He wanted to borrow her gun so *he* could check out the house, but he knew better than to ask. "If you would be so kind," he replied and gave her a sweeping bow as he pushed the door wide enough to admit her.

Starting with his mother's suite, she walked through every room and looked under the beds and inside the closets. She searched the attic, too. "No bogeyman," she announced, even though he'd followed her every step of the way and could see that for himself. "I'm guessing it was a crank call, a false alarm."

Although something *had* disturbed his sleep. Was it just the storm, as he'd first thought? "If you say so, Chief."

"There's no evidence to indicate otherwise," she said as they walked back to the entry hall. "But I'd lock the door from now on, if I were you."

"It might've been locked."

"The fact that you don't know is the problem. I'd double-check."

"Got it. Will do."

Instead of leaving, she hooked her thumbs into her utility belt and openly appraised him.

He smoothed down his hair, which was probably standing up. He had, after all, just rolled out of bed. "What is it?" he asked when she didn't speak.

"I'm curious about you."

"Why?"

"On the one hand, you're everything I was expecting."

"And on the other?"

"*Nothing* I was expecting."

"The fact that you're familiar with my reputation doesn't surprise me."

"You *are* the Coldiron Prince." Her lopsided grin said she was teasing, making fun of his family's lofty status.

"In what way have I lived up to your expectations?" He'd told himself he wouldn't ask but couldn't resist.

"You're handsome as the devil. I'm sure I can't be the first woman to tell you that."

He breathed a little easier. "Handsome" wasn't the negative comment he'd anticipated, but he could tell she wasn't finished yet. "I hope the comparison stops there."

She laughed. "Do you and the devil share other traits?"

"Some would say we do. Just so you know, I'm completely reformed."

"We'll see," she said with a wink and reached for the door handle.

"Chief?"

She turned.

"Any chance you'd give me Hugh Pointer's number?"

"You're coming dangerously close to interfering with my investigation, Mr. Lazarow."

He rested his hand on the doorknob. "I'm still waiting for the file."

"Les is still working on that."

"I'll get Hugh's number when you return my mother's phone and computer, anyway. I behaved myself at the morgue, didn't I?"

"You told the coroner's technician that the coroner doesn't know what he's talking about. You call that behaving?"

"I said he was *human*. Anyone can make a mistake."

He got the impression she found his interaction with Dean Gillespie amusing, wasn't really put out by it. "Fine. Give me your number. I'll text you in the morning when I get to the office."

"Thanks." He did as she asked, watching as she added him to her contacts.

"What are you doing?" he asked when she proceeded to key in a text.

She didn't answer, so he assumed she was letting dispatch know she hadn't found an intruder. Or maybe she was sending Les Scott a message, telling him to get Pointer's number in addition to copying that darn file.

When she finished, she slid her phone into the pocket of her uniform. "Have a good night, Mr. Lazarow."

"You, too, Chief." He stepped out on the porch until she could get into her squad car. Then he shut and locked the door. It wasn't until he reached his bedroom and saw his phone on the nightstand that he realized she'd been texting *him*. Only she didn't mention Pointer. He supposed that information was still coming in the morning.

I probably wouldn't refuse if you asked me out. Harper Underwood

He had her first name now, which seemed like a victory in itself. And that "probably" made him eager to test her. He hadn't planned to date while he was on Fairham, but he figured befriending the chief of police couldn't be a *bad* thing. Perhaps once they got to know each other, he could convince her that his mother hadn't committed suicide.

Dinner Friday night? he wrote.

Pick me up at six.

He smiled as he sank onto the edge of the bed. He'd never dated a cop before.

I hope you're not texting while driving—and in the rain, no less.

My phone takes voice commands. Why, were you considering a citizen's arrest?

I wouldn't dare.

Do I detect sarcasm? Forget protecting you from an intruder. I might shoot you myself.

No sarcasm on my part. I'm impressed that you came out to defend me. So impressed that I'm not sure you'll ever be able to top that.

Do I have to?

It could make Friday more interesting...

Then I'll see what I can do.

Sounds promising.

Don't get your hopes up too high. It won't entail removing my clothes.

Then I won't remove mine, either.

Turning the tables on me?

I already pegged you as a Goody Two-shoes.

Someone has to tell you no.

Chuckling at her response, he put his phone back on the nightstand and went downstairs to dig through the refrigerator. He was halfway through a turkey-and-Swiss sandwich when he noticed wet footprints on the floor, coming from the back entry. He and Chief Underwood had turned on the light and looked around the kitchen, but because they could see that the back door was locked, they hadn't walked all the way over.

They should have. Where the hell had those footprints come from?

His heart pounded as he followed them into the pantry. Once he checked it more thoroughly than the cursory glance they'd given it before, he found a dish towel on one shelf. The fact that it was wadded up and damp made him think someone had come in out of the rain and used it to wipe off.

So where was that someone now?

His voice was deep and resonant, like that of a radio host. He sounded handsome, well-polished, but given his mother's taste, Keith had expected nothing less.

"I'm terribly sorry about your mother."

Keith pivoted at the window and started back across the room. The weather had cleared—not that he was paying much attention. "*Are* you?"

"Of course."

"Good. Then maybe you can tell me what happened to her."

There was a slight pause before he said, "I wish I could. But I don't know any more than what the police told me the morning she was…er…found."

"And what did they say?"

"That she…that she took her own life. I'm sure, by now, they've told you the same thing?"

As Pointer spoke, Keith listened for signs of pain or grief. He couldn't detect any, and yet Pointer came across as sincere. "Do you believe that?"

"I don't know what to believe," he replied. "Do *you* believe it?"

"Not for a second."

"What else could've happened?"

Keith headed back to the window and that ray of sunshine he'd noticed before. "Someone killed her."

This declaration was met with silence.

"How do you know?" he asked at length.

Now Keith detected some alarm. But was Hugh Pointer alarmed for the right reasons? "Because she didn't commit suicide. The autopsy hasn't been done yet, but the coroner doesn't believe it was a heart attack, a stroke or an accident. If he's right, that leaves only one other option."

"Murder."

"Yes. And I'm going to find out who did it and make that bastard pay."

Another long silence. Then he said, "I hope you're not intimating that *I* might be that bastard. I'm as shocked and upset as you are. I would *never* hurt your mother."

"Of course you wouldn't." Keith didn't bother to keep the sarcasm out of his voice. "Did she know about your *wife*?"

Hugh cleared his throat. "I won't pretend that what I did was right. We should never have gotten involved. But it wasn't as if I was actively looking for opportunities to cheat. Other than the...relationship I had with Josephine, I've been faithful to my wife. It's just that, when I met your mother...well, you know what she was like. I couldn't take my eyes off her."

"Does your wife know about the affair?"

"No. And I hope she doesn't have to find out."

"You're not going to tell her?"

"Considering my actions, you may not believe this, but I can't stand the thought of hurting her. I get why *you'd* want to see me punished, however. You view me as the bad guy in all of this. But I didn't harm your mother. She was taken from me, the same as she was taken from you. Don't you think that's punishment enough?"

"I think it gets you out of a tight spot. It's got to be hard, juggling someone as demanding and used to attention as my mother when you already have a wife and family."

"That's true, but I couldn't have killed her even if I'd wanted to. I lived for every moment we were together."

Oddly enough, Keith's anger was beginning to ebb. The emotion he hadn't been able to detect at first was now apparent in Hugh's voice, and he couldn't believe the man was faking. "You loved her," Keith said, voicing the realization the second it dawned on him.

"With all my heart," he admitted. "Besides, I was here in Perth, waiting for her to join me, and I can prove it. If someone killed her, it wasn't me."

Keith raked his fingers through his hair. It'd been so much easier to villainize this man, who was cheating on his wife and misleading Josephine—something not many people could pull off—when he'd only been a name and not a real person with feelings. "Did she love *you*?" Keith asked.

"Yes."

That was convincing, too—the way he stated it without reservation. Hugh felt confident with Josephine; very few men had ever felt like that.

So had his mother finally fallen in love? Had she met someone who could gain her respect as well as her heart? Someone who could even out the balance of power?

Although Keith hadn't expected it, this man seemed capable of that. "Were you aware of her financial difficulties?"

Keith had been trying to shock him, to get under his skin so he could elicit a reaction. But *he* was the one who turned out to be surprised.

"I was," he replied. "I helped her as much as I could, without alerting Lana. My wife is no fool. She's always been a big part of my business. She handles most of the money."

Keith pulled out his desk chair and slumped into it.

His mother had been up-front with Hugh. That, right there, changed Keith's opinion of the relationship. She hadn't been using her beauty and her charm to trick him into marrying her so she could exploit his fortune, as they'd assumed. "Shit," he muttered.

Hugh didn't respond immediately. He gave Keith time to absorb what he'd learned. And to his credit, when he did speak, it wasn't to make further denials or protestations of innocence. His voice was soft, beseeching. "She spoke of you often, you know."

Keith sat up. He really didn't want to hear what Hugh had to say on *this* subject. "I'm sure she did. She had more than a few complaints. And I won't lie. A lot of them were legitimate." He had some complaints of his own, also legitimate. But he wouldn't share them with the one person she seemed to care about, especially since she could no longer defend herself.

"It wasn't like that," Hugh said. "In the end, she went over and over the mistakes she made with you. Blamed herself for the majority of your troubles. She loved you a great deal."

A fresh wave of guilt crashed over him. He'd *had* to get away. He wouldn't have survived if he hadn't.

But could he have come back? Should he have? Tried to make amends once he was on his feet?

The answer to that question wasn't quite so clear, and that was where the bulk of his guilt came in. He feared that at some point, anger and resentment, rather than the survival instinct that'd taken him away, were what had stopped him.

"She didn't blame you for anything," he added, as if he could guess Keith's thoughts. "That's important for you to understand. I'm *glad* you called me. I considered calling you. I wanted to tell you that, since she wasn't the type to say it herself. But I wasn't sure you even knew I existed."

A baseball-sized lump rose in Keith's throat, making it impossible for him to speak.

"She was proud of you," Hugh said and hung up.

Tears dripped from Keith's chin as he sat staring at the phone. He'd called a total stranger, full of indignation and judgment—and Hugh had done all he could to mitigate Josephine's mistakes and ease Keith's conscience at the same time. That, more than anything, convinced him Hugh Pointer was telling the truth. He really had loved Josephine, and he'd known her well, probably better than anyone else. Keith couldn't name a single other person she'd ever confided in like that.

But the fact that Hugh hadn't had anything to do with Josephine's death only made what Pippa had told Keith that much more disconcerting.

Nancy had just finished a bridal bouquet and was starting on the smaller bouquets for the bridesmaids when she heard the bell over the door. "Coming!"

After taking a few seconds to add some white roses, she abandoned her worktable—only to bump into Keith, who came striding confidently around the corner.

She put up her palms to avoid a total face-plant into his chest, and he grabbed hold of her shoulders to steady her. She dropped her hands as soon as she touched him, but he didn't let go of her. He gazed down at her, wearing an intense expression—one that made it seem as if he'd missed her, as if he was tempted to pull her the rest of the way into his arms.

Telling herself she had to be *crazy* to attribute emotions he couldn't possibly feel to him, since he'd never cared about her to begin with, she stepped out of reach. "Sorry. I had no idea you...that you... What are you doing here?" She looked behind him, thinking she might see Maisey, but he appeared to be alone.

He blinked at her question. "I'm pretty sure I own this place now, so I'm checking in. You doing okay with the store?"

So *he* was going to inherit Love's in Bloom and not Maisey?

Nancy couldn't help being disappointed by that. She doubted he'd be as easy to work with—or as amenable to her plans. "I'm doing fine. Thank you. Maisey already checked."

"That's good. I don't want you to feel you've been abandoned in all of this."

"Don't worry. I can handle the shop. Unless... Are there any immediate changes you'd like me to make?" She'd assumed it would be business as usual, at least until whoever inherited had a chance to take over. But maybe Keith had other ideas. He was enough like his mother that she could see him diving right in. They always had to be in charge...

"No, not at this time," he said.

She was glad she'd worn her nice black slacks with her gray sweater. This outfit made the most of her more slender figure, so she looked better than she had yesterday when he'd seen her carrying Simba home. It was a relief to not be at that kind of disadvantage again. "Okay. If you think of anything you'd like me to do differently, just let me know."

He nodded as he glanced around. If he were Josephine, she'd be about to get a long list of "change this and change that." But she sensed that he wasn't paying close attention to the shop. He just wasn't ready to leave—was obviously searching for something else to say.

"Is there more?" she asked.

"No." With a frown of disappointment, he turned to go. But then he swung around to face her again—and reversed his answer. "Yes."

She took another step back, just because she liked—a little *too* much—the way he smelled. "What is it?" Had he learned what really happened to his mother? Was she about to hear the shocking or not-so-shocking details?

"I said I was sorry, Nancy. I'll apologize again, if it'll help."

So this *wasn't* about Josephine. He was referring to their personal history. "No, one apology is enough. I said everything was fine between us, and it is."

"It's not," he argued. "I can feel the chill. You haven't forgiven me."

Because she *couldn't* forgive him. She needed to finish getting over him first, or she'd only end up as miserable as she was before, wanting something she couldn't have.

But he probably didn't understand what having him back in her life could do. She felt sure he'd never been so head over heels in love with *anyone* that it would require months, let alone years, to cope with a breakup. "I don't get why it matters one way or the other," she said. "As long as we're cordial to each other, and I continue to do my job until you…you sell this place or whatever else you're going to do with it, we should be good."

"It matters because I care about you," he said. "You

took me in when I was at the lowest point in my life. That means a lot to me. I'm grateful."

She brushed a few clinging leaves from her work apron. "Don't bother with any gratitude where I'm concerned. You don't owe me anything. We had a…a short fling, that's all. Nothing serious." At least on his part; *she* would've given anything to spend the rest of her life with him, despite his problems at the time. "Anyway, I'm happy you've turned your life around. Not many people have the strength or the courage to do that. I don't mean this to sound condescending, but I'm proud of you."

He grimaced. "I'm not looking for praise or acknowledgment. I should never have allowed myself to fall so low. But I've told you things, trusted you with details I haven't shared with anyone else—"

"I would never share anything you told me privately."

"It's not that. It just feels like…something's missing now that I'm back. I never wanted you *out* of my life."

She managed a casual chuckle. "I'm not out of your life. I work for you, don't I?"

He didn't laugh at her little joke. "That's not the same. I'd like to be friends."

She closed her eyes for a moment. "Okay, then we'll be friends." She didn't care what label he put on their relationship, as long as there wasn't much contact. Because even now she could remember the taste of his kiss, the way his lips moved over hers and then trailed down her neck to—

She cut off her thoughts.

He peered at her. *"Honestly?"*

"Of course." Once he obtained her agreement, he'd be satisfied and move on. So she couldn't see any reason to hold out, to make him come around a second time. She wasn't out to punish him; she only wanted to stop the ache in her heart. At last. To be as fine without him as he was without her. Was that too much to ask?

He grinned at her, and she cursed the way that grin turned her knees to jelly. "Okay," he said. "Does that mean you'll let me take you to lunch?"

"Right *now*?"

He checked his watch. "Why not? It's noon."

She wasn't sure how to respond. "I... I can't leave the store."

"You could close down for an hour. We've done it before. Lots of people do that here on Fairham, especially in the winter when business is slow."

"I brought a sandwich today. And since I was off yesterday, I've got too much work to take lunch. Maybe... next week."

His mood dimmed, as if he understood she wasn't eager to spend time with him, regardless of his attempts to make up. "Okay."

She stiffened when he hugged her, refused to close her arms around him in response, mostly because she was afraid she wouldn't be able to let go. It'd been *so* long. But if he noticed her less-than-enthusiastic reaction, he didn't comment on it. "Thank you. It's great to see you again. You look gorgeous," he said.

Not compared to the women he normally dated. She'd seen the Facebook and Instagram pictures he'd been tagged in. Nancy probably weighed more than any of those women. But she told herself to quit being nasty and bitter. She had so much to be grateful for. She loved the town where she lived. She was near her sister and stepfather and wouldn't be if she had to live anywhere else. She enjoyed her work, and she was healthy. So what if she couldn't have the man she wanted? "Thanks."

"I'm going to prove that I'm not as bad as you think," he said and turned to go.

When she called his name, he stopped as if he'd been waiting for some sign from her. She considered telling him the truth—that she'd never thought he was "bad." She'd understood and sympathized, and wanted only the best for him. But what was the point in going over all of that? Their one-sided love affair was ancient history. "Not to put any added pressure on you, but when this is all over, and you're ready to go back to California, I'd like to meet with you if you can spare me a few minutes."

"You mean outside of our lunch date? Because you already committed to that."

She wiped her palms on her apron. "Um, yeah. Right. It can be over lunch. I'd just like to…to make you an offer."

"Now you have my attention."

He was joking—maybe even flirting with her. Feeling a rush of the love-drunk high she used to get when he gave her that look, she moved over to her worktable so she'd have something else to concentrate on. "It's a business offer. I—I'd like to buy the store, if possible. But I'll understand if you'd prefer to hang on to it and let Maisey run it, or…whatever."

When he said nothing, she forced herself to meet his eyes.

"This is what you'd like to do for the rest of your life?" he asked.

She hauled in a deep breath. "Yep."

"That'll lock you into staying on the island."

"I was never the one who wanted to leave," she said. That was him. He'd been angry, unsettled and looking for something that might ease his resentment and dissatisfaction. If he wasn't fighting his demons, he was running from them.

"It's easier to meet people on the mainland," he said. "You know just about everyone here."

Where was he going with this? She opened her mouth to say she didn't need anyone beyond her current circle of friends and her family. But then she caught on. "If by 'people' you mean 'men,' I'm already dating someone."

"That's what Maisey said." He slid his hands into his pockets. "Is it serious, then?"

She placed some more greenery in her current work-in-progress bouquet. "It could become serious. I'm not ruling anything out."

He came over to lean on her worktable. "I see. Where does he live?"

"The Isle of Palms."

"So…he'd move here if you married?"

"If I bought the store, I guess he'd have to." Since marrying Tom wasn't even a possibility, she wasn't worried about that. There could be someone else later who didn't live on Fairham—so far, none of the men on that dating site did—but she couldn't defer her plans forever, waiting to fall in love.

"Okay," he said. "I'll keep that in mind."

"I'd appreciate it."

With a nod, he straightened and walked out, and this time Nancy *did* allow herself to go to the window, which proved to be a mistake. Almost as soon as he reached his car, he walked back to the store, and she had to scramble to return to her worktable before he could step inside.

"Nancy?" he called after the bell went off.

She hurried around the corner. "Yes?"

"Have you ever met Landon?"

"Your brother-in-law?"

"Yes, Roxanne's husband."

A memory came to mind, but it was one that sent a prickle of foreboding down her spine. She didn't want to talk about Landon, especially with Keith. "I've met him. Why?"

He didn't explain; he just asked another question. "When was he on the island last?"

"A few weeks ago for Christmas, as far as I'm aware."

"He was with Roxanne and the kids?"

"Of course. It was the holidays. I can't imagine he'd come here without them." Why wasn't Keith asking Roxanne this? Or Maisey? They'd be in a better position to answer his questions.

"So you've never known him to come to Fairham on his own."

"No. Never," she said, and that was the truth.

"You've never seen him in the store or around town?"

"Not since your mother's Christmas party." For years, Josephine had had an annual celebration at Cold-iron House, during which she handed out the holiday bonuses to all her employees. "Landon was there. So were Roxanne and the kids. Maisey and Rafe weren't. They had another event. To my knowledge, that's the last time Landon was here."

Keith rubbed the beard growth that darkened his

square jaw. "Did Mom and Landon seem to be getting along?"

She'd seen them together briefly, standing alone in a small piano room off the foyer. Whatever they were talking about had seemed…serious, but she had no idea what they'd been discussing because they'd gone silent the moment they saw her. Nancy could've told Keith that, but she was afraid it could be misconstrued. It was just a split second. She couldn't come up with any good reason why that sight had made her feel so…odd. And since she had nothing concrete to offer as a reason, she figured it was better to keep her mouth shut. "Far as I could tell."

"And… Maisey's never mentioned if there's been any problems between him and Roxanne?"

"Not to me."

"Okay. Thanks." He raised one hand to signal that he was leaving.

"Wait," she said. "Why are you asking about Landon?"

"Pippa told me something that made me wonder if she's remembering the past few weeks as well as she should. That's all."

Maybe Pippa had seen more than Nancy had at that party and could accurately interpret what was going on… "Pippa may have a few gray hairs, but she's absolutely reliable. Your mother counted on her a great deal."

"Until the end?"

"Until the very end," she confirmed.

Her answer did little to ease the lines of concern in his forehead. If anything, he seemed *more* troubled. "Good to know," he said. "Give me a call when you're ready to take me up on that lunch. I'd like to hear what's going on in your life."

"I will," she said, but she was pretty sure he understood that she wasn't going to call. She couldn't. She didn't even have his number.

And she didn't ask for it.

11

"What are you talking about? Landon hasn't been on the island since Christmas." Maisey looked upset despite her denials. "They live in Louisiana. It's not as if he can jump in his car and drive here whenever he wants."

Keith picked up the coffee Maisey had poured for him. He was sitting at her kitchen table while she fed Bryson lunch. Laney was at school; Rafe was at work. Her house, a clapboard bungalow built up off the ground to protect against hurricanes and flooding, wasn't large, but it was comfortable. He could see why she'd be happy here, right off the ocean in one of the vacation rentals their father had built. She'd always been partial to Smuggler's Cove—she used to accompany their father whenever he came down to check on the development. Keith had secretly envied her those trips, all the time she spent with their dad, but he'd never said anything.

Because Maisey and Malcolm had been so close, he'd expected her to inherit the rentals. And she would, if Keith could save them from whatever his mother might've done in an effort to preserve the rest of her holdings after the loss she'd suffered with that Jamaican resort.

At least Maisey and Rafe owned the home they lived in. Rafe had purchased it from Josephine before he ever got together with Maisey, so there was no danger of their having to move. Thank God. For now, Keith had other things to worry about, although he knew he'd have to deal with his mother's financial woes soon.

"Pippa *saw* him, Maisey," he said. "After you guys left last night, she told me he'd been to see Mom the day before she died."

"Why didn't she say something about that right after she found Mom?"

"I'm guessing she was too shocked and upset to even think of it. The police, the coroner, everyone said it was suicide, and she was trying to accept that."

"We still don't know it wasn't!"

"Come on. She knows Mom would never kill herself. It just took a few days for her suspicion to overcome the shock."

"*Suspicion?* So she thinks *Landon* might've killed our mother?"

Tears were filling Maisey's eyes, so he reached over to squeeze her hand. He'd been hesitant to mention what he'd learned, but he felt he needed to find out *why* Landon might've visited Fairham without his family. Short of going to Roxanne, which he wasn't prepared to do until he knew more, he felt that Maisey would be the most likely person to have that information.

He hadn't expected her not to know about Landon's visit. That was a bit worrisome. "Suspicion that something isn't right. She doesn't know who did it. She merely wanted me to realize that something…irregular happened before Mom died."

"She's casting doubt on our sister's husband!"

"That wasn't her intention," he said calmly. "Or she would've told you, the police and everyone else. She's trying *not* to cause trouble. She told me discreetly so I could protect Roxanne and her family. She was letting me know that the police might look at Landon if they start digging around."

Her throat worked as she swallowed. "That means she's worried. She's afraid there may be some connection between his visit and Mom's death."

"She's nervous. I'll give you that."

"Because he showed up? Maybe he had a good reason for meeting with Mom!"

"That's what we'd all like to believe. So, *did* they have business together?"

"Not that I've heard, but that doesn't mean anything."

Their mother was pretty closed-mouth about her business dealings and her financial situation. She always had been. Still, Maisey lived so close, he'd felt certain she'd be able to tell him something. The fact that she couldn't made him regret coming to her, but it was too late to handle the situation any differently. "They argued," he said. "That also raises a red flag."

She gave Bryson another spoonful of cottage cheese. "What did they argue about?"

"Pippa couldn't tell. She was in the kitchen working, and they were in the drawing room. When she heard raised voices, she came out to see if everything was okay. But as she approached the drawing room, everything suddenly got quiet. Then Landon whipped open the door and nearly knocked her flat as he stormed out of the house."

"What'd Mom say when he left? Was she upset?"

"Pippa stuck her head in to check, and Mom told her to go back to work and close the door."

"That's it?"

"That's it. Except… Pippa said she looked pale. And she didn't come out of the drawing room for some time."

Maisey bit her lip. "That's crazy. There can't be anything to it."

"I agree. But what could they possibly have to fight about?"

She blew a strand of hair out of her face. "With Mom, it was possible to fight about anything. Have you asked Roxanne?"

"No. I figured I'd poke around a bit first, try to get a feel for what might've happened." He loved Rocki, and couldn't bear the thought of her worrying. Since they'd once lost her, she was such an unexpected blessing. He never wanted her to regret having them back in her life.

"Don't tell me you're afraid she'd lie to you…"

"No. I'm not saying that. I'd just like some context for what Pippa overheard before I talk to Rocki, that's all. Maybe Rocki doesn't even know Landon was here."

"She'd *have* to know," Maisey said. "He wouldn't fly off without telling her. The day before Mom died was last Saturday—a weekend."

"Yes, but Saturday isn't necessarily a family day for them, if that's what you're driving at. Landon's busier on weekends than weekdays. He could've told her he had a tour." He'd frequently spoken to his sister on various weekends when Landon was working…

"Mo!" Bryson demanded, pounding on the tray of his high chair.

Maisey had been so distracted that she'd been holding his spoon in midair, and he was tired of waiting.

"There's not much going on with the tourists at this time of year," she said as she brought the spoon to his lips.

Keith took another sip of his coffee. "Doesn't mean he couldn't get a group interested in seeing the swamps. That could happen in any season."

"If he was here, Rocki would know," Maisey insisted.

"Then why didn't she mention it to you? Why didn't *you* know?"

"Why didn't *you*?" she countered.

"Because I live in California. She'd have no reason to mention it to me."

Bryson hit his high chair again, which kept enough of Maisey's focus on him that she continued to shovel food into his mouth. "I can't imagine why she wouldn't tell me." She used the back of her free hand to wipe her damp cheeks. "I guess that's why I'm upset. I was already reeling, what with Mom's death and the question of how she died. To learn that my brother-in-law, and maybe my sister, too, came to town without even calling me…"

Keith hadn't called her the other day, when he'd arrived on Fairham, either. But he didn't remind her of that, and he was glad she didn't bring it up. "Why don't you check in with her?"

"Right now?"

"I'd like to hear the conversation."

Maisey rinsed Bryson's empty bowl in the sink and began washing his face and hands. "I'm not going to set her up, if that's what you mean."

"I'm not talking about *setting her up*. I love her as much as you do. That's why I'm being so cautious here. But because you live on the island, this call would seem more…normal if it was from you. Just ask why Landon

came to Fairham. And what he and Mom were fighting about."

Now full, Bryson rubbed his eyes. "Let me put him
down for a nap," Maisey said. "Then I'll give her a call."

Nancy couldn't concentrate. In fact, she'd been struggling to concentrate ever since Josephine Lazarow died.
Losing her employer so unexpectedly made her feel
she might be on the brink of an opportunity, made her
dream of one day owning the shop herself. But that
wasn't the only reason her mind was wandering. Now
that Keith was in town, she caught herself remembering
that lopsided grin of his, the weight of his hands gripping her shoulders when they'd nearly collided, the solid
feel of his body as he gave her that final embrace. It'd
been too long since she'd been with a man. She missed
the intimacy, and it didn't help that he was the last guy
she'd been with. She'd never had a very robust sex life,
but it'd been virtually nonexistent the past five years.

Determined to combat the desire aroused by knowing he was so close, she stopped working and returned
Tom's call. She needed a distraction. And he'd tried to
reach her earlier. She'd let it go to voice mail.

"Hey, there you are," he said when he answered.

She pulled herself onto her counter-height worktable
and swung her legs as she talked. "Sorry, been busy. I
told you my boss died, right?"

"Yeah. Are you okay with that?"

"I guess. It's just that I have more responsibility now
and need to make sure I do a good job, for Maisey's
sake." Although the shop might be going to Keith...
She'd do almost anything for Maisey, who she consid-

ered a close friend. But, in all honesty, looking out for Keith's best interests motivated her even more.

"Didn't you pretty well run everything before?"

"As much as my boss would let me. But she was a bit controlling, and stopped by quite often to…to let me know how I could improve." And to remind her that she still needed to get off those last few pounds. Josephine Lazarow had even offered to pay for Nancy to join a gym. *You'd be the prettiest girl on the island if you could just slim down*, she'd say.

"Then I won't take up much of your time," Tom said. "I'm busy all afternoon myself. I have three new personal injury cases."

"Sounds like business is good."

"It's building," he said proudly. "Anyway, the reason I called is to see if I could take you to dinner tomorrow night."

Nancy weighed his offer in her mind. She felt so torn about him. "I don't know, Tom," she said at length. "I'm not sure I'm feeling what I should feel in order for us to continue seeing each other."

"Whoa, wait," he responded. "Then you're taking it all too seriously. Don't. We get along great."

Was it really that simple? "'Getting along' doesn't mean we're falling in love. Isn't that what you're hoping for?" He certainly kissed her as if he was feeling *something*.

"Eventually, yeah. But who can say what might develop over time? We barely know each other."

That was what she kept telling herself. According to her sister, who analyzed all her dating errors, she had a tendency to bail out too soon. But she didn't want to mislead anyone. "I like you. A lot. I just—"

"Don't say the rest," he broke in. "I like you, too. Let's leave it there. If something comes out of that, it does. If it doesn't, we'll move on."

"As long as you won't feel I took advantage of you. Maybe if we each pay our own way—"

"You're not going to pay. Not when you're with me. I'm old-fashioned enough to believe that's the man's responsibility. But I'm mainly looking for companionship. Going out with me isn't a promise to marry me—or even to sleep with me." He lowered his voice. "Although I wouldn't mind that," he added with a suggestive chuckle.

Her queasy reaction to his innuendo was partly what worried her. She'd been without sex for five years, and she *still* couldn't imagine taking her clothes off for him. She was afraid she'd only fantasize about Keith. She'd wanted Keith to touch her almost from the moment they'd first met. What was it about him?

She couldn't explain it. Her heart was…stubborn, didn't know what was good for her.

She was about to reiterate her refusal when Tom said, "Come on. It's dinner. No strings attached. You don't have anything else planned, do you?"

Tomorrow her sister had the day shift at the inn. They'd talked about going to Charleston after work, to see if they could meet some interesting romantic options at a club. Nancy hadn't done that in ages. Even another night spent watching TV alone with Simba and eating a quart of Ben & Jerry's sounded better than seeing Tom. There were some interesting shows on Friday nights.

But she could go out with Jade another time, and she could record her shows. She'd never get her weight off if she continued to shut herself up at night, drowning her loneliness in ice cream. "No, I don't have any plans."

"Then let's grab a bite. It'll be good for you to get out."

She rested her head in her hand. She wished she could feel some enthusiasm for Tom—or any of the other men she'd dated since Keith. But Keith was the only one who made her pulse race. Still, if she didn't keep trying, she'd *never* get over him. "Okay, sure. Why not?"

"There you go." She heard the pleasure in his voice. "I'll pick you up at six."

Nancy thought of her lingerie drawer and how nothing in there fit anymore. Maybe she needed to force herself to be intimate with someone else. It could be that she only *thought* she was in love with Keith because she'd had sex with him so many times—they'd been living together, after all—and the depth of that connection kept her hanging on.

After saying goodbye, she set her phone aside and hopped off the table so she could get back to work. But she decided she'd hurry to the mall in Charleston as soon as she closed for the day. So what if she hadn't lost all her weight? She looked better than she ever had. She might as well enjoy the improvements she'd made. She'd buy a new dress for dinner. And she'd buy some lingerie, too. If she could bring herself to get physical with Tom, maybe she'd surprise him after dinner.

Keith sat on the edge of the couch while Maisey called Roxanne. "Are you going to let her know I'm here?" he asked.

"Yes. Of course. Why wouldn't I? I don't suspect her

or Landon of anything. I have no doubt there's a perfectly good explanation for his visit."

"I agree. I'd just like to understand why he was here. And maybe he can tell us what frame of mind Mom was in."

"Exactly," Maisey said. But once Roxanne picked up, she must've changed her mind because she didn't mention his presence.

Keith listened to Maisey's side of the conversation as his two sisters indulged in some chitchat. Updates on the kids. Latest career endeavors. A few words on the weather. After that they talked about the autopsy coming on Sunday. Fortunately, Roxanne seemed to support his decision to use someone who wouldn't be influenced by what the coroner had already decided, which made Keith feel a bit better. She wouldn't support a thorough autopsy if her husband had any culpability in Josephine's death.

It was ludicrous to even *think* he might be involved…

When Maisey seemed to feel the time was right, she sent him a nervous glance and started in on what Pippa had told him.

"It was so good to see you and the family over Christmas," she said. "I bet you're especially glad you made the effort now that…well, now that we know it was our last Christmas with Mom."

Keith motioned for her to sit beside him and share the phone so he could hear Rocki's response. When Maisey hesitated, he thought she'd refuse. But, with a grimace, she conceded.

"We should've moved to Fairham," he heard Rocki say. "I was taken away so early that I don't remember a lot about my childhood. And Mom only came back into my life five years ago."

"You know how Keith and I felt about living close to Mom," Maisey said.

"I do, but…losing a mother is still losing a mother. And now I've lost two."

That sounded sincere. She certainly didn't seem *happy* to have Josephine gone, which came as a relief. Surely that was a promising sign that Keith would be able to keep what was left of his family together.

"What does Landon have to say about Mom's death?" Maisey asked.

"Landon?" Rocki echoed. "He feels bad, of course. Same as me. But mostly for my sake. He and Mom didn't have much to do with each other. I'm the one who always talked to her on the phone."

But Landon had spoken to her before she died. He'd had an argument with her…

Keith nodded when Maisey looked at him, encouraging her to press harder.

"They didn't have any business dealings?"

"Mom and *Landon*? No. Why would they?"

Roxanne didn't know her husband had visited the island. Otherwise, she would've volunteered that information by now. That made Keith uneasy again. He could tell by the tension in Maisey's body that she was getting the same feeling—and that she was just as apprehensive about it.

"Pippa told Keith that Landon visited Coldiron House the day before Mom died, Rocki."

"No way!" their sister said.

"Pippa says she saw him. She said they argued."

Dead silence.

"Rocki?"

"That *can't* be true," she said. "Landon was at a gaming convention in Las Vegas. He has to stay on top of all the new video games so he knows what to order for the store."

"So...you think it must've been someone else Pippa saw?"

Landon was nearly as tall as Keith but bigger, thicker. His size made him distinctive. Keith doubted Pippa could've confused him with anyone else. Besides, she'd seen him over Christmas...

"Or she's lying," Rocki said.

Maisey jerked back. "Why would Pippa lie about that?"

"I have no idea," Rocki responded. "But he wasn't there. It's impossible."

She sounded upset—causing Keith even more concern. Did she know something about Landon and their mother they didn't? Or was it the possibility that there might be something Landon hadn't told *her* that was making her voice rise?

"Could you ask him?" Maisey said. "I mean, to be sure? If this turns into a murder investigation, I'd like to have a good explanation for why he was on the island."

And why he didn't call her while he was here. Maisey had to be thinking that. But she didn't say it.

"Of course," Rocki said. "I'm on my way to get some groceries. I'll swing by the store and talk to him. But I can already tell you what he'll say. He was in Vegas. He called me from Vegas on Saturday night."

He called her from *somewhere*—but if Pippa was right, it wasn't Vegas. Keith hated that this might create problems between his sister and her husband almost as much as he hated all the other possibilities.

"Will you let me know later, then?" Maisey asked.

"Yeah," she replied, but she sounded preoccupied. Maisey even commented on that once they'd said good-bye.

"So…is he lying to her?" Keith asked.

"*Someone* has to be lying. Either him or Pippa."

"True."

"You were the one who talked to Pippa. How convincing was she?"

Keith remembered her earnest expression, the frantic way she kept wringing her hands. "She seemed absolutely sincere. What reason would she have to lie?"

"No reason. Unless *she* had something to do with Mom's death and is trying to throw us off track."

"You told me yourself that Pippa would never hurt Mom."

Maisey jumped to her feet. "I can't believe she would. But I can't believe Landon would, either!"

Keith dropped his head onto the back of the couch. He didn't want to believe it could be Pippa *or* Landon any more than Maisey did. But there were no obvious signs of a break-in. And nothing had been taken.

Whoever killed their mother had done it for a reason, with forethought and planning, and that told him one thing. The culprit knew her.

12

That night Keith couldn't sleep for entirely different reasons than usual. Maisey had called to say that Landon denied having been on Fairham the day before their mother died, which bothered Keith, because it didn't ring true. And he was hoping his mysterious visitor would return—so that he could figure out who it was and what he wanted. He traipsed through the house, checking rooms, staring out windows, visiting the garage and the apartment over it, where his grandfather's driver had once lived, only to go through the whole circuit again.

Tonight he carried a baseball bat instead of a vase, so he felt more prepared. But he heard no unusual noises, saw nothing out of the ordinary. Fatigue made him groggy at about one thirty, but he was so afraid he'd miss the intruder that he fought through it. Then he *couldn't* sleep, because he'd pushed himself too far. That was when a craving for cocaine set in—so razor-sharp it felt like breathing in broken glass.

He'd been doing so well that he was back in the midst of that battle almost before he knew it. While he was away from his usual routine, he hadn't been working out enough to siphon off the excess energy that flooded his body whenever the desire flared up. Neither did he have the usual challenges and responsibilities that went with running his multimillion-dollar company.

In an attempt to cope the same way he did in California—by turning his attention to work and stubbornly ignoring everything else—he carried his computer to the study and handled all the email he hadn't responded to before now.

His business seemed to be running smoothly. He'd received permission from the city to put up a sign for one of his public storage companies on the busy street closest to it, which was a win. He'd received notice that the strip mall he'd most recently purchased had closed escrow. And his assistant had informed him that the broker with whom he'd listed an office building had a possible buyer.

Satisfied with all of that, Keith emailed a different Realtor to say he wouldn't be submitting an offer on the apartment complex he'd been considering. That was a project he couldn't focus on right now. Then he answered whatever questions he'd received from his various employees and did a little surfing for new opportunities.

Normally, he enjoyed sifting through the various properties for sale. He could spend hours researching demographics, establishing value, calculating ROI and evaluating the potential upside. But tonight, probably because he didn't feel he could move forward on anything until he understood what it might take to deal with his mother's debts, he quickly lost interest. Getting high. That was all he could think about. The rush. The euphoria. The exquisite, painkilling escape. Coming home to Fairham tempted him to revert to his old self…

"Don't tell me I'm going to fail despite everything I've done," he muttered, alarmed by the strength of that dark lure.

He was checking the house again, searching for that damned intruder and finding nothing, when Nancy came to mind. He missed her. While he was in California, he'd refused to even think about Fairham. He'd cut off everything and everyone associated with his past, other than his sisters. Doing that had felt crucial, as if he might not survive if he did anything less.

But since he'd returned? He'd been shocked at the number of times his thoughts had drifted to the woman he'd been sleeping with before he left. He wished he could go see her—but he'd promised Maisey he wouldn't.

Instead, he logged in to Facebook and found Nancy's page. She'd never accepted his friend request, but her settings were such that "friends of friends" could view what she posted. Since she was friends with Maisey, he was able to see pictures of her celebrating her step-father's birthday with a huge cake, riding bikes around the island with her sister and lying out on the beach.

She looked sexy in her bikini. He was happy that she'd lost some weight, since it was so important to her.

He scrolled through several humorous memes and smiled at a video of Simba, in which she was trying to teach him to catch. Every treat she tossed in the air hit him in the face and fell to the ground before he could snatch it up. That made Keith laugh, just like Nancy was doing while she filmed.

"That's a major fail, buddy." Keith started it again as he began to toy with the idea of driving over. He needed a friend, and she'd been such a good one. It wasn't as if he'd ever *tried* to hurt her.

Didn't matter, he reminded himself. He needed to leave her alone, as Maisey said. Nancy didn't want anything to do with him.

But his next thought was of "Speed" Harbinger, who lived down the street from Nancy and had been a drug dealer since Keith could remember, which was even more dangerous.

Was Speed still in Keys Crossing? Was he still dealing?

The answers to those questions were irrelevant, because *he* was no longer using, Keith told himself and put on some workout clothes before heading to the gym in the far wing. With a string of rock classics pounding through his smartphone, he did several circuits on the expensive Nautilus equipment his mother had purchased.

The strain on his muscles felt familiar, comforting, but he couldn't quiet his damn mind. He kept turning down the music to listen for the intruder who'd come last night. Kept trying to piece together a logical explanation for why Landon had flown to Fairham Island to speak to Josephine, what the two of them might've argued about and why he was lying about it.

Keith was on his way back to his room for a shower when he decided to finish up with a run. He hoped the exertion would finally exhaust him.

But he should've known where he'd wind up. Twenty minutes later, he was sweaty and cold, since he hadn't bothered to throw anything on over his T-shirt, and standing on the curb of Nancy's house.

Fortunately, the lights were off. If he'd thought she was up, he would've gone to the door.

When Keith opened his eyes, he was back at Cold-iron House and he was alone.

Was he drug-free?

It took him a few minutes to fight through the grogginess so that he could remember the long run home and establish that he hadn't screwed up. The knowledge came as a relief. Remaining clean hadn't been easy. Leaving Nancy alone hadn't been easy, either. He'd hung out in her front yard for at least fifteen minutes, wrestling with himself.

Go to the door and tell her how much you've missed her...

Don't you dare get involved in her life again.

There's nothing wrong with being friends. Maisey shouldn't be able to dictate that.

But you're not looking for friendship—not tonight. You're looking for consolation and support and the same warmth and acceptance that saved your life once before.

Finally, frustrated and shivering against a stiff wind, he'd ambled over to Speed's, which wasn't a wise decision. He could tell just by looking at the junk in the yard and the beat-up cars in the drive that nothing had changed.

Whether it was smart or not, he sort of missed Speed, too. Not in the way he missed Nancy, but Speed wasn't a bad person. He was caught in the same cycle of addiction that had trapped Keith for so long, and he was dealing to support his habit.

Keith wasn't sure how he'd managed to avoid knocking on *that* door. He'd known he'd be far more welcome there than he would at Nancy's, which had added to the temptation. But, somehow, he'd found the strength to return home just as the sun was coming up and had fallen into a deep, dreamless sleep.

Thank God he hadn't ruined five years of sobriety, he thought as he stretched. Seeing the sun shining through the shutters gave him hope that returning to Fairham wouldn't set him back, after all. But staying clean was always easier during the day. Nights were much harder, and in seven hours it would be dark again…

He reached over to get his phone so he could see if Chief Underwood had responded to the text he'd sent in the middle of the night, asking if she'd been able to track the person who'd made that phone call.

She'd responded, all right. Judging by the time on the text, she'd gotten up at the crack of dawn, right when he was falling into bed. But she hadn't shared any information. We'll talk tonight.

With a sigh, Keith tossed his phone on the carpet beside him, rolled over and went back to sleep. And he didn't wake up until it was almost time for their dinner.

"You look *amazing.*"

Nancy managed a rather wobbly smile. Tom had told her that *so* many times since he'd appeared at her door: *You bought a new dress…? Wow, you're hot… I'm going to take you to some other fancy places so I get to see you in that dress again!*

Those compliments fed her ego, especially since she'd never felt attractive enough for Keith. But Tom had been touching her at every opportunity, which reminded her of a dog that wouldn't stop licking. He was too eager, and it made her shrink away.

"Thank you," she murmured and hoped, by keeping her response short and simple, he'd get the hint and talk about something besides her appearance.

Sadly, he missed that subtle cue. "I mean it," he said. "I've never seen you looking so good."

She barely managed to keep her smile in place. Who knew that having someone compliment her too much could be as off-putting as feeling overlooked or inferior? "It's just a new dress, okay?" A Herve Leger off-the-shoulder bandage dress that'd cost almost two days' wages, but still... It was black, so she could wear it to the funeral—whenever that was. Even Josephine couldn't have looked down her nose at *this* number.

He leaned away from the table as their waiter, Bobby LaSalle, came with the wine. "Isn't she gorgeous?" he said to Bobby.

They hadn't left the island. They were in Keys Crossing, eating at the nicest restaurant in town—down by the wharf, near the water. Nancy knew Bobby, and that added to her embarrassment. "Stop." She gestured for Bobby to forget the question, which he could answer only one way. "I'm flattered," she said to Tom. "But, please, that's enough."

Bobby winked at her. "As far as I'm concerned, she always looks like a million bucks," he said and hurried back to the kitchen.

"Bobby's mother cuts my hair," she whispered to Tom. "I've known him since I was twenty-four and he was in middle school."

He reached for his wine. "You're talking about our waiter?"

"Yes. Bobby." She'd introduced them when Bobby first appeared and announced he'd be "taking care of" them. That was only a few minutes ago.

"Nice guy," he said and took a sip.

Tom's words were appropriate—she couldn't fault him there—but his throwaway tone told Nancy he wasn't really paying attention, and he obviously hadn't been paying attention before. He liked her dress, liked the cleavage and skin it showed, and that was the only thing on his mind.

She'd just decided it was going to be a long night— and that she wouldn't be using the new lingerie she'd bought, after all—when she saw something that made her wish she was anywhere else.

Chief Underwood had traced the phone call to a disposable phone. She'd also been able to determine that the caller had been somewhere near the lighthouse, which was the farthest point from Keys Crossing. Other than the occasional home built way back in the vegetation, there weren't many people living in that area.

Did that mean the caller had *intended* to mislead the police? That he was actively avoiding identification and might be savvy enough to pull it off?

Harper had told Keith what she'd learned while they were driving to the restaurant. She'd also said she hadn't given up yet. She was trying to track the serial number of that phone to the store where it'd been purchased, hoping to find an image of the person who'd bought it on security video.

Keith appreciated the effort. Given the odds, though, he wasn't particularly optimistic. Most of the bigger stores had security cameras, but what about the mom-

and-pop places that didn't? There had to be at least a few of those, especially on the islands. Smitty's, for instance, was the biggest store in town, yet it didn't have security cameras. Or did it? He hadn't been there recently, but there'd been no cameras when he'd lived here before. And even if she found the store and it did have cameras, unless there was a burglary or some other obvious problem that required visual proof, a lot of places simply recorded over earlier stuff. That meant timing could be an issue, too.

"Let's talk about *why* someone might send you to my house in the middle of the night," he said as they entered the restaurant.

"I don't have an answer to that. Do you? I've thought about it, but I can't believe the intruder who came in that night *wanted* to get caught—a plausible assumption since he purposely avoided detection. If you hadn't seen those wet footprints, we wouldn't even have known he was there. We would've continued to think it was a false alarm."

The intruder could've called afterward because he *wanted* them to know he'd been there. But that didn't seem too likely, either, considering the time of Chief Underwood's arrival. "So if it wasn't the intruder, who made the call?"

"A father, brother or friend? Someone who did it secretly so the intruder wouldn't know?"

Keith didn't respond. They'd reached the hostess station where a heavyset, middle-aged woman was gathering menus so she could lead them to a table. His mind was still on their conversation—until he saw Nancy sitting near the window with some guy in a suit. Given the size of Keys Crossing, he understood that he could run into her anywhere. But he hadn't expected to see her *here*.

He got the impression she'd actually spotted him first. She was digging into her small black purse in such a preoccupied way, it seemed contrived.

He halted the hostess so he could greet Nancy in spite of that. He couldn't help it. They'd once been close; it seemed ridiculous to ignore each other now.

Besides, he was curious about her date.

"Nancy! Great to see you again."

Sure enough, he detected no surprise in her expression when she looked up. She gave him a polite half smile. "Good to see you, too, Keith."

He glanced expectantly at her date, but she didn't speak up so he introduced Harper. "You might know our chief of police."

"Of course. She's been to the shop." Nancy shifted her attention to Harper. "Thanks for all you do."

Harper acknowledged her gratitude with a nod. "You bet."

Nancy seemed perfectly willing to let them move on without mentioning *her* companion, so Keith turned to him. "I don't believe I've seen you around the island."

"I don't live here." Tom stood and offered his hand. "I'm Thomas Humphries, an attorney from Charleston."

"What kind of law do you practice?" Keith asked as they shook.

"Personal injury."

"You must get involved in a lot of…intriguing cases." Truth was Keith had zero interest in that, but he figured everyone was different.

"I do. And business is booming."

Tom obviously took pride in his accomplishments.

"There are a lot of people getting hurt in Charleston who have reason to sue?" Keith asked.

He'd been joking, but Tom didn't seem to catch on. Or maybe he had. There was a hint of defensiveness in his posture when he replied. "Probably no more than any other big city, but I've established a name in the business. I work mostly off referrals."

"Referrals are always nice," Keith said. "Advertising can get expensive." He didn't mention ambulance-chasing and the other tactics some personal injury attorneys employed.

"Yes." Tom glanced uncertainly at Nancy, since she hadn't provided Keith's name or any point of reference. "And you are…"

Once it became plain that she couldn't avoid it, Nancy spoke up. "This is Keith Lazarow, Tom—my boss's son."

Tom's eyes widened. "The one who…" He stopped and finished with, "Whoa, I'm sorry about your mother. Losing a parent is always rough."

Keith could've pointed out that his connection with Nancy wasn't nearly as loose as she'd implied. He could remember one night when they'd made love three or four times in an eight-hour period. But the way she'd clasped her hands tightly in front of her told him she preferred to end this encounter as soon as possible. "You're right," he said. "It's not easy, but it happens to most of us."

"True." Tom sat back down. "Still, you have my condolences."

Keith turned to Nancy. "You look beautiful in that dress."

"Thank you," she muttered, but he could tell she immediately discarded the compliment as if it was meaningless coming from him.

"Have a nice dinner," he said.

Tom responded with something equally banal and the hostess finished leading them to their table.

"You used to date Nancy, didn't you?" Harper asked after the hostess had provided them with menus and walked away.

"For a few months. Why? Who told you that?"

"I must've heard it around town somewhere. But it was also obvious by her body language just now."

"How?"

"She was visibly uncomfortable."

"I didn't notice," he lied.

As Harper started to open her menu, she paused to give him a skeptical look. "I'm guessing she's not over you."

He opened his own menu. "Of course she's over me. It's been five years."

"Time isn't always a deciding factor." She perused her food choices. "Did you love her?" she asked, raising her head.

"No. I wasn't capable of loving anyone back then." Maybe he still wasn't. That was why he was trying so hard to stay away from her, why his sister demanded it. He'd hurt Nancy badly enough. He didn't want to hurt her again.

Nancy couldn't taste her food—and yet she'd ordered the Cajun blackened shrimp scampi, which was spicy. She no longer had an appetite, anyway. She wished she could ask Bobby to box up her dinner so she could get out of the restaurant and escape the attraction that kept drawing her gaze to Keith. The way the hostess had seated them, she and Keith were facing each other. Every time she glanced up, their eyes would meet. She'd pretend it was inadvertent, as if she hadn't intended to look at him, but her face would heat, and she was afraid he could see that.

"You seem sort of distracted tonight," Tom complained after the waitress delivered their cherries jubilee.

"I'm sorry. It's…all the stress I've been under at work," she said. But it was a lot more than that. Seeing Keith with the pretty chief of police made her nauseous, although she had to admit they were a magnificent-looking couple. Maybe Harper Underwood had what it took to hold him. Harper was a confident, bold, take-charge kind of person. She was also thinner than Nancy.

"I brought you here so you could unwind," Tom said.

She could feel Keith's eyes on her again but kept her gaze riveted on her own date. "I'm trying."

"It might've been better to stay in tonight."

"No. This has been great," she lied.

Covering her hand with his, Tom leaned close. "I'm glad. Should we go back to your place and watch a movie, then?"

Under the guise of reaching for her drink, she slid her hand away. "I don't think so."

"Why not?"

She fumbled around for an excuse. She could hardly say that the only man she'd ever loved was sitting across the restaurant, reminding her of what it felt like to *really* want someone. "I…need a good night's sleep."

He scowled at her. "So I drove all the way to Fairham Island just to buy you dinner?"

She could understand why he'd be put off and felt bad for disappointing him. That hadn't been her intention. She'd just purchased some sexy lingerie, for crying out loud. If that didn't indicate that she'd hoped for more, she wasn't sure what would. They just hadn't been able to establish any kind of rapport or chemistry. And maybe that was her fault, because her stubborn heart would not forget Keith.

Either way, the confusion she'd been experiencing lately had cleared, leaving her with the sad realization that she couldn't continue to see Tom. She wasn't sexually attracted to him. She'd rather remain single for the rest of her life than try to make something out of nothing. "I'm sorry. This place is expensive. I'll pay."

Bobby had slid the leather case containing the bill onto the table shortly after bringing their desserts. Nancy reached for it, but Tom grabbed it first.

"No, I didn't mean that. I understand if you're a little out of sorts. Everyone gets that way once in a while. Why not let me come over and give you a back rub? I bet that'll help."

His earlier comment went through her mind—*Going out with me isn't a promise to marry me or even sleep with me, although I wouldn't mind that*—and knew he'd been making himself sound more patient than he really was. She shook her head. "No, thanks. I think I'll stop by my father's house, check in on him since my sister went out tonight."

He put the bill holder back down. "*What?* He lives here, doesn't he? You can see him anytime."

"True. But… I'm sorry, Tom. It's just not going to work out between us."

"We talked about this on the phone. You haven't given it a fair shot."

"I don't think we should see each other anymore."

Shaking his head, as if he couldn't believe she'd be so stupid as to turn away such a fine catch, he sighed. Then he made his reaction worse by adding, "You have no idea what you're missing."

"You're probably right," she agreed. "You're a *great* guy and…and no doubt you'll make some other girl very happy."

He glared at her without responding. Then he let her pay the bill.

When Nancy and her date got up, Keith lifted his hand to wave, in case she glanced over. She didn't, but he did get a better view of her in that dress. She looked stunning, whether she believed him or not.

When Harper noticed his preoccupation, she twisted around to watch Nancy go. Then she said, "I take it your relationship with Nancy didn't end well."

"Nothing I did five years ago ended well," he said drily.

"Whoa! *You're* taking the blame?"

He'd been in a terrible situation long enough that almost everyone else had given up on him. Nancy was the only one who'd been willing to listen, to try to help. She gave him a place of refuge, cooked for him, washed his clothes, lent him money and encouraged him to get off drugs. "Completely."

Harper held her wineglass loosely. "You're more honest than I was expecting."

"That doesn't say much for what you were expecting. Are you still concerned about my reputation?"

She put down her wine and took a bite of her sole. "No. Just thankful that you've reformed."

He'd ordered crab legs. He held the seafood cracker in one hand as he responded. "Because…"

She offered him a flirty smile. "Because if someone like Nancy can't get over you, you must be more than just another pretty face."

"Nancy's a nice person. I feel bad about…about how I behaved with her." He was tempted to explain that he hadn't hurt her intentionally, but he figured that was a moot point.

"If there's no magic in a relationship, there's no magic. You can't fake it."

He supposed that was true. He felt that way about Dahlia back in LA. But Nancy was different. He respected her. He cared about her, too—enough that he'd shown up at her door last night and felt a strange sort of envy when he'd seen her with another man tonight. Why? He rarely thought of any of his other old girl-friends. Was it simply that he hadn't treated Nancy the way she deserved to be treated—and he regretted it? Or was it a desire to reconnect with the one person who was most comfortable and familiar to him while he was going through this difficult time?

He chose not to answer those questions, preferred not to examine his feelings for Nancy too closely. "That's true," he told Harper. "There's no forcing those things. So maybe we can talk about something else—like who might've killed my mother…"

She gave him a look that said she found his reluctance to talk about Nancy sort of curious. But she didn't push the issue. "Have we established that your mother's been murdered?"

"There *was* that intruder."

"The entire island had heard of your mother's passing. With her gone, and the family plunged into grief and confusion, perhaps some opportunistic and unprincipled person decided it would be a fine time to break in."

"Except they didn't take anything."

Her fork clinked against her plate as she set it down and wiped her mouth. "They didn't expect to find you home. When I got there, the place was dark, and your rental car wasn't in the drive."

"There's no need to park in the drive when you have an abundance of garage stalls." Especially now that he'd put a garage door opener in his rental.

"That's my point. There was nothing obvious to show you were home."

"From the front. I fell asleep with my light on, so there was definitely something at the back of the house."

"People often leave lights on, even when they're not home."

"So you believe it was an attempted burglary."

"I'm saying it *could've* been."

"It could also have been the person who murdered my mother returning to the scene. That happens, too, doesn't it? At least it does in the movies."

She chuckled. "Yes, it's possible. *If* your mother was murdered. I'm keeping an open mind."

"Really! That's a positive change," he teased.

"From what I hear not many people are capable of opposing you," she joked back.

"Somehow I doubt *you* have that problem." He dipped his crab in the warm butter and offered her a bite, which she took.

"Thank you," she said. "Anyway, just to be clear, I'm still leaning toward suicide. There's more evidence to support that than anything else."

"You mean like the fact that her bags were packed? *That* evidence?"

"I mean that the ferry captain doesn't recall seeing anyone who looked suspicious either coming or going on the night of your mother's death."

"That doesn't mean there wasn't someone. Maybe the ferry captain was preoccupied. Maybe whoever it was didn't stand out. Or the culprit lives on the island."

"True. That's why I'm not *completely* convinced. Just taking the measure of it all. It'll be interesting to see what they find at the autopsy on Sunday."

"Who told you we scheduled it for Sunday?" Although he'd been planning to get to that, they hadn't spoken of it yet. "Did Dr. Pendergast call you?"

She wiped her mouth again. "No. I ran into Maisey earlier at the grocery store. I'm sorry you felt you had to get involved. Because the coroner doesn't have an 'agenda.' We all want the same thing. The truth."

"I feel more comfortable calling the shots."

"Obviously," she said, and he could tell she was suppressing a smile.

He scowled at her. "Why do I get the impression you're laughing at me?"

"I'm not *laughing.* You have to be in charge, and that's fine. Obviously, that's your approach to life— which isn't too different from the way your mother handled things. So I can see where it comes from. Anyway, I'm hoping Dr. Pendergast will be able to tell us more. Regardless, I'll keep digging. See what I can come up with. My tech is still going through your mother's computer."

"I can't imagine he'll find anything there."

"Don't kid yourself," she said. "Almost everything is electronic these days—work documents, financial records, even social interactions. She was older so there may be less than there'd be for someone, say, our age. But I'm guessing there'll still be plenty to tell us what her last few months, weeks, even days were like."

He mulled over what he'd learned about Landon from Pippa. He knew he should probably say something, but he was so protective of Rocki, he couldn't bring himself to do it. It was much easier to insist that Landon's visit meant nothing, that he could never have hurt Josephine, so his being on the island had no bearing on any of this.

"She'd hate the invasion of her privacy almost as much as hearing you say she was 'older,'" he joked.

"Then she should've thought of the consequences."

"Trust me. She would have. She thought of everything. That's why I don't believe she committed suicide." After cracking the shell of his last crab leg, he held out some more meat. "Would you like another bite?"

The way she licked his fingers when she accepted his offering took him by surprise—and told him he probably wouldn't have to spend the night alone. She liked him, and she wasn't making a secret of it. "That's delicious," she said. "I wonder if you have anything else I'd enjoy."

He considered paying the check and taking her home. He was eager for company, didn't want to deal with the slow march of time until the sun came up. Getting naked with a beautiful woman would be the perfect distraction…

But a vision of Nancy in that dress made him hesitate. As pretty as Chief Underwood was, she wasn't the one he wanted. "I won't be staying on Fairham for long, Harper."

She stopped chewing. "Whoa. I didn't see that coming."

"See what coming?"

"Rejection."

"I'm not rejecting you. You're a very attractive woman."

"'No' is still a rejection," she said with a laugh.

"I'm flattered. I just don't think you're the type for casual."

She sobered. "Is that really all you're interested in?"

He wasn't convinced of that anymore. He'd been single for a long time; casual had grown ho-hum. The beautiful Dahlia was a case in point. She had a perfect body, and she knew what she was doing in bed. Most guys would kill to be with a woman like her, yet he'd hardly thought of her since arriving on Fairham.

Something was missing in his life. He suspected it was the kind of deeper commitment Maisey and Roxanne had found with Rafe and Landon. But he wasn't ready to admit it. "From your text the other night, I assumed sex wasn't a possibility. So I guess I'm surprised, too."

"I expected I'd be able to talk myself out of it," she said.

"What changed?"

"My opinion of you."

"I'm happy to hear *that*, at least." He lowered his

voice so she'd know he was sincere. "And I'm sorry to disappoint you."

She put her napkin on the table. "It's okay. It's probably for the best. I haven't been with anyone since my husband. I'm not sure I'd be any fun, anyway."

"I have no doubt you'd be fine." He slid his plate away. "And if not, whoever you choose for that honor should be willing to help you work through any...difficulties."

Her lips curved into a sad smile. "Sounds to me like you'd be a good man for the job. If you change your mind, you have my number."

Keith *almost* reconsidered. At that point, it felt as if he'd be doing her a favor. But he couldn't get that damn vision of Nancy out of his mind. He knew he'd only think of her, want to be touching her instead.

Besides, whoever initiated Harper back into the world of intimacy after the loss of her husband should feel more excited about it. She deserved a partner who was totally engrossed in *her*.

"You're not making it easy," he said.

She started to laugh.

"What?"

"You're not even tempted. Why? Is it Nancy?"

Although the word *no* was on the tip of his tongue— since it came more naturally for him to deny it—he didn't see any harm in being honest. "Yeah."

"Oh, my God!" she exclaimed. "She got under your skin, after all. If she only knew..."

"She wouldn't believe it anyway," he said and gave the waitress his credit card.

13

When he dropped Harper off, she gave him the file he'd been asking for, but Keith wasn't ready to go home, even with that. And he sure as hell didn't want to drive by Nancy's and see some other man's car parked at her house. So he drove out to the lighthouse. He'd been on that side of the island when he visited Maisey, but he hadn't looked around. Now that he'd learned the call that had brought Harper to his house two nights ago had been placed from this area, he wanted to see it through more careful eyes, to determine who was living out here and whether any of those people might be likely to place that call.

Without any streetlights and no moon to speak of, it was darker than he'd expected, but at least it wasn't raining. He pulled up to the lighthouse and watched the beacon swoop around for several minutes. Then he got out and walked as far as he could toward the ocean without getting his feet wet. The ground here quickly became soft and marshy.

Had someone stood where he was standing, or somewhere close by, while making that call Wednesday night? Had that person stared out at the waves as he was doing now? Or—Keith turned to look behind him—was it someone who lived in one of the homes hidden behind the thick foliage?

Bracing against the wind, which seemed to pass right through him, he squinted at his watch. It was after ten. Too late to knock on any doors. But because that call had been placed in the middle of the night, he hoped *someone* had noticed *something.* This side of the island didn't get many visitors, especially after midnight.

Tomorrow he'd canvass the area, he told himself and, with a sigh, trudged back to his car. He was close to Maisey's. He could've driven over there in just a few minutes, shown her the file. But Chief Underwood told him there wasn't anything in it he didn't already know. And his sister would be busy putting her kids to bed— or if she'd already done that, she'd be spending some quiet time with Rafe.

Feeling he belonged in that picture either way, he chose to call her instead. "Any word from Rocki and Landon?" he asked when she picked up.

"No. Which is odd, considering we normally talk every day—sometimes more than once."

She sounded worried. "Have you tried calling them?"

"Once, before I left for dinner, but she didn't pick up."

"Well, I've called three times. Voice mail every time."

"Any idea what might be going on?"

"None. Not since she told me Landon wasn't on the island last Saturday. She's pretty much clammed up since then."

"Do you think she's mad that we asked?"

"Who knows? Rafe says I need to reserve judgment

and be patient. She'll call when she can. I'm trying to do that, give her the benefit of the doubt."

Five years ago, they'd been so excited to find Roxanne—who'd been called Annabelle when they were children. They'd embraced her immediately, welcomed her back with such relief and excitement. And she'd become a big part of their lives. "I'll call her again."

"Okay. Let me know if you get through."

He tried to reach Rocki but, like Maisey, he got only her voice mail. He waited through her greeting so he could leave a message. "Hey, Rock. This is your brother. Can you call me? Doesn't matter how late."

After he disconnected, he thought about going over to Maisey's, after all—just to burn some time. He'd slept all day, so he wasn't remotely tired. And he couldn't face returning to the empty mansion where his mother had died. He knew Maisey and her family would welcome him.

However, he didn't go there, because he really wanted to be somewhere else.

He told himself that if he saw Nancy's boyfriend's car out front, he'd continue down the street. But there was no evidence that she had company. And she was home. He could see the flicker of her TV reflecting off the front window.

So he parked at the curb.

Nancy was surprised when she heard the knock at her door. She wasn't expecting anyone. As she threw on a robe so she could answer, she worried that Tom had come back to try to talk her into changing her mind. He'd had a difficult time accepting "no." Even after

they'd left the restaurant he'd spent twenty minutes trying to convince her it was a mistake to break things off.

But the person on her front step was too tall to be
Tom. When she pushed a barking Simba aside so she
could peer through her peephole, she could see nothing
except a man's chest.

That was enough. She'd seen the same view many
times before—knew exactly who it was.

Self-consciously tightening the belt of her robe, she
drew a deep breath. Then she pulled Simba back by the
collar and told him to be quiet and sit.

As soon as she opened the door, Keith's gaze swept
over her as if he liked what he saw, but she told herself he must've struck out with Chief Underwood, or
he wouldn't be here. And she wasn't going to be anyone's "if all else fails." Especially Keith's. She'd played
that role in his life once before. It wasn't a flattering or
pleasant position.

"Sorry to bother you." His lopsided grin acknowledged that he knew he was somewhere he shouldn't be.

"No problem." She liked his endearing expression,
but she told herself she was a fool to find him endearing at all. *Stay on your guard.* She'd let him hurt her
before; she wouldn't let him do it again. "Is there…
something you need?" she asked when he didn't volunteer the reason for his visit.

Her response caused that gorgeous smile to wilt.
"You said you were hoping to buy the flower shop. I
thought you might like to talk about it."

"Tonight?"

He shoved his hands in his pockets. "Is this a bad
time?" he asked with the reappearance of that sheepish smile.

Simba was inching closer to the door, hoping to slip through, so she barred him with her leg. The fact that her leg was bare seemed to catch Keith's attention. When he glanced down, he paused to stare for a moment, but he didn't comment.

"Um…" She was searching for some reason she shouldn't invite him in, but couldn't come up with one. She really *did* hope to buy the flower shop, which meant they had to have this conversation some time. Why not tonight? "Sure, okay. Come on in."

The moment he crossed the threshold, he crouched to scratch a tail-wagging Simba, who was exhibiting more than enough excitement for both of them. "Good boy! At least *you* still like me, huh?"

Ignoring that, Nancy proceeded to slide the sacks from her shopping excursion to one side of the table. She could've invited him to sit in the living room, but the kitchen table felt more businesslike.

"Simba's foot is healing," Keith said. "He's not even favoring it anymore."

"Yeah. I'm relieved about that. I don't know what I'd do if anything happened to him." She gestured toward a chair. "Would you like to sit down?"

He peeked into one of the Victoria's Secret bags she'd just moved and lifted the black teddy inside with one finger. "Looks like you went shopping."

"I did."

"Aren't you going to get dressed?" he asked when she sat across from him.

"Why?" she replied. "I'm covered."

"It's a little…distracting to think you're naked under there. That's all."

"I'm *not* naked!"

He tilted his chin up as he tried to peer down the opening of her robe. "Looks that way to me."

"Yeah, well, looks can be deceiving. Anyway, don't worry about it."

"I'm not *worried*, exactly. Just curious. If you're not naked, what are you wearing?"

She gestured toward the sacks. "What do you think?"

"Oh. Right. Lingerie. Imagining you in something black and sheer—that's *much* less distracting."

She knew he loved that sort of thing, but so what? She'd worn plenty of lingerie for him before and it hadn't changed the outcome of their relationship. Purposely ignoring his sarcasm, she stood up to get a pad of paper and a pen. "About the flower shop—"

"Did you buy all this for Tom?" He waved at the pink sacks.

She'd bought it to help her forget about *him*, but it hadn't served its purpose. "More or less."

"Wow." He whistled. "I hope he appreciated it."

"He didn't get the chance."

"Because…"

She wasn't sure she should tell him, but she also felt it was pathetic to lie. That was what had gotten her into the date with Tom to begin with—trying to pretend she felt more than she did. "Because I broke things off with him."

"Why?"

"He isn't right for me."

"That's what *I* thought!"

She barked out a laugh. "As if you'd know!"

"I met him. You can do better. A lot better."

"He's a nice guy. We're not…sexually compatible.

At least, I don't think we'd be. I'm not attracted to him in that way."

Leaning back, he folded his arms across his chest. "You were attracted to me."

She said nothing.

"Anyway, what a shame," he added.

"I'll live. I'll find someone else," she said with a shrug.

"Until then you'll have all this lingerie going to waste."

She raised one finger. "Don't even suggest it."

He spread out his hands. "I'm not suggesting anything. I'm concerned for you."

"For *me.*"

"Yes."

"*Sure* you are." She shook her head. "It can go back to the store. That's why I was trying it on, so I could decide what to return."

"Why don't you let me be the judge of that? If it looks terrible, I'll tell you."

"Nice try. Now about the *shop.* I won't have a big down payment, but I've got *some* savings. And my stepfather said he'd lend me a few thousand. I'll give you whatever I can get together. I'm hoping we can work out monthly payments from there, if you're open to the idea of…of accepting terms."

"Sure. I'll give you a good deal," he said, but he didn't seem to be paying attention to the business side of their conversation. He was too preoccupied with her robe and what was in those Victoria's Secret bags. "About all this lingerie…"

After being cast off by him as if she was nothing, she couldn't help feeling more than a little gratified that he was so interested. She leaned forward, letting her robe gape open, and felt a corresponding zing when his jaw dropped. "What about it?"

"It might be useful to have a man's opinion on what you should keep and what you should take back."

"So I should…what? *Show* you?"

"Why not? I'm happy to do you a favor. As a friend."

Nancy couldn't explain how they'd come to this, especially so fast. He'd been inside her house for only a few minutes. When she'd answered the door, she'd thought she had everything well in hand. And yet…here she was, heart thumping and body tingling.

She had no intention of letting Keith touch her, or touching him. But the hunger in his eyes fed a primitive part of her—a part that had been starved for male attention. She couldn't resist taking this one step further.

And why not? she asked herself. Nothing she'd bought was any more revealing than the average bikini. "As a friend," she echoed.

He leaned back on only two legs of his chair. "We're only talking about feedback."

She wanted to make him salivate, push him even further toward the edge of that metaphorical cliff. "Fine." Untying her robe, she let it fall open.

He stared for several seconds without speaking.

"This is called a Chantilly lace babydoll with sheer skirt and V-string panty." Dropping the robe off her shoulders, she pivoted as she modeled it for him. "So? What do you think? Would a man like this? Should I keep it or take it back?"

"That's gorgeous," he said.

His response answered *that* question, but she wasn't finished with their game quite yet. He'd beaten her at everything else they'd ever played, because *she'd* been playing for keeps. Now *she* was the one who wanted a cheap thrill and nothing more. That gave her a certain power she'd never possessed with him before.

"I don't know." She licked her bottom lip provocatively. "The dream angel lace bustier might be more... *me*."

"Let's see it," he said.

She took the remaining sacks into the bedroom to change. Once she was out of his sight, she leaned against her closed door and tried to calm down. But that look on his face... She'd never seen that much appreciation there before... "What about this one?" she asked, leaving her robe behind when she walked out.

"Turn around." His voice was deeper, more gravelly. She might not be as skinny as the women he usually slept with, but he seemed to be enjoying the show.

"Well?"

"I love your curves, Nancy. You're so soft."

As far as her "curves" went, she found his admiration a little hard to believe. Very few of the other women he dated had any curves to speak of—except maybe a pair of silicone implants. So she ignored the compliment. "Is this better or worse than the other one?"

"It's every bit as good. I say keep them both. Are there any more?"

"Just one. A lace-and-mesh teddy. In black. With garters. But...you've helped me enough. I'll keep these and take that one back."

"Whoa, wait. You can't quit now. Put it on," he said, but once she changed and came out to show him, he insisted she had to keep that one, too.

"You were supposed to help me decide what to take back," she said with a laugh.

"I can't. They *all* make me hard."

She ignored that, too. "But I can't keep them all."

"Why not?"

"Because they're expensive. I have no one to show them to. And I'm trying to buy a flower shop, remember?"

His gaze was riveted on hers. "I'll buy them for you. I'll buy all the lingerie you want. I'll buy you a lot of other things, too."

Nancy's heart seemed to lodge in her throat. She knew what her part in that deal would be. This titillating game was going too far. "No, that's okay," she said and immediately hurried back into her bedroom, where she donned a pair of sweats.

When she returned, Keith's hair stood up as if he'd been running his hands through it, and he was pacing her living room. "I promised Maisey I'd leave you alone," he announced.

"Leave me alone?"

"Yeah. You know. That I wouldn't try to get anything going."

"Okay. I'm surprised she requested that, since it's been...forever."

"To me it seems like only yesterday."

"Because you're out of your element."

"Stop it. Stop downplaying everything I say. I've missed you," he said point-blank. "We were good together."

She figured he was talking about the sex, since he'd mentioned that earlier and they didn't make what would be considered "a good couple" on any other level. His mother had considered her so far beneath him that she'd refused to even acknowledge that they were dating, never mind living together. Anyway, the sex *had* been exceptional—beyond anything Nancy had ever experienced with anyone else. Not that she'd been with very many guys. "There's always the next girl, right?" she said and softened that with a little laugh.

He didn't laugh with her. "I'm not talking about the next girl. I'm talking about you."

"I'm not interested, Keith."

"Because…"

Her mouth was so dry, she could hardly swallow. "Because you're not really offering me anything," she managed to say.

"Come on. You bought all that lingerie for a reason. You must be looking for some excitement, some physical satisfaction. I can give you that. All you can take. Right here. Right now."

Wonderful! Making love again would be fun, exhilarating. Just like before. Until he left the island without a backward glance. "Thanks, but I'm looking for something a little deeper and more permanent this time around."

He rubbed his jaw. "You never know what might develop."

"Actually, I do. I've been there before, remember? I'm holding out for a more meaningful relationship."

He made an impatient gesture. "Fine. Wait for Mr. Right. But you don't have to hide out alone until then, do you?"

He sounded like her sister. Why couldn't either one of them understand that casual sex wasn't so easy for her? Keith had a profound effect on her, one she couldn't counteract—which meant she'd be left brokenhearted. She might as well have a *little* pride and be the one to say no. "It would be a mistake."

"One night couldn't hurt. But I won't push you. Just...consider it and...and give me a call if you'd like to come over."

"What about the shop?" she asked before he could leave.

He seemed taken aback by the question. "What about it?"

"You'll still sell it to me even if...even if I don't call, won't you?"

"Shit, Nancy. I'm the first to admit I've been an asshole. But that's all in the past. I'll be fair with you, no matter what."

Relieved to hear it, she crouched down to hug her dog. Simba was the one who'd consoled her when she'd been crying over Keith before. He'd have to console her tonight, too. "Thank you."

Keith stood there for a few seconds, watching as she stroked Simba's fur. "I want to make love to you again," he said. "I want to feel you clinging to me, gasping my name like you used to."

Nancy's chest tightened until she couldn't seem to breathe. She'd fantasized about having him back in her bed—plenty of times. But she understood his limitations a little better this time around.

Or maybe she was just more realistic about what she could and couldn't tolerate. "I'm sorry. I shouldn't have...shouldn't have been messing around with that lingerie. I know you don't have access to...to your usual sexual outlets right now. But even if Chief Underwood shut you down, there are other women on Fairham who wouldn't *think* of telling you no."

He scowled. "What makes you assume Harper Underwood shut me down?"

"Well, you're not at *her* house, are you?"

"Because I chose to come here!"

Sure he did. Harper was gorgeous!

"Women aren't interchangeable to me, Nancy," he added when she didn't respond. "At least, you're not. I hope you'll call."

After he let himself out, Nancy sat on the floor and tugged Simba into her lap. Her dog was big for that sort of thing, but he didn't seem to mind and she needed the love. "How can I even be tempted?" she groaned, resting her forehead against his.

Simba pulled his head away so he could lick her cheek.

"I know. True love is the goal. I won't accept anything else." She kissed the side of his furry muzzle. "I hope."

14

Keith hated to leave Nancy's. He had to fight the impulse to turn around and go back, to talk to her some more. What he'd seen of her in that skimpy lingerie was messing with his head and his heart, which was racing. He told himself he was feeling deprived only because he was used to getting what he wanted. That he was frustrated because he'd finally met up with a woman who was rejecting *him*.

But that wasn't it. He honestly cared about Nancy, more than any other woman he'd ever been with. He hated that he'd hurt her badly enough that she'd built such a high wall between them—even though he respected her for doing it. Since he couldn't seem to leave her alone, she *had* to protect herself from getting hurt.

He knew she'd probably be surprised by his true feelings, but he didn't have any negative intent toward her. He missed her. Wanted to be with her. That was all.

To distract himself from the impulse to go back, he called Maisey as he drove around the island.

"Any word from Rocki?" he asked as soon as she answered.

"No."

"Me, neither. So what should we do? If Landon did

come here, there'll be ways to prove it. Chief Underwood could check the airlines, for instance."

"No. Don't involve her. We should just…let it go. If Rocki says he wasn't here, he wasn't here. I'd rather believe her than Pippa."

As much as he loved Rocki, Keith wasn't sure he could go along with that, mostly because he had no doubt Pippa was telling the truth. *He* was the one who'd spoken to her, had seen the earnestness in her face. He could tell she, too, was concerned by what she'd seen. Why else would she have told him at all—and told him privately?

He remembered his conversation with Chief Underwood at dinner. She'd said the ferry captain couldn't remember seeing anyone he didn't recognize or that he thought might be connected to any trouble. But if he was shown a picture—of Landon, for instance—what would he say then?

"It's possible she and Pippa are both telling the truth," he said.

"How?"

"Maybe Landon's lying to Rocki. Maybe he *was* here but he told her he wasn't."

"No…"

Keith didn't want that to be true, either. Because then he'd have to believe Landon had a reason to lie, which would cast even more suspicion on him. "Yeah, you're right. Never mind. I'm sure she'll call soon, let us know that everything's okay, that this has all been a misunderstanding. I'll be in touch as soon as I hear from her and you do the same."

"Okay," she said, but he stopped her before she could hang up.

"Maisey?"

"Yes?"

"I have something else to say."

"I'm listening…"

"I can't make you any promises where Nancy's concerned."

After a brief pause, she said, "Why not? She never mattered that much to you before."

He remembered that strange knot in his chest at dinner, when he'd had to sit there and watch Nancy give all her attention to someone else. Harper had been nice, and they'd had plenty to talk about, but whenever possible, he'd been straining to hear what Nancy was saying to that personal injury attorney. "That's not true," he said. "She made a big difference in my life, and I'd like to spend some time with her, if she'll let me."

The silence stretched.

"I'm sorry," he added as he reached the gates of Coldiron House. "I'm not out to hurt anybody. Especially her. I just…think we should be friends." His life wasn't complete without her in it…somewhere. He'd realized that since he'd come home…

"It's not as simple as it sounds, Keith. She doesn't look on you as a friend. She's in love with you."

"She *was* in love with me. It's been five years. Maybe now she can handle a different type of relationship."

"So you're saying it'll be platonic?"

"I'm not promising anything," he said again. "But whatever happens should be up to her, not you."

"That doesn't sound platonic. Which means you're not really offering friendship. Can't you leave her alone? There are so many other women in the world."

Once again his mind conjured up images of Nancy

in that lingerie. His hands literally *itched* to touch her. He'd never experienced that before. And not being able to act on what he felt left him feeling so frustrated, so restless.

"What about Chief Underwood?" Maisey asked. "When I saw her at the grocery store this morning, she said you guys were going to dinner tonight—and I didn't get the impression it was police business."

"I like Harper. We had a good time."

"Then what about her? She's beautiful, don't you think?"

She wasn't any prettier than Nancy. And even if someone else thought she was, so what? What he felt for Nancy wasn't based on her appearance, which was why it felt odd when his sister or anyone else tried to compare her with the other women in his life. She was different. She looked different; she acted different. He didn't even think of her in the same light. "Harper's okay."

"Seriously? You don't feel more enthusiasm than that?"

"I'd rather spend the time I have here with Nancy."

"Damn it," she muttered. "Here we go again."

He punched in the code for the gate. "Gee, thanks for that, sis. You act like I'm an ax murderer or something!"

"Metaphorically speaking, maybe you are! You hacked her heart to pieces!"

"I didn't make her any promises I didn't keep—in the end, anyway. And you covered my debt until I could get on my feet and attempt to repay her. I just wasn't ready for a serious relationship."

"But she isn't capable of any other kind."

"That's not true. What's wrong with having more people who care about you in your life?"

She started to explain how confusing that would be to Nancy, but his phone beeped. Someone else was calling in.

He checked the screen. "That's Rocki," he told her.

"Finally!"

"Let me talk to her, and I'll get right back to you." He switched over before she could respond. He couldn't miss Rocki's call; he had no faith that she'd pick up when he tried to phone her back. "Hey, there you are."

He heard her sniffle, which immediately put him on edge. "What's wrong?"

"Everything," she said.

He pushed the clicker for the garage and watched the door roll up. "You're making me nervous here. Can you be more specific?"

"Landon lied to me. He wasn't in Vegas at a convention last Saturday. He was on Fairham Island, like Pippa said."

Instead of pulling into the garage, Keith kept his foot on the brake. "He admitted to coming here?"

"He had to. He can't continue to lie, not with Pippa telling everyone that he was at Coldiron House."

Keith parked, then let his head fall back against the seat. "Did he say what that meeting with Mom was all about?"

She sniffed again. "Money. What else? Apparently the tour business isn't doing so great—well, either of our businesses. To avoid worrying me, he kept insisting we were fine, that we were getting by, but…"

"He turned to Mom for help."

"Yes."

"But why didn't he just call her? Why would he spend the money to travel so far?"

"He thought she might be more receptive to a personal visit."

"And yet she still said no." After what he'd learned from Chief Underwood, he knew their mother probably didn't have much choice.

"Right. That part isn't the problem, though, especially considering what we've learned since. If she didn't have it, she didn't have it. But she didn't *tell* him she didn't have it. She told him we were stupid to invest in those businesses to begin with, that they're surefire losers. She said we'd have to shut them down and move to Fairham if we wanted her help. When he refused, she called him a fool, and said he'd only throw good money after bad if he kept trying to save them, and… I guess they had an argument."

Keith got out of the car. "Are you behind on your bills, Rock? If so, why didn't you tell me? How much do you need?"

"I don't even know. I didn't ask him. I think we're okay for now."

But it was winter. They couldn't expect their tour business to pick up until spring. "Let me know if you're in a bind. I'll do what I can."

"I appreciate that. I really do. But I'd rather not borrow from anyone."

"Maybe you're more like Mom than I thought," he said.

"What does that mean?"

He pocketed his keys as he went into the house. "You're too proud for your own good."

"I'm no prouder than you are."

"I've borrowed money when I've been in a jam."

"When you were on drugs, maybe."

He flipped on the lights and locked the door behind him. "Listen, don't be too hard on Landon. I wouldn't want to go to my wife with that sort of news, either."

"He should *never* have approached my mother without my knowledge. That's…humiliating. Embarrassing. Especially because Mom and I were only reunited five years ago. It's not as if she raised me. That changes the mother-daughter relationship, makes it more…cordial and less motherly."

She wasn't very "motherly" with any of them, hadn't particularly liked the responsibility and sacrifice that went along with having children. "I understand, and I agree. I'm sorry."

"It'll be okay. With time. I think," she added glumly.

He stood at the kitchen sink, staring out at the dark night. "Is Landon there now?"

"No. We've been fighting all evening. He just stormed out."

"Wow. I'm sorry about that, too. I hope he calms down."

"So do I," she said and disconnected.

While Keith understood why Roxanne was upset, *he* felt a whole lot better about the situation. Landon had been on Fairham the day before their mother had been found in that tub. And he'd been upset. Those two things had been confirmed. But Josephine's refusal to give him a loan wouldn't lead a reasonable man, a family man such as Landon, to murder. Even if Chief Underwood found out about that visit and turned her attention to Rocki's husband, they wouldn't have to fear any unpleasant surprises.

"Thank God," he muttered and called Maisey as he walked up to the office, where he'd left his computer. After he told her they could relax, they laughed that they'd been nervous to begin with. All that angst seemed silly in retrospect. Then he got off the phone and spent several hours reading through his mother's police file and then catching up on work. When he was done, he even managed to get some decent sleep. It wasn't until the following morning, when he received an email from Chief Underwood, that he began to feel uneasy again.

Can you tell me who this man is? Because...maybe I'm wrong, but he looks an awful lot like your brother-in-law. I've never met Landon—never seen him in person, that is. I have seen the photos that were taken when he was in town for your mother's Christmas party, however.

Keith downloaded the attached file. He kept thinking, *So what if it is Landon?* Rocki had already confirmed he'd been on the island, and Keith now understood the reason. It all made sense.

But as soon as the image popped up on his screen, he could see why Chief Underwood would find it disturbing. It was a selfie of Landon, all right—standing naked, except for a tie, in front of a mirror. And he was showing off a major erection.

Where did you get this? he wrote back.

Her answer came immediately. It was on your mother's computer.

Roxanne woke with a start. She'd fallen asleep on the couch, so she was stiff and a bit disoriented. She glanced at the clock on the mantel, realized it was nearly ten and jumped to her feet. The kids! She hadn't gotten them up for school.

She was halfway to her thirteen-year-old daughter's room before her mind latched on to the fact that this was Saturday. They didn't have school. That was a relief, but with proper brain function came the memories of last night, and those memories made her feel sick. Landon hadn't come home. He'd never done that before.

She paused in the kitchen, stared at the island he'd built, the cupboards he'd installed, the flooring he'd put in. Then she went back into the living room to look for her phone.

She found it on the floor under the couch, where it had apparently dropped after she'd fallen asleep. She checked to see if he'd tried to reach her, but there were no missed calls and no answers to her many texts.

Where are you?
Why are you doing this?
Surely you can understand why I'd be upset.

Had he gone home to his parents' house? She hoped not. In twenty-one years of marriage, that'd never happened. But he was close to his folks. His father owned half of their swamp-tour business—or, rather, they owned half of his father's swamp-tour business, which meant Landon worked with his dad almost every day.

That had to be where he'd gone. Where else could he be? Lafitte, Louisiana, wasn't a big town. Sometimes Landon's nephew, a high school senior who ran the video game shop for them on weekends, had something come up and she or Landon would have to fill in. That was the case this weekend, but Landon wasn't supposed to spell Jackson until later this evening—two hours before closing. And she couldn't imagine Landon paying for a motel. Dandra Huxtable ran the closest one. Rocki wouldn't want Dandra to wonder why Landon was checking into a motel in his own hometown any more than she'd want him going to his folks'.

"How embarrassing," she murmured to herself. Not to mention upsetting and painful. Rocki returned to the couch and went through her contacts, scrolling for her mother-in-law's name. She was about to swallow her pride and call Suzanne when Zac, their ten-year-old, shuffled into the room.

"Hi, Mom."

Hoping he wouldn't ask about his father, Rocki put down her phone. She didn't want to lie to him, but she also didn't want to admit that Landon had left and hadn't come back.

Thank goodness her oldest daughter was away at college, and her middle child, also a girl, was spending the weekend with a friend. Zac had been listening to his music and playing around on his computer during her heated discussion with Landon last night. His earphones had kept him oblivious. And he was so used to his father working, there was a chance he wouldn't ask where Landon was. "Hi, honey. Still tired?"

"Kind of." He didn't seem to notice that she was wearing yesterday's clothes. Fortunately, he wasn't the most observant kid in the world. Over the years, she and Landon had had very little marital strife, so their children weren't trained to look for signs of trouble.

Her son yawned as he came over to give her a hug. The pressure of his body was reassuring, so reassuring it was difficult for Rocki not to hold him a few seconds longer. "What's for breakfast?" he asked.

"Cereal?"

"You always make pancakes on Saturday."

The complaint in his voice told her he wouldn't be happy to settle for anything less. "You're not tired of pancakes?"

"No. I love them."

"Right. Then...pancakes it is."

He flopped onto the couch and used the remote to turn on the TV while she took her phone into the kitchen. She managed to get all the ingredients out for buttermilk pancakes, but then she had to pause to fight her tears. Why was Landon doing this? She hadn't gotten *that* angry last night, still couldn't figure out how their argument had ignited. The way he was acting, she had every right to question his whereabouts, his actions and his motivations...

Her phone rang and she snatched it up to check the caller ID.

It wasn't her husband; it was Maisey.

She stared at her sister's image on that small screen, wondering if she could rein in her emotions long enough to have a conversation that didn't include tears. But every time her thumb hovered over the accept button, the lump in her throat swelled and she knew she wouldn't be able to talk without breaking down. So she let it go to voice mail.

He'll be home soon, she told herself.

"Why would your mother have this picture on her computer?"

Keith had no answer. Chief Underwood had brought

his mother's phone and her computer to Coldiron House, and they were both seated at the dining room table. She'd logged on to his mother's laptop and had shown him exactly where she'd found the picture—in a file named "Tuesday."

"Keith?" she prompted when he didn't reply right away.

It felt odd looking at something like that for a lot of reasons, but especially with his grandfather, in the portrait behind him, peering over his shoulder. "I can't even begin to guess," he admitted. "What was on her phone?"

"Nothing like this. Just pictures of the family."

"That's good," he said. "The fewer pictures she has like this, the better."

"Isn't one enough?"

He sighed as he remembered feeling that everything with Landon was going to be okay. That was just last night. "*More* than enough."

"The fact that there weren't any on her phone tells me she probably received this little 'gift' in an email rather than a text."

Or she went to the trouble of saving it somewhere she thought it would be safe before deleting it from her phone.

But why would his sister's husband be sending his mother a naked photo of himself in the first place?

"How well do you know Landon?" Harper asked.

"Not as well as I do Rocki. I've been on the West Coast since I left here. But she and I talk all the time, and I've always had the impression that her husband's a decent guy."

"How long have they been married?"

"They were high school sweethearts, and they've

been a couple ever since. Went to college together and got married right after. They have three kids, one of whom is in college now."

She put her hand on his arm in a gesture of comfort. "I'm sorry. I know this doesn't look good."

He frowned at the screen. Should he tell her what Pippa had told him? Why not? She'd find out, anyway. Now that she'd discovered this, she'd be asking about Landon—and if she asked Pippa directly, Pippa would probably repeat what she'd told him. His mother's housekeeper hadn't volunteered that information to the authorities, but she'd be unlikely to lie to them. "He came here and argued with my mother the day before she was found," he said.

Harper dropped her hand. "How do you know?"

"Pippa saw him, heard the raised voices."

Her lips parted in surprise. "When did you learn this?"

"A couple days ago."

"And you weren't going to tell me?"

"I thought it was irrelevant."

"What were they fighting about?"

"She couldn't tell. They stopped talking as soon as she came out of the kitchen to see what was going on. Then he stormed out. But I've asked Rocki why he was here. She says he tried to borrow money from Mom and the request wasn't well received." He left out the lie about Vegas. Landon was looking bad enough.

Harper seemed to be mulling over that tidbit. "Pippa didn't mention Landon to *me*," she said at length. "She said that nothing unusual occurred before your mother's death."

"Seeing a member of the family wouldn't be 'unusual.'"

"If that was the case, she wouldn't have told you, either."

"Everyone was saying it was suicide. Because of that, Pippa had no reason to believe that what she'd heard and seen might be connected to my mother's death."

Harper didn't defend the suicide conclusion. Her expression was thoughtful as she continued to stare at the picture.

"What are you thinking?" he asked, but he was almost afraid to find out.

"You keep asking if I believe your mother's death was a suicide."

"And…?"

She tapped her fingernails on the table. "I'm less convinced of it now than I was at dinner. Are you sure they were arguing over money?"

He sighed. "I'm less convinced of it now than I was before."

At the echo of her own words, her lips curved into a rueful smile.

"Why would she label this file 'Tuesday'?" he asked, wondering if that small detail could clarify or illuminate anything.

Harper leaned back. "It's innocuous—nothing that would attract attention if someone were to get on her computer. That's my guess."

That was his guess, too. Because there wasn't one other picture or document in the same file.

"Or Tuesday held some special significance in their relationship," Harper added. "Maybe that was the day of the week they first slept together—if they went that far."

Keith winced at the image *that* presented, but his mind had jumped to the same conclusion. An affair. "I can't imagine my mother would ever be interested in a man with so little money," he said. "Landon had nothing to offer her."

"I wouldn't call that *nothing*."

Keith couldn't even laugh. He merely grunted to let her know how unappealing that comment was to him—connecting his mother to his brother-in-law as it did.

"Not only does that look like a pretty impressive… um…erection," she said, "he's significantly younger, and he's attractive. Being able to catch his eye probably fed her vanity."

If anything would tempt his mother to make such a terrible mistake, it would be her fear of getting old, her need to remain desirable. That had to be the reason Keith felt slightly nauseous. Considering the way his mother had behaved around men—the way she reveled in their attention—he could actually see something like this happening.

"She was in a relationship with Hugh before she died," he said, but it was a feeble attempt to resist believing what he was seeing, and he wasn't surprised when Harper immediately shot it down.

"Shocking though it may be, some women sleep with more than one man at a time. It wouldn't be unheard of. With Hugh in Australia, they couldn't see each other often."

And when it came to the opposite sex, his mother had always had her pick. Old, young, it didn't matter. They *all* loved her. Keith could see her dangling several guys at once, especially if she knew Hugh was married. She'd feel perfectly justified in pursuing other men. She could collect hearts as easily as other people collected seashells along a sandy beach.

But wouldn't she draw the line at her *daughter's husband*?

Keith gestured toward his mother's computer. "Any other pictures of him on there?"

"None like that," she said. "There are a few of him with his wife and kids. That's it. My tech has scoured both devices." She picked up his mother's phone to show him the family shots.

Keith pored through the photos, grimacing when he saw one with Landon, Rocki and the kids posed in front of his mother's ornate Christmas tree. According to the date, that was taken just a month ago at his mother's party. There were other shots and short videos from the same night. In one picture, Keith saw Pippa carrying in a shrimp platter. In the longest video his mother had, which had obviously been taken by someone else, she presented each of the employees with his or her Christmas bonus. That included Nancy, who thanked his mother politely but didn't seem too keen to accept the hug that went with it.

"Did my mom and Landon ever call each other?" he asked. "Text?"

"If so, she deleted their correspondence—or someone else did—before she died. The only texts that show up on her phone are to Rocki, and they're what you'd expect them to be."

"But you can still get any texts that've been deleted, right?"

"Yes. I'll be able to see how often and how long they talked, even when they talked. And I'll be able to read their texts. I've already prepared the subpoena for the cell phone company. I'll submit it first thing tomorrow morning."

"How soon will they respond?"

"It should take a day, maybe two."

"That's fast."

"Hey, it's the digital age."

"Well, shit." He scratched his head. He knew he was making his hair stand up, but he didn't care. He didn't like where this was going. "Are you positive he sent this picture to her?"

"It's a selfie, Keith. How else would she get it?"

Rocki wasn't likely to send it to her; that was for damn sure.

Keith nearly shoved the computer away. He couldn't bear to look at that picture anymore. But then he noticed a detail that made him sit up. That tie! It was the same tie Landon had been wearing in the family picture in front of the tree. And now that Keith was over his initial shock and could focus on something besides the fact that a nude picture of his brother-in-law had been found in his mother's possession, Keith could tell the photo had been taken in one of the bathrooms at Coldiron House. He recognized the bust behind Landon; it was in a guest suite, near the jetted tub.

So why, if Landon was staying in the house, would he send Josephine this picture?

Because they'd been flirting, and he wanted to take the next step, but Rocki was awake in the adjoining bedroom? Was he titillated by the thrill of sexting someone else right under his wife's nose? His wife's *mother*, for God's sake?

"I can tell you when and where that picture was taken," he said.

"I already know *when* it was taken," Harper said. "December 26. At least that's the date your mother saved the file on her computer."

"No, it was taken on the thirteenth, the night she threw her big Christmas party."

"How do you know?"

"Look at his tie."

"It's the same. I saw that. But maybe that's his favorite, and he wears it often."

"No. He doesn't wear any tie often. I'm surprised he even owns one. Rocki probably bought it for the party. Anyway, he's standing in a bathroom off one of the guest suites here at Coldiron House. He took that picture on December 13."

"Hmm. Okay. I'll talk to Pippa, see if she can tell me how they were acting toward each other that night."

"She would've been working, very busy. I doubt she noticed. Besides…"

"What?"

"I'd rather keep this quiet if we can. The suspicion alone will destroy what's left of my mother's reputation. And news of this could really hurt my sister and her kids. I know it doesn't seem likely right now, but… maybe there's some explanation other than what we're thinking."

"Like…?"

"Landon was trying to send this to his wife, and accidentally texted it to the wrong person?"

"That would be embarrassing, wouldn't it?" she said with a laugh.

"The worst possible outcome."

"Not as bad as what we're thinking. And it's feasible, I suppose. Only I'd guess he meant to send it to someone besides his wife. Rocki was with him that night at the party. Why would he try to send her a naked picture of himself from the bathroom?"

Keith scrambled to come up with an explanation that would preserve Landon's dignity. "Maybe it was a joke, a game. Stranger things have happened. But...until we know more, can we be careful with this information? Let me ask a few discreet questions to people I trust before you take this public?"

"People you trust? Who might that be?"

"Pippa, of course. And Nancy. She was at the party, too. Maybe she'll have something to add."

"Did you see her last night?"

He felt bad letting Harper know he'd gone to see another woman after dropping her off, but he'd already admitted his interest at dinner, so he told her the truth. "I did."

"How'd it go?"

"Not too well."

She chuckled softly.

"What?"

"It's funny that she doesn't realize how much you want her."

"She's not interested in what I have to offer."

She gave his shoulder a reassuring squeeze. "Maybe she'll move in your direction. Or—" she winked at him "—maybe you'll move in hers."

After he showed Harper to the door, he went in search of his keys. He was taking Nancy out for that lunch she'd agreed to. After last night, he wasn't convinced she'd give him the time of day. But he figured it wouldn't hurt to ask. She might be able to shed some light on how his mother and Landon were behaving at that party.

Even if she couldn't, he wanted to see her.

15

Nancy was starving when Keith knocked on her door. She had Saturdays off and had spent the morning cleaning, too intent on finishing her housework to take a break, even to eat. She was also afraid that if she stopped, she'd only start obsessing over last night—what she'd said and done and how Keith had responded. What on earth had possessed her to be so bold? She'd *never* been a tease, but she'd definitely been out to make Keith sit up and take notice.

And she'd achieved her goal. She'd felt so vindicated to see the desire in his eyes, that rapt look on his face. But she'd been just as affected as he was.

Anyway, he'd probably forgotten about her and her silly lingerie as soon as he drove off—went to Harper's or somewhere else, while she tossed and turned all night, imagining his hands on her body.

"Have you come to talk business?" she asked, because she had no interest in doing anything else.

"No. I've come to take you to lunch. Do you have an hour or so?"

She glanced over her shoulder at the vacuum, which was still in the middle of the floor.

"Come on, Nancy. Cleaning can wait until you get back."

He was right. She was almost done, anyway. But she hadn't showered yet. "When?"

"How about now?"

"You couldn't have called? I need time to have a shower and get changed."

"I like you just the way you are."

"Well, thanks for that, but there'll be other people in the restaurant. Can't we talk here?"

"We can if you're willing to let me in."

She remembered where that had led last night and didn't dare take the same chance. "Never mind. I'm fine with going out."

She expected him to chuckle at that, but he remained somber. "Thank you."

She hurried to brush her hair into a ponytail and pull on a sweater, some jeans and a pair of boots. When she walked out, she found him wandering around her living room. "I'm ready."

"Great. Let's go." He waited as she locked up. Then he gestured toward his mother's Mercedes.

"You took your rental back?"

"Not yet. I should do that in the next few days. Didn't see any point in letting a nicer car sit in the garage unused."

"Makes sense."

"Where should we go?" he asked.

"You like burgers. Why don't we go to Billy's?"

"What would *you* like?"

She preferred a salad. Buying that lingerie had renewed her motivation to lose those last twenty pounds—

and to find someone who'd appreciate all her effort. "A salad at the Wild Rose Café sounds good to me."

"Fine." He opened the door for her and waited until she got in before walking around to the driver's side.

She breathed deeply, taking in the scent of the expensive leather. She could also smell a hint of Josephine's perfume, which made her a little uncomfortable. Fortunately, the heater came on as soon as Keith started the engine, quickly concealing that scent. But then *his* cologne reached her nostrils…

"What's going on?" she asked as he backed out of her drive. He seemed so serious today.

He shrugged off the question. "We're having lunch."

"You said you wanted to talk to me. That suggests you have a purpose in mind."

"We'll get to it."

"Where's Maisey?"

"Haven't talked to her today."

"Maybe she'd like to join us. Should I call her?" She'd feel safer in a group, but he shot her a look that left little question as to his feelings on the matter. "You'd rather she didn't come?"

"We'll be fine on our own."

They rode the four blocks to the café in silence.

"I'm sorry about last night," she said as he parked. "I was out of line. I really can't explain what got into me."

"The part when you sent me home was the only part I didn't like, so unless that's what you're apologizing for, forget it."

He didn't wait for her to respond. He got out and came around to her side. But this wasn't a date—not to her—so she opened her own door.

He motioned for her to climb out. Then he shut the door and hit the button that would lock the car.

Although Rose's had a brisk business in the summer, it was never very busy in the winter—except on weekends. Nancy was just regretting that she hadn't insisted Keith wait until she could shower when her neighbor, Justin Cruz, who worked at Rose's, said, "Hey, good-lookin'. Haven't seen you in forever."

"I was at your New Year's party!"

"That was *weeks* ago," he teased. "You should stop by the house more often."

"I'll do that." She liked going there. Justin and his significant other really knew how to decorate and cook.

He nodded at Keith. "Two for lunch?"

Nancy answered since Keith was checking his phone. "Yes, please."

Before Keith looked up, Justin waggled his eyebrows at her as if to say she'd found a "hot one," and she gave him a slight shake of her head to let him know Keith was not a romantic possibility.

"Where'd you meet the guy who seated us?" Keith asked after Justin left them with menus and went to get their water.

"Justin? He and Tyler are partners. They live down the street from me."

"Tyler who?"

"Broome, the owner's son."

"Oh! Right. I remember him. I never knew he was gay."

"He had several girlfriends when we were growing up. He hadn't come out then. Or he could be bi, I guess. I've never asked."

"Then we'll have to clarify *that* as soon as he gets back."

When she glanced up, he flashed her a smile to indicate that he was joking.

"So why have you brought me here?" she asked once she was ready to set her menu aside.

He put his menu on top of hers. "Because we're friends, remember?"

"Friends?" She lowered her voice. "Not quite yet—I mean, if last night is anything to go by."

"Friends with benefits if I have *my* choice. But you're being stubborn."

She rolled her eyes. "You're unbelievable! You were out with the chief of police only minutes before you propositioned *me*."

"That was a business dinner."

"Yeah, right. It looked like one," she said with a laugh. "Anyway, the point is you have plenty of other options."

"It's not about options."

"Then what *is* it about? Taking care of your, uh, needs while you're on the island because you can't go without for a few weeks? Or one last screw for old times' sake?"

He scowled at her but didn't answer. Leslie, their server, was approaching the table.

Keith ordered chicken potpie; she went with the Cobb salad.

"I need to talk to you about something," he said once Leslie had moved away.

Nancy was surprised that he hadn't picked up the conversation where they'd left it. "So this *isn't* about friendship."

"That's a separate issue."

Feeling both relieved and curious, she took a sip of water. "What do you want to discuss?"

"How well do you know Landon?"

He was wearing a blue sweater that molded to his broad shoulders. She found him so damn handsome—not that she cared to acknowledge that. "This is the second time you've brought up your brother-in-law since you've been back."

"I realize that."

"What's going on?"

"You were at my mother's Christmas party."

"Yes…"

He put his coffee cup right side up and pushed it to the edge of the table. "Landon and Rocki were there, too."

She slid her cup next to his. "They were. I'm the one who told you that."

"I remember. Did you see Landon interact with my mother at all?"

The question was a simple one, but Nancy felt that a lot depended on her answer, and Keith was edging close to a memory she'd rather not speculate on. Something about what she'd seen that night had felt *off*, but what if she was wrong?

"I saw them interact…a little," she hedged.

He waited for a server carrying a coffeepot to pour them each a cup. "Did that interaction seem…normal?" he asked as he added cream.

When she didn't reply, he looked up. "No answer?"

"I'm thinking."

"Yes or no will do. Don't hold back. Just tell me."

She opened a packet of sugar for her own coffee. "I'm

not sure I *should* say anything. That's why I haven't spoken about it to anyone."

"I'm going to share a few details with you that I hope you won't tell anyone else."

He was taking her into his confidence, once again involving her in his problems. She doubted letting him do that would be wise, but she was too curious to object. "Of course."

"Chief Underwood found a naked picture of Landon on my mother's computer."

She'd just taken her first sip of coffee. At this, she coughed and then wiped her mouth. "What kind of naked picture?"

"What could be unclear about *naked*?"

"The intent behind it, I guess. Was it…pornographic or something else? I mean, a picture of Landon mooning his mother-in-law would be different from a picture of him…say…touching himself."

He lowered his voice. "He took a selfie in front of a mirror while he had an erection—wearing nothing, I might add, except the tie he'd had on at the party. Does that clarify things?"

She grimaced. "I'm afraid it does."

"I'm guessing he texted it to her that night, since the picture was taken in a bathroom at Coldiron House."

The odd feeling Nancy had gotten at the Christmas party welled up again. "That's…revolting."

He sat back and studied her. "And yet you don't sound surprised."

"I was hoping I was wrong."

"About…"

She took another sip of coffee because she needed an extra second to examine the memory. "I saw him…

whisper to her. That's all. A brief moment when he leaned close to her, bent his head and said…something."

"You don't know what?"

"No."

"So…what makes you uneasy about that moment?"

Keith knew there had to be some hint that Landon wasn't merely telling Josephine what he'd bought Rocki for Christmas, or Nancy wouldn't have reservations. He watched as she put her coffee cup down.

"The way he touched her when he did it, the look on his face after. All of it. It…made me uncomfortable."

"Did you get the feeling there was some *romantic* interest between them?"

As soon as Landon noticed she was observing them, he'd dropped his hand and straightened. "Honestly? Yes."

When Keith propped his elbows on the table, rested his chin in his hands and began rubbing his temples, Nancy wished she could smooth his hair back or do something else to comfort him. She used to rub his back and neck when he was at his most troubled. He'd ended up resorting to drugs on some of those nights. But there'd been other instances when she'd been able to calm him.

So many people thought he'd been born with a silver spoon in his mouth and acted out in later years only because he was spoiled. They didn't understand the abuse he'd suffered and how hard he'd tried to figure out some way to get along with his overpowering mother while still retaining a connection to the grandfather he'd adored. One had to know Josephine Lazarow to understand just how narcissistic and controlling she could be. That was why Nancy couldn't hold any of his actions—including what he'd done to her—against him. She'd been close enough to see his pain.

Was that the reason she couldn't get over him? Because she'd forgiven him even before he asked?

"I could be wrong," she said. "It's important to keep that in mind."

He straightened his silverware. "You weren't wrong."

"We can't be sure," she insisted. "How much contact could they have had? It's not like he's ever *lived* on Fairham."

"He brought his family to visit a few times each year."

"Only once or twice—not often. If he was coming here every week or two, Pippa would know. And Rocki would probably suspect."

"If my mother was expecting him, she could easily give Pippa the day off or the afternoon off or whatever. Pippa only works five days a week and those days are flexible. She wouldn't know what went on in her absence. Or my mother could've met Landon elsewhere—someplace she considered more exciting, like New Orleans. She loved to travel, and New Orleans was one of her favorite destinations."

This was sounding worse by the moment. "How close is New Orleans to Lafitte?"

"Less than an hour's drive."

"But your mother was seeing someone else before she died—someone from Australia." Nancy toyed with the empty sugar packet next to her plate. "At least, that's what I told myself after catching that odd…caress or whatever."

"Hugh Pointer? He's married, Nancy."

She blinked at him. "Oh. Wow. You're kidding. Did she know he had a wife?"

"Apparently she did."

"I wouldn't have expected her to be so tolerant."

"That came as a surprise to me, too."

"So, what now?"

The waitress arrived with their food. Keith held his tongue until she was gone. Then he said, "I'm beginning to wonder if Landon could've killed her."

Nancy's stomach knotted. Although she didn't know Rocki well, she understood how deeply that would hurt her—and that it would negatively impact her kids, as well as Maisey and Keith. "That *can't* be the case."

"It *could* be. Which is why I'm feeling sick to my stomach."

Rocki heard her husband's truck in the drive. Fortunately, Zac had gone skateboarding and Chloe wasn't due to return from her friend's house until tomorrow. Rocki was home alone, and was so grateful for that. Coping with whatever was going on would be much more difficult if she had to suppress her emotions until she and Landon could speak privately.

Digging her fingernails into her palms, she stayed in the kitchen while waiting for him to come through the door. What would he say? Where had he gone? She'd called his parents' house. They'd acted surprised that she didn't know where he was and claimed they hadn't seen him.

Were they lying?

They had to be, didn't they? She couldn't think of one other place he might've gone. His best friend lived nearby, but Landon hated his best friend's wife. Most people did. Chrissy wasn't an easy person to get along with. Rocki couldn't imagine that he'd put himself at *her* mercy.

Just when she thought he wasn't coming in, after all, that he'd gone around back to mow the lawn or do some other chore instead of greeting her, she heard the door creak open. Her eyes began to burn but she blinked back the tears. She'd promised herself they'd have a calm conversation—that she'd say what she was thinking and feeling without creating another argument.

She hoped she'd be able to accomplish that.

Whenever Landon got home from work, he'd yell, "Rock? I'm home!" But this time he didn't call her name, as he'd done so many times over the years.

She moved to the entrance of the kitchen, and he stopped in midstride the second he saw her.

"Hey," he said, standing awkwardly in the living room as if he didn't know what to do with himself.

She wished he'd close the distance between them and pull her into his arms, tell her he was sorry and that he loved her. He'd been acting so strange, so aloof the past few weeks—even before he'd gone to Fairham.

But he didn't reassure her, which was completely un-like him. They'd had so few arguments over the years, hardly any that were serious and none that had lasted. And if they did have an argument, he was generally the one who made it possible for her to put it behind them. "Hey," she responded.

He glanced toward the hallway. "Where're the kids?"

"Zac's at Jeffrey's. Chloe's at Amy's."

With a nod, he shoved his hands in his pockets and shifted from one foot to the other. "Any word from Brooklyn?"

Their oldest daughter had been texting her. "Yes. She has a big dance tonight."

"She's sure enjoying college."

"So did we," Rocki said. "Remember?"

He shifted uncomfortably. "I remember."

"Where've you been?" she asked.

"I drove down to New Orleans."

"New Orleans?"

"Yeah."

Anxiety left her stomach churning. "What was in New Orleans that you wanted to see or do—alone?"

His big shoulders lifted in a shrug. "I just needed to get away, do some thinking."

"So you stayed at a motel?"

"A casino."

When she moved closer to him, she could smell cigarette smoke. That made her believe he *had* gone to the casino, since he'd never smoked himself. "You were up all night gambling?"

"I did a little gambling, yeah."

The defensiveness that crept into his voice put her on edge, too. "And?"

"And I lost a few hundred bucks."

That should help their financial situation, she thought sarcastically, but managed to bite back the words. He looked hungover, so she assumed he'd been drinking *and* gambling. "I wasn't asking about your losses. I was wondering…what you had to decide."

"We're in trouble with the businesses, Rock. I have to do something about it or we're going to lose them both, *and* our house."

"That's why you went to Fairham and then lied about

it? You thought my mother was the answer to those problems?"

"Yes! I told you that already!" he said, but then his eyes skittered away from her.

That anger, when he'd never been an angry man—and the fact that he wouldn't look at her—only made Rocki feel worse.

Somehow she swallowed around the lump in her throat. "And were you trying to protect me last night when you walked out and didn't come home?"

He rubbed a hand over his face. "I don't want to talk about last night. I don't even want to *think* about it. I really don't understand why asking your mother for a loan was such a big deal. I thought she had a lot of money and wouldn't mind."

But he had too much pride to ask anyone for money. She'd never known him to do it in the past. So why would he embarrass himself—and her—by going to her mother? And without even speaking to her about it? This was nothing like the man she'd married. "It wasn't the money that was the problem," she said. "It was the lie."

"You've told me that. A dozen times, at least."

"So why can't you understand it?"

"I understand. I'm just done fighting about it. Why can't we forget about Fairham and your mother and move on?"

"*Forget about my mother?* She just *died*—or was killed. You're acting so strange! Is there something else?" she asked. "Something I don't know?"

His lip curled with impatience. "Will you quit asking me that?"

"I can't! There's a barrier between us. I don't understand what it is, but it's tearing us apart. I mean...the argument we had before you left hardly seemed like sufficient grounds for you to walk out on me. And... and to stay gone so long, without even a call to let me know where you were or when you'd be home."

"I needed a break, okay? It's not like I'm gone very often, not unless I have work that keeps me away. Besides, you don't need to monitor my actions. I'm not a kid."

"Then why don't you stop acting like one?" she said quietly and hurried down the hall to the bedroom, where she closed the door because she could no longer hold back the tears.

As Keith drove Nancy home, he hated to think about what Rocki and her children might face in the near future. He didn't want to tell Harper Underwood what Nancy had told him—didn't want to tell *anyone*. His first instinct was to protect those who were still living. But he couldn't let the person who killed his mother get away with it, even if that person was a member of the family. Who could say what Landon might do next— who he might get involved with, what he might do to Rocki if she ever became a nuisance to him.

"Are you okay?" Nancy asked as he pulled into her drive.

"I'm fine. Just worried about Rocki."

Her troubled expression suggested she shared his concern. She'd always been empathetic, probably too empathetic for her own good. That was how she'd gotten emotionally involved with him during that period of time when most other people were steering clear.

"Even if Landon and your mother were having an affair, it doesn't mean he killed her," she said.

"He was one of the last people to see her alive." Funny how quickly one's perspective could change. He'd really liked Landon, thought he was an impressive husband and father. And now he was wondering if Landon could be a murderer...

"Still, maybe you should give him the benefit of the doubt, at least until the police come up with some hard evidence. Everything we've talked about is circumstantial."

"*Someone* killed her," he said.

"We don't even know that for sure—and we certainly don't know it was Landon."

He put the transmission in Park so he could get out, but she shook her head. "There's no need to walk me to the door."

She started to get out on her own, but he caught her by the chin and turned her face toward him. "Fine. Then I'll take my kiss here."

"What kiss—"

Eager to feel the comfort he remembered so well, he leaned forward and covered her mouth with his.

She didn't stop him. She resisted only when he ran his tongue along her lips. He was hoping she'd part them, let him take the kiss deeper, but she didn't.

Disappointed, he pulled away, but then her hand slipped into his hair, tugging him back to her, and her tongue met his in a series of thrusts and parries that instantly made him hard.

She tasted exactly as he remembered. He wished he could caress the soft skin under her shirt, but he knew he'd be a fool to push her too far. A kiss was a good start, especially a kiss like this one that spoke of so much pent-up desire.

"Come over tonight," he said.

She looked as dazed as he felt. Obviously, the moment that kiss had gotten away from them had surprised her, too.

"Come on," he pressed. "You're all I can think about."

She seemed uncertain, as if she believed only an idiot would fall for that line.

"It's true," he said. "If you want to be with me as badly as I want to be with you, why waste the time we've got left? I won't be on Fairham very long." He remembered telling Harper the same thing—for very different reasons.

"We'll see," she said and got out of the car.

16

Since Landon had driven over to the store to relieve his nephew, who wanted to attend a going-away party for a friend, Rocki was once again alone. She embraced the silence, the solitude and relief from the tension that'd been humming through the house like electricity while he was there. Her home was her refuge, where she'd felt happy and safe for so many years.

That wasn't going to change, she promised herself. They'd figure out how to get on top of their financial difficulties. And just because her husband had lied to her, that didn't mean he wasn't the same person he'd always been or that he didn't love her anymore. She *knew* Landon— better than anyone else did. She'd been with him since she was sixteen. Those twenty-seven years had to count for something, didn't they?

That was what she'd been telling herself since the Christmas party, when he'd started acting so strange…

Her phone dinged as she received a text from her oldest daughter, who was at Louisiana State University.

What are you doing?

Just housework, she wrote back. I thought you had a dance tonight.

I do, but it hasn't started yet, and I was just wondering how you were feeling about Grandma Josephine. You haven't said much lately.

I'm handling it okay. It was just everything else that was getting to her, but she wasn't about to draw her daughter into her pain. What about you? How are you feeling about your grandmother's death?

Fine. I really didn't spend much time with her. It's not like it was my other grandma. That probably sounds harsh, but you know what I mean.

I do. You grew up with your father's mother. I think it's more the circumstances surrounding Josephine's death that are hard for me.

I understand. Have you heard anything new?

No, not yet.

Should I come home? Be with you until the funeral?

What about your classes?

I'll muddle through, study at home.

No. I appreciate the offer. But there's no need for you to miss too much school. Let's wait until we know when the funeral is before you take off.

Okay. Have to go. My ride's here for the dance.

Have fun!

How do I look?

Despite the pain she was feeling, Rocki couldn't help smiling at the selfie Brooklyn sent her. Thank goodness Brooklyn wasn't around to see what was going on.

Gorgeous, as usual. Love the boots!

Rocki felt her smile fade as she carried her phone into the bedroom. She shut the door, although there was no one around to hear, and stared down at her list of contacts. It was time to call Maisey back, time to tell her sister that she stood behind her husband—and that she expected her and Keith to do the same. So what if they hadn't grown up together? They'd built a relationship over the past five years that shouldn't allow for this kind of suspicion.

Before she could make that call, however, another text popped onto her screen.

Mom? Can I skateboard for a little longer?

Relieved that her son was happy at his friend's, and that she'd have more time to herself, she replied that he could before returning to Maisey's number on her contacts list.

"I'm so glad you called," Maisey said the moment she answered. "Are you okay? I've been worried about you."

Those damn tears threatened to well up again. Rocki

was so confused, so uncertain. She couldn't remember a time, except maybe in the weeks following her abduction, when she'd felt so bewildered.

Swallowing hard, Rocki kept her voice as steady as possible when she responded. "I'm fine. I've been... busy with the family."

"I didn't want you to think that Keith and I were accusing Landon of anything. We were just surprised that...that he'd been to Coldiron House and didn't stop by to see me and Rafe and the kids. That's all."

"I understand. But he wasn't there long enough. He went to see Mom, to work out a loan. A proper loan, with interest." That was what he'd said, anyway. And she wanted to believe it.

No, she *did* believe it.

"Completely understandable. Like I said, we were a little surprised, that's all."

"I hope that's true, Maisey—that you don't believe he could hurt anyone."

"Of course he couldn't! Besides, maybe *no one* hurt Mom. The autopsy hasn't even been done. Suicide is still a possibility."

Rocki prayed the autopsy *would* indicate suicide. If not, there'd be trouble. She could feel it coming, feel everything crumbling, everything she'd been trying to shore up since that damn Christmas party at Coldiron House... Why had they even gone? They hadn't really had the money. They should've stayed home. "You said the autopsy's tomorrow, right?"

"Yeah. Nine in the morning."

Rocki couldn't wait for that to be over. If the pathologist ruled Josephine's death a suicide, maybe things would start to get better. Her marriage couldn't survive a lengthy police investigation, not with the strain that currently existed between her and Landon—and the doubts. Those sickening doubts had been eating her alive for weeks, well before the argument that had sent him to New Orleans. "You told me Mom was facing bankruptcy. Losing her money, her holdings. That would've been catastrophic for her."

"I agree," Maisey said. "But why would she throw such an elaborate Christmas party if she was stressed and worried about money? That party had to cost several thousand dollars."

"Because she did it every year. Old habits die hard. Perhaps she justified spending the money by telling herself she was keeping up with tradition. And knowing her, she probably didn't want anyone to realize she was in trouble."

"I could see that. Mom was all about appearances. But if she was distraught enough to take her own life, don't you think someone would've noticed *some* sign of her distress? Rafe and I had dinner with her on Friday night—and she was fine, wasn't behaving any differently."

"She didn't seem to be uptight at the Christmas party, either," Rocki admitted. On the contrary, she'd been flirting with almost every man in the house, including Landon. As far as Rocki was concerned, Josephine's behavior had been embarrassing, if not downright disgusting. But Josephine had always had a great need to be admired. The fact that Landon had seemed to enjoy her attention didn't mean anything. He'd gone back to Coldiron House to get a loan, as he said, and not for any other reason.

She hoped. God, did she hope...

"I wish we could've been there," Maisey said.

Laney's school play had been the same night, but their two families had gotten together the following morning. "Has anyone told Hugh Pointer that she's dead?" Rocki asked.

"Chief Underwood did. She called him right away."

"Could *he* have had anything to do with it?"

"No. He was in Australia."

"He could still be responsible. Don't they always look at the love interest first?"

"Hugh has an airtight alibi."

"What about his wife?" If she knew about the affair, she could easily want to kill Josephine…

"She has no clue that he was cheating."

"Are you sure?"

"That's what he said. And since the coroner believes that Mom killed herself, Chief Underwood hasn't pushed it. She doesn't see the need to destroy more lives. But I suspect Lana Pointer will find out what her husband's been up to if the autopsy proves otherwise. Chief Underwood will definitely be calling her then, since she'll have to investigate anyone who could possibly be involved."

Desperate to establish a plausible scenario that wasn't fraught with danger to her own family, Rocki tightened her grip on the phone. "It's possible she does. Maybe she's the one who killed Mom—out of jealousy." Jealousy was a powerful motive. After what she'd experienced in the last weeks, Rocki understood that in a way she never had before.

"She was in Europe when Mom died. She might still be there, on some class trip, touring with their eighteen-year-old daughter."

"She could've hired someone—"

"Rocki!"

She winced at the concern in her sister's voice. "What?"

"You sound…odd. What's going on?"

Rocki squeezed her eyes shut. She was so torn. Should she wait to see what was going to happen? Continue to keep her secret? Or should she act to defend Landon, just in case?

"Rocki?"

Determined to act now, she took a deep breath. "Mom's relationship with Hugh wasn't exactly what you think, Maisey."

"How do you know?"

"Gretchen told me."

"Gretchen? The woman who raised you? *That* Gretchen? How? I don't mean to sound callous, but she's been dead for some years. There's no way she could know about Hugh."

"His relationship with Mom wasn't new, Maisey."

"What are you talking about? Of course it was new. Mom said she met him when she flew to New York a few months ago—in first class."

"That part may be true, that she met him on a plane. But I'm telling you it wasn't a recent trip."

A brief silence told her Maisey was as shocked by this news as Rocki had expected her to be. "You're saying the affair went on much longer?"

"For years. More than forty. Don't get me wrong, it was probably on and off. Obviously, Mom would get with other men and then go back to him. I guess no one could really replace him. How else could the relationship have lasted all those years? But it started a long time ago. That's how Gretchen knew."

"How could that even be possible?"

"I know it sounds bizarre. But during my first year of college, my mother and I—*Gretchen* and I—went to some movie about a woman who cheated on her husband. The husband went crazy and killed his wife and her lover. So…we were talking about it as we drove home. That was the first time Gretchen ever brought up the fact that my birth mother had a lover. But she mentioned it several times after."

This silence lasted even longer than the first one. Hoping that she was doing the right thing, Rocki squared her shoulders. "Are you still there?"

"Yeah. I'm just… I'm not clear on where you're going with this. After Dad died, Mom was with a lot of men."

She was ignoring or discounting the fact that Rocki had said Josephine had first met Hugh more than forty years ago. "This was before that, Maisey. Gretchen claimed that this man, who owned a pharmaceutical company down under, was—" she drew another deep breath before blurting out what she'd been holding back "—Keith's father."

"No!" Maisey cried. "Keith is… Keith's as much of a Lazarow as we are. He looks exactly like us."

"Because he resembles Mom. He's part Coldiron. But there are differences, too. His height, his lean build. Our dad was five foot eleven and stocky."

"That doesn't mean he's not our full-blooded brother. Gretchen would say anything to tear Mom down. We've talked about this before. She tried to make you feel lucky *she* was the one raising you, even though she couldn't give you all the things you would've had as a Lazarow."

"Maisey—"

"No, you can't believe her. She kidnapped you because she felt Mom was an unfit mother, to get you out of a bad situation—and she probably had to keep reminding herself how pure her motives were. Otherwise, how would she ever excuse the fact that she'd stolen another woman's child?"

Rocki loved Gretchen as the mother she'd known for most of her life. She'd been well cared for. And yet that woman was her kidnapper, someone who'd taken her away from her real family. When she thought of Gretchen, there was tenderness and gratitude and resentment and outrage all wrapped up together. Even worse, Rocki couldn't speak to Gretchen about the past, couldn't get any sense of resolution, since Gretchen had passed away before Rocki learned that her birth family *hadn't* died in a car accident. All she had left were memories of Gretchen and conjecture about what those memories might mean. It was Landon who'd made her feel loved and whole all these years, in spite of her past. And now he wasn't acting anything like the man she knew…

But she wouldn't think about that. She had to focus on making sure no one suspected him of murder. They could deal with their other problems later.

"That's all true," Rocki admitted. "But when Josephine first mentioned to me that her new 'boyfriend' was from Australia, a chill went down my spine. That moment was like déjà vu, as if I could hear Gretchen talking to me in that car after that darn movie, telling me how terrible my real mother had been. How she'd beaten Keith. How she'd cared only for herself and her beauty. How she was a harsh and unforgiving employer. And how she'd been unfaithful for almost the whole length of her marriage."

"I can't believe it!"

"I can see why. Most people don't maintain such a long-lasting relationship with someone they've had an affair with. But what are the chances Josephine would get involved with two different men, both of whom she met in first class, both of whom were from Australia, both of whom were extremely wealthy and owned pharmaceutical companies? She wasn't the only one who was married back then, and that could explain why she didn't break up her own marriage to be with him."

Nothing. No response.

"This could be important, Maisey. Gretchen even told me that she had overheard Josephine on the phone talking to her lover, who *had* to be Hugh, saying he was the one true love of her life."

"Shit," Maisey said, her voice small.

"I'm so sorry."

"Do you think there's any proof?"

"Beyond the fact that Josephine thought he was the father of her second child? No. Why would she get a paternity test? That would only prove her infidelity. It's not as if she was going after Hugh for child support."

"So maybe it's *not* true."

"That's a possibility. But the timing, or the way Keith looked, or *something* convinced Josephine that he was Hugh's."

"What are we going to do? We can't tell Keith. That could destroy all the progress he's made. You didn't know him when he was going through those dark years, but they were awful. I thought he might never over-come the past."

Rocki hated putting Keith at risk. She understood how this might hurt him. But what she knew estab-lished how much Lana Pointer would hate Josephine if she ever learned about her. "He's shared enough with me about those years that I understand what's at stake." Which was what made this so hard…

"Did he tell you he once tried to commit suicide?"

"We haven't discussed that specifically, but I know he got pretty desperate."

"It was terrifying," Maisey said.

Rocki couldn't think about that. She loved Keith. "But he's well beyond that kind of thing now, isn't he? He's so functional these days."

"It all depends on his sobriety. If he relapses, who can say how far he'll fall? That spiral only moves in one direction—and that's down."

"So we won't tell him," she said. "Hopefully, we won't have to."

"Hopefully?" Maisey echoed.

Rocki grimaced at herself in the mirror. She hadn't showered yet, had gone most of the day without even combing her hair. She'd been too distraught—and she hadn't wanted to see her red, puffy eyes staring back at her as they were now. "I'll have to speak up if the po-lice start investigating Landon. As much as I care about Keith, this gives Hugh's wife a strong motive, and that could save my husband."

Maisey sighed audibly. "I understand."

"You'd do the same for Rafe."

"Yes," she said. "I would."

* * *

After Keith left Nancy's, he drove over to Maisey's to talk to her in person and weigh some of his concerns. But she wasn't home. When he texted her to see where she was, she told him she was helping Rafe's mother clean her house, since her arthritis was so bad, and would be home soon.

Leaving his car in the drive, he went down to the beach and walked along the water's edge. His family didn't need any more problems. He and his siblings had survived their grandfather's death, their father's death, "Annabelle's" supposed death and their subsequent re-union, Maisey's baby's death and divorce from her first husband and his own addiction. Would they really have to cope with learning of an illicit affair between their mother and Landon, in addition to Josephine's death?

The questions Keith needed to ask could drive a wedge between Rocki and her husband. And what if, in the end, the police couldn't prove Landon guilty *or* innocent?

That would mean they'd have to live with some level of doubt and suspicion.

Either way, Rocki's family would probably be torn apart. Even if she managed to bear up under an intense police investigation, maybe a prosecution, she'd likely become estranged from him and Maisey. Five years of a relationship might not be enough to survive that kind of upheaval and the destruction of her marriage. Unless Chief Underwood could quickly eliminate Landon as a suspect, there'd almost have to be a split *somewhere*. Keith had seen several true crime shows where part of the family—a son or daughter or parent—remained firmly loyal to the defendant despite overwhelming evidence that suggested the defendant had murdered another loved one. On one episode of *Dateline*, everyone except the suspect's children believed he'd murdered their mother.

If Landon became a suspect, would Rocki stand behind him? Even if she didn't, there'd be far-reaching consequences. The more Keith thought about what those consequences might be, the more convinced he became that there was nothing he could do to change the future. He hated that Rocki and her children might be hurt. He hated that Maisey might be hurt, too. But they *had* to have answers, had to at least seek justice. Otherwise, it was possible that Landon would get away with murder, and Keith, for one, wasn't about to allow that.

The wind ruffled his hair and his clothes as he headed back to Maisey's house. The darkening sky told him they were about to get more rain. It'd been so wet since he'd arrived on Fairham. He missed sunny Los Angeles, but only because of the weather, he realized. *This* was home. This was where he belonged.

Surprised to feel that connection, when he'd always been so restless, so unhappy and dissatisfied here, he stopped and looked around as if he was seeing Smuggler's Cove for the first time. Despite everything that was happening right now, he was more settled, more grounded than he'd ever been.

Who would've guessed? he thought and, tilting back his head, he closed his eyes and filled his lungs with the same salty air he'd breathed as a child.

When she returned, Maisey found Keith waiting on the steps of her bungalow and felt a heightened sense of foreboding. In spite of her concern, she waved cheerfully as she cut the engine. Then she hopped out, putting a spring in her step, all in an effort to act as if she hadn't just learned that they might not have the same father.

"Where're Rafe and the kids?" her brother asked, getting to his feet.

Maisey kept her chin up and a smile on her face. "At his mother's."

"Still?"

"They're getting a pizza for dinner."

He gave her a funny look. "You could've stayed with your family and stopped by Coldiron House to see me on your way home. Why didn't you say you had plans?"

"Because you wanted to talk to me." So she'd dropped everything and arranged for Rafe to stay with the kids. After what she'd learned from Rocki, she hadn't been able to pay attention to what was going on at her mother-in-law's, anyway. She'd been too worried about her brother and what might happen if he were to find out, or even suspect, that Hugh Pointer from Australia was his father and not Malcolm, the calm, steady man who'd raised them.

At first, Maisey had tried to deny that Keith could belong to someone else. She didn't want to believe it, but there were a few things that suggested what Rocki had told her could be true. Keith was far more high-strung than they were. Malcolm had had a difficult time relating to him, which might've been caused by some intuition about his wife's behavior, if not outright knowledge that Keith wasn't his. Their mother had always loved Keith best, despite their frequent clash of personalities. And last, but not least, what about all those trips her mother used to take? Was she traveling with Hugh? Meeting him at exotic places? Malcolm had rarely gone with her. He preferred to stay on the island with them and work on his vacation rentals and other developments, most of which were in Charleston and had long since been sold...

Keith blew on his hands. "I do need to talk to you, but I didn't mean to ruin your family outing."

"I was afraid it might be something I wouldn't want Laney to hear."

Her brother acknowledged this by grimly pursing his lips. "That's probably true."

She braced for more bad news. Surely, Rocki hadn't hung up with her and then immediately called Keith. This *couldn't* be about what Rocki had just told her, could it? "What's going on?"

"I was hoping you could tell me what Landon was like around Mom."

She swallowed a sigh as she unlocked the house to show him in. "Not Landon again. You're barking up the wrong tree, Keith. I've decided there's no way he could be responsible for Mom's death. You know him as well as I do. He isn't capable of murder."

"How can we be sure of that? I like him, don't get me wrong. But murderers don't walk around with Post-it notes on their foreheads. A lot of killers have wives and children."

"But *Landon*? Really?"

He didn't speak again until she'd closed the door, removed her coat and gazed up at him expectantly. Then he said, "I think he and Mom were having an affair, Mais."

"What?" She held a hand to her chest as if he'd just slugged her. "That *can't* be true!"

"Yes, it could."

Her mind raced as she tried to make sense of his outlandish comment. First Rocki claims Keith isn't Malcolm's son, and then Keith claims Rocki's husband was having an affair with their *mother*? Like Alice in Wonderland, Maisey felt as if she must've fallen through the rabbit's hole. "She was sixty-three!"

"She didn't look a day over forty-five."

"So?"

"Forty-five is actually very close to his age."

"That's crazy!"

"Not really. Not with a mother as beautiful as ours," he said.

Maisey had just opened her mouth to argue when he showed her a picture he had on his cell phone.

"Where did you get that?" she gasped.

"It was on Mom's computer."

Fortunately, he was using his thumb to cover Landon's genitals. A naked picture of her brother-in-law in her mother's possession was shocking and upsetting enough.

She shoved the phone out of her sight. "There must be some other explanation. Mom wouldn't sleep with Landon, even if he wanted to sleep with her. What would she have to gain?"

"Rocki's a beautiful woman. Maybe Mom felt threatened by her own daughter. Maybe she wasn't ready to be upstaged. Maybe she was out to prove she could still get any man she wanted."

Her knees were suddenly so weak Maisey had to sit down. "That makes me sick."

"Because it sounds plausible?"

She imagined her curvaceous mother, dressed like someone out of a Ralph Lauren ad and smelling like the perfume section of an expensive department store.

She turned male heads wherever she went… "No! Only the vainest person in the world would behave like that. Our mother was vain, no question, but I have to believe she had more integrity." Maisey had never been able to get along with her. The past five years had been the best period in their relationship, but only because she hadn't taken their mother as seriously as she had before. There was no need to. She'd had Rafe to lean on, to love her, to comfort her when her mother made her feel two inches tall, the way Josephine had such a habit of doing. "She was difficult on so many levels. But she wouldn't have actively *enticed* Landon…would she?"

Keith perched next to her on the couch. "Have you talked to Rocki today?"

She averted her gaze—and lied because she didn't feel she could cover for what she'd been told. "No. I've tried calling. She hasn't gotten back to me. But that in itself doesn't mean anything," she added quickly.

"She's not herself right now."

"She's under a lot of stress. They run two businesses. They've got three children. And they're having trouble paying the bills."

"We're all stressed, coping with Mom's death." He lifted his phone, referring to what he'd shown her, even though that picture was no longer on the screen. "So do we tell her about this?"

As much as Maisey feared the fallout, she couldn't see any way around it. Her sister had to know, couldn't be kept in the dark. *She'd* want to know if it were Rafe. No one relished the thought of being duped.

But then what Gretchen had told Rocki would also come out. All the terrible secrets of the past would be spilled on the table. "Son of a bitch."

"No kidding," he said, although he had no idea just how torn she was—or why.

He watched her for several seconds. "Well?"

"We have to," she said. "We don't have a choice."

"And if he's innocent? If there's some other explanation for the photograph?"

"Then he can give it to us. That's why we tell her—and him. So he'll have the chance to explain and clear his name. He deserves that."

Keith pinched the bridge of his nose, then dropped his hand. "Fine. We'll tell her. But when? Now? Later? Chief Underwood's getting Mom's cell phone records, which should provide more definitive information. I bet she's getting Landon's, too."

"Then we'll wait until we have those and possibly know more." At least that would buy some time. Maybe they'd learn something that would change the situation, put fewer people at risk. Leaning forward, she rested her chin on her fists. "This really sucks, doesn't it?" she said. "We were all doing so well, were *finally* sailing through smooth water."

He put his arm around her. "We'll get through this."

Surprised that *he* was the calm one, that *he* was encouraging *her*, she looked into his face. "I'm so proud of you."

"You were expecting me to slip up while I was here?"

She could feel his chest hum when he spoke. "I was worried. If you fell apart... I couldn't take that, too."

He kissed the top of her head. "I'm not going to fall apart. I hate to admit it, but getting Mom out of my life five years ago was a game changer—despite the guilt I feel now."

"Why do you feel guilt?" she asked. "You pulled

yourself out of a bad situation and built a life. You did the right thing. And you made her proud in the end."

"But could I have done it a better way?"

"Doesn't matter. You recovered. That's what counts. Anyway, what about *her* guilt? She should've been riddled with remorse for being such a bad mother."

"According to Hugh, she *was* remorseful."

She stared out over her front yard. "You've spoken to Hugh Pointer?"

"Yes."

She clasped her hands together—tightly. "And? How'd he treat you?"

"He was very nice."

"He brought up your relationship with Mom?"

"He did. Said she blamed herself for the rift between us."

"That surprises me." Unclasping her hands, she wiped her palms on her jeans. "Maybe she was closer to him than we thought," she said, just to see how her brother might respond.

Fortunately, he didn't seem to place much importance on her comment. "Maybe," he agreed. "But the bottom line is that we couldn't get along. And I'm sure it wasn't *all* her fault. Some of it was my own insecurities and immaturity and how much I resented her control and manipulation."

"Don't gloss over the pain she caused. That was at the root of everything."

"But which came first, the chicken or the egg? I was a difficult kid. Could be I provoked her."

"She beat Rocki, too, when she was Annabelle."

"She didn't beat *you*."

"I came last, and I was dead set on staying out of her way. You defied her."

"That's what I'm saying. I kind of asked for it."

"There were certainly times… But she was the adult, and she went too far."

He didn't seem entirely convinced.

"It's true," she insisted.

"I'm willing to accept my share of the responsibility. The helplessness was the worst, feeling I couldn't take control of my own life. Doing so has made a big difference."

"We all have to set boundaries." She took his hand. "So…does this newfound optimism and strength mean you're not tempted to relapse?"

"I'd be lying if I said it didn't cross my mind at least once a day." He offered her a rueful and yet endearing smile. "But I can overcome the temptation. I don't need to escape the life I'm living. I'm becoming more and more satisfied with what I'm doing and who I am."

She wished that was enough to reassure her. But he didn't know that everything he'd come to terms with was about to be upended. "Still, Mom's death and all of this with Landon…that's not going to set you back?"

"I don't get it, either." He shrugged as if his reaction was inexplicable. "I'm concerned. I'm sad. I'm angry. I'm determined. I'm dealing with a lot of emotions. But I'm okay in a way I've never been before."

What she knew would probably reverse all the progress he'd made. With a heavy heart, she rested her head on his shoulder. "Then that's the ray of sunshine we hang on to."

She just hoped it would carry him through.

17

"I want to see you. Have you decided yet?"

Nancy shouldn't have answered Keith's call, but she'd felt such a surge of excitement when she saw his name that she'd picked up despite her better judgment. Now her eyes inadvertently shifted to the bags of lingerie she'd left on her kitchen table. She planned to take everything back. She'd thought that might help her resist him...

But those things hadn't been returned yet.

"It's not even six o'clock, and you're already asking for an answer?" she said.

"Do I have to wait until a certain time?"

"We just had lunch a few hours ago."

"So? What are you doing for dinner? I'll take you to Charleston."

Oh, boy. He was pouring on the charm. Nancy didn't know a woman who could refuse him when he did that. But she *had* to learn from experience. *Had* to guard her heart. "I was heading over to my father's. I make dinner for him and Jade every Saturday."

"Great. I'm in."

She hesitated. "You're kidding, aren't you?" If anything, she'd expected him to try to convince her to cancel. He'd never been interested in her family, hadn't cared to spend any time with them—which was part of the reason her stepfather had warned her not to get involved with him. According to Martin, that kind of behavior said a lot about a man, as well as that man's level of interest in a woman.

Her stepfather's logic had been sound, but nothing she'd been willing to hear back then. She was determined to be smarter this time, since Keith had proved him right before.

"No, I'm serious. What're we having? Any chance you're making that Mexican steak dinner you used to make?"

She hadn't intended to make her Mexican steak dinner, but it was easy enough to do. She *could* change her plans. But why would she? The fact that she'd even consider it made her mad at herself. She was already trying to please him. "No. I'm making my taglierini dish."

"The one with tomatoes and garlic?"

She'd often cooked for him. Although she'd enjoyed it, she'd also felt she'd *had* to cook to compete with the professional chef his mother had hired at Coldiron House. Josephine's standards were so high—for everything—Nancy had felt she'd never measure up. And Josephine had made it abundantly clear that she agreed.

Still, Nancy had tried, had given it every effort, and there'd been times when she'd succeeded in making life a great deal easier for Keith. She was just surprised all of that hadn't meant anything to him in the end.

It said something that he remembered those meals, though. "That's the one."

"I like that, too. When should I come over?"

"To eat or to help with the cooking?" she countered.

If the challenge put him off, he didn't show it. "To help, of course. I'm ready now if you want."

"Fine. Come pick me up."

"I'm on my way."

He hadn't balked at anything. Nancy was smiling when she hung up, even though she wasn't sure how her stepfather would react to having Keith in his house.

Landon walked into the house before supper. But he didn't kiss Rocki or tease her as he usually did. He didn't pull her down on the couch with him, either. He showered, did a few things outside, judging by various noises around the house, and came inside when she called everyone to the table.

Although he was quiet throughout the meal, he also seemed a little less defensive than he'd been before. It probably helped that Rocki hadn't said another word about his trip to Fairham. She'd showered, put on her makeup and made pot roast. Although Zac was home, Chloe was still out. Rocki knew their son would go to his room and play on his computer after dinner—weekends were the only time she allowed computer games—which would give her and Landon a few hours alone. She was looking forward to clearing the air, to finally understanding what he thought and felt. How was *he* the injured party if he was also the one who'd lied?

She couldn't answer that question, but she promised herself she wouldn't be accusatory. Although he'd been acting strange ever since her mother's Christmas party, he'd been much worse the past week. They needed to find common ground again, needed to get back to where they'd always been. Her marriage had never felt fragile to her before, but everything she'd taken for granted suddenly seemed to be in jeopardy. Was Landon unhappy with her? Had she missed signs she should've seen? Had he fallen out of love? If so, when? Was this serious enough to tear them apart? Or something they'd be able to work through?

With a shake of her head, she tried to pull herself out of the doldrums. *Of course* they'd be able to overcome their problems. A marriage as good as hers didn't collapse in a few days—or even a month.

"The pot roast is delicious, Mom. I love it when you make this."

Rocki smiled at her son. "I'm glad. I also made a chocolate cake."

"Wow!" he exclaimed. "Is it someone's birthday?"

"No. I just thought it'd be nice to have dessert for a change."

Zac wrinkled his nose. "Dessert to you is usually fruit."

"Because I happen to care that refined sugar and processed food aren't healthy for you. Mothers are like that, you know. Besides, you *like* fruit."

"Not as much as I like cake—especially when it has tons of frosting!"

Landon glanced at their son's plate. Zac was avoiding his carrots and peas and filling up on bread. Normally, Landon would've said something, but tonight he didn't, and Rocki ignored it, too. She was trying to stay positive, which was something of a chore, since Landon wasn't contributing to the conversation. She struggled to carry it herself, to keep Zac occupied so he wouldn't feel the strain. She asked about his visit with his friend and where they'd gone skateboarding. Then she recounted a story she'd seen in the paper about a dog that had saved his human—a five-year-old child who'd fallen through the ice into a lake.

Relieved when Zac finally carried his plate to the sink and went to his room, Rocki stood up to clear the table.

Landon helped her do the dishes. But they danced around each other as if they were polite strangers, careful not to touch. Rocki hated the strangeness of it all, wished she could smash through his sudden reserve. Where was the man she'd married?

As soon as they finished, he went into the living room and turned on *SportsCenter*. He was avoiding her. She wanted to follow him, to turn off the TV so she could try talking to him again. But Zac was still awake and could possibly hear if the conversation erupted into another heated argument.

Forcing herself to leave Landon alone, she went into the bedroom and picked up a mystery novel. She usually loved to read, but tonight she couldn't concentrate. The lines blurred together until, mercifully, her eyelids grew heavy and she drifted off to sleep.

At worst, Nancy had expected her stepfather to be unfriendly to Keith—at best, remote. But she had seriously underestimated Keith's ability to win people over. Martin Dellinger had melted like butter on a hot sidewalk, and it had taken only a few minutes, just long enough for Keith to shake his hand, sit down with him on the couch and begin a conversation about the Gamecocks, her father's favorite college football team. She could hear them trying to remember which players would be returning, who would start, if the coach would be replaced, if they'd have a better season. Keith had mentioned helping her cook, but she hadn't been serious when she'd acted as if she was counting on that. Taglierini didn't take long, and he'd just get in her way, so she'd insisted he visit with Martin while she made dinner.

Jade came home from a friend's house not long after Nancy had started pressing the garlic cloves that went into the pasta sauce, and made a beeline for the kitchen.

"Whoa, what's going on?" she whispered as the kitchen door swung shut behind her.

Nancy put a finger to her lips even though the men were in the other room and her sister was speaking softly. "Nothing. We've decided to be friends. That's all."

"Friends? That doesn't make sense."

"Of course it does."

"Then what's he doing *here*?"

"He's here for dinner. What do you think?"

"He doesn't need to be here for dinner. He has a housekeeper who cooks."

"Pippa doesn't work on weekends—not unless he makes special arrangements with her."

"So that means he's helpless? He'll starve without you?"

Nancy rolled her eyes. "I'm guessing he didn't want to eat alone."

"He could always eat with his sister! Last I checked, she lived on the island, too. And she has kids he might enjoy seeing. Yet he chose *you*."

"I don't know why he asked to come!" she finally admitted. "It's a mystery, okay?"

"He wants to be with you!" Jade said. "Admit it!"

Nancy didn't need her sister working against her. She'd be foolish to get her hopes up. She couldn't win

Keith's true affection. She'd already tried everything—let him live with her, slept with him, cooked for him, lent him money. None of that had made any difference. He'd been with her before only because he was hitting rock bottom and had no one else. Why would he choose a simple flower arranger, who had no money or influence to speak of, when he was now on top and no longer needed that kind of support?

With a scowl to show she disagreed that this meant anything at all, Nancy went back to pressing garlic. "No. Not in the way you think." He'd expressed sexual interest, but even that didn't mean anything. He'd slept with her before. Now that he'd stumbled back into her orbit, he wanted to fall into bed with her again. He wasn't geographically near the women he'd been sleeping with lately—and Keith liked sex too much to go without it.

"He's never come over *here* before," Jade said.

"He's trying to make up for being such a jerk."

"That's sweet."

She shrugged. "He's basically a nice guy. He just isn't the type to settle down. And that's the only type I'll be satisfied with. We're looking for different things in life."

"Anyone can fall in love and change their plans, Nance."

She put the garlic in a skillet and began to brown it in olive oil. "Not Keith."

"Yes, Keith."

"Apparently you're more of a dreamer than I am," she said as she washed the garlic press. "He lives in California and won't be here long. These days he's a wealthy man in his own right, with a company to run. Not to mention he's handsome and charismatic and—"

"And you love him," she broke in.

Nancy turned off the water. "Stop it, Jade! He could have *anyone*."

"So what? No one else is as good as *you*," her sister said.

All of Nancy's pique flowed out of her body like air from a punctured balloon. "Come here." She pulled her sister into an embrace. "What would I do without you?"

"You'd forget how great you are, that's what," Jade teased.

Movement at the door caught Nancy's eye. Keith had just poked his head in the room. "Am I interrupting something?"

Jade pulled away. "I was just telling Nancy about this new technique of giving a blow job that makes the pleasure so intense it melts a man's bones."

Nancy sucked in her breath so fast she nearly choked. She couldn't believe what'd come out of her sister's mouth—and yet she should've expected *something* outrageous. Leave it to Jade. Jade didn't feel comfortable with displays of emotion; shocking Keith put her back on stable ground.

Keith coughed in surprise. Then his lips twisted into a crooked grin. "I'd say that's good information to have. Who was telling you about that?"

"A couple of gay friends. They claim to have perfected the technique. But it'll take a lot of experience to get it right," Jade said as she headed for her room. "Too bad Nancy rarely has an opportunity to practice."

Nancy covered her face. "I'm going to kill her," she mumbled into her hands.

"Don't do it before she finishes teaching you that technique," he said, and ducked as she threw a garlic clove at him.

* * *

Landon sat, bleary-eyed in front of the TV, wondering what the hell he was going to do. Thanks to Pippa, everyone now knew he was the last person to see Josephine alive. That was damning enough. If they found out any more...

He tried to imagine the embarrassment and humiliation his family would suffer. The betrayal. Rocki would never speak to him again. Once she learned that the truth extended far beyond what she already knew, she'd abandon him. The kids would, too. And the agent of his destruction, that damn picture he'd taken while he was drunk, could still be out there, somewhere. He'd insisted Josephine delete it from her phone. He knew it was gone from there, but the fact that he'd sent it in the first place made him sick with anxiety. He'd spent the past several days in an utter panic, hardly able to function, fearing someone might stumble upon it.

God, how had he let his life spin out of control? How had he done the terrible things he'd done? He'd always considered himself "a good guy." His mother, his father, his wife and children—everyone believed he *was* a good guy.

Bile rose in his throat as he realized just how soon they could be disabused of that notion...

He thought of Rocki in her bedroom, reading or whatever, and felt infinitely grateful that she hadn't followed him into the living room. He couldn't even look at her right now, couldn't face the devastating truth about how far he'd fallen and the price they'd *all* have to pay.

"Daddy, will you read this for me?"

Tired of being away from home, Chloe had decided not to stay the whole weekend at her girlfriend's and had come home shortly after Rocki disappeared into their bedroom. When he heard her voice, the guilt he'd been feeling became that much worse. His daughter didn't deserve what he'd done. No one in the family did. Why hadn't he been more careful? Kept his thoughts and desires in check?

He stared down at his hands as if they'd betrayed him on their own...

"Daddy?"

Chloe sounded confused. And she had reason. He hadn't even looked up at her, wasn't thinking straight, wasn't acting normal. But he couldn't act normal when it felt like he had a semi parked on his chest.

After he took a deep, calming breath, he switched off the television and forced himself to face her. "What, sweetheart?"

"Mom's asleep and I'd rather not wake her. I think she might've had a hard day. So I was hoping you could read over my English paper. I really want to get a good grade in this class."

She fought for a good grade in every class. She was a straight-A student, part of the student government and should be a strong contender for "kindest person in the school," because she had more empathy in her little finger than most people had in their whole bodies.

"Of course," he said, but her paper was an autobiography that praised her parents, gave thanks for her loving home and shared her dreams—which would soon be crushed beneath the selfish desires that'd somehow, inexplicably, snuck up and taken control of him. His eyes burned as he read and reread each paragraph.

"Are you okay, Daddy?" Chloe bent close to look into his face.

He nodded because he couldn't speak for the tightness in his throat, and she placed a soothing hand on his arm.

"You seem sad," she whispered. "What is it?"

He couldn't remember the last time he'd shed tears. He was pretty sure it was at Zac's birth, when the miracle of watching his son being born had overwhelmed him. But he felt like sobbing now, felt like throwing himself into his daughter's innocent arms and crying his eyes out.

"I'm fine," he said. But that couldn't be further from the truth. He'd destroyed *everything*...

18

Keith loved sparring with Jade. All evening they ganged up to tease Nancy. Actually, he liked Martin, too. He wasn't sure why he hadn't paid more attention to Nancy's relatives before, because they were engaging and unique. Nancy didn't have the stereotypical "step" family. She loved them and they loved her as much as if she was related by blood—maybe more. Keith could finally understand why Nancy would never leave the island. Why would anyone ever walk away from these kinds of relationships? Although they didn't have a lot of money or worldly possessions, they were the happiest people he'd ever met.

He felt happier himself just being around them. He'd filled his life with work and belongings rather than people. Trust, especially emotional trust, didn't come easily for him. But he'd reached the point where he could finally see what he was missing. "Hey, where are you going with my dessert?" he said. "I'll have one more slice."

Nancy had just taken the pie off the table so she could bring it to the counter, where her father and sister were doing the dishes by hand because they didn't own a dishwasher. "You've got to be kidding me," she said. "You've eaten enough pie for three people."

"But is it polite to mention that?" he said. "What kind of hostess are you?"

"One who's been counting calories for a long time."

He chuckled at her "sour grapes" face. "So you're jealous."

"Of the fact that you can eat whatever you want and never gain an ounce? Yes. I'm absolutely *green*. Who wouldn't be?"

Remembering Jade's blow job comment, he gave her the once-over. He doubted Jade could teach her anything that might improve her technique. She'd always been a sensitive and passionate lover. But he was certainly willing to experiment. "You look good just the way you are."

She glanced behind her, as if she couldn't believe he'd say that in front of her family, and steered away from the innuendo in his voice. "One would think you didn't have a full-time cook, Mr. Lazarow."

"Pippa's off this weekend," he said as she cut him another slice.

"But if I know Pippa, your refrigerator is fully stocked." She set his plate in front of him. "Heaven forbid you ever had to fend for yourself."

"That's probably true." He licked meringue from his fork. "You'll have to come over and help me empty it out so she's not offended."

She placed her hands on her hips. "The problems of the rich and good-looking. They're insurmountable."

"Not all of us can have the life you've lived here," he said, gesturing around the kitchen.

She seemed to understand that it was an honest compliment, since she smiled at him instead of taking offense.

"I have some errands to run," he said as she placed the pie under a domed cover. "Any chance you can go with me?"

"Errands?" she echoed. "On a Saturday night?"

He wanted to drive over to the other side of the island to see if he could learn any more about the person who'd called to alert the police about that intruder. He'd meant to go this morning, but there'd been that business with Landon's nude photo. That had distracted him, for sure, but now he felt a renewed conviction to find that caller. It was the break-in that gave him hope Landon *hadn't* killed Josephine, even if he'd been sleeping with her. Rocki had told him Landon was home with her Wednesday night, so he hadn't returned.

Keith hesitated to explain all of that to Nancy, however—at least while her father and sister were in the room. "Yeah. I need to drop by Maisey's."

"Go." Jade spoke up, addressing Nancy before Nancy could refuse. "Dad's about to sit down and watch some TV while I finish the dishes. We're fine."

"What are you talking about—Dad's about to sit down? I can help," Martin protested.

Jade nudged his hands out of the sink. "Go take a load off, Dad."

"I hate to leave you with all the cleanup," Nancy told her.

"Why?" Jade tossed a dish towel over her shoulder. "You did all the cooking."

"But you do the cooking and cleaning all week. Saturdays are *my* turn."

"This Saturday isn't. Go with Keith. You love Maisey's."

"It *has* been a while since I've seen her kids…" Nancy said.

Martin used the back of a chair to steady him as he came around the table. He looked as if he feared that Nancy was being drawn in by Keith again and they'd done nothing to stop it. But he didn't argue. He embraced her when she went over to kiss him goodbye.

"Dinner was delicious, sweetie," he said. "You're too good to me."

"It's because I feel sorry for you being stuck with Jade all week," she teased.

Jade flicked water at her, then glanced over to where her father was humming to himself as he shuffled into the living room. "Don't forget what I told you about that special…um…technique with your tongue."

She gave Keith a sly wink to remind him, too, but *he* wasn't likely to forget. Since Jade had first made that joke, he'd thought about having Nancy's mouth on him almost every time he looked at her.

"Isn't Chief Underwood trying to track down the person who made that call the night after you got here?" Nancy asked from the passenger seat.

Keith adjusted the heater so it wouldn't blow so strongly. "She is, but police work takes time. And she's looking for a needle in a haystack, so…she could probably use some help."

But would she welcome it? That was the question. Even a small force like Fairham's, which consisted of only three officers besides Chief Underwood, didn't usually appreciate the involvement of civilians. Civilians didn't understand what to reveal, what not to reveal, the rules of gathering evidence, etc. But maybe Underwood was different. Nancy was still a little confused by her and Keith's relationship. She was fairly certain they'd gone out on a date last night, and yet Keith had classified that dinner as "business."

Despite her curiosity, Nancy wasn't going to ask him to clarify. He had his freedom, the right to do anything he wanted. And so did she. She couldn't justify being friends with him if she became possessive. "Okay, but… shouldn't we have started a bit earlier?"

"Not necessarily. For a Saturday, it's not too late. We should be able to hit every house before ten."

"I doubt we'll find anything."

"Whoa, now *you're* the pessimist?"

Her shoulder bumped against the door as the road curved. "The realist." The sun had gone down while they were eating. She gestured at the darkness outside. "I just don't want you to panic and assume it must be Landon if we don't find anything. Look how dark it is. What are the chances that someone could've seen someone else making a call on a cell phone?"

"People have headlights."

"But that call could've come from inside a house or car."

"There's always the chance that someone happened to see a man who was acting furtive or didn't look as if he belonged—or even a car that seemed out of place. I've got to be thorough. My brother-in-law's freedom could hinge on finding whoever called in that night. This is something that needs to be checked out, even if it's just to eliminate the possibility."

She agreed, but didn't see why he'd brought her with him. She wasn't sure why he'd joined her family for dinner, either. They'd already had lunch together and, as she'd told him at her stepfather's place, he probably had a whole refrigerator stuffed with delectable meals. "What do we know so far about the night your mother died?"

"We know there was no evidence of forced entry."

"Meaning your mother answered the door?"

"Possibly."

"Perhaps she recognized her visitor, invited him in and they ended up having an argument..."

"Or the door wasn't locked in the first place. It's even possible that whoever killed her knew where she kept the spare key. Some crazed psychopath would likely kill in a more violent fashion and he wouldn't bother staging the scene with drugs and alcohol, so I think we can safely rule that out."

"You're right, staging the scene would take time and thought," she said. "But your mother lived alone, so he probably *had* time."

"Then maybe we can't rule anything out."

"The autopsy's tomorrow?" Keith had mentioned that at lunch...

"Yes. Why?"

"I was wondering about DNA evidence."

"If there is DNA, I hope to God it's not Landon's."

They wound their way on ever-narrower roads into the heavy vegetation that covered the far side of the island. Every now and then Nancy glimpsed a half-moon, grinning at her through the trees. But mostly it was just the twin beams of their headlights cutting through the darkness—until they reached their first stop. Then a dim yellow porch light acted like a homing beacon, guiding them to the front door.

The people who lived on this end of Fairham weren't

the more affluent islanders. But the child who answered their knock, a boy of about ten, looked well cared for and opened the door to a neat and clean living room.

Although he called his father as soon as she and Keith identified themselves, they didn't learn anything new. Keith was right—they found most folks at home—but no one had any information.

By the time they approached a house made partially of plywood, with plastic covering the roof and a blanket over the main window, Nancy could tell that Keith was getting discouraged.

"This looks a little sketchy," she murmured as they got out.

"Why don't you stay in the car?" Keith suggested.

When she followed him to the door anyway, he waved her back, but she ignored that and knocked.

They heard the drone of a television, so someone was home. That became even more apparent when the blanket at the window moved. Nancy got the impression a tall figure was peering out at them, but it was hard to tell. Except for the flicker of that TV, it was just as dark inside the house as out.

And no one answered the door.

"Should we go?" she murmured.

"Not yet." Keith rapped on the window and the blanket fell back into place. "Hey! Will you open up for a second? Give us a chance to talk to you? We just have a couple of questions. Then we'll leave you alone."

When there was no response, they assumed his persistence wasn't going to pay off. They'd both started walking back to the car by the time the door opened.

They turned to see a bulky, thirtysomething male dressed in baggy sweat bottoms and a white T-shirt.

"Sorry to intrude on your evening," Keith said.

The guy was almost as tall as Keith, which wasn't that common. He had at least fifty pounds on him, too—all of it muscle. But it was his expression that unnerved Nancy. He wasn't pleased by their visit and didn't care if they knew it. "What do you want?" he growled.

Taking her hand, Keith tugged her slightly behind him. Although it was a subtle move, Nancy understood that he recognized the potential for danger and was trying to place himself in front of her. "My mother was killed last Saturday night—"

"I heard," the man interrupted without the slightest show of sympathy.

Keith froze. "You know who I am?"

The guy could've said, "Who doesn't?" Most people on the island, if they'd been here for any length of time, would recognize Keith. The Lazarow/Coldirons were notorious, especially Keith because of his good looks and bad behavior. But the guy said, "You don't know who *I* am?"

Keith hesitated before shaking his head. "No. Sorry. Did we go to school together or something?"

"My dad works for your mother—well, for *you* now."

"And your dad is—"

"Tyrone Coleman."

The mention of Tyrone's name siphoned off some of the tension that seemed to be flowing through Keith. "Of course! I haven't been around in a while, didn't know you were back on the island."

He rubbed his hand over his shaved head. "Just moved back a few months ago."

"Let's see…you must be…Marcus?"

"Yeah." Despite having Tyrone as a connection, this guy didn't offer them so much as a smile. He wasn't interested in becoming friends. "So what's goin' on? Why are you here? I had nothin' to do with your mom's death. That I can tell ya."

Keith raised his hand, palm out, in the stop position. "I'm not here to accuse you. Someone made a call to the police from this side of the island on Wednesday—to notify them of a break-in. It was a male voice, but the caller wouldn't give his name. I was hoping you might be able to help me figure out who it was."

When he said, "That was me," Nancy's jaw dropped and she stepped closer, hoping to get a better look at Marcus's face.

"You?" Keith echoed.

"I was driving home, past the turnoff to your place, when a woman flagged me down. Said she thought someone might be breaking into Coldiron House. Told me her phone was dead and asked me to call the cops."

"What'd this woman look like?"

"I couldn't tell ya. It was pitch-black and raining, and she was bundled up from head to toe in a raincoat. Had a scarf covering most of her face. I couldn't even tell you the color of her hair. She was white, though."

"Any idea of her age?"

"I'd say she was in her thirties. But I wasn't paying a whole lot of attention. I just wanted her to get out of the way and let me pass."

"What was she driving?"

"There was no car that I could see. I'm guessing she parked up the cliff, toward the house."

"You didn't turn down that way to see what was going on? Didn't go to the house yourself?"

"No. Once she moved off to the side, I went on my way. I figured she could be wrong. I wasn't going to call. But then I thought of my dad and I knew he'd care what was going on at Coldiron House even if I didn't."

Nancy didn't feel he'd needed to add that last part, but he was obviously an angry person. "So...why wouldn't you give your name when you called in?"

He leaned to the right, peering at her in the darkness. "That's none of your business, but I'll answer, just to show you how honest I am. I don't like authority. That's how it is when you serve time. You don't like talking to the cops. You get me?"

"You used an untraceable phone," Keith pointed out.

"So?"

Keith came right back at him, *"Why?"*

He spread out his hands. "What can I say, man? That's all I got. I don't have any credit, and I sure as hell don't have the piles of money you do. So until I pull my life together, I probably won't have anything better."

Keith ignored the reference to his wealth. "Did you pass any other vehicles on the road that night?"

"Not once I got out of Keys Crossing. Or I would've let them handle it."

"So there were no other people lurking around the turnoff to Coldiron House?"

"Just that one woman."

"Who you didn't recognize. She wasn't an islander."

"I didn't recognize her, but you can't take that to mean she don't live here. I just got out of the slammer. I was locked up for fourteen years, man. A lot's changed since I left."

With a sigh, Keith scratched his neck. "Chief Underwood will probably want to talk to you—to confirm what you just told us."

"That's what I was afraid of. See? I shouldn't have called. It's been less than a week since I did and already I'm gettin' dragged into somethin' that ain't none of my business—and I didn't even leave my name," he said in disgust and shut the door.

They walked back to the Mercedes without speaking. Once they were inside and they'd pulled out of the rutted drive, Nancy broke the silence.

"Nice guy," she said sarcastically.

"He's not a happy person."

"Poor Tyrone."

Keith shot her a look. "People used to say that about my mom because of *me*."

"Except it was your mother who was the difficult one. I can get along with most people, but even I had trouble with her." She loosened her seat belt. "Anyway, do you believe him? Tyrone's son?"

"Yeah, I do," he replied. "Don't you?"

"I don't know. He *does* have a record. And if they put him away for that long, he must've done something pretty bad."

"If he was the one who broke in the night my mother was murdered, he would've taken stuff."

"He could've broken in for other reasons."

"Like…"

"Revenge. Maybe he was angry with your mother. Maybe he tried to get a job at Coldiron House, and she wouldn't hire him because of his record. Or he didn't believe his father was being treated the way he should be."

"I still say someone like Marcus would've helped himself. He needs too many things to walk away from everything in that house—and if you're going to commit murder, why not get a computer?"

"Because then you might have to explain where it came from."

"Who'd tell on him?"

"A friend or neighbor."

"Out here? No. He wouldn't have admitted to being our caller if he was also the person who murdered my mother."

"Unless he was afraid we'd eventually figure out it was him and was covering for that."

Keith shrugged off her words. "He's been in the system. He knows that kind of phone is untraceable."

"Okay. Well...we'll see what they find at the autopsy tomorrow. Maybe that'll clarify a few things—since this didn't."

He called and told Chief Underwood what they'd learned. Then he surprised Nancy by taking her hand. She thought he might try to persuade her to stay the night, since he'd mentioned it before. But they passed the turnoff to Coldiron House and continued to Keys Crossing with his fingers threaded through hers.

"It's good to see you again," he said.

Although he sounded sincere, she refused to read anything into that comment. "It's good to see you, too."

19

You still awake?

Nancy was scratching Simba's belly, since he was lying on the couch with her, when Keith's text came in. Keith had said good-night when he dropped her off so she hadn't expected to hear from him again. But it wasn't all that late—only eleven.

Yeah. I'm up, she wrote back. You okay?

Fine. Just worried about Rocki.

When are you going to tell her about Landon?

Not until after the autopsy. I hope Dr. Pendergast determines that it was suicide. And that I'll be able to accept and believe it if he does.

I think you already know how you'll react. Isn't that why you hired him in the first place?

Maybe that's why I can't sleep.

You've got to try. You need your rest.

Any chance you'll come over and keep me company? We could play some pool or darts or watch a movie. There are so many rooms here. You can use one of them after we're done. You don't have to sleep with me.

He didn't want to be alone. He'd never liked being alone. His demons came out at night. For her own sake, Nancy wanted to say no. Being around him was increasing the desire to touch him and be touched by him. But she cared too much about Keith not to support him during what had to be a difficult time.

Somehow she'd deal with her own feelings. Plenty of people suffered broken hearts. At least she'd never been through anything like he'd been through.

What about Simba? she wrote.

His response was almost immediate. Bring him.

Nancy tapped her fingernails on her phone. "I know better than to do this," she told her dog. But Simba sat up and wagged his tail as if *he* didn't see anything wrong with going.

Her phone vibrated to signal a new text. Are you coming? I have food. Loads of food. And I'll give you a back rub, if you want.

She wanted a lot more than a back rub. That was the problem. But she couldn't refuse him. This was as close to a plea for help as he ever got. Just the thought of him prowling around that big house, on edge and unable to relax, made it impossible to say no. If she did, she'd ramble around her own house, feeling miserable and worried about him. Yeah. I'm coming.

Once Nancy got to Coldiron House, Keith was as good as his word. He offered her food, did everything he could to entertain her. And he didn't make one sexual comment—didn't even try to touch her. He seemed grateful just to have her there.

After they'd eaten and he'd won several games of pool—except for the one time he let her win—they put on *Last of the Mohicans*, which he happened to remember was her favorite movie.

By then, it was late—nearly two. Nancy had to open the flower shop at ten. She'd be tired most of the day if she didn't sleep soon. But she didn't care. She was enjoying every minute of this night and was glad she hadn't turned Keith down when he'd asked her to come over. As dangerous as it was to feel the way she did, she was so happy right now that she didn't even *want* to sleep. She couldn't remember ever finding so much satisfaction in simply being with someone.

She could tell Keith was getting tired, too, that he was struggling to stay awake. She had the feeling that he was afraid she'd leave if he fell asleep. But while they lounged on one of the big, soft couches in the theater room, with Simba at their feet, he started leaning more heavily against her as his body relaxed. She helped him get comfortable by letting him lay his head on her lap. As she combed her fingers through his hair, his eyelids fluttered open for a brief second and he looked up at her with a grateful smile. Then he drifted off as if he found her touch so soothing he couldn't fight the fatigue any longer.

Nancy didn't mind. She was glad to see him get some rest. She had the movie to keep her entertained—not that she was paying much attention to it. She'd seen it so many times she could almost recite the actors' lines. She was just enjoying the darkness, the drama of the sound score and, more than anything, finally having the freedom to once again touch the man she loved.

Five years have changed nothing, she thought. Except…it had changed *him*. Keith was different these days, more mature, more emotionally stable, less volatile. That she was proud of him for hauling himself up by his bootstraps—all on his own—didn't help her maintain any emotional distance. The tenderness she felt nearly overwhelmed her as she watched him sleep.

When the movie ended, she used the remote to turn off the projector. Then she scooted down beside him as she pulled up the blanket that'd been covering their legs and fell asleep snuggled against his warm body.

Someone was jiggling his arm. Keith dragged himself out of the heavy but healing darkness he'd had so much trouble finding since he'd come home and opened his eyes, half expecting Pippa to be standing over him. But it was Nancy, freshly showered and dressed for the day.

The fact that she'd stayed all night was a welcome surprise.

"I'm leaving for the store," she said. "Your phone's been going off. Your sisters are trying to get hold of you. With the autopsy under way, they're probably nervous. But I wanted to let you sleep as long as possible, so after I took Simba out, I brought your phone into the bathroom with me while I got ready. I didn't want it to wake you. I hope that's okay."

"You're leaving?" That was about all his groggy mind could grasp—that and a certain reluctance to see her go.

She put his phone in his hands. "Yes. I have to work."

"Will you come back?"

When she hesitated, his mind started sifting through everything he'd said and done last night. "I was on my best behavior, right? I didn't… I didn't try anything."

She chuckled. "No, you were perfect."

"So we'll have dinner tonight?"

"I don't know. Pippa's going to think we're seeing each other again…"

"She won't even be here today. It's Sunday—" he said, then caught himself. He'd told Pippa she could come in to make up for one of the days she'd been off last week. He'd told her not to worry about it, that she'd still get a full paycheck, but she'd insisted. "Never mind. I just remembered. She is coming."

"Then there's that. And if she says something about finding me here, it'll spread all over the island…"

"Does that matter? What do we care what people think?"

"You're going back to LA. I can see why you wouldn't care. You've never cared. I'm the one staying here, so *I'll* have to deal with all the questions—*You and Keith aren't together anymore? He left for LA? Is he coming back?* Then there'll be the pity I'll get for being dumped again."

"Tell them you dumped me. I'll say the same. Just come back."

"We'll see."

"Great. Dinner it is."

"I said we'll see," she said with a laugh.

She called for Simba but he stopped her. "Give me the keys to your house. I'll bring Simba home later."

"Why? If I leave now, I should have time to drop him off."

"There's no need. I'll do it. Have you fed him?"

"Of course."

"Then he's fine until dinner."

"He should be, as long as you let him out once in a while and there's water in his bowl."

"Does he know where the bowl is?"

"Yes. In the kitchen." She looked as if she was suppressing a smile. "Now you both know."

He caught her hand. "Why don't you bring over some of that lingerie tonight?"

"What happened to being on your best behavior?"

"It's the least you can do if I'm going to watch your dog."

She gaped at him. "I didn't *ask* you to watch my dog!"

"Well, it's nice of me, isn't it? Better than leaving him alone all day. I'll even take him out for a run."

"That'll be good for *both* of you. Maybe it'll help pass the time until the autopsy's done. But be forewarned, he won't run far. He is my dog, after all."

He seemed to find that amusing. "Duly noted. So about that lingerie…"

She just gave him a look.

"What? If I want something, I ask for it."

She tossed him a grin but didn't commit herself on the lingerie. "I'll see you tonight. Take good care of my dog."

"Of course! Simba loves me as much as he loves you," he called after her.

"Don't kid yourself," she called back.

He let his head drop onto the couch pillows they'd been using and checked his call history. He could hear Nancy talking to Pippa, knew Pippa would assume, as

Nancy had said, that they were sleeping together. He was pretty sure last night was the first time he'd ever spent the night with a woman he *didn't* touch in that way. He wouldn't admit it to Nancy, or anyone else, but being with her had been gratifying in its own right.

He remembered the moment she'd first shifted so she could hold him on her lap and the soothing way she'd run her fingers through his hair. That was when the anxiety that so often plagued him had released its death grip, had all but disappeared. Her calming influence created a solid defense against the turmoil that crept up and threatened to overcome him at night. He hadn't thought of cocaine once the whole time he was with her.

He had, however, considered stripping off her clothes. That idea had cycled through his head at least every five seconds.

His phone rang. Maisey again. She'd already tried to reach him twice.

He pushed the answer button. "Hey," he said and pulled himself into a sitting position. God, it felt good to have slept deeply for a change. "I was just about to call you."

"So you're up?"

He covered a yawn. "Sort of."

"I wish *I* could've slept in. Took me until almost dawn to fall asleep. And then I had to get up with Bryson so Rafe could take Laney to his mother's before church."

"I'm sorry you had a bad night. That's miserable. I know the feeling." He shoved a hand through his hair. "What are you doing this morning?"

"Just looking after Bryson and worrying. You?"

"I hadn't started worrying quite yet, but now I'm

right there with you. Thanks for making sure I was on the same program."

"You're welcome." She didn't sound repentant. "What do you think the pathologist will find?"

"Evidence of murder."

"How long do you suppose it'll take?"

"We may get some information later today—perhaps the cause of death. Dr. Pendergast told me he'd call me afterward and give me his thoughts. But all the toxicology reports and such…that could take weeks, depending on how backed up the lab is."

"Bottom line, we're not going to receive the quick resolution we're hoping for."

"True. But that phone call last week? The one that brought Chief Underwood to my door?"

"Yeah?"

"I found out who placed it."

"Who?"

"Tyrone's son, Marcus. He just happened to be passing the turnoff to Coldiron House when a woman flagged him down, said there was something going on at Coldiron House and asked him to call the police."

"What woman?"

"He didn't recognize her and can't describe her. It was dark and rainy out, and she was bundled up."

"So what does that tell us?"

"Nothing new," he admitted. "The break-in could be a separate crime, or it could be part of Mom's murder."

"Which one are you leaning toward?"

"I don't believe in coincidence. As far as I'm concerned, it's related."

"Keith…"

Her tone had become even more somber. "What is it?" he asked.

"No matter what happens, I love you. Nothing else is important, right? It's love that makes people family, that holds a family together."

That was certainly true for Nancy's family. They weren't connected by blood; love was all they had. But Maisey wasn't usually so maudlin and sentimental. Their mother's death was really getting to her. "I haven't broken down, Mais. Not once. In case you're wondering."

"What are you talking about?"

"Drugs. Isn't that what *you're* talking about?"

"Not this time. I have confidence in you. You understand that drugs wouldn't help anything, even if… even if we get bad news, right?"

"What's going on with you? The way you're talking— don't tell me *you* killed Mom," he joked.

"That's not the slightest bit funny!" she cried. "I can't *believe* you said that!"

"I'm sorry," he said. "Sometimes I need an outlet, and laughing helps. But don't worry. I'm doing great." Last night was his best night yet. He was excited to think Nancy would be coming back. Maybe, instead of taking her out, he'd have Pippa make them a fancy steak dinner. Served with some flowers and candlelight, dinner in the dining room would be private and romantic…

"I just…want you to know how much you mean to me. That's all," she said. Then she mumbled something about Bryson getting into the wrong drawer and told him she had to go.

Keith was still a little perplexed when she disconnected, but he didn't have time to think about their conversation because Rocki called him next.

"Morning," he said, falling back on the couch.

"Morning."

"How are you feeling?"

"I've been better." She sounded tired, stressed.

"Don't get too worked up. Dr. Pendergast is performing the autopsy today, but that doesn't mean he'll have much to tell us. He has to send slides of Mom's organs out to various labs and—"

"Please, don't give me the gory details," she broke in. "I'm only calling to tell you that you don't have to worry about Landon. He didn't hurt Mom, and we can prove it."

Keith got to his feet. "How?"

"Don't act so damn relieved! I thought you were on *our* side."

"I *am* on your side. Always." Just not Landon's—not after seeing that photo. "So...what do you have?"

"A plane ticket. Landon did go to Fairham, and he did argue with Mom. But he flew out of Charleston early Sunday morning, before the first ferry. That means he got off the island on one of the last ferries Saturday night. And Mom was still alive then. I know because I talked to her myself."

"Why didn't he tell us this before?"

"He and I were too busy arguing over the fact that he'd been there at all. It wasn't until I explained what was at stake that he realized we had more to worry about than whether or not he'd asked my mother for a loan without my knowledge or consent."

There was that loan business again, but Keith no longer believed a word of it, not after seeing that damn picture. "So what time did he take the ferry off the island?"

"Five."

That meant it was the second-to-last ferry of the day. Keith would've been more reassured if Landon had never even gone to Fairham, but he felt confident that five o'clock would exclude him.

"I'm glad to hear it, Rock," he said. "Chief Underwood should have no problem confirming that he was on a plane. And once she does, he has an airtight alibi." Then maybe what he, the police chief and Maisey knew about Landon's sending that naked photo could be forgotten. They could assume it was a mistake, couldn't they? Give Landon the benefit of the doubt and leave Rocki and her husband to carry on just as they had in the past? Because even if Landon *had* slept with Josephine, maybe it was a one-time thing. The desire to possess something exotic for a change. She'd mentioned that he seemed to be going through a midlife crisis. A single night of stupidity didn't need to destroy an entire family.

Keith wasn't convinced he could get Maisey to agree with him on that, though. She'd been pretty definite when they were talking about telling Rocki—and he had a tendency to be more practical in the first place. But keeping quiet might be the best approach. Especially since they were all trying to cope with Josephine's death. He could always hire a private detective to make sure Landon wasn't cheating on Rocki now, have him watched for a year or so and then decide what to do, based on his behavior.

Relieved that their mother's death might not cause a domino effect, after all—that the rest of his family might be safe—he looked up at the ceiling. *Thank you, God.* He wasn't religious, but he was grateful. "I'm glad you called. I'll let Chief Underwood know right away," he said, but he didn't have to call Harper. She called him just as he and Rocki were signing off.

Unfortunately, she didn't have good news.

20

"Hopefully, that'll be the end of that," Rocki said as she put her phone down on the counter. But she wasn't nearly as confident as she was pretending.

Her husband was sitting at the kitchen table cradling a cup of coffee that had to be cold by now. She hadn't seen him take one sip since he'd poured it. He'd brought the kids to his mother's, who'd asked to have them for the day, but he hadn't gone to work. He'd called his father to say he needed a day off, and she hadn't gone to open their video game store. They didn't get many patrons first thing on a Sunday morning, anyway. But even if it had been Saturday, their busiest day of the week, she wouldn't have bothered. Some things were more important than work and routine. Some things were more important than money. This was one of them, especially since she was pretty sure there'd be nothing left to save once the whole truth came out. And she had a feeling she was about to get the truth. She could tell Landon had worked his way through whatever he'd been feeling; he was finally willing to talk.

"I never intended to do anything that would hurt our family. I hope you know that," he said. He'd been watching her with hollow eyes during her conversation with Keith.

She drew a steadying breath, trying to overcome the jitters that had set in once Landon had come to bed last night—at four in the morning. They'd remained on their own sides of the mattress, staring up at the ceiling without touching or speaking. She'd refused to initiate the conversation. She knew he was the one who needed to do it. That was when he'd mentioned that his ferry had left Fairham before Josephine was dead. That was when something that should've been obvious seemed to come to him, to them both, and it came as an afterthought because he couldn't even imagine being seriously suspected of murder.

"Was that trip to Fairham really about getting a loan, Landon?"

She'd asked him before, many times—and he'd claimed it was. Today he said nothing, but he couldn't meet her eyes. That told the truth. So did the way he was sitting, hunched over and more miserable than she'd ever seen him.

"Well?" she prompted.

"How will it help to know the details?" he asked without looking up.

Closing her eyes, she leaned against the counter so she wouldn't sink to the floor. The fact that she'd been right all along—that those terrible suspicions were true—cut like a knife. She wished he'd deny it again, wished she could believe him if he did. But she knew it wasn't possible. That was the very reason she kept asking.

"So it *wasn't* about a loan."

"No, it… I can't even say it."

"Why?" That came out as a whisper despite the volume she tried to put behind it. "What'd I do to deserve what you did?"

He winced as if she'd struck him. "Nothing," he said. "It had nothing to do with you. You've always been everything I could ever want in a wife, in a lover. It was all my fault. I was feeling like a failure, like everything I'd ever done was a big waste. Her...*interest* somehow made me feel bigger, more important than I was. It was an escape, and I just...got caught up in it. I can't explain what happened any better than that."

Her nails bit into her palms as she clenched her fists. "So you slept with her."

He said nothing.

"God, Landon." Covering her mouth, she ran to the sink. She was going to throw up. She swallowed hard, trying to stop the bile rising in her throat, but it didn't work. What little breakfast she'd eaten came back up, soured by the coffee she'd drunk with it.

As soon as she stopped retching, she rinsed her mouth, closed her eyes and tilted her head back to catch her breath.

When she faced her husband again, she could see tears streaming down his cheeks and dripping off his chin. "I'm sorry," he said, meeting her gaze. "I'd do anything to take it back. But I can't."

"Why didn't you tell me sooner?" she asked. "Why didn't you tell me when I first asked you—that day after her Christmas party?"

"Because it was already too late."

"You slept with her that night? While we were staying there for the party?"

"Yes."

The way he answered let her know the truth had been excruciating to admit. "And after that?"

He stared into his coffee mug. "Never. That was it. One time. But it was enough. I knew you'd never be able to forgive me."

"That's why you didn't tell me."

"I didn't want to lose you."

She felt light-headed, as if she might faint. After running cold water over her hands, she patted her face. "You didn't care about losing me when it was happening? When I was sleeping in another room in the same house?"

It took him a few seconds to answer. When he did, he said, "That's the thing. I was so…caught up that… that my own selfishness was all that mattered. I wasn't thinking…about anything. I just…wanted to be someone else for a while."

"And what was my—" she couldn't bring herself to say *mother* "—Josephine's part in this? Who instigated the…affair?"

"This is so humiliating." His words were barely a whisper.

"I guess that goes with the territory," she said sadly and rinsed her mouth again. "Who instigated it?"

"I think you'd be safe to blame both of us."

"You're not going to blame it on her?" After all, Josephine wasn't around to contradict him.

"No. She let me know that she had…an interest in me, but I never should've responded. Now that whatever spell I was under's been broken, I can't believe I ever did."

"And that fight you had with her on Fairham the day before she died?"

"That wasn't about money. I would never borrow from your mother. That would only have convinced her you were a fool to marry me. I went there to…"

"To have sex with her again?"

"No!" He shook his head vigorously. "She'd invited me to come for the weekend. But all I wanted to do was end the whole mess. I couldn't eat, couldn't sleep."

She remembered. That was what had told her something was wrong.

"I went because she was expecting me."

"And you *paid* for it, even though we're struggling."

"Yes, of course. I have *some* pride left. And I thought it was worth it. I just needed to speak to her, face-to-face, so I could get back on stable ground."

"You didn't touch her…"

"No, Rocki. I swear it. She…she tried, but I wouldn't. I suggested we approach you together and explain what happened, apologize. I didn't think it would be fair if I cleared my conscience on my own. She'd just come back into your life five years ago. I didn't want to take your mother away from you again. So I was hoping that by some miracle, we could all work through it together."

When she gasped, his voice faltered.

"I know. It was…idealistic of me to think either one of us could save our relationship with you."

She didn't comment, had no idea if she'd be able to continue their marriage. "What'd she say when you told her that?"

"She wasn't interested in confessing. She said if I ever told a single soul, she'd tell a very different story—and make it believable enough that you'd never let me within ten feet of you or the kids again. She said she wasn't going to lose you because I couldn't keep my dick in my pants."

Rocki laughed at the irony of Josephine's audacity, but her response had more to do with hysterics than humor. "And *this* was the woman you loved instead of me?"

He grimaced. "No! God, no. Never. It wasn't love. It was…lust, I guess. Wanting to feel singled out. Special. I became a victim of my ego and my sex drive."

"So you told her you wouldn't tell anyone and left Coldiron House."

"Yes. I've never felt so much hatred or anger in my life. But I hated myself even more than I hated her."

She turned to stare out the window, at the lawn he'd planted and mowed regularly. Everyone in Lafitte saw them as the perfect American family… "And that's where you left it?"

"She was so vengeful I didn't feel I had a choice. I was afraid of what she might do—to tear our family apart—if I didn't. So I decided to forget, to act like it never happened. To try to put it behind me."

"And then?"

He looked up as if he wasn't sure what she was getting at. "And then she was found dead."

Rocki got her keys.

"Where are you going?" he asked.

"I don't know."

When Keith walked into the flower shop just after noon, Nancy could tell right away that something had changed—and that it wasn't a positive development. "What's wrong? Is the autopsy over?"

"Yes."

"What'd they find?"

"There was no water in Mom's lungs. She didn't drown."

Nancy put down the greenery she was about to use in an arrangement. "So how did she die?"

"She was suffocated."

"And the pills? Did they play a role?"

"The toxicology reports will take a few days. But Dr. Pendergast doesn't believe they'll reveal any drugs or toxic substances. He thinks someone held a pillow over her face."

Suffocation wasn't a pleasant way to die. That sort of thing took time... "But the fact that it was murder doesn't really come as a surprise. You guessed as much."

"Yes, but I never guessed her murder could be tied to my own family."

"None of that's been confirmed—has it?"

"It's not looking good. Chief Underwood received Landon's phone records from his cell phone carrier this morning."

"And?"

"He and my mom were definitely having an affair."

Although she'd been hoping against it, Nancy had expected that. She'd seen that questionable encounter at the Christmas party, which had prepared her. "Give me a sec." She put up a sign indicating the flower shop would be closed for a few minutes. Then she gestured for him to join her in the back, where they wouldn't be seen through the windows and could have a little privacy.

"Want to go into the office, sit down?" she asked when he stopped as soon as they reached her work area.

"No. I have too much adrenaline going through me to sit down."

Nancy cleaned off a spot on her worktable and pulled herself onto the edge. "So Chief Underwood has Landon's cell phone records, and those records show there were a lot of calls between them?"

He paced in front of her. "Yes. For a short time there were a lot of calls and texts, which they both deleted."

"Underwood could access them in spite of that?"

"Fortunately—or unfortunately, depending on how you look at it."

"What'd they say?"

"Nothing I'd ever want to read, coming from my mother. The fact that they were sent to my brother-in-law only makes it worse."

"Are you going to tell Rocki?"

Pivoting, he walked back toward her. "You know what scares me the most?" he said in lieu of an answer.

Sensing that he was about to tell her, she waited.

"I think she already knows."

Nancy frowned. "Why do you think that?"

"Landon's cell phone puts him in Charleston at the time Mom was most likely killed."

"Which was…?"

"Around eleven. That's the latest estimate I've been given."

"So…that's good, isn't it? Landon couldn't have killed Josephine if he wasn't here."

Wearing a tortured expression, Keith stopped in front of her and rested his forehead against hers.

She knew she shouldn't let him get this close, simply because she wanted it so badly. She told herself not to react, but her arms automatically went around him. "What is it?" she whispered.

He lifted his head to look into her face. "Chief Underwood subpoenaed Rocki's cell phone records, too."

Nancy could tell something unpleasant was coming… "And?"

"They put *her* on Fairham Saturday night, after Landon left."

"No!" she gasped.

When he closed his eyes, she knew his mind was a million miles away.

She slid her hands up to gently cup his face. "Don't tell me she figured out that Landon wasn't in Vegas and came here looking for him."

"Stands to reason, doesn't it?" He took her hands. "She's had plenty of opportunities to tell me she was here that weekend, Nancy. She *had* to know it would be relevant."

"And yet she hasn't mentioned it."

"Not a word."

She stared down at their clasped hands. It felt so natural to touch him, to caress him. How was she going to get away from the desire she felt for him?

She had no idea, but she couldn't worry about it now. His distress mattered more than anything else. Whatever she could do to comfort him, reassure him… "I've met Rocki. She isn't capable of murder, Keith. It wasn't her."

"Having your mother cheat with your husband could drive *any* woman to murder. Can you imagine the jealous rage?"

Nancy couldn't argue with that. "Still," she insisted.

"Rocki's not the type. She's…easygoing, like your dad was. At least, that's what Maisey's said about her."

"I haven't told you everything," he said.

"There's more?"

His troubled eyes focused on hers. "Chief Underwood was holding something back, something she didn't want to tell me because it didn't fit with what the coroner was saying."

"Which was suicide."

"Yes. She even made sure there was nothing about it in the file she gave me."

"What is it?"

"They found a long dark hair in the tub with my mother's body."

"Your mother had long dark hair—"

"Yeah, at first they assumed it was hers. But it's a slightly different shade. Now they're taking a closer look at it, admitting it might belong to someone else."

Nancy's stomach tightened. "Did it come from Rocki, then?" Rocki also had long dark hair.

"There's no follicle, so they can't get any DNA."

Maybe that was a good thing. "Does Maisey know?"

"Not yet. I haven't been able to make myself call her."

"Why didn't Chief Underwood tell you both?"

"She's under no obligation to tell either of us anything. I think she only told me because I've been so involved in the investigation."

"So what does it all mean?"

"It means they'll examine that hair under a microscope and compare it against samples from any and all suspects." Which now included Rocki.

"What if it *was* your older sister?" she asked. "How

will *you* feel? Will you try to save her from prison—
or fight to see that she goes away for life?" And what
would Maisey do?

He shook his head. "That's an impossible question
for any brother to answer."

21

Keith couldn't bring himself to call Rocki. He had the time; he was driving back to Coldiron House from the flower shop. But he couldn't confront his sister quite yet, and he was just as hesitant to call Maisey. He'd gone to see Nancy instead. She was the easiest person for him to talk to because she understood him and the situation in a way none of his newer friends in LA could. They had no idea of the kind of man he once was, or the family he came from. He presented a very different image to them.

Nancy always offered sound advice, and she could sympathize without being devastated. Maisey, on the other hand, would feel like he did. Shocked. Saddened. Sickened. And angry at their mother for getting involved with Landon in the first place. *What had she been thinking?* She had so much male attention; she hadn't needed Landon's, as well. Rocki wasn't the type to hurt anyone. Not without a powerful trigger. But Josephine had threatened Rocki's marriage, and therefore her family's well-being. So...did that make what might've happened all Josephine's fault? Was there a line beyond which murder became justifiable?

Keith could understand the rage that must have

boiled up when Rocki learned about the affair. He'd felt his own share of rage over the years, his own desire to see the last of their mother. But *murder*? Even if *he* sympathized with his sister, the law would not.

As he drove through the gates and into the garage, he told himself to stop thinking the worst. They'd thought maybe Landon had hurt Josephine, and they'd been wrong. Keith felt a little guilty about those suspicions now that Chief Underwood had confirmed Landon wasn't even on the island.

Could they also be wrong about Rocki?

Sure. The police had no forensic proof that Rocki had killed their mother. The strand of hair found in the tub indicated only that the culprit was someone with long brown hair, but a lot of people had long brown hair— some of them men.

"She didn't do it," he said, as if saying it aloud might ward off the doubt. Then he shut down the engine and called her from inside the car. He didn't want Pippa to overhear his conversation. He saw no need for this to go around the island, for his sister to be convicted in the minds of Fairham's residents before there was any actual proof.

She didn't pick up. So he texted her. It's important I talk to you as soon as possible. Please answer.

A minute or two later, she called him.

"What's going on?" Her voice had a nasal quality that made him wonder if he'd interrupted her during a crying jag.

He slid his seat back to create more legroom. "Are you okay?"

"No."

That didn't exactly shore up his hope. She didn't even know she'd been found out... "Why?"

"Family stuff. Between Landon and me." She told him to hang on while she blew her nose. "What's happening with the autopsy?" she asked when she came back. "Are they finished?"

"They are. I just heard from the doctor. He couldn't provide a lot of details yet, but he did give me the manner of death."

"Murder."

"Yes."

There was a brief silence. Finally she said, "You expected that."

Did *she*? He noticed she didn't ask *how* Josephine was murdered. Was she too distracted? Or did she already know? "I wish that weren't the case."

"Me, too." She'd supported his decision to get a pathologist of their own. Why had she done that? Why hadn't she stood behind the coroner's initial assumption of suicide? *There I go again. She's innocent.*

"Is that why you called?" she asked. "Because this isn't really a good time—"

"When were you going to tell me, Rock?" he interrupted.

Another silence greeted this question. "Tell you what?"

"About Mom and Landon."

"I don't know what you're talking about."

"I think you do."

The silence grew even heavier.

"Rocki?" he said. "Hard as it may be, you need to open up, to trust me."

Nothing.

"Are you still there?"

"This is a nightmare," she mumbled more to herself than to him. "And it's getting worse by the day. I keep hoping I'll wake up, that my life will go back to normal, but…"

"We have to deal with what *is*. When did the affair start?"

"How'd you find out?" she asked instead of answering.

He wished he didn't have to tell her about the photograph. That would add insult to injury. But he felt they both needed to be as open and honest as possible. Complete transparency might be the only way to survive this emotional maelstrom. "There's a picture of him on Mom's computer that's…shocking."

"What picture?" She sounded scared.

"He's naked. With an erection."

When he heard her gulp, he felt a renewed anger at Josephine and Landon. Not only had they ruined their own lives, they'd probably caused Rocki to ruin hers. "I'm sorry."

"How'd she get that?" she asked when she could speak.

"He must've sent it to her, right?"

The sound of water rose to his ears—the taps going on? "Rocki?"

He heard retching next and felt his muscles tense. After a minute or two, she picked up again. "I'm here." She didn't explain what she'd been doing; she didn't need to.

"Where's here?" he asked softly.

"My…my house. My bathroom."

"Where's Landon?"

"His dad wasn't feeling well and needed him to handle a tour."

"So he went to work? You're alone?"

"Yes."

"What about the game store?"

"It's closed today."

"I'm glad." He paused. "Why don't you tell me exactly what happened."

"How can *anyone* explain the past week?" she said. "No, it's been longer than a week. The past month and a half?"

"Please try, and I'll do everything I can to help you."

He heard the rasp as she sucked in a breath. "Okay."

"Whenever you're ready."

The volume of her voice dropped so low that Keith had to hold his phone tightly to his ear, but he didn't dare interrupt in case he couldn't get her talking again. "I first noticed something...odd a little over a month ago," she said. "Landon was more preoccupied than usual, not as engaged with the family. He was nice enough, just...not as attentive and not as interested in sex, which I found unusual. I didn't let it bother me too much, though. We've been under a lot of financial pressure lately, and I was busy with the kids."

"You noticed nothing before that?"

"Nothing that stood out. A month ago is when it got...serious. If that's the right word. Landon can't give me a specific time. He said it began subtly. A few years ago. Whenever we'd visit Fairham, Josephine would flirt with him, touch him on the arm or shoulder, lean in close when she spoke to him. I was oblivious to it until Mom's Christmas party. But while I was there, I got a strange feeling about them. They joked and laughed too much, seemed to be in their own little world, and I wasn't part of it. I'd never seen Mom do that with anyone else."

"Because you weren't around to watch her target so many other guys over the years."

"I'm embarrassed to admit this now, but at first I was flattered that she liked my husband so much. And then… It's hard to verbalize. At that party, as the night wore on, I started to get a bit uncomfortable. She'd look at him too long or something. It was weird."

"Did you confront her? Or him?"

"No. You know Mom. She was above question. I didn't confront either one of them. I ignored what I'd seen—talked myself out of it. I couldn't believe that Landon would have any interest in a woman so much older, no matter how pretty she was, especially my own *mother*."

"I can see why you might discount it."

"I'm glad to hear you say that, because now I feel like a fool for being so blind. I thought once I got Landon home, everything would be okay. After all, we don't live close to Fairham and we rarely saw Mom. But then he told me he had to go to Vegas, and that made me uneasy all over again, because we'd already decided we didn't have the money to attend the convention this year."

"You suspected he might be coming here?"

"I didn't *suspect*, exactly. I was…worried, concerned. Enough that I checked up on him after he left."

"How'd you do that?"

"I put an app on his cell phone that's designed to show where everyone in the family is."

"Without him finding out?"

"I had all the pings and other notifications go to an

email account he and I created years ago that we no longer use."

"But couldn't he see the icon on his phone?"

"He has loads of apps. I knew he'd never notice."

"So that's what gave him away."

"That's what gave him away," she echoed. "The app showed him on Fairham, not in Vegas, although he called me, pretending to be at the MGM Grand. So I arranged for the kids to stay with their friends, and I went to Fairham to confront him—and Mom."

Keith released his seat belt; he hadn't even noticed that he still had it on. "When was this?"

"A week ago Saturday night."

The night Josephine was killed. Keith rubbed his eyes. "What'd he have to say when you surprised him?"

"I never actually saw him. By the time I got in, the app showed him as disconnected, so I assumed he'd realized I'd put that location device on his phone and deleted it. I found out later that he'd turned off his phone because he was on a plane to Vegas."

"You told me he left on the five o'clock ferry."

"He did."

"Does that mean you arrived on the eight o'clock?"

"Yes, I barely made it."

If only she'd missed it… Keith felt a chill that had nothing to do with the cold air creeping into the car. "And did you see Mom?"

"I did. She was packing for her trip."

"Did you see anyone else?"

"Like who?" She seemed surprised that he'd asked such a seemingly unrelated question, but he was keeping track of timelines, wanted to determine exactly who knew what and when everything had happened.

"The ferry captain. Tyrone. Pippa."

"The ferry captain *might've* noticed me, but it was dark and rainy and we didn't speak. It's not like I was driving Mom's Mercedes, or there was anything else to connect me with Coldiron House. I'd rented the cheapest economy car I could find. I doubt he paid me any attention."

"What about Pippa and Tyrone?"

"They were both off by the time I got to the house. And I was glad. As you can imagine, I wasn't at my best. I didn't want Maisey or anyone else to even know I was on the island. I was hurt and angry and reeling at the thought of my mother and…"

When her words fell off, he could tell she was once again fighting to suppress her emotions.

"…and my husband," she finished a few seconds later.

Keith twirled the keys around and around his finger. "So you came across on the ferry and drove to Coldiron House in the rain without speaking to anyone."

"Yes."

"What happened next?"

"Like I said, Mom was packing for her trip. She didn't want to talk to me, kept trying to put me off. Said I didn't know anything. That nothing was how it appeared. That she couldn't deal with my *issues* right then."

"And you…"

"I told her she was the most despicable human I'd ever met. That I was glad Gretchen stole me and raised me. That Gretchen, despite her faults, had more integrity in her little finger than Mom had in her whole body. That she'd ruined my family. That I'd never speak to her again as long as I lived." She paused, then said, "I can't even remember it all."

"So you didn't leave."

"Not right away. I wish I had, though. I wish I'd never gone there, never spoken to her."

"Why?"

"Because those are the last memories I'll have. And whether she deserved what I said or not, those memories are ugly."

"How did it end?"

"She was mortified. I don't think she'd ever been caught so red-handed. She always acted as if she had more to be proud of than the rest of us did, that she had more dignity...or more *something*. She was so damn arrogant. She tried to ignore me while she packed. Kept saying Landon meant nothing to her. But that only made me angrier. If he meant nothing to her, why'd she have to do what she did?"

Keith wished he could answer that question. "Some sick desire to be more attractive, more appealing than you?" Her *daughter*. He didn't say anything about Landon's role in the whole mess...

"I guess. Anyway, in the end she apologized that I was 'upset.' That was when I knew staying wouldn't help anything. So I screamed a few more terrible things and ran out."

Keith was relieved to hear that she'd left. But she couldn't get off the island until the ferry started running the next morning. Did she return to Coldiron House later, hoping to see their mother again, hoping to achieve more satisfaction the second time around? "Where'd you go after that?"

"To Smuggler's Cove. I wanted to go to Maisey's,

but I was too humiliated, didn't want anyone to know what Landon—and our mother—had done."

"Then why didn't you stay at the Drift Inn? There are always vacancies in the winter."

She laughed without humor. "I didn't have the money—and no room on my credit card. I'd gone over the limit paying for my airfare, which wasn't cheap since I booked at the last minute."

He felt so guilty about what she must have been feeling that night. It couldn't have helped that she had such limited resources. "So where'd you sleep?"

"I managed to get inside one of the rentals. It was cold, because I couldn't get the heater to work. The pilot light must've been out, but I wasn't about to try to deal with that."

So how did their mother wind up dead? "Did you go back to see Mom again that night, Rocki?"

He had to wait several seconds for her response, but then she said, "Are you asking me if I killed her, Keith?"

He could hear tears in her voice. "I'm afraid so. I *have* to ask, Rock. I have to know what really happened."

"It wasn't me," she said fervently. "I've never hurt anyone in my life. Ranting and raving the way I did— that's the most violent I've ever been. I could never have…drowned anyone. Even her."

Keith's breath lodged in his throat. *Drowned?* The pathologist had determined that there was no water in Josephine's lungs, which meant she'd been dead when she was placed in the tub. Rocki was still going on information she'd received when the police had found Josephine.

But was it an attempt to mislead him? Rocki wasn't stupid...

"Maybe your cell phone records will prove you were on the far side of the island." Chief Underwood had been able to pinpoint where Tyrone's son had called dispatch, hadn't she?

"I doubt it. Once I left Coldiron House, I had to turn my phone off. I'd rushed off without a charger and I needed to conserve the little battery power I had left."

Keith bit back a curse. But since she'd paused, he felt he had to fill the silence. "You realize what that means, don't you?"

"I don't have an alibi."

Exactly. The police probably wouldn't be able to place her outside Coldiron House at the time their mother was murdered—if she *was* outside Coldiron House...

"I didn't kill her, Keith," she said. "Please, you have to believe me. I wasn't capable of carefully planning to sneak back and set the scene so that it looked like a suicide. Whoever murdered Mom was one cool customer. Even if I *could* kill someone, I wasn't capable of that kind of precise strategy—not that night."

What she said made sense, but was she telling the truth? Or was this sister, who he'd known for only the past five years, such a good actress that she could pretend to be distraught while hiding the fact that she'd taken the ultimate revenge?

Keith *tried* to remain skeptical. She hadn't come forward with the information that she'd been on the island when Josephine was killed until she was forced to. That didn't lend her a great deal of credibility. But she was his sister. And he could understand why she wouldn't want anyone to know she'd followed her husband to Fairham. "I believe you," he said. "And I'll do everything I can to protect you."

When she broke down and started sobbing, he felt tears fill his own eyes. "This whole thing has been terrible, Rocki. I'm sorry. I really am."

"Are you going to tell Maisey about Landon?"

"She already knows."

"And she didn't call—didn't tell me she knew my husband was cheating?"

This was another blow. "She wasn't sure of it. We were hoping that picture didn't mean what we thought it might. I haven't told her yet what Chief Underwood found when she subpoenaed the phone records."

"Even without that… I can't imagine what she must think."

"She feels bad for you. Like I do," he said. "What's going to happen between you and Landon?"

It took her a long time to answer. When she finally did, she said, "I don't know."

"Does he want to try to work things out?"

"He says he does. But I'm not sure this is something we can recover from."

"Has he moved out?"

"I haven't asked him to. We don't have the money to get him a place, and we're trying to maintain as much stability as we can, for the kids' sake, until we each decide what we want."

Keith couldn't bear the thought of them splitting up. Since he and Maisey had discovered Roxanne, living with her husband and children in Louisiana five years ago, they'd thought Rocki was the lucky one. She'd been raised by a much less complicated and far more loving person.

But maybe Rocki hadn't escaped the wrecking ball that was Josephine, after all...

22

Keith was just finishing up several things he had to take care of for his business in California when Nancy called. He jumped at the buzz of his phone—and grabbed it—because he'd been expecting to hear from Chief Underwood. Some technician at the lab she used was supposed to be examining the hair found in his mother's tub to see what information, if any, could be gleaned from that small piece of evidence. Even if they couldn't recover any DNA, she'd told him they should at least be able to determine the race of the person who'd left that hair. If it wasn't a Caucasian, maybe she wouldn't even need to ask for a sample of Rocki's hair…

"You haven't brought my dog home," Nancy said by way of a greeting.

Simba, who'd followed him around the house ever since he got back, was lying at his feet. He lifted his head and his ears perked up, suggesting he could hear Nancy's voice.

"I'm holding him ransom," Keith said, leaning over to scratch under Simba's collar.

"How much is it going to cost me to get him back?"

"We are having dinner together, remember?"

"I don't remember agreeing to that."

She hadn't decided against it, though. He could hear the playfulness in her tone. "You can't disappoint Pippa. She's spent the past hour making us a delicious meal."

"I *am* hungry," she confessed as if that was the only reason it tempted her. "What'd you order?"

"A pomegranate and feta salad. Two steaks, grilled to perfection. Some kind of vegetable—I left that to her, but now that I think of it, I hope it's asparagus. And a fancy dessert, something with chocolate."

"If I come, I'll have to skip dessert. I'm on a diet."

"You can't miss Pippa's dessert."

"I'll have to. I need to look good. I just accepted a date for Friday."

Keith frowned as he stood up. She'd inserted that information for a reason—to keep him from getting too close. "Who with?"

"Some guy I met online."

"On a dating site?"

"Living in such a small town, that's pretty much what I've been reduced to. It's sort of pathetic, but there you have it."

"It's not pathetic. A lot of people meet that way. But…you can do better than whoever he is."

She laughed. "You haven't met him."

"If he's anything like the last one. Are you sure you shouldn't just hang out with me until I leave?"

"Are you suggesting I put my life on hold?"

He grimaced. *Was* he? No, he wanted her to be happy. He just wished she could be happy in a casual relationship with him until he went back to California. "When you put it that way…"

A beep signaled that he had a call coming through. "Chief Underwood's trying to reach me."

"Okay. I'll let you go."

"You're coming, though, right?"

"Yeah. I'll be there soon."

He gave her the entrance code but was still thinking about that date she had on Friday when he switched over. "What's the latest?" he asked.

"Are you ready for this?" Underwood replied.

"I'm not sure. Am I?"

"That hair isn't a hair at all."

"What do you mean?"

"It's a synthetic fiber—from a wig."

"So whoever killed my mother was in some sort of disguise?"

"That's one possibility. Unless she was wearing a wig herself that day and one of the fibers clung to her body. Have you ever known her to own a wig?"

"No. But I can't speak for the past five years."

"I didn't see anything like that in her closets. What about Rocki?"

He hated that Rocki's name even had to come up. "No. Her own hair's great. Why would she wear a wig?" Unless she was trying to disguise her appearance...

"Well, if we can find the wig that fiber came from, we might have something to work with. I'm going to talk to the ferry captain again, see if he noticed anyone who might've been wearing a wig coming or going around the time of your mother's death."

"Would the ferry captain even notice, especially with the kind of weather we've been having? Whoever was wearing it could easily have worn a hat or a hood—or used an umbrella. That person could also have taken off the wig after leaving Coldiron House."

"It's worth asking—him and others. I need to do everything I can. Look everywhere. Now that the autopsy's been completed, the fact that your mother's death wasn't a suicide will hit the press—and you won't be the only one demanding answers."

The pressure to solve the case had just gone up. He hated to think of all the attention that would focus on his sister. "It wasn't Rocki," he said. "Just so you know."

"I'd like to believe you. Can you tell me anything that would exclude her?"

Nothing Chief Underwood would be able to accept. Just his love for his sister and his faith in her. And then there was that intruder... As far as Keith was concerned, that *had* to be related. Who was the woman on the side of the road who'd stopped Tyrone's son? And why? "No. Not yet."

"That's the problem. Until I have proof that she's not our culprit, I can't show her any special consideration. But I'm hoping something will turn up. I don't want it to be Rocki any more than you do."

"We need to ask the ferry captain if he noticed anything unusual the night I found those wet footprints in the kitchen. That's what we need to ask him. We also need to check with Nancy's sister over at the Drift Inn to see who was staying there that night. And we should ask the gas station attendants in town if they saw a woman in a trench coat and scarf, like the woman who stopped Marcus Coleman. If we could figure out what kind of car she was driving, maybe we could track her down."

"We?" she challenged. "I've been open and honest with you, shared more than I should—"

"You held out on that hair."

"I've still shared more than I should. But don't stretch my courtesy too far, Keith. Now that things have…gone the way they've gone, I need you to stay out of it and let me do my job."

"I'm just telling you that incident *has* to be related to my mother's murder, and I know that the woman who stopped Marcus wasn't my sister. If Rocki couldn't afford a cheap motel room when she came the first time, she wouldn't have had the money to fly back only a few days later."

"I'm not ignoring Wednesday night. I've already established that your sister was in Lafitte and can't be related to what happened when dispatch got that call. Her cell phone records confirm it. I also spoke to her son's schoolteacher, Mr. Pembroke, who saw her drop him off on Thursday morning. If she was here late Wednesday, she wouldn't have been able to get off the island until the first ferry the next morning, which was when she was at her son's school. So we can exclude her from the list of possibilities for Wednesday night."

Thank God. That might be the thing that saved Rocki. "We have to find that mystery woman," he said. "She's the answer to everything."

"*I'll* find her," Underwood responded. "You just sit tight until I do."

Nancy slipped her phone into her purse. She'd done well. She was supporting Keith without getting too close. And she was continuing to live her own life while she was doing it. She'd spent a good hour on that dating site earlier in the afternoon. She wasn't going to let Keith's coming home turn *her* world upside down.

Before she closed the shop, she called her sister. Jade had left a message earlier, when Nancy was helping a customer. "How're things at the motel?" she asked.

"Not bad," Jade replied. "It's quiet tonight."

"It's quiet all winter," she joked.

"True. What are you up to? Any chance you'd be willing to bring me a sandwich for dinner?"

"You didn't pack anything?"

"I did, but it's leftovers that aren't my favorite."

"Not what I made last night…"

"No, from before. Besides, I thought you could keep me company for a little while—tell me what happened after you left with Keith."

Sometimes she went over to help Jade at night, when business was slow and the ferry wasn't running. "I'm sorry. I'm afraid I can't come over right now," she said. "I'm going to Coldiron House for dinner."

"Whoa!" Her sister's voice warmed with interest. "Last night must've gone well then."

"Not according to *your* criteria. We didn't have sex. We played some pool and watched a movie." She didn't add that they'd slept curled up with each other. That wouldn't have happened if Keith hadn't fallen asleep before the movie was over.

"No clothes came off?"

Her disappointment rang through loud and clear. "None," Nancy confirmed.

"Damn! Even after I got him all hot and bothered with that blow job bit?"

Just remembering what her sister had said made Nancy groan. "I can't believe you embarrassed me like that. I almost died when that came out of your mouth."

"Why? He took it well."

"He's a guy! And he likes you."

"I like him, too—although I don't know why. Everyone here's so sure he's a spoiled brat with more money than morals. But... I see something in him. I think he's grown up, matured."

Did Jade's opinion matter? She wasn't a good judge of character. She was far too forgiving.

"Maybe you'll get lucky tonight. You do have birth control, don't you?"

"Are you joking? I haven't had sex with anyone in five years, so it's not like I've had any reason to visit a doctor to get an IUD or go on the pill."

"Then buy some condoms," her sister said. "You need those for safe sex."

"Oh, that would tell him I'm not interested!"

Her sarcasm didn't faze Jade one bit. "You're forgetting the fact that you *are* interested."

"Okay, maybe I am," she admitted. "But I'd be embarrassed to whip out a box of condoms."

"It's a brave new world, Nance. Women don't have to be shy and retiring about sex anymore. Anything goes. We're all freethinkers now."

"Forget it. There's nothing to worry about, because I won't be sleeping with him. Anyway... I didn't call to talk about Keith. I called to tell you I have a date on Friday."

This took her sister aback. "Who with?"

"That Warren guy I told you about a couple of weeks ago."

"The one whose profile you liked? He got in touch?"

Technically she'd initiated the contact; it was her second attempt since he hadn't responded to her first message. But after Keith left the flower shop, she'd needed something to get her mind off him, and she felt Warren might be the one guy who could distract her.

Fortunately, it'd worked. He'd responded with an apology for not getting back to her the first time, said he'd been out of town. And now that she had another possible contender, she felt she'd be less likely to get in too deep with Keith.

"I sort of prodded him a bit, but yeah. He invited me to dinner."

"Nice! I'm proud of you!"

"At least I'm not moping around over Keith anymore."

There was a momentary hesitation.

"What?" Nancy said.

"Are you sure that isn't because he's back in your life? Why would you mope if you've got him?"

"We're just friends, Jade!"

"Okay, but I'll bet you fifty bucks you won't be singing that tune in the morning. Going over there tonight is like walking into a lion's den. You realize that."

"I spent last night there and nothing happened." Nothing on the scale of what Jade was expecting, anyway.

"Because he's biding his time, waiting for the right opportunity. Listen, there's a condom machine here at the motel. Will you swing by and pick up a couple? Who knows who he's slept with since he left here. The women in LA get a lot more action than you do—I can promise you that."

"I'm hanging up now," Nancy said, and she did.

When he answered the door, Keith was wearing black pants and a lightweight, fitted sweater. With his thick, dark hair, a broad smile on his full lips and those thick-lashed eyes, he was beautiful—not a term Nancy generally applied to men, but in his case it was true. He'd always been beautiful. He and his mother had simply been blessed, more than other people, when it came to physical beauty.

"Took you long enough," he grumbled.

She could tell he was teasing, but she came back at him, anyway. "What are you talking about? I didn't even go home to change." She was still wearing the black leather skirt and sheer black blouse, with a lacy camisole underneath, that she'd worn to work. And now she was glad. She would've been woefully underdressed if she'd pulled on a pair of jeans. Apparently, even without Josephine, dinner was a formal affair at Coldiron House. She supposed that came with living in a mansion and having a housekeeper who did the cooking.

"You didn't need to change," he said. "You look great in that."

"You look great, too," she said and immediately cursed the excess enthusiasm that oozed through that statement. She'd meant to act indifferent to his appeal in the hope that she'd eventually *become* indifferent. How would she get past her romantic attraction to him if she was constantly admiring his physical assets?

Fortunately, he didn't seem to notice the longing in her voice. "Pippa took Simba out to go potty. They'll be back any second."

"Great."

"I hope you're hungry."

She held out the wine she'd brought. As far as she was concerned, that bottle was what, more or less, kept this evening from being a date. Contributing to the meal was something a friend would do. "I picked this up on the way."

He lifted up the bottle to study the label. "I've never tried this brand but it looks good."

"I hope it will be."

The tingle that went through her when he looked at her—as if he *was* just biding his time until she succumbed, as Jade had said—told her she didn't have the willpower she would need to maintain platonic.

"Is something wrong?" he asked when he started toward the dining room and she hesitated.

"Maybe this isn't such a good idea, after all," she replied, and tried to reclaim her coat.

He held it away from her. "Whoa, hang on. Everything went according to plan last night, didn't it? You seemed happy enough when you left this morning."

Last night had been wonderful. She'd enjoyed every second of it—talking and laughing with him, but especially being free to touch him again after so long. She'd listened to him breathe for what seemed like hours, because she hadn't wanted to miss a single second of being with him. But he'd been asleep and couldn't respond. She doubted that would happen tonight. "Last night went well," she admitted.

"So what are you worried about?"

She looked around the vaulted entry hall with that winding, *Gone With the Wind* staircase, the giant flower arrangement and all the expensive paintings and furnishings. "I've never been invited to Coldiron House for dinner before." His mother would roll over in her grave if she knew—except she wasn't in a grave yet, so that cliché didn't quite work. "It feels…odd." As if she was trying to climb too high and would only fall and land on her ass again...

"That's because you haven't had a glass of wine. Come on. You need to wait for Simba, anyway."

She could grab her dog on the way out. He had to be on the grounds somewhere. She knew better than to agree to wine with Keith. Who had she been kidding? She was still madly in love with him. All her efforts to fight what she felt, to be satisfied with the friendship he offered, amounted to nothing. So what if she had a date with the "best profile" on her dating site? If she stayed, she'd share Keith's bed. At this point, she wanted him so badly she no longer cared what it would cost. Which meant she was backsliding, exactly as she'd feared she would...

"Nance?" He could sense her uncertainty, could tell she was hovering on the brink of flight.

She raised her eyes to his.

"Don't go. I really want you to stay," he murmured. And the fact that he seemed so sincere was all it took to get her to accept the hand he extended.

"What's one night?" she said.

Although he seemed a little uncertain as to what that might mean, he didn't question it. Maybe he would have, but at that moment Simba came bounding toward her from the kitchen and she let go of Keith to kneel down and embrace her dog.

23

Delicious as Pippa's dinner probably was, Keith didn't enjoy it as much as he'd anticipated. He could hardly taste his food—he was too eager for the meal to be over. Something had changed with Nancy soon after she arrived. He could sense the difference in her. She was no longer resisting the attraction they felt. She didn't glance away when he studied her, didn't bring up her date on Friday. And there was no reticence or hesitation in her manner. She looked boldly back at him as if she was imagining the same kind of after-dinner entertainment he was, as if she was finally going to take what she wanted and make no apologies. The promise of what he saw in her eyes had him so aroused he couldn't even think of anything to say.

Fortunately, conversation didn't seem necessary. She didn't say more than a few words herself. Didn't eat much, either. As the minutes ticked by, the tension grew, until Keith wondered if Pippa could hear his heart pounding whenever she brought them a new course.

"Now that you've finished dinner, would you like a cup of coffee with your dessert?"

Keith tore his gaze away from Nancy in order to respond to Pippa, who was standing dutifully at the entrance to the dining room. "No, thank you." He had no intention of dawdling over coffee…

"I'll pass on coffee, too," Nancy said, more proof that she felt the same.

Their desserts arrived a few minutes later. They were beautiful creations—a molten lava cake with a fancy lattice-like chocolate swirl on top. They both complimented Pippa, but ate only one or two bites.

"Leave our desserts here. We'll finish them later," he told Pippa. Then he suggested she clean up in the morning and gave her the rest of the night off. He wanted Nancy to feel comfortable and he was willing to bet she'd feel much more comfortable if they were alone in the house.

"Yes, sir. I already handled most of it, anyway." Pippa smiled as her eyes flicked toward Nancy. "Enjoy the rest of your evening."

Keith wasn't sure he or Nancy even answered. They stayed at the table, staring across at each other until they heard Pippa leave. Then he stood up. "Did you have enough to eat?"

"I did," she replied. "It was a wonderful meal."

He walked around to tug out her chair and took her hand as she got to her feet. "You're not going to back out on me, are you?" he murmured, searching her eyes for any sign of the reluctance that had been there before.

She didn't ask what he was talking about. She didn't need to. "No. But I didn't bring the lingerie. If you want that to be part of tonight, we'll have to go pick it up."

Obviously, she had no idea how eager he was. He had no patience for driving over to her place. He couldn't wait a moment longer. "We'll save the lingerie for next time."

"Next time?" she asked as if she wasn't committing

to anything beyond this one encounter, and he recalled her comment when she arrived. *What's one night?*

"I'm hoping there *will* be a next time."

"It's not entirely up to you."

"Which is why I'm going to do everything I can to convince you."

She didn't continue to argue, but he didn't really give her a chance. He kissed her before they could move away from the table.

When her lips parted beneath his without resistance or restraint, his heart pounded even harder. *This* was the woman he knew, the woman who'd saved him from himself at the most critical moment of his life. The familiarity of her kiss, the fact that he'd missed her so badly, swept over him, creating more longing than he'd ever felt. He could hardly breathe as he slipped his hand up her blouse. The smooth texture of her skin had always been unique to her. No other woman had ever felt quite so soft.

"You're shaking," she whispered as she tilted her head back to gaze up at him.

"Because you taste even better than I remember," he said and swept her into his arms.

"Put me down! I'm too heavy," she cried but he didn't. Thanks to all the cross-fit training he'd done, he had no problem carrying a 160-pound woman, even up the stairs.

"Don't say a word about your weight," he warned. "Don't act as if you're afraid you're too heavy or that you don't want me to see your body in the light, like you used to. No more of that bullshit, because you look exactly the way I want you to look—like *you*."

"I'd rather you didn't hurt your back—at least not before I get what *I* want," she joked.

He laughed as they reached his room and he set her on the bed. "Nothing's going to stop us now. After five years, this is going to feel so good," he promised. Then he stripped off his shirt.

Nancy could've drowned in Keith's sexy grin, in the sound of his voice and especially the sound of his laughter. Even his pseudo-harsh admonishments about her insecurity when it came to her body did nothing to diminish the moment. He made her feel beautiful, desired, and she was simply going to enjoy it. Forget five years ago, forget the future. She was throwing all those cares aside to have one magical night with the man she loved, even if she wasn't wise to love him in the first place.

He took his time removing her blouse and camisole. Then he paused to admire what he'd uncovered. "*Look* at you!" he breathed.

He was no longer laughing or teasing. His expression had grown intense, as if he really was stunned by the beauty of what he'd uncovered.

Nancy felt her nipples tighten.

"Have I told you that you have the nicest tits I've ever seen?" he asked.

"No."

"It's true." He lightly caressed her right breast before he climbed onto the bed, held her hands over her head and straddled her hips. Studying her one last time, he lowered his mouth to hers and kissed her so tenderly, so sweetly, that she could only groan from the exquisite pleasure. His tongue met and moved against hers, but also explored the sides and roof of her mouth as if he didn't want to leave *anything* untouched.

"You taste so good, Nance," he whispered and let

go of her wrists to slowly slide her tight-fitting skirt up to her waist.

Shifting to straddle her knees instead, he smiled at the sight of her lacy black thong. She'd bought those panties, as well as the sheer bra she'd been wearing, when she'd purchased that lingerie from Victoria's Secret—and was now glad she'd gotten a few more practical things, too. Thank God she was wearing them.

"You always liked sexy underwear," he said. "I love that contradiction. You're so sweet and good no one would expect you to be wearing something naughty like this."

The desire she felt had already settled between her legs and throbbed there. Now that he was no longer re-straining her hands, she grabbed fistfuls of his com-forter so she wouldn't jump as he ran his finger over the small triangle of fabric that covered her.

"I think we've found a sensitive spot," he joked and slid her panties aside as he lowered his head.

Nancy moaned and arched her back when his tongue touched her as gently as his fingers had. She could feel his warm breath on the wetness he created, could feel the scratch of his beard growth on her thighs… "Oh… God," she gasped as he slid her legs up over his bare shoulders and anchored her hips in place with his hands.

"See? This isn't too bad, is it?" he murmured against her.

She couldn't help writhing beneath him. The plea-sure was intense—and building quickly. But he didn't let her climax. She was just on the verge when he stopped and lifted himself above her. "Enjoying your-self yet?" he asked as he got rid of her skirt, which was bunched at her waist.

"I was *so* close," she complained with a scowl, but he wasn't the least repentant.

"It'll be stronger if I make you wait," he said as he nuzzled her neck.

"Wait for what?"

"For me. I want to be inside you when you get there."

She watched as he removed his pants and kicked them aside. He'd definitely put on some muscle; he wasn't nearly as skinny as he'd been five years ago. Back then she could almost count his ribs. Now he looked... healthy, strong, fit—and very obviously aroused.

"I'll get my revenge," she promised.

His smile told her he wasn't worried about that threat. He understood her frustration and was going to make it pay off. And he did. Once he put on a condom and pressed inside her, she forgot all about revenge.

"It's been so long." She hadn't realized she'd said that out loud until he paused.

"Too long," he agreed as he began to thrust.

As much as she wanted to draw out their lovemaking, he'd gotten her too excited. She couldn't take it slow. Insisting he let her get on top, she propped herself up with her hands on his chest and struck the perfect rhythm. He fondled her breasts, clearly enjoying their close proximity to his face, until the pleasure began to get the better of him, too. Then he grabbed for the bedding and muttered a hoarse warning. "Nancy..."

She didn't stop. She didn't need to. The satisfaction he'd made her postpone ripped through her at that very moment. She felt her body clutch him—and saw the satisfaction on his face just before she heard him groan.

The past fifteen minutes had gone beyond anything Nancy had ever experienced. The fatalism with which she'd approached this particular encounter had allowed her to cut loose with him for probably the first time, at least to *that* degree. And she'd been well rewarded. But she wasn't about to admit that he'd given her anything special. It was bad enough that she felt so much more for him than he did for her.

Unfortunately, her silence didn't fool him.

"That was good, right?" he said as she slumped over to catch her breath. "I told you it'd be better if I made you wait."

"What are you talking about?" she murmured. "I didn't like that one bit." She had her cheek to his chest and licked his nipple.

He moved a sweaty tendril of hair off her forehead as he laughed at her response. "You sure looked like you were enjoying yourself."

She raised her head to give him an exhausted grin. "Looks can be deceiving." Assuming that he'd want her off him now, she started to slide to one side, but he pulled her back where she was and, using one leg, managed to get the covers over them.

"You hated it so much, you're going to be bugging me to do it again in a few hours," he predicted.

"That might be true," she said. "But you're the one who keeps saying you won't be here very long." She had to make up for lost time—as well as the fact that he would soon be gone and she might never get over him…

Some loves lasted a lifetime.

She was afraid this might be one of those.

As it turned out, Keith woke Nancy. She was no longer on top of him, the way they'd fallen asleep. They must've shifted afterward, because she was on her side, with his bigger body curled around hers. At first, since it wasn't dark, she thought she'd slept the whole night away. But then she realized that the light was on because they hadn't bothered to turn it off. It wasn't even close to morning when she felt him kissing the nape of her neck.

As one hand cupped her breast and the other moved lower, she made no effort to return to full awareness. She liked letting him make love to her when she was half asleep, liked the haze of sensation that was beginning to envelop her. But he wasn't willing to accept passive involvement. She got the impression that he was intent on enticing her to respond to him as she had before, with that same peculiar blend of focus and abandon.

"Tell me you want me," he whispered as he slid a finger inside her.

"No," she whispered, refusing to comply even as she covered his hand with hers and pressed that finger deeper.

"Don't be stubborn," he said, his voice husky in her ear. "Admit it. No one can make you feel the way I do."

She had limited experience, but so far that was true. It frightened her to think how bleak her life was going to be without him. It felt as if the last five years had been spent waiting for this very night. But he was joking, trying to provoke her. So there was no need to inflate his ego—not that she would have, anyway. "You're okay, I guess. Beggars can't be choosers," she teased and gasped as he nipped at her neck.

"Ouch!" she complained, but he'd given her the kind of love bite that hurt in an exciting way—so exciting that she hoped he'd do it again.

He rolled her onto her back and braced himself over her. "Tell me you want to fuck me again."

That was too close to the truth. "And if I won't?"

"You'll have to be punished."

He'd never played with her like this before. "How?"

He slid his hands underneath her to squeeze her buttocks. "You could be spanked…"

She touched his face, let her thumb move over his bottom lip. "Do I have any other choices?"

"I could tie you to the bed."

"With…"

"The sheet."

"That wouldn't be easy."

"Because…"

"Unless you're going to tear it, which I wouldn't do with the price of *your* linens, a sheet's a bit unwieldy, don't you think? And I won't just lie here and let you do it."

"I doubt I'd have any problem, even if you decide to make it difficult."

She raised her eyebrows. "Feel free to give it your best shot."

A wrestling match quickly ensued, which messed up the expensive linens on his bed. She was easily overpowered, was no match for his strength or his size, but she resisted as long as she could. And even after he had her mostly subdued, she wouldn't lie still long enough for him to tie her to the bed. She was laughing so hard by the time he managed to get one of her hands anchored to the bedpost that she was nearly crying.

"You are being so stubborn!" He was scowling *and* laughing.

"Fine! If it means that much to you, I'll lie still," she said.

But once she gave up the fight he stopped trying to

restrain her. He held her face between his hands. Then he kissed her, slowly and so seriously that it surprised her—because that kiss felt...meaningful.

As she gazed up at him, he pecked her lips. "I'm glad you changed your mind about being with me."

Slipping her hand out of the knotted sheet, which hadn't been tight to begin with, she grabbed fistfuls of his hair to gently draw his face back to hers. "It was worth it," she said and closed her eyes as he put on a condom and buried himself inside her again.

This time the passion built slowly. He seemed intent on drawing out the pleasure of every thrust. She could hear the rasp of his breathing, feel the thud of his heart pounding against her chest, and felt utterly lost in her emotions. She was hopelessly in love with him. But there was nothing she could do about it.

"You ready?" he asked in a low voice.

"You go." She wanted to watch him, to experience their lovemaking in a different way than being consumed with achieving orgasm.

He seemed grateful for the license to be selfish, to just enjoy what he was feeling without having to time it perfectly.

Just before he climaxed, however, he pulled back to stare down at her—and she told herself she had to be mistaken, but there seemed to be a certain...possessiveness in the way he looked at her.

24

After driving through the swamps for hours, Rocki came back home for the sake of her kids. She wasn't sure what Landon had told them about where she'd been when he picked them up from his mother's, who'd made them dinner, according to a text she received, but she hadn't been able to face returning any sooner. It wasn't easy even now, after spending most of the day trying to come to terms with what she'd learned. She'd never felt so betrayed, so heartbroken—not since she was six years old and Gretchen told her that her entire family had died in a car accident.

Was this another of those life-altering events?

She didn't want that. Maybe she hadn't had *every-thing*. She and Landon had struggled to get by financially. But she'd been happy.

She expected to find the house quiet and dark—and it was. So she almost jumped out of her skin when, just after she let herself in, Landon spoke to her from where he sat alone on the couch. "Are you okay?" he asked softly.

"What's okay?" she responded.

"I've been so worried about you."

The break in his voice made her think he was sincere in his concern, but she rolled her eyes, anyway. "I'm sure you have."

He didn't attempt to convince her. No doubt he'd heard her sarcasm, knew he didn't have a chance of playing the dutiful husband now. "I told the kids you were helping a sick friend today."

"What friend?"

"I didn't give them a name."

"And they believed that?"

"Seemed to. If you hadn't come home, I'm sure they would've pushed me harder. But I thought you and I should talk first, decide how we're going to approach this together before we…before we tell them what's happened."

She'd ignored most calls and texts, couldn't handle communicating with anyone—especially her children. Although, she had responded to Keith, and she'd sent a reply to Chloe, who'd texted her a message. Hi, Mom. I finished that stained glass window I was making for art. Wanted to show it to you. But I'll show it to you tomorrow. I'm heading to bed now. Love you.

"I appreciate the consideration," she said stiffly.

"I'm not asking for any credit for…for such a small courtesy," Landon said. "I just… I wanted to let you know where things stood since…since the kids mean so much to you."

"Too bad they don't mean more to *you*," she snapped.

He winced but didn't respond.

"I'm tired. So…are you going to sleep here? Or am I?" she asked so he wouldn't try to join her.

He cleared his throat as if he was still struggling to overcome the accusation that he didn't care about their children. "You can have the bed. I'll tell the kids I fell asleep watching TV, if they ask."

Rocki could hardly breathe for the painful pressure in her chest, but she was all out of tears. She'd cried most of the day. "Good night," she said.

"Have you decided anything?" he asked before she could reach the hall.

"Yes," she replied.

There was a long pause. Then he said, "Before you tell me what it is, I want you to know I've been doing some thinking, too."

"Good. I'm sure we came to the same conclusion. Have you already packed?"

He bowed his head as if she'd just slapped him across the face.

"Is that a yes?"

"No. Not yet. I will, though. I expected as much and I don't blame you for hating me. I hate myself for what I did. But I'd give *anything* to be able to go back and… and be less of a fool. I hope you can believe that."

"I loved you," she whispered. "I trusted you more than anyone else in the world. I wanted to spend the rest of my life with you."

It took a moment before he could speak. He cleared his throat again and dashed a hand across his face. "Like I said, I deserve your hatred."

"She was my *mother*!"

He nodded, then dropped his head in his hands. "I'm sorry," he said. "I'm so sorry."

She knew their situation wasn't completely normal. As far as he was concerned, Gretchen had been her mother. Josephine hadn't come into their lives until five years ago. And she'd certainly never acted very motherly. Not only was she far more beautiful than most mothers—than the average woman, period—she'd had a gift for capturing male attention. A gift and a *need*.

In order to be fair, Rocki told herself she should cut Landon a little slack. At least he hadn't stayed on Fairham when he'd secretly gone there. He could have, if he'd been interested in continuing the affair. It wasn't as if he'd known his wife was on her way. To this day, Rocki hadn't told him that she'd followed him there. But even if her head could acknowledge all the circumstances that made it possible to understand how a man *could* get tripped up by that situation, her heart couldn't accept it. Because this wasn't just any man. It was *her* man. Someone who should've been above temptation.

The betrayal cut too deep.

"Like you say, it's too late to take it back now," she said and left the room.

After that, she sat on the bed in her clothes for probably another hour. She could hear Landon moving around, knew he couldn't sleep, either. But she didn't go out to confront him again. She stayed right where she was and eventually fell asleep. She was dreaming of last summer, when they'd taken the kids to see Keith and they'd all gone to Disneyland, so she was reluctant to wake when someone pounded on her door. It was early, too early for her alarm, so she was confused by the fact that she was still fully dressed and Landon wasn't with her.

Then she heard him say, "Rocki, open up," and it all came tumbling back.

The urgency in his voice put her on edge. What was wrong now?

Staggering to her feet, she used the furniture to

steady herself until she could find her equilibrium and opened the door.

He pushed her back inside so he could come in, then shut the door behind him. "The police are here," he whispered. "And they have a search warrant."

She blinked at him, still confused. "For…"

"They're going to search our house!"

"Why?"

"I told them I have proof that I wasn't even on Fairham when Josephine was killed, that I was on a flight to Vegas that left before the ferry started on Sunday morning. I thought that would stop them from…from barging in here and upsetting you and the kids, since they could easily check. But I was told—" his eyes searched her face "—that *you* were on Fairham after I left."

Rocki's heart sank to her knees. She would've crumpled to the floor if he hadn't caught her.

He helped her over to the bed. "That's not true, is it?" he asked.

It wasn't that cold in the house, but her hands felt like blocks of ice. "Yes," she said, "it is."

"You need to get up."

Keith opened his eyes, squinting at Nancy. At some point, they'd turned off the light, but now the sun was glinting through the shutters, nearly blinding him. "Why?"

She was standing over him, just like yesterday. Only this time she wasn't ready for work. Her hair was mussed, her makeup smeared, and she was wearing *his* robe, which was so big it nearly dragged on the floor. "Because we did a number on your bed. I'm going to straighten the bedding so I can get out of here."

"Right *now*?" He hid a yawn. "You haven't even showered."

"I'll do that at home."

"What's the rush?"

"It's seven forty, and that means Pippa's going to be here soon. I'd like to get out of the house before she or Tyrone shows up."

"Tyrone won't care. And I bet Pippa's already guessed that we're sleeping together. Last night, I wanted you so badly I almost took you on the table right in front of her. I doubt she could miss that level of sexual interest. So see? You don't have to shower at home. You can shower here. And you certainly don't have to make the bed."

"I'd still like to make the bed." She motioned at the rumpled bedding and the sheet that was tied to one post. "Otherwise, I'm afraid of what she might imagine…"

He couldn't help grinning at the mental image her words evoked. "Whatever she imagines, it won't be as good as the real thing. I can't remember when I've had sex so many times in one night, especially *that* kind of sex."

She managed to untie the sheet and started trying to put it back on the bed. "Come on. Cooperate with me, okay?"

Tugging the fabric out of her hands, he pulled her back into bed with him instead. "I say we have twenty minutes before she gets here. Let's make better use of that time."

"You've got to be kidding me! You can't possibly want more. We hardly got any sleep as it was."

"That depends." He opened his robe so he could see

her breasts. "Is this my last chance? Or will you come back tonight?"

His phone buzzed before she could reply, and because she was on the side where he'd dropped his pants, she crawled off the bed to get his cell out of his pocket. She was smiling playfully when she picked it up, giving him the impression that he could talk her into seeing him again. But when she glanced down, her smile disappeared.

"What is it?" he asked.

She handed him his phone. "Some woman says she's missing you and can't wait until you get home."

He checked the text. Dahlia had sent him a picture of herself, naked and bending over in a seductive posture, with the words "Missing you" written in lipstick on her ass.

He deleted that image, but Nancy wasn't climbing back onto the bed with him. She was gathering up her clothes.

"It's not serious with this woman," he said.

"No. I'm sure it's not. I get that. We just spent the night together, but we're not serious, either. I'll be careful never to send you something like this in case it puts you in an awkward situation with the next girl."

"Nancy—"

"I'm joking. I would never send anything like that, period. Anyway, I have to go. I have things to do at home."

He was getting up so he could stop her—he didn't want their fabulous night to end on such a sour note—when his phone rang. If it had been Rocki or anyone else, he might've let it go to voice mail, thinking he'd call back in a few minutes. But it was Landon, and

Landon rarely, if ever, called him. That made him hesitate, and by the time he glanced up, Nancy had taken her clothes, hurried into the bathroom and shut the door.

Planning to talk with her after she got dressed, he took the call. "Hello?"

"Keith?"

"What is it?"

"The police are here."

"They're *what*?"

"They're searching our house. They have a warrant and everything. I've never been in a situation like this, never been so filled with self-hatred. What the hell have I done? If anything happens to her, I'll never be able to forgive myself."

"She didn't kill Mom, Landon. Like you, she had an argument with her, but Mom was alive when she left the house."

"I know that. And you know that. How do we convince *them*?"

Keith remembered Chief Underwood telling him not to get involved in her investigation. But he couldn't sit idly by. He had to do something to protect his sister. "We'll figure out who really did it."

"How?"

"We have to find the woman who stopped Marcus Coleman on Wednesday night."

"I don't know what you're talking about."

"I've got it. Just take care of your family like you should've done from the beginning," he snapped and hung up. Poor Rocki. He could only imagine what she was going through, having the police toss her house on the heels of her husband's infidelity.

Keith was so immersed in the news of this latest development, and his worry for Rocki, that Nancy startled him when she came out of the bathroom. "Thanks for everything," she said. "Last night was fun."

She was being a little *too* casual, and her careless attitude didn't ring true.

"You're not upset, are you?"

"No. Of course not. What do I have to be upset about?" she asked, and yet, despite all the intimacy of last night, she wasn't coming near him. Apparently, she wasn't even going to kiss him goodbye.

"That picture Dahlia sent—"

"Is none of my business. Have a good day," she said and, with a cheery wave, called her dog, who'd been lying on the floor next to the fireplace.

"Are you coming back?" he called as she walked out. He would've hurried after her, but he was stark naked and could easily run into Pippa on her way in.

"Nancy?" he yelled.

He never got an answer.

She was an idiot. Not for doing what she'd done. She'd wanted to sleep with Keith, and she'd enjoyed it. But she hadn't kept it strictly physical, as she'd promised herself she would. She'd let herself believe that she mattered more to him than she really did.

The funny thing was…she knew better! He was just so damn convincing. The way he made love, as if he was so consumed with her and only her, would've thrown any woman off.

Damn, he was good. No wonder Dahlia was sending him pictures of her bare ass. She wanted him back. Who wouldn't?

Nancy puttered around the shop, mostly cleaning and

rearranging and waiting for new business. She didn't have many orders to fill, and the ones she did have she couldn't start on quite yet. Since flowers lasted only so long, and the events she was servicing weren't until the weekend, she couldn't work on those arrangements until Thursday. She wished she was busier. Then she'd have less time to obsess over Keith and the exquisite pleasure he'd provided—

The bell over the door rang. She hoped it was a customer coming in with a huge order, one that would make her work a lot harder than she was right now. If she had to stay late, she'd have a good excuse for not heading back to Coldiron House.

But it wasn't a customer. When she turned the corner, she saw her sister.

"Brought you lunch," Jade announced.

Nancy cringed at the reminder that she hadn't shown up at the motel with dinner for her sister last night. She'd chosen to stay with Keith instead. "I'm sorry I couldn't come by," she began, but Jade put up a hand.

"No apologies necessary—" her grin turned slightly wicked "—*if* it was because you were too busy at Coldiron House."

"I was...pretty busy," she admitted and quickly pulled Jade in for a hug so her sister wouldn't be able to tell that she was suddenly and inexplicably on the brink of tears.

Jade stiffened. She wasn't much of a hugger; she preferred to show her affection in other ways. But Nancy was used to that, so she wasn't offended.

"And? How'd it go?" her sister asked.

That split-second reprieve, during which she'd managed to dodge her sister's piercing gaze, helped. By the time Jade could see her face, Nancy was once again able to fake a smile. "It was…incredible."

"Wow. That's better than good."

"Easily the hottest thing *I've* ever experienced."

"Really? But wait, maybe I shouldn't be so excited. The hottest thing *you've* ever experienced isn't saying much."

Nancy managed a laugh. "Not all of us can be as adventurous as you are."

"I'm a lesbian. I *have* to get creative. I could tell you—"

Nancy shook her head. "Enough!"

"It's so much fun to shock you. You're one of the few people I know who can still blush. Which means I probably won't get many details about last night."

"You'll get this—he's a talented lover."

"Whoa! Big deal. You told me that before, remember? Did he ask to see you again?"

"I could go back over, if I want."

Jade's eyebrows knitted. "He doesn't care one way or the other?"

"He asked me to return tonight. He sounded as if he'd really like that, but…"

"But *what*? You had fun! Why the hesitation?"

"I'm just another girl to him, Jade—someone to keep him busy while he's here."

"I doubt *that's* true."

Nancy recalled the text she'd seen from "Dahlia." "Trust me. It's true. I'm afraid of getting in too deep. I'd rather not be devastated when he leaves."

Jade bit her lip. Nancy expected her to immediately change her position, to retrench, but she didn't. "You're strong. You can survive it," she said at length. "Life is all about taking chances. If you care about him, go with it and see where it leads."

"Last night you told me I was walking into the lion's den. Now that I'm agreeing with you, telling you I nearly didn't make it out alive, you're saying I should *go back in*?"

"Someone like you...you deserve to find love. That won't happen if you're always protecting yourself. Sometimes you've got to reach for what you want."

Nancy cocked her head. "I'm not sure whether you're good for me or not."

"Don't you think he's worth it?"

If he was as invested as she was, Nancy knew she'd make any sacrifice. But a relationship that was too one-sided wouldn't go anywhere. "I think you're blinded by the love you have for me," she said. "You want me to be happy."

"I won't deny that."

Nancy caught a glimpse of something that stopped her from making any type of rejoinder. A black Mercedes had just pulled into the lot—and she recognized it. "He's here!"

"Who's here?" Jade turned around to see for herself. "Aw, lover boy," she said with satisfaction.

"Please don't embarrass me! And in case that isn't clear, that means no more talk of blow jobs or...anything along those lines." Nancy whispered this, even though there wasn't any chance that Keith could hear her from outside. He was just getting out of the car.

"I won't embarrass you." Jade threw her a look that suggested Nancy was being ridiculous to mention it. But Nancy shouldn't have believed her. As soon as Keith walked through the door, Jade gave him an obvious once-over and said, "I hear you really know how to please the ladies."

Keith's eyebrows slid up but, fortunately, he didn't act too shocked. "Glad I can do something right."

"That's it," Nancy said. "You're leaving," she told Jade.

"Oh, relax." Jade waved her off. "He can take a joke."

He blocked her path to the door. "And she can't leave. I need to talk to her."

Although he'd played along with Jade so far, Nancy could tell he wasn't in the mood for jokes this morning. "What is it?"

"It's about my mother."

Jade sobered, too. "You want to talk to *me* about your mother? Should I be worried?"

"Not at all. I'm hoping you can help me."

"How?"

"Someone broke into Coldiron House last Wednesday night."

Jade glanced at Nancy. "I don't mean to be callous, but...wasn't your mother already dead by then?"

"Jade—" Nancy said, but Keith cut her off.

"Yes, she was. That's why it's odd—that four days later someone would break into the house."

"I still don't understand what I have to do with any of this," Jade said.

"I'm trying to find a certain young woman who flagged down Marcus Coleman as he passed the turn-off to the cliff late that night. She could be an islander, but he didn't recognize her, so...maybe she wasn't."

"I know Marcus. I remember him from high school. He just got out of prison and is *not* a nice dude. I certainly wouldn't put him at the top of my list of people here who can be trusted."

"I think he's telling the truth," Keith argued. "I also think…if this person came here from somewhere else, she would've needed a place to stay, since she couldn't get off the island in the middle of the night."

"You're wondering if I had a young woman staying at the Drift Inn last Wednesday night."

"Yes. A woman wearing a trench coat and a scarf."

"To be honest, I don't remember anyone like that. But you know how the Drift Inn's built. It's garden-style. You don't have to go through the lobby to reach the rooms, so I would only have seen her if she was the one who checked in."

"You don't remember anything unusual about that night?"

"No. And I was on duty. But…let me check the registration records. Maybe that'll jog my memory as to who was there."

"Any chance we could do that right now?"

Jade pursed her lips. "I'm all for helping out a friend, but since that information is supposed to be kept private, I'd rather have Chief Underwood make the request, if that's okay."

"I'm sure she'll do that eventually. But by the time she knows what I already know, and makes those registration records a priority, the trail could be cold."

"What are you talking about?" Nancy asked. "What do you know?"

He shoved his hands in his pockets. "That she's focusing on the wrong person."

Fresh worry made Nancy grip the edge of the counter. Rocki, Maisey, Keith—they'd all been through enough. "Landon?"

"Rocki."

"You're kidding!"

"No. Underwood's in Louisiana now. Along with the Lafitte police, she's searching Rocki's house."

Nancy nudged Jade. "Let him take a look at the registration records. If that turns up nothing, no one'll have to be the wiser."

"Except that Violet's working today," Jade said. "She'd love to take over as manager if I get fired."

"Can't you act like you're there to get something else and make a copy of the records at the same time?" Nancy asked.

"Probably could, but...what if it goes the other way? What if I *do* find something?"

"That would be a *good* thing," Keith said. "You could help solve a murder *and* keep an innocent person from going to prison."

"You haven't mentioned the part where I could lose my job," she grumbled.

"If it comes to that, I'll buy the Drift Inn so Violet never takes your place," he told her.

Jade threw up her hands. "Oh, what the hell. It's not like I plan on managing a motel for the rest of my life, anyway. And you're not going to use the information to harm anyone, so I don't have to worry about that. Come on."

Keith started to follow her out. Then he turned at the door, walked back and kissed Nancy. "I'll call you later," he said.

25

Jade had him wait in the car while she ran in. Keith watched through the window as she spoke with the woman behind the counter before disappearing into the back.

It took longer than he'd expected, but when Jade finally came out, she hurried toward him with a coat draped over one arm. Thanks to a sudden gust of wind, he could see she had a file hidden underneath it, which was encouraging.

"Everything go okay?" he asked as she climbed in.

Tilting her head to peer into the lobby, she slid the file into view, careful to keep it below the dash. "Yeah, but let's go before Violet realizes I wasn't just picking up the coat I left here last week."

He put the car in Drive and pulled out of the parking lot. "That took a while."

"Violet was all worked up. Chief Underwood sent Les Scott over first thing this morning to get copies of the records, so she was kind of freaked out. 'Do you think whoever killed Josephine Lazarow was staying *here*?' That sort of thing."

"Were you working the night my mother was killed— or was she?"

"She was. That's partly why she's so worked up. 'Whoever it was could've killed *me*.'"

"Did she say if Les found anything?"

"She has no clue. She copied the records, put them in a manila envelope and he came by and picked them up."

Keith had tried to call Chief Underwood earlier, as soon as he'd heard from Landon. He'd wanted to ask if she'd found some piece of evidence he didn't know about. But she hadn't picked up. He was fairly certain she was avoiding his call. Now that she felt Rocki might be his mother's killer, she didn't fully trust him, or she would've said something about the search when he spoke with her last night. She must've been talking to him from a motel room in New Orleans or somewhere closer to Lafitte than South Carolina, since she'd arrived at Rocki's house so early.

"Tell me you got the records for Saturday *and* Wednesday."

"Of course."

"Did you see anything that stuck out while you were making the copies?"

She removed the sheets of paper from the envelope. "I didn't even look. I was in too much of a hurry. But I can go through them now." She frowned as she perused her own handwriting. "Okay, of the forty rooms we have available, we rented nineteen last Wednesday night."

"That's more than I was expecting—for winter."

"We usually get forty to fifty percent occupancy on weekdays, which, during the winter, are busier than weekends."

"Do you recognize any of the people?"

"Quite a few. Peter Mann was in town. He comes over to sell restaurant supplies every six months or so.

Leland and Tina Hatch are hoping to open a B and B here in a year or two, when Leland retires. There were some biologists researching the marine fauna. They took two rooms. Leslie Harrison checked in." She shot him a look. "But she only needed the room for a few hours."

Leslie Harrison ran the ice-cream parlor and could've been Dolly Parton's twin sister. She'd been fooling around on her husband for years. "Leslie's still cheating?"

"She pretended she and Jeff were having an argument, so she needed the room all night because she wasn't 'about to stay under the same roof with him.' But I wasn't fooled. I saw her 'guest' sneak up to the second story. And I saw them both leave an hour later."

Keith was driving, so he couldn't read the list, but he gestured to it. "And the others?"

"We had a family—the Wilkersons. Mom, Dad and both kids. They have this goal of visiting one hundred lighthouses before the year is out and came to see ours."

"They don't sound like suspicious characters."

"Definitely not. But neither are any of the others."

"Any women who were alone?"

She lifted the top page to check the one underneath. "None."

"Were any of the people who stayed on Wednesday the same as those who were at the motel on Saturday?"

She shook her head. "No. Completely new tenants. All of them."

Damn. He'd had such high hopes for those records.

Once they reached Coldiron House, he'd look over what she had. Then he'd check to see who was staying at The Carriage Inn. That motel was smaller, and set on a back street, so he'd felt a stranger might not know about it. But there was always a chance.

His phone buzzed. When he stopped to put the code in at the gate, he glanced down to see why. Rocki had sent him a text. They took my computer.

He parked in the drive. It wasn't raining, so he didn't see any point in using the garage. He and Jade wouldn't be at the house long enough to bother.

"Holy shit," Jade said. "This is gorgeous!"

"You've never been here?" he asked as they climbed the steps to the porch.

"I'm not exactly someone your mother would invite to tea. I saw her all over town, but I bet she only knew me as 'that lesbian sister of Nancy's.'"

"That's entirely possible." He let her in the house. Then he texted Rocki back. What will they find?

On my computer? My plane reservations to and from Fairham.

Your phone already placed you on Fairham. Anything else?

I don't know. I have no idea what they'll perceive as incriminating. My life is falling apart so fast I can't even think straight.

Don't worry. Everything's going to be okay. I'm doing all I can to find the real culprit.

What if they charge me?

They're not going to charge you. But if they do, don't say a word. Tell them you'd like a lawyer.

You believe I didn't do it, don't you?

Absolutely.

He started to put his phone away, then pulled it out again. Did they find a wig?

A wig? Like for Halloween costumes? I'm sure we have a few—one for a witch, that kind of thing.

The fact that she didn't immediately know what he was talking about encouraged him. I'm asking about a regular brown wig.

No. I've never bought a wig in my life. They can check anything, anywhere. I wouldn't even know where to get a decent one.

That's good news. It's going to be okay, like I said. How are you and Landon getting along?

We're not. We're like strangers. We barely talk. I heard two cops whispering about that naked picture Landon sent Mom. They said, "Who could blame her? My wife would probably do the same thing." Everyone thinks I did it.

We're going to prove you didn't.

She didn't reply, so he tried calling her, but she wouldn't pick up.

"Everything okay?" Jade asked.

"No," he said. "But let's see what we can do to fix it."

After slipping his phone in his pocket, he led her to the dining room, where they spread the papers she'd copied at the motel on the table. He recognized the names she'd mentioned in the car and asked about the rest. As she'd told him before, there were no women who'd rented a room alone. But he didn't believe the woman who had stopped Marcus on the road that night *had* been alone. Someone had been inside his house…

"Could any of the females who were there be in their thirties?"

"No. They were all older."

He made his way down the list, eventually pointing to a name three-quarters down. "What about this guy? Did he have a wife?"

"Yeah."

"Do you remember her?"

"Not really. I never actually saw her. But she called the front office later that night, asking for an extra blanket. I was shocked that she'd need one. We have the big feather comforters on the beds at this time of year. They're so warm. But she said she wasn't used to the cold weather. Said it was summer where she lived."

An uneasy feeling prickled Keith's spine. "She said it was *summer* where she lived?"

"Yeah. They were from Australia. She and her husband had the coolest accents."

Now Keith's whole body was tingling. "Did she give you *her* name?"

"She might have. I don't remember it, though. And her husband didn't put her on the room, so…"

"How long did they stay?"

"Just the one night. Checked out early the next morning."

He stared at the name "Harry Middleton" again. Was

it merely a coincidence that there'd been a man from Australia staying at the Drift Inn on the night there'd been an intruder at Coldiron House?

It could easily be a coincidence. Keith had to acknowledge that. But "Harry Middleton" bothered him as much as the Australian accent. He couldn't help wondering if it'd been fabricated by meshing the first name of England's Prince Harry with Kate Middleton's last. Some lies went that way—they sort of evolved from easy associations. "Did you check his ID?"

"I always check ID, but I admit I didn't check his very carefully. He was *totally* credible, and he'd already paid for the room online, so I wasn't worried that we'd get stiffed."

"Was it a driver's license or..."

"It was a passport with a blurry picture, which didn't do him justice. He had to be sixty or so, but he was handsome in a polished sort of way. Reminded me of George Clooney."

Keith rubbed his chin. Could this be who he thought it was? The age and accent certainly fit...

"Did you get his license plate number?"

"Why would I do that?"

"A lot of hotels ask for a license plate number, even with a rental."

"Maybe in the big city, where parking's a problem. Not out here, especially in the winter when the lot's half empty."

"Hang on a sec," he said and went upstairs to get his mother's phone. Fortunately, Chief Underwood had returned it to him when she'd brought it over, along with Josephine's computer.

When he found it, he searched through his mother's

pictures until he came to one that showed her with a George Clooney type, as Jade had indicated. This had to be Hugh Pointer. Josephine had a lot of pictures of him and with him—especially over the past year.

Taking the phone, he hurried back downstairs to find Jade wandering around the house, admiring the furnishings.

"What's it like to be so rich?" she asked.

"I'm not going to lie. It has its benefits." He held out his mother's phone to show her the picture he'd pulled up. "This isn't Harry Middleton, the 'credible' older guy who checked in last Wednesday night, is it?"

Her eyes widened in surprise. "Yes!" she cried. "How'd you know?"

Landon could hear Rocki cleaning up in the bedroom. The kids were at school. He'd gotten them there late but, after the initial disruption of having the cops show up first thing, they were out of the house. He'd wanted Rocki to take them, to spare her the humiliation of watching the police search the house, but she was too upset to go anywhere. He sensed that by staying, she somehow felt she was protecting her belongings.

After dropping off Zac and Chloe, however, he'd come home to find that the police weren't taking much care with the house, in spite of her presence. He couldn't do anything to change that, either. He and Rocki could only stand by as half a dozen men, along with Fairham's chief of police, ransacked every drawer, cupboard and closet and inspected every nook and cranny. They even rummaged through their underwear and the shoebox hidden in the closet where they kept their sex toys so the kids wouldn't find them.

After the initial shock of being invaded by police officers, Rocki had watched in silence, tears streaming down her face.

Seeing her so devastated had nearly killed Landon. He wasn't sure if Chief Underwood found anything she deemed "telling" or important. She hadn't been particularly friendly to him, and he could understand why. She identified with the pain his actions had caused Rocki. That seemed to hold true even for the men on the Lafitte force, most of whom he knew from school, sports or business.

He'd destroyed his wife and created the worst experience of his life…

In the end, the police had taken Rocki's hairbrush, her computer and a wig that she'd purchased with a Disney costume for Chloe some years ago. But at least it was over, and they hadn't taken more. Although the search seemed to have lasted for days, the officers and Underwood were gone.

He called his mother to see if she'd get the kids and take them to her place after school, said he and Rocki were dealing with some "problems" and was grateful when she agreed. He hoped that brief respite would give him and his wife a chance to regroup before they had to face Chloe and Zac. If they could pretend that what had happened this morning was just some big misunderstanding, maybe the kids wouldn't have to suffer along with them.

But he wasn't convinced Rocki would be able to bounce back. The invasion of their privacy, especially at such a difficult time, had been hard on her.

Closing his eyes, he let his head fall against the couch, where he'd dropped a few seconds earlier. If only he'd never gotten involved with Josephine. Then he wouldn't have had any reason to go to Fairham instead of Vegas, and Rocki wouldn't have followed him there and this would never have happened.

But, bad as it was, he feared the worst was yet to come...

What if she went to prison? That wasn't unheard of, even with people who were innocent.

His phone pinged, signaling a text.

Daddy, what's going on? Chloe texted me that the police came to the house this morning! I'd call, but I'm in class.

Thank God for small favors, because he couldn't bear to talk to Brooklyn right now, feared she'd see right through his "everything's okay" act. It's nothing, babe, he wrote back. A misunderstanding about Grandma Josephine. When someone's been murdered they have to look at everyone who was close to her.

I knew she didn't commit suicide!

You were right. I think we all felt pretty strongly about that. Anyone who knew her would have a hard time believing she'd do something like that.

But why would they bother you guys? You live in Louisiana!

They're just being thorough. We have nothing to worry about. But please don't bother Mom right now. It's been a hard morning.

I won't. I have to put my phone away before I get in trouble. But call me later, okay?

I will.

He sat on the couch, listening to the oppressive silence in the house for another fifteen minutes. Then, unable to endure the strain between him and Rocki any longer, he got up and walked down the hall.

When he opened the door, she turned from putting her jewelry back in its box. But her eyes didn't light up the way they used to when she saw him. They shifted dully back to her task, as if he wasn't standing in the doorway.

"Can we talk?" he asked.

"I tried talking to you—for days. All you wanted to do was get defensive and yell, and then you went to *New Orleans.*"

He raked his fingers through his hair, which was already standing on end from the number of times he'd done that before. "Where I got drunk because I couldn't face what I'd done. I was...trying to cope with the disappointment I felt in myself, with the truth that I wasn't the man I thought I was—that *you* thought I was. I couldn't bear how badly my actions would hurt you."

"And now?"

"And now I realize that running from it will get me nowhere. In the end, there's no changing what I did, and there's no hiding from it, either. All I can do is take responsibility and tell you how sorry I am."

"I don't understand how or why it even happened," she said, looking shell-shocked.

He let his breath go in a long sigh and bumped his

head repeatedly against the door frame. The impact hurt, but he didn't care. He wanted to do a lot worse. "I don't, either. But I know everything I want is still right here. I've never stopped loving you."

She quit working and sat on the bed. "Why did *she* do it?" she asked. "To prove I was nothing next to her? To show everyone that she could take the one thing I loved more than anything else?"

He couldn't help wincing at the past tense of "love."

"I don't think that was it at all. I believe she was lonely, and because I made you happy, she thought maybe I could make her happy, too."

"What did she say when you told her you didn't want to…to carry on the affair?"

"She said she had never wanted me, anyway. That I wasn't worth her time. That Hugh loved her and that eventually they'd be together."

"She was in denial. I don't think he ever planned on leaving his wife."

"Which was why she was so lonely, I guess."

"She really loved him."

"That's my take. Like Gretchen said, he was the one she's always wanted."

"But she couldn't have him, and she wasn't used to being denied. He wouldn't do what he needed to do in order for them to be together."

He shoved away from the door frame and sat on the end of the bed, facing her. "I believe that all her life, she's been looking for something or someone to make her feel whole. Malcolm, as good a man as he was, didn't satisfy her, or she wouldn't have been looking elsewhere. Hugh might have done it for her, but she was never able to have all of him."

Rocki closed her eyes. "I still can't believe she chose *you*."

"She was going through a bad time, losing everything—her money, her status, maybe even Coldiron House—and Hugh, the man she loved, wasn't coming to her rescue the way she wanted him to. I'm guessing she thought that after waiting so long and with his daughter getting older, he'd finally leave his wife and marry her. The more she had to settle for 'same old, same old,' the more upset she got."

"She told you that?"

"Not in so many words. But she told me I reminded her of Hugh. That might've had something to do with... what happened, too."

She smoothed her hand over the duvet. "If I didn't kill her, and you didn't kill her, who did?"

He took a deep breath. He'd been asking himself that question all along, wondering if he might've seen some sign of trouble if he hadn't been so immersed in his own desperate struggle to get back on the right course. "I have no idea. But I hope they find the bastard soon."

"What would you say if I said it *was* me?" she asked.

He hesitated for a second, a little freaked out by the deadpan tone of her voice. "I wouldn't believe it. You're not capable of something like that."

She went back to reorganizing her jewelry. "Yeah, well, I never would've thought you were capable of what you did, either. Maybe you never really know someone, huh?"

26

Keith sat with Maisey in her living room. Rafe was at work, Laney was at school and little Bryson was playing with his toys a few feet away. "Have you told Chief Underwood?" she asked. After telling her about Rocki's cell phone records placing her on the island and the police search of her house, he'd mentioned the Australian named "Harry Middleton," who was actually Hugh Pointer.

"I have. I called her as soon as Jade identified him. I knew Underwood wouldn't be able to tell just from looking at the registration records collected by Les that Harry Middleton was Hugh Pointer. And that's pretty significant."

"So significant she probably feels bad about searching Rocki's house."

"I doubt it," Keith responded. "I hate to admit it, but Rocki had as much motive to murder Mom as anyone, and she hasn't been eliminated from the pool of suspects. Underwood has to treat all persons of interest the same. She has to do her job or this could backfire on her."

Maisey grimaced, obviously angry that anyone could

suspect their sister, whatever the reason. "It's Landon's fault, not Underwood's."

"True. He's put Rocki in an impossible position."

"Do you think she'll ever be able to forgive him?"

"I doubt it, although I hope she will."

Maisey came halfway off the couch. *"After what he did?"*

"Don't get me wrong. What he did was bad. But I've spoken to him. He's completely distraught—suffering as much as she is because he knows he's to blame for everything."

"Yeah, well, apparently I'm not as forgiving as you are."

"Maybe it's because I've fucked up before. If you've never needed that kind of forgiveness, it's different."

"You didn't cheat on anyone."

"Because I never made a commitment in the first place. What's worse?" He picked a speck of lint off his shirt. "At least he was the one who cut off the affair. He got involved and made a mistake, but then he tried to undo that mistake. He didn't wait until he was caught."

"Having an affair is not a 'whoops, I'm sorry' kind of thing."

Given her ex-husband's history, Maisey was especially sensitive to this type of betrayal. "True, but it's not as if he went out searching for another woman. I get the feeling he's been happy, in love and faithful for all the years they've been married—until this. It wasn't as if he was in love with Mom or ever fell out of love with Rocki. He was just…captivated by Mom's wealth and beauty and attention."

"He slept with his wife's mother!"

"Who he didn't know until five years ago—and he

didn't see very often, even after he was told she was his 'real' mother-in-law."

"Stop making excuses for him," Maisey snapped. "It's pissing me off."

He chuckled. "Okay. Calm down. I don't think I can save him from his actions, anyway. So I'll move on to what I might be able to do—and that is save Rocki from being unjustly prosecuted."

"Now you're talking," she said sullenly. "So...are you thinking Hugh was here on Saturday, too? Under a different alias or maybe at the other motel?"

"No. Underwood claims that's impossible. He was in Australia. She has witnesses who saw him there on Saturday."

"Then he came here after that."

"Apparently." That made Keith wonder if he was actually in Charleston or somewhere much closer when Keith spoke to him on Thursday morning. He'd have to be. He couldn't have gotten back to Australia that quickly.

Bastard. And to think Keith had liked him...

"But if he wasn't here on Saturday, he couldn't have killed her," Maisey said.

"I think *she* killed Mom."

"His wife? So she *did* know about the affair? And she wasn't in Europe?"

"It's possible. Maybe Mom was pressing Hugh to divorce her, and Lana Pointer was fearful enough to take matters into her own hands. Sounds like he had her with him on Wednesday, so obviously she wasn't touring Europe with their daughter at that point."

"Then where was their daughter? Were there three people in that motel room?"

"Not according to Jade. But the daughter is technically an adult, old enough to do as she pleases. She could've been back in Australia, in Europe or even here in the States, maybe in Charleston, both on the night Mom was killed *and* when Hugh—with Lana as the person who likely stopped Marcus—broke into Coldiron House four days later. I doubt it would be difficult for them to get away from her. She's about to graduate from high school this spring. Remember what we were like back then? She was probably *glad* to be left on her own for a while."

"If she were to admit that her mother wasn't with her on the night of the murder, that'd be huge. Underwood needs to get on that right away."

"Underwood probably would've confirmed it by now, if that naked picture of Landon hadn't taken the investigation in a completely different direction. I know she established that Lana and her daughter went to Europe. I'm not sure she ever verified that they *stayed* in Europe."

"Then she needs to do that." Maisey got up to help Bryson reach a car he was having trouble retrieving from his toy box. "So why'd Hugh and Lana come here after the murder? To get an expensive piece of jewelry or something he gave Mom?"

Keith remembered finding the door to his mother's suite open that night. "Possibly. But that's a big risk to take for jewelry. I bet when he found out what his wife had done, he was afraid she'd left something incriminating behind—maybe she even realized she had and told him so—and he came to clean up."

"So he was protecting her."

"He probably feels responsible because of the affair."

"Do you think he knew you were at Coldiron House when he broke in?"

"No way. It wasn't until the following morning that I called him. I'm assuming he thought the place would be empty, figured he could waltz in and do what he wanted. He'd probably know where the hide-a-key was, which explains how he got in. I'm sure he's visited Mom at Coldiron House once or twice since I left. Maybe he arrived late at night and she told him to just let himself in."

Bryson brought her a toy that had colored wooden pegs he could hit with a small wooden hammer, and she held it while he pounded. "But if he was here to protect his wife, to clean up, why would she flag down Marcus? That doesn't make sense."

"Unless she wanted to see him punished for having the affair."

"Wouldn't dragging him into the spotlight only lead the police back to her?"

"She might not have realized that, might not have understood exactly what the police can do these days, what with cell phone records and such. She might've been trying to frame him. You have to admit, to a twisted mind, getting Hugh arrested would sound like the perfect revenge. Her rival dies, the man who betrayed her goes to prison and she and her daughter live happily ever after with his money."

"I suppose," Maisey said.

Keith scratched his head. "I wish I could talk to Lana."

"Wouldn't Chief Underwood frown on that?"

"Absolutely. She's asked me not to even call Hugh for fear I'll tip him off that we've found a connection."

"What does she think he'll do?"

"Who knows? He has the money to disappear if he wants to."

"That means you're going to respect her wishes, right?"

"Wrong."

"What?" She startled Bryson so much that he began to cry. She picked him up to calm him, but she didn't look away from Keith.

"I'm going to call him." He held up a hand to stop her before she could interrupt. "Don't worry, I won't give anything away. I want to see if he'll say something that could be used against him later."

"Like?"

"Who knows? But I plan on recording the conversation, just in case."

"Then why don't you call him from here? Now?"

"It's too late there."

"Assuming he went home."

"I'll bet he hurried back to Perth as soon as he could. I want to catch him when he's awake and willing to talk, and hopefully when his wife isn't around."

He coaxed Bryson over to him with a plush football. "Here you go, buddy," he said, then dropped a kiss on his soft cheek.

Bry scowled and wiped his cheek, but he was interested enough in the football not to go anywhere.

Maisey checked her watch. "I've got to pick up Laney. She stayed after school to teach a few friends how to crochet. But I have to be there by three forty or so, and it's a bit of a drive, what with waiting for the ferry. If you'd like to come back in an hour or two, I'll make dinner."

He thought of Nancy and that text she'd seen from

Dahlia this morning. "I was hoping to grab a bite with Nancy."

Maisey got up and swung Bryson into her arms. "How're things going with her?"

Keith could tell she still wasn't pleased about the fact that he was seeing her. "Good."

"I just got off the phone with her before you arrived."

Had she outed him about that text? "And?"

"She told me not to worry. That she understood the limitations of the relationship."

That was the look he'd seen on her face when she handed him his phone—a sort of fatalistic expression that suggested she would've been a fool to expect anything more from him. He hated the way that made him feel. "I'm not sure I'm happy you two are friends."

"She also said she has a date with a really hot guy from her dating site," she said with a wink.

Keith cleared his throat. "She mentioned that."

"You don't mind?"

"No," he lied and helped her load Bryson into the car so she wouldn't be late.

Nancy told herself she should head home and get a few groceries—everything she hadn't remembered the last time she went to the store. She couldn't stop living her life just because Keith was on the island. He and Jade had both called, separately, to tell her what they'd learned from the registration records at the Drift Inn. She supposed Keith would be meeting with Chief Underwood tonight. As much as she cared about Rocki and Maisey and especially *him*, he could handle that without her. She'd received quite a few messages on that dating site, and it was rude to let the men who'd sent them wait.

She needed to show others the same consideration she hoped they'd show her. She also needed to keep her relationship with Keith in its proper perspective.

So she was prepared to tell Keith no when he called to see if she'd be joining him for dinner. "I've actually got some things to do," she said.

"Like…?"

"I have to run to the grocery store."

"I have plenty of food here. I think you know that."

"Dog food probably isn't something Pippa has in stock. And speaking of Simba, I should spend some time with him, take him for a walk."

"No problem. Grab some dog food on your way over. It's a little windy out, but it's not raining. We'll take him down to the beach when you get here. It's secluded, so he can go off-leash and run in the surf."

That sounded tempting—almost as tempting as seeing Keith again. But she'd decided to cool things off a bit, so she flailed around for something else she needed to do, something a bit more crucial than picking up a few groceries. But what? Business was slow at the flower store and Jade was working again tonight. Her house was spotless, since she'd just cleaned it on Saturday and hadn't been home much since. "Don't *you* have stuff to do?" she asked.

"Not until later."

"What's happening later?"

"I'm going to call Hugh Pointer, see if I can get him to talk to me."

"About…?"

"My mom."

"Won't he find that odd?"

"Not if I act like I'm calling to give him the results of the autopsy."

"Why don't you do that now?"

"It's pretty early in the morning over there."

"Oh. Good point. That's all you have to do?" She thought of that text from "Dahlia" and wondered if he'd already responded to it—and what he'd said.

"That's it."

"Okay. Maybe I'll stop by."

"*Maybe?* I can tell you're blowing me off. Look, I'm sorry about that text this morning. As you've probably guessed, I *have* slept with Dahlia, but I have no real interest in her and don't plan on pursuing a relationship."

Was that supposed to make her feel better? Didn't he understand it was that behavior pattern she objected to? Why would she want to be another "Dahlia," settling for a few crumbs of his attention while knowing there'd be no progression to their relationship? She had to have more respect for herself. "Right. I understand. It's just... I have some messages to return on that dating site."

"To hell with the dating site! We spent an incredible night together. Can't you wait until I'm gone to respond to all the men who'd like to take you out?"

"I'm not sure it's fair to ignore them just because you're in town."

"Why not?"

"Because one of them could be my husband someday!" Which was far more than she could say for him.

"Fine. If you'd rather be with someone else, I won't get in the way," he said and hung up.

She sat staring at the phone. She'd accomplished what she'd set out to do. She was staying home tonight. But she certainly didn't feel good about it. Why did "having more respect for herself" make her feel so damn bad?

She almost broke down and called him back. That was what she *wanted* to do. So she turned off her phone and promised herself she wouldn't turn it back on until morning.

Almost immediately, Keith regretted responding to Nancy the way he had. He could understand why she'd be leery. She had every reason to be. What if he'd seen a text like Dahlia's come in on *her* phone, especially after having sex with her for the first time in more than five years?

He wouldn't have been happy about it. Besides, he'd already proved that he wasn't emotionally reliable. He couldn't expect her to ignore everything that had happened in the past.

He paced for fifteen minutes, wrestling with his Coldiron pride—the same pride that had so often interfered with his mother's happiness. She could never simply accept responsibility for her mistakes, could never apologize when she was wrong. She'd lost several friends by trying to prove she didn't care, didn't need anyone. Unless he wanted to follow in her footsteps, he had to be more honest, had to be willing to show his vulnerability to those he cared about.

So he called Nancy back. She didn't pick up, but he didn't blame her for that, either.

He waited for her voice mail.

"Nance, I'm sorry. I wish I'd acted differently a few minutes ago. I know I'm not someone you consider emotionally 'safe.' There's good reason for that. If I were a woman, I'd probably steer clear of me, too. But I would never intentionally hurt you. I hope you believe that. Anyway, I already miss you and hate that you're not coming over. So if you change your mind…" He wasn't sure how to end his message, except with the one thing he knew to be true. "I hope you'll change your mind."

He hung up and waited. But when he didn't hear from her, the clock seemed to tick more and more slowly. So he began to tear apart the house, looking for whatever Hugh had been after. It probably wasn't worth the effort, which was why he hadn't searched extensively before. But looking filled the time—kept him from thinking too much about Nancy or the addiction that tried to grab hold of him whenever he was frustrated, upset or unable to sleep.

"Shit," he muttered when, several hours later, he still hadn't found anything. At that point, he stopped pulling things out of cabinets and drawers and threw himself into a chair in the drawing room. Nothing was particularly comfortable in this room, since it had been furnished for show. But he was too stubborn to move to the living room or the library or even his bedroom.

He checked his watch. Had Nancy finished grocery shopping yet? Fed Simba? Walked him?

Most likely. It was ten.

Why hadn't she called him back?

Hoping to see her headlights, he peered out the front window. But she wasn't in the drive, and he had the terrible feeling she wasn't coming.

Fortunately, it was finally late enough to call Hugh. Figuring that would distract him, at least, he walked to the study so he could be at his computer when they spoke.

"Hello?"

"Hugh, it's Keith."

"I recognize your number. How are you?"

Was this man protecting his wife? He almost had to be. "I'm fine. You?"

"Still reeling, of course. I'm sure you are, too."

Was he sincere? Keith supposed knowing that his wife had killed his mistress, if that was what happened, wouldn't be an easy thing to live with—so maybe he was. "They've completed the autopsy."

"I put a call in to Chief Underwood, but haven't heard back from her. What'd they find?"

"Mom didn't drown. She was smothered."

There was another pause. "You're saying she was murdered."

You already know that, you bastard. He *had* to know, didn't he? Otherwise, why had he come to Fairham on Wednesday night—with his wife? "I'm afraid so."

"Do they have any leads on who might've killed her?"

Wouldn't you like to find out? "Right now my sister seems to be the primary suspect."

"Maisey?"

"Rocki."

If Hugh had information that could save Rocki, and he had any conscience at all, he should come forward. "Why?"

"Jealousy."

"I'm not sure I follow you. What kind of jealousy?"

"There was one night when Rocki's husband, Landon, and Mom became a little too affectionate." He didn't feel it was necessary to say more than that.

His words were met with silence. Then Hugh said, "Men were always drawn to her."

She did what she could to reel them in, too. Couldn't stand not to be admired by every man in the room. Perhaps that was why Keith had some sympathy for Landon; Landon probably didn't know what hit him. But Keith didn't point out that his mother was very likely as culpable as his brother-in-law. He thought it wiser not to incite Hugh's jealousy, felt it might make the man more talkative if he steered away from that as much as possible. "Yes."

"But Rocki lives in Louisiana. How could anyone think *she* might be to blame?"

"She was on Fairham that night."

"Oh, God." He seemed genuinely distressed by this news.

"Exactly. She's going through a very hard time. The police searched her house today."

"Did they find anything to implicate her?"

"Not that they told me about. But that doesn't necessarily mean anything. Now that the investigation's so close to home, Chief Underwood isn't being nearly as open with me."

"Makes sense, I suppose."

What was this guy thinking? Keith wished he could somehow climb inside his head. He considered mentioning that strand of hair the police found; he wanted to see how Hugh might react. But he was afraid that if Hugh's wife had the wig the fiber came from, they'd destroy it, if they hadn't done so yet.

"How've things been with your wife?" Keith asked. "Does she know?"

He lowered his voice. "About your mother? No."

Chief Underwood had been too busy chasing other leads and searching Rocki's house to take a very thor-

ough look at the Pointers. She'd made a few initial inqui-
ries, learned that Hugh—and his wife, ostensibly—had
an alibi and turned her attention away from them. But
now that Jade had placed him and Lana on Fairham so
soon after the murder, she'd be investigating them further. "Is she still in Europe?"

"Not anymore."

"When did she get home?"

"Not too long after you and I talked last time. She
came home early."

Which couldn't be true because she was on the island with him last Wednesday. He'd caught Hugh in a
lie right there. "Why'd she cut the trip short?"

"She got sick, so she came home."

"And left your daughter there?"

"It's school trip, so there are teachers and other chap-
erones." Which explained where Marliss was when
Hugh and Lana came to Fairham. Lana had probably
left Marliss as early as the Friday before Josephine was
killed—and had come straight to South Carolina.

"I'm sorry to hear Lana didn't get to finish the trip."

"As we know, worse things can happen than missing
out on part of a vacation."

"Right. Well, I hope she's feeling better."

"I'm sure she'll recover soon." After that, Hugh was
eager to get off the phone, but Keith didn't mind. He
was already on his computer, searching Facebook for a
Marliss Pointer from Australia. If she'd just been to Europe, she might've posted a few pictures of her mother
on social media...

Fortunately, Marliss wasn't a common name. Only
one profile came up—one that showed a pretty girl
with blond hair and blue eyes who looked to be about

the right age—and, in the details section, he saw that she was from Perth. She'd recently posted several pictures of herself standing in front of the Eiffel Tower with an older woman he could only assume was Lana. Their eyes were unmistakably similar—deep-set and an identical blue.

After pulling up the same profile on his phone, Keith went over to show Marcus Coleman.

27

"Marcus Coleman believes Lana Pointer was the woman who flagged him down," Keith told Chief Underwood, who'd answered even though he'd called after midnight.

"I thought this person was too bundled up for him to see what she looked like."

"Her eyes weren't covered," he said. "He told me she had blue eyes—and Lana's definitely got blue eyes."

"I don't know that we can bank on 'blue eyes,' Keith. Or on the word of an ex-con."

"He has no reason to lie."

"Maybe not, but what about the age discrepancy? You originally told me he said the woman he saw on the side of the road was in her thirties. Lana's a lot older than that. She and Hugh have been married for forty-two years."

"Getting the age wrong would be an easy mistake to make, given the circumstances. But Lana and Hugh had to be the ones who broke into Coldiron House. He used a fake name when he checked into the Drift Inn. That tells you something right there."

"It makes me believe he's probably involved on some level—"

"He would *have* to be. It doesn't make sense otherwise."

Chief Underwood yawned. "I hear you, Keith. Just… let me figure it out, like I asked you before. Right now, I'm completely exhausted. I've gotten very little sleep since your mother died and I need to grab a few hours before my flight in the morning."

"You're still in Louisiana?"

"Yes."

"But you'll verify where the Pointers were as soon as possible?"

"Keith, I'm capable of doing my job. I don't need you riding herd on me."

He understood that. She just didn't have as much at stake, and that made it difficult for him not to push. "Okay, I'll let you go."

"I'll be back on the island tomorrow night," she said. "We'll talk then."

He disconnected, but he wasn't ready to call it a night. He took up the search he'd started before he left for Marcus's house with renewed determination and purpose. It stood to reason that Hugh Pointer didn't get what he'd come for. Thanks to Lana having someone notify the police, he didn't have much time. And even though the doors to Josephine's suite had been open when they should've been closed, suggesting Hugh had made it that far, Keith had searched her suite extensively the first two nights he was here and found nothing he recognized as valuable to the investigation. Not only that, but nothing in there had been disturbed since he discovered those letters. Unless Hugh knew exactly where to find what he was after, Keith figured there was at least an equal chance that he'd left empty-handed.

Problem was… Keith had no idea what "it" could be. He only knew the item was important, or Hugh wouldn't have taken the risk of coming here immediately after Josephine's murder.

Keith had gone through all the lived-in parts of the house—the kitchen and pantry, the drawing room, the living room, the library, the dining room, his mother's atrium, her sitting room, the small art gallery and the entry area, and was currently working on the study. He hadn't yet tackled the gym, the apartment over the garage or any of the guest rooms. Taking on the nether regions of the house felt like a daunting task. He couldn't imagine that either his mother or her killer would've left anything there, anyway.

After emptying the shelves in the study, to no avail, he slumped into the chair behind the desk. What a waste of time and effort. It was nearly four. Pippa would arrive at eight. He doubted she'd be happy to find the house torn apart when she arrived. She'd definitely earn her paycheck over the next week as she put it all back together…

So what now? Did he go after the garage apartment? The guest rooms?

"Damn it! What were you after?" he shouted as he glowered at the empty bookshelves. Rocki was counting on him. He couldn't let her down. He had to pull his family back together, and if he could prove that someone else murdered their mother, maybe he'd be able to do that.

Think. Frustrated, he rubbed his temples as he stared at the empty bookcase. "Whatever it was, it's not in here," he grumbled and got up to leave. But a small book he'd knocked to the floor—a travel book on Perth—

caught his attention, because it had a piece of paper or something jutting out like a bookmark.

He doubted that paper or whatever it was would be any more than a place marker or a few notes his mother had jotted down, but the fact that the book was about Hugh's home city made him take a closer look.

And that was when he found it.

When Landon first woke Rocki, and she was staring up into his face during those few seconds, she smiled in relief. She thought everything that'd happened had been a nightmare. Here was her husband, the same as he'd always been. But then her memory returned, and she realized that nothing was the same. At her request, he'd spent the night on the couch again. And to make matters worse, Zac and Chloe had figured out that there was something serious going on. Although she'd attempted to reassure them, had told them the police were merely doing their jobs by searching the house, since they had to look at everyone who was close to "Grandma Josephine," the kids had been oddly subdued. They'd begun to watch her and Landon with unease. They'd also noticed that their father wasn't sleeping with their mother anymore.

"Why are you so mad at Daddy?" Chloe had asked Rocki. "What'd he do? Is everything okay? Are *you* okay?"

Rocki had told her that she and Landon were dealing with some "adult" business and they'd eventually work through it.

But she wasn't entirely sure that was true. And now that Chloe had become aware of the turmoil under the surface of the polite exchanges between her parents, she couldn't be fooled. She'd spoken to Brooklyn, which meant Rocki also had to soothe *her* fears. But at least Chloe tried to play along with them for the sake of her little brother, who seemed more willing to take them at their word.

"It's Keith," Landon said, holding up his cell phone.

"Where's *my* cell?" Her words came out as a raspy croak; she had to clear her throat before she could speak in her normal voice.

"I haven't seen it, but you didn't answer. That's why he called me."

Sitting up, she pushed her hair out of her face as she pressed Landon's phone to her ear. "Keith?"

"Rocki, I'm sorry to wake you, but… I had to tell you the news."

He sounded excited, which brought the first glimmer of hope Rocki had felt in what seemed like a long time. "What is it?"

"I found some letters in a book in the study."

"What kind of letters?"

"One from Lana Pointer to Mom, which proves Lana *did* know about the affair. And one to Lana that Mom was in the process of drafting."

Rocki still felt groggy. "You—you found those in a book?"

"Yes. The book was on Perth, but it was a miracle I stumbled across it. I wouldn't have if I hadn't pulled everything off the shelves. Anyway, I'm guessing Mom hid them because she didn't want Pippa or any of the other help to come across them. They were her own private business."

Relief helped clear the cobwebs, and gave Rocki

the energy to sit up. "Which means…what? I'm off the hook?"

"Maybe not completely, not yet. But it's definitely a step in the right direction. This proves Hugh was lying when he said his wife didn't know about Mom. It also proves that Lana was extremely upset over what she'd learned. You should read the letter. 'If you know what's good for you, you'll stay away from my husband… I won't allow you to break up my family, or my marriage—not after more than forty years…'"

Rocki clutched at her comforter. "That gives Lana motive!"

"Yes. Some of this stuff—it could almost be interpreted as a threat."

"What did Mom write in reply?"

"You know Mom. She was never one to back down from a fight. She says stuff like, 'I told you last time that you can't hold him forever,' and 'The only reason he's still with you is because of Marliss, but she graduates this spring. Good luck then.'"

After being awakened from such a deep sleep, Rocki was still struggling to process everything she was hearing. *"Last time?"*

"Yeah. I caught that, too. They'd obviously communicated before. I don't know where those other letters could be. Mom probably burned them. I'll bet the only reason I found this one is because she was still referring back to it. But the tension between them was definitely escalating."

"I can't believe Mom didn't finish the letter and send it."

"No doubt she saw the foolishness of riling Lana up just before Lana was supposed to go to Europe to act as chaperone for Marliss's trip. If Lana canceled, Mom wouldn't be able to see Hugh."

"I bet Mom assumed she was finally winning the fight, if he was willing to have her come to his home *after* his wife found out about them."

"She probably demanded that, thought she was on the brink of getting what she'd always wanted."

The pieces of the puzzle Keith had presented to her were beginning to fall into place. "Thanks to Marliss's graduation, it sounds like everything was coming to a head."

"I bet Lana's suspicion got the best of her, or something tipped her off that Mom and Hugh were going to meet up, and she left Europe to fly here."

Landon stood, watching her expectantly, hopefully. "What is it?" he asked.

She gestured for more time. Keith was telling her that he was certain Hugh had come back to Coldiron House last Wednesday, looking for the letter or letters his wife had sent.

"So you don't believe he was in on the murder."

"No. He had nothing to gain from her death."

"Peace at home. That's something."

"All he'd have to do was cut it off. Problem was, he didn't want to give up either woman."

"Then Lana came here on her own?"

"Here's my theory. After Lana left for Europe, she was overwhelmed by suspicion. She might even have learned that she had *reason* to be suspicious, that Mom was coming to Australia. She'd already written more than one letter, asking Mom to back off, and knew she wouldn't. So she decided to take matters into her own hands. She flew here, saw the packed luggage and the flowers from Hugh and lost it. She killed Mom. Then she called Hugh in a rage over 'what he'd forced her to do.'"

"At which point *he* panicked and flew over here to make sure there was nothing connecting Lana to the crime scene, nothing that would lead the police to her," Rocki added.

"Exactly. Because he'd caused the mess in the first place, he felt he needed to step in and protect Lana, or he was going to lose *both* women. Only I was home—something he didn't expect so soon, since Mom and I were estranged—and he never got the chance to go through the house the way he planned."

"Sounds plausible to me." Rocki rubbed her face. Could the police—or Keith—solve Josephine's murder? *Was* it Lana? Keith was certainly making a good case. "Wow. I'm so glad you found those letters. They could make a big difference."

"You're going to be okay, Rocki. I love you. Just hang in there." There was a slight pause and then he said, "You probably don't want to hear this, but regardless of Landon's...*mistake*, I believe he loves you, too."

She wasn't going to argue with him while Landon was standing at the side of the bed. "Thanks. For everything."

After she disconnected, Landon sat down next to her, careful not to touch her. "Well? What'd he say?"

She explained what Keith had found and what he thought it might mean.

"That's hopeful, isn't it?" he said.

She nodded and, for the first time, noticed how haggard Landon had become over the course of the past week. He hadn't been sleeping. She could tell by the lines of tension and exhaustion in his face. He hadn't been eating, either. She couldn't remember when she'd seen him do more than push his food around the plate.

"Good," he said, giving her a sad smile.

Keith called Nancy as soon as he got out of bed. Pippa had already come upstairs an hour ago and knocked softly at his door—shocked, no doubt, by the state of the house—but he'd refused to let her interrupt his sleep.

Nancy answered on the first ring. "Hello?"

"Seriously?" he said. "You're holding a grudge?"

"No, of course not."

He shoved a pillow behind his back. "Then why didn't you come over last night?"

"Because I didn't get your message until this morning."

That made him feel slightly better. At least she wasn't angry. "Would you have come over if you'd gotten it?" he asked and smiled when he heard her laugh.

"I'm sure I would have, since I'm here now."

"Here…*where?*" Suddenly, he was afraid *she* was the one who'd knocked and not Pippa. He would've responded…

"On your beach, with Simba. I didn't want to wake you too early."

"So you haven't been inside the house."

"No."

He pulled on a pair of basketball shorts so he could go to the front windows without fear of shocking Pippa, should he bump into her. Sure enough, Nancy's car was parked in the drive. "What about work?"

"Marlene's filling in for me today. Said she could

use the extra hours. And I was interested in having some time off."

The wind was playing havoc with their connection, but he was able to make out her words. "Perfect. Why didn't I think of that yesterday? We could've spent the whole day in bed."

"I'm not sure my boss would've liked that," she teased.

He lowered his voice. "I can guarantee he would."

"Are you coming out?"

"Yeah." He could hear Pippa moving around downstairs. From the sound of it, she'd decided to reassemble the kitchen before turning her attention to the rest of the house, which made sense. It wouldn't be easy to cook in the mess he'd left last night. "I'll be there in a minute."

Once he'd quickly dressed, he went to acknowledge Pippa and found her in the pantry, putting away all the stuff he'd torn from the shelves. "Sorry about the mess," he said.

She looked a little uncertain when she poked her head out. "Are you okay, Mr. Lazarow? At the risk of being…impertinent, I'm thinking some grief counseling might be in order."

He waved her words away. "I appreciate your concern, but I'm fine. I wasn't being destructive. I was looking for something—and I may have found it," he added with a wink.

She pursed her lips. "Too bad you couldn't have found it a bit sooner."

"You should be grateful I never made it to the far wing," he said and they both laughed as she peered around at the mess that remained.

"No problem," she said. "The challenge will keep my mind occupied. I'll get it taken care of."

"Thanks. I appreciate your help."

"Of course."

He'd just started to go when she called him back. "Mr. Lazarow?"

He turned expectantly. "Yes?"

"I don't mean to pry, but if it's not a secret, I'd love to hear what you found. I cared a great deal about your mother, so if it has anything to do with her death…"

"I found some letters, Pippa—from Hugh Pointer's wife. Did you know anything about them?"

She shook her head. "No. Nothing."

"Did you ever meet Lana Pointer? Ever hear my mother talking to or about her? Do you have any knowledge of her whatsoever?"

"None. I was completely shocked to learn that he was married."

Keith turned, once again, to leave. Then she said, "But," and that caused him to hesitate in the doorway.

"What?" he prompted.

"I don't believe your mother only started seeing him recently, sir."

"What do you mean?"

"She's been speaking to a Hugh Pointer ever since I came here. She was very clandestine about it at first, but I definitely heard his name—now and then from almost my first day. I even answered a few calls from him, when he couldn't reach her on her cell. So I'd say she knew him for fifteen years, at least."

Up until five years ago, Keith had been in and out of the house. He didn't remember his mother *ever* speaking to or about a Hugh Pointer. But he'd been completely caught up in his own life and his addiction. When he and his mother did talk, they generally fought, so he tried to avoid her as much as possible. She could've been dating a whole host of men he knew nothing about, especially if she was keeping her mouth shut about them. Besides, for a while there, she'd flown to one destination after another, only to come home briefly before setting off again. "So they were friends before they got involved."

"No, sir. I think they've been involved for ages— on and off."

"Then…why was it such a secret?"

"Pride, I guess."

Of course. That would be his guess, too. His mother wouldn't relish playing the role of "the other woman," especially if Hugh wasn't going to leave his wife and prove to the world that *she* was most important to him. But how long had the relationship been going on?

It wasn't like his mother to spend too many years with one man…

"Thanks," he told Pippa and hurried down to the beach. Now that Nancy was at the house, he didn't want to keep her waiting another minute.

The weather was drier and warmer than it had been since before Christmas, but it was still cold enough for a coat and there was a steady wind. Nancy wished she'd tied back her hair. She held a hand against her forehead to keep it from blowing into her eyes as she watched Keith descend the steep stairs from the house and stride toward her on the beach. "Morning," she called out.

He didn't say anything. He glanced at Simba, who was completely enthralled with chasing the waves in and out. Then he grabbed her and kissed her soundly—and somehow he never pulled away. Before she knew it, they were both reaching under each other's clothes to touch bare skin.

"We're outside on the beach," he said when she slipped her hand inside his pants instead of up his shirt, where it had been a moment earlier.

"It's a private beach," she responded. "Cut off from the rest of the coast."

"But I'm afraid you'll get too cold. Shouldn't we go in?"

"No." Pippa would be there, and Nancy would suddenly feel self-conscious. She didn't want to change anything. The beach was secluded, they were alone, and the sea made a lovely sound. So, cold though it was, she wanted Keith right here, right now, before all the doubts and self-reproach could overwhelm her again.

"Are you sure?" he breathed when their excitement escalated.

"Do you have a condom?"

"In my wallet."

She got it out for him, and that was all the encouragement he needed. A second later, he was stripping off her jeans.

At first, the cold air stung. But when he put on the condom and lifted her up, holding her in his arms, she locked her legs around his hips and threw her head back, reveling in his warm body. She loved feeling so carefree and lost in the moment.

But then Simba decided he could leave his fun long enough to greet the new arrival. Her dog came bounding over and jumped up on Keith, and with his pants partway down, that made them both fall onto the cold, damp sand. They laughed as Simba stuck his head between their two faces to see what strange thing was going on.

"Go back to the water, Simba," Keith said, shooing him away.

They continued to laugh, but their levity didn't last. Simba returned to his fun, and soon Nancy grew numb to everything except the heat and pleasure generated by Keith. She could feel the tension mounting as she stared up at the morning sky over his shoulder and watched the wisps of clouds drifting across it. She felt like she was floating on top of those clouds, propelled who knew where by the wind. "That's it," she said. "Oh!"

She gasped as the pleasure washed over her like a particularly strong wave and saw Keith close his eyes as if he'd been awaiting her signal. His body jerked several times, and then he dropped to his elbows to prop up his own weight.

"What?" she said, when she noticed him grinning down at her.

"Nothing," he replied.

She narrowed her eyes. "Looks like you're pretty pleased with yourself."

He kissed the end of her cold nose. "I am. I admit it. I love watching you come in my arms. The way your lips part as you gasp and your body grips mine. Just thinking about it makes me want to do it again."

Her smile faded as she smoothed the hair off his forehead. Then, before she could stop herself, she did what she swore she'd never do again. "I love you," she whispered. "More than anything."

The second those words were out of her mouth, Nancy wished she could take them back. They were true; they'd come from the very depths of her being, which was probably why they'd welled up almost of their own accord. But she knew there was nothing to be gained by putting Keith in such an awkward situation. He'd only back off. What the hell was wrong with her?

She thought he might make a joke, so it wouldn't be quite as obvious that he couldn't say the same. But he didn't. He stared down at her with an inscrutable expression on his face. "I'd love you, too, if I was capable of it," he said.

Suddenly far colder than she'd been before, she started to wriggle out from under him so she could get into her clothes. "That's okay," she said, forcing a smile that felt frozen on her face. "It's not as if I expected anything more."

He took her arm before she could escape him. "It can't be much consolation, but you're the closest I've ever come to that sort of thing, Nancy—the only woman I completely admire and miss, the only woman I think about."

Somehow, she managed to broaden her smile to mask the gut-wrenching disappointment. "That's nice. Thanks for...trying, I guess."

He looked at her as if he wasn't sure how to take her words, but she didn't want to elaborate—or ever address this again. She grabbed her clothes and, with shaking hands, pulled them on while he fastened his pants.

When he was finished, he reached out for her, and she felt she had no choice but to take his hand. "Let's go have breakfast," he said.

What a fool! She felt like one of the countless admirers who'd fallen at his mother's feet only to have her step over them. But what could she say? She'd just told him she had the day off, so she had no excuse to leave.

Besides, he hadn't done anything wrong. He couldn't *make* himself love her. "Breakfast sounds great," she mumbled.

On the pretext of adjusting her clothes, she let go of his hand as soon as possible and called her dog. Simba had disappeared behind a rocky outcropping, which didn't alarm her until he didn't come as he normally would.

Turning, she shaded her eyes against the sunlight, watching for any sign of him. "Simba!" she yelled again, putting more authority in her voice.

Finally, he came trotting into sight. But he had something soggy and hairy in his mouth. Nancy wrinkled her nose in distaste as he dropped it at her feet, proudly wagging his tail.

"What the heck is *that*, Simba?" Assuming it was the remains of some dead animal she didn't care to investigate, she grasped his collar to drag him away.

But then Keith, a shocked expression on his face, bent to retrieve what Simba had found.

"What are you doing?" she cried, backing away.

"This is the wig," he said as he picked up the dripping mess. "Oh, my God! This is the wig!"

28

After his two great finds—the letters and the wig that'd been thrown out to sea—the next few days seemed entirely anticlimactic to Keith. Nothing noticeable had happened with his mother's case. Chief Underwood told him she was still digging and sent the wig to the lab that had the single fiber from the tub. Pippa slowly but surely put the house back together while he continued to run his business long-distance. And Nancy hung out with him whenever she wasn't working. She was the bright spot of every day, and even stayed with him at night. But she seemed…guarded again, ever since that morning on the beach, and he could understand why. He wished he *could* fall in love with her. He didn't want to prove Maisey right—that he should've kept away from her. But, like his mother, he seemed to be fundamentally flawed. He and Josephine had been blessed with the ability to attract just about anyone who caught their interest, and yet they couldn't fulfill their partners emotionally, which made their good looks and whatever else drew people to them more of a curse than a blessing.

Although he checked in with Chief Underwood daily, it wasn't until Friday afternoon, when he was approving payroll for his own business as well as his mother's employees, that she called with any news.

"Have they examined the wig fibers?" he asked first thing.

"They have—with a microspectrophotometer, which can discern the seven thousand commercial dyes used in the United States."

He put down his pen. "And?"

"The fiber found in the tub was from the wig you gave me. Both were dyed the same color and to the same industry standard. They were even from the same dye lot."

"So that's a perfect match."

"Yes."

He slowly let his breath go. "Now we just need to connect that wig with whoever tossed it in the ocean."

"That would be a nice touch, but it's no longer essential."

At this, he shoved his chair away from the desk so he could get up and move. He could hear a note of triumph in her voice. "What does that mean? Don't tell me...you've got her."

"I do, Keith. Lana Pointer confessed. Can you believe it? It's official. I wanted to call you first thing."

"So she *did* come to the States."

"Yup. And Marliss confirms it."

"How can *Marliss* confirm it?"

"She brought her daughter with her."

"Lana brought her daughter to a *murder*? That's sick!"

"She claims she wasn't planning on hurting anyone. She merely wanted to confront your mother, to finally have it out with her. Also, Hugh had given your mother some money that Lana felt Josephine should repay."

Keith thought that could be true; Hugh had told him he'd tried to help Josephine financially. "Is that how she found out?"

"Yes. She discovered he'd been sending money to your mother—quite a bit. She wanted to get it back and tell Josephine not to contact Hugh again."

"I still don't understand why Marliss didn't stay with her friends from school and finish the trip," Keith said. "That's what I would've done—what most teenagers would do."

"She refused to continue the tour without Lana. Apparently, they're very close. And she's so spoiled. God forbid they ever say no to that child. I could tell just by talking to her."

"If Lana *was* planning a murder, that must've been damn inconvenient."

"I don't believe she was, Keith. Or she wouldn't have brought Marliss. I believe her about that. She was pretty convincing, in tears and all of that."

He got up and started across the room, doubling back when he reached the far wall. "How did the confrontation and a demand for repayment turn into murder, then? There didn't appear to be any type of altercation in the bathroom…"

"I'm getting there. They landed in Washington, DC, the Friday before your mother was murdered and rented a car, which they drove to Charleston. Once there, Lana got a motel room, left Marliss at seven to order room service and watch a movie and hurried to catch the last ferry of the day to Fairham. Lana claims that when she first got to the house, there was a car in the drive. So she waited until whoever was inside had left."

"Rocki."

"Judging from the description of the vehicle, it was the rental your sister was driving."

"And that's something only the killer would know."

"Yes. I'm telling you, we've got her."

"Then what happened?"

"She knocked and your mother came to the door and let her in. That's why there was no forced entry. But she admitted that Hugh used the spare key when they returned on Wednesday. He knew all about it."

As Keith had thought... "I can't imagine my mother was pleased to see her."

"No. Josephine was in a bad mood. She'd already had an argument with Landon, and then Rocki. And when Lana demanded the money, your mother told her she didn't have to pay it back, that Hugh loved her and *wanted* to help her. Then she proved it by showing Lana the flowers he'd sent."

"And that's what pushed Lana over the edge."

"That's what did it. Your mother threw her out, but she didn't leave the island."

"She couldn't. Not until morning."

"Right. So she drove around, waiting and steaming for hours over her husband's infidelity before she went back."

"How'd she get in the second time? I can't imagine Hugh told Lana about the spare until they needed to use it after the murder, and I doubt my mother would've answered the door again."

"Lana claims it was unlocked."

"That seems careless."

"I'm sure your mother was quite upset, probably wasn't thinking straight, and she'd gotten rid of Lana. She must've believed that was the end of it. Anyway, Lana let herself in, quietly climbed the stairs, entered your mother's bedroom and, when she didn't see her, checked the bath."

"That's where she was."

"Sleeping in the tub."

"Which made killing her easy."

"Yes. Lana took a pillow off the bed and used it to suffocate her."

"Lana's sixtysomething years old," Keith said. "Would she be strong enough to do that?"

"Standing above her, using her weight to bear down? Absolutely. She said the bottle of sleeping pills was on the counter. She was convinced Josephine had taken one, because she was so groggy she couldn't even put up much of a fight."

"And that's what gave her the idea of staging the scene."

"Yes. She got a bottle of wine and a glass from the kitchen, to make it look as if Josephine had also been drinking. Then she flushed all of the pills down the toilet and dropped the bottle on the floor as if it had been knocked over."

"Where did she go after?"

"She slept in the car near the lighthouse and returned to Charleston on the first ferry."

"Marliss confirms that?"

"Marliss claims she doesn't know when her mother got back, but Lana was there when she woke up around noon."

"Did Lana have her phone? Did she use it that night—maybe to check in with Marliss?"

"She had it with her, but they'd been traveling so much and she was so angry and eager to confront Josephine, she hadn't remembered to charge it. The battery was dead. She couldn't call anyone, and no one could call her."

Keith scowled as he gazed out at the ocean, which was roiling with the promise of another storm. "Did Hugh know she was coming here? Maybe she did know about the spare key. Maybe he put her up to the murder."

"No, I doubt it. He's heartbroken. This means he'll lose both women."

"Despite his best efforts to save Lana. Did he admit to coming here and using that alias at the Drift Inn?"

"He did. He said when Lana returned to the motel, she sent Marliss to the front desk to ask where the ice machine was and phoned him to say, quite calmly, that it was over between him and Josephine *for good*. When he realized she was in the States and not Europe, he started to really question her, and that's when she broke down, began to cry and told him what she'd done."

"At which point, he caught the first flight out of Australia to help her cover it up."

"Yes, he admits to that."

Keith shoved his hands in his pockets. "Will he be prosecuted?"

"No. He didn't actually do anything, not that would warrant extradition. Once he arrived at Coldiron House, he found it wasn't empty, as he'd expected, and he took off. I doubt we can get Australia to bother going after him for that."

The wind lashed the trees outside. "Is it going to be a problem that *she* lives in Australia?"

"No. Murder is different."

"Wow." Keith couldn't believe it. His mother's murder was solved; he finally had resolution—something he hadn't been sure he'd ever get. But he still had questions. "Why was Lana down by the highway the night Hugh broke in?"

"She was supposed to be his lookout. Was supposed to call him if anyone came."

"Then why did she flag down Marcus? Hugh was there to *help* her."

"Sounds illogical, I know, but she blamed him for what she'd done, and I guess part of her wanted to see him punished for all the pain he'd caused her."

"She could've called the police herself."

"She didn't dare go that far. She thought if he was caught breaking in, the investigation would take off from there and would focus on him, not her."

"It's too bad for everyone that Lana found out about Mom. But I guess it was inevitable. Pippa told me that the affair lasted for at least fifteen years. That wasn't a quick fling. That's love, and the emotional attachment would hurt more than anything else."

"One of the reasons she wanted to strike back at him, no doubt."

Keith returned to his chair. "So you're satisfied?"

"I'd be happier if we could put that wig in her possession, but…she claims she never wore one."

"Because that would show premeditation, and would carry a stiffer sentence."

"I'm still doing what I can, checking all the shops near Perth, where they lived, and along her travels to see if she bought one. But even if we can't prove pre-meditation, she's going away for a *long* time."

And since she was sixtysomething, maybe a long time would be forever. Maybe he didn't need to worry about it.

A sense of relief swept through Keith. It was over. Rocki, who'd been traumatized by the fear that she or Landon would be charged with Josephine's murder, would be able to relax and focus on mending her marriage—or leaving Landon. They could go ahead and bury Josephine, knowing that the person who'd killed her would be punished. And Keith could try to save Coldiron House and set his mother's finances in order, then go back to California to continue building the life and business he'd started there. His employees were getting restless, wondering when things would return to normal.

Now *everyone* could get on with their lives.

"Keith?"

He realized that he was still on the phone with Chief Underwood. "Yes?"

"Are you happy about all this?"

"Completely." He thanked her. Then he hung up to call Rocki. He figured she deserved to hear the news first.

When Nancy saw Keith's number on her cell phone, she didn't pick up. They'd spent a lot of evenings together this week, and always had a wonderful time. But she had a date with someone else tonight—and she knew, whether Keith loved her or not, he wouldn't like that.

He shouldn't have any say, she told herself. And she

wasn't going to cancel at the last minute. So, deciding she'd call him in the morning, she let the call transfer to voice mail. It wasn't as if she'd be standing him up. She'd told him about this date. It'd been a few days since she'd mentioned it, but whenever she did, he'd quickly gloss over it as if he didn't want to hear.

Once she listened to his voice mail, however, she couldn't resist calling him back immediately. His mother's murder had been solved. He and his sisters could have Josephine's funeral and bury her in the family cemetery.

Nancy was *so* relieved for Rocki—and for Maisey and Keith. But she was also a little anxious. Soon Keith wouldn't have any reason to stay on Fairham. Then he'd be gone again—back to LA, where he'd continue to see Dahlia or some other woman. She was going to be so lonely when that happened. She'd allowed herself to get just as involved with him as she'd been before.

Problem was…she couldn't stop loving him. Lord knew she'd tried.

"There you are," he said when he picked up. "Did you get my message?"

"I did. Congratulations! That's great news."

"Let's go celebrate. I'll take you wherever you'd like to go. Should we get off the island, drive over to Charleston?"

She sank onto her couch. "I can't go out with you tonight, but we could do that tomorrow, if you want."

He hesitated. "What's wrong with tonight?"

"I'm not available. I have a date, remember?"

"You're going out with someone else?"

She inhaled a deep breath. "I'm afraid so. I told you about this, remember?"

"I do now. But… I guess I put it out of my mind, figured you'd wait until I left to see other guys. I mean, won't there be plenty of time for that later?"

"I'm sure there'll be lots of time, but I accepted this date before we…we started sleeping together regularly—" how else could she refer to their relationship since that was all they had? "—so I didn't feel it'd be very nice to cancel." Especially for a guy who couldn't love her back. She shouldn't be seeing Keith at all, let alone sleeping with him every night.

"That sucks," he said.

She smiled at his sulky tone. "I'm sorry. I didn't plan to ruin your Friday night."

"I know that. I'm just saying…it sucks," he repeated. "I'd like to see you."

"Tomorrow, okay?" There wasn't any point in staying on the phone. She'd been struggling to drum up enthusiasm for this evening. She didn't want to regret that she couldn't be with Keith any more than she already did. "I'd better go. I have to meet him."

"What're you wearing?" he asked.

"I haven't decided yet," she replied, but that wasn't strictly true. She was fairly certain she'd wear her gray slacks from White House Black Market with a white blouse and a black, jacket-like sweater she'd purchased at Banana Republic.

"The dress you wore for that other guy?" he guessed.

"No. This isn't quite as formal."

"Where are you going?"

She rubbed her forehead as she spoke. "A Mexican place."

"Sounds good."

"I hope it will be. He says it's the best one in Charleston."

"Does he now?"

She said nothing.

"Did you ever take back that lingerie?" he asked.

"I haven't had a chance."

"So it's still at the house."

"I'm not going to sleep with him, Keith. If that's what you're worried about. This is a first date."

"I'm not worried. I just… I don't know. It feels weird to think of you with someone else."

"I'm sorry. I've got to go."

"Fine. I don't want to hold you up."

"Thanks."

She was about to disconnect when he said, "Seriously? Are you *really* going out with him instead of me?"

"I am," she said. "But I hope you'll enjoy your night. I'm very excited about your news."

"Will you call me later, when you get home?"

"Um… I'm not sure. It might be late."

"Mexican food doesn't take that long."

"I don't want my feelings for you to get in the way of being open to other people, Keith. You can understand why."

"Right. Of course. Because *I* can't deliver."

"Except in bed." She thought that little joke would lighten the conversation, remind him of why he wanted to be with her in the first place, but he didn't laugh.

"Thanks," he said with a touch of sarcasm. Then he was gone.

Nancy released her breath as she pushed the end button. It was almost impossible to keep from calling him back. But she had no intention of being unfair to the guy who was taking her out. He'd asked in good faith, and she was going to respond in good faith.

"It'll be fun," she told her reflection as she started to get ready, but she wasn't convinced she could enjoy anything when she really wanted to be with Keith.

Rocki was sitting at the kitchen table when Landon got home from work. The kids were both out—one at a school dance and the other at a movie. He walked in, took one look at her and came closer, wearing an expression of concern. "What is it?"

She shook her head because she didn't trust her voice. She'd hung up with Keith fifteen minutes ago, but she still hadn't processed the tremendous relief her brother's words had brought. She cleared her throat to steady her voice. "They found Josephine's killer."

She hadn't been able to call Josephine "Mom" since she'd learned of the affair. Somehow, reverting to Gretchen as Mom made it easier to cope with the betrayal.

He pulled out the chair across the table from her and sat down. "Who did it?"

"Lana Pointer, Hugh's wife."

"I thought she was in Europe."

"Apparently not. Chief Underwood traced her movements to Charleston, and then to Fairham. Anyway, she's confessed."

"So you're no longer a suspect. Nothing's going to happen to you."

"No. Thanks to Keith. If he hadn't found those letters and swung the investigation back in that direction, who knows what might've happened?"

"That's fantastic!" For the first time in probably two weeks, his face relaxed into the smile she'd always loved. "I've been so worried, felt so terrible."

She was tempted to tell him he *should* feel terrible. But the bitterness and anger that welled up, sometimes when she least expected it, wasn't constructive. Since the police search, he'd been working long hours—dawn until well after dark. When he did come home, he'd drop onto the couch for a few hours of sleep, then get up the next morning and start the whole process all over again.

But he'd *always* worked hard to support them. Rocki chose to focus on that, to feel a little gratitude for the good in him. He'd done so many things right in their marriage. Other than that one indiscretion with Josephine, he'd been a sensitive lover, a supportive husband, a devoted father. Was it fair to judge him, and to throw away so many years of marriage, because of one selfish and stupid act?

She didn't know the answer to that question. He'd hurt her deeply. But if she left him, if she broke up her family, would anyone be better off?

She didn't want to let Josephine destroy all the happiness she'd known in her life, most of which was connected to Landon. She just wasn't sure she was capable of forgiving something that intimate, that…painful.

"It's a relief," she said simply. She had to overcome the inclination to place blame. He felt bad enough. He was beginning to lose weight, quite a bit of it, and that concerned her, even though she hadn't mentioned it to him.

"Do you need any help around here?" he asked.

She knew he hadn't eaten dinner. She'd been saving it for him since six; it was now after nine. "No. Everything's handled. I'll warm up your dinner so you can eat."

She put a big bowl of beef Stroganoff in front of him. But he took only a few bites before he thanked her politely, cleaned up his own dishes and crashed on the couch.

29

Nancy had expected her date to be a disaster. She'd thought she'd be able to muddle through the evening, but had no real hopes beyond that. If she wanted more than a week or two of happiness whenever she saw Keith, she had to take the painful first step of meeting someone else. Keith had talked about having her fly to LA to visit him once he returned, so he was acting as if he assumed their relationship would continue. But there was no sense of permanence in the way he spoke about her—about *them*—and that sometimes left her with an odd, hollow feeling. It meant settling for so much less than she really wanted. She figured it'd be different if she were still in her twenties. A decade ago she could afford to take a few wrong turns, give him more time, hope his feelings might grow stronger. But she was thirty-five and ready to start a family. She deserved more than to spend her life loving someone who couldn't love her back.

So she'd gone into the evening with a "grin and bear it" attitude, and was completely surprised that the date wasn't bad at all. Warren Castillo, a divorced pharmacist from Charleston with two children, eight and ten, turned out to be funny as well as nice. She liked him.

There were even a few moments when she *almost* forgot about Keith and the fact that she could've spent the evening with him instead.

By the time they'd finished eating and Warren walked her out to her car, she was more encouraged than she'd been in a long while—so encouraged that she accepted his invitation to see a movie the following weekend.

Since she had to catch the eight o'clock ferry, or stay the night in Charleston, it wasn't late when she got home. She could've hurried over to Coldiron House. Keith probably expected it. But if she was going to give Warren, or any other man, a chance, she needed to quit wasting her time with Keith. The more she was with him, the more she *wanted* to be with him. That hardly helped in her quest to meet someone else.

She was on the dating site, catching up on all the messages she'd neglected, when she received a text from him.

Hey, you home?

Nancy experienced the same pull she always felt when she heard from him. She suddenly missed him, even though she'd been feeling so hopeful and strong and determined just a moment before. She told herself she shouldn't respond, but cutting him off abruptly seemed rather…unkind after their closeness over the past couple of weeks. So she texted him back.

Yeah.

How was it?

Fun.

What'd you do?

Just had dinner.

Do you think you'll go out with him again?

We're seeing a movie together next weekend.

Nice.

Without any context or body language, she couldn't tell if he was being facetious. But, considering how he'd acted before, she guessed he was. So she decided to leave it there and put down her phone.

Fifteen minutes later, he called.

By then the afterglow of her date had worn off, and forcing herself to stay away from Keith was making her downright miserable. "Hello?"

"What are you doing?"

Reluctant to say she was on the dating site, she told him she was watching TV. She had turned it on; she just wasn't paying any attention to it. "What about you?"

"Maisey, Rocki and I have been planning the funeral. We're going to have it on Thursday."

"In Charleston?" There were no mortuaries on Fairham so that was almost a given.

"Yeah. At two. Can you make it? If not, we can move it."

"No. There's no need for that. Marlene will trade days with me again. I can make it."

"If she wants to come, too, she can close the shop."

"I'll let her know."

"Good."

"Can you text me the address?"

"Sure. Or you can get it while you're here. You're coming over tonight, aren't you?"

She got up to pace her living room. Simba seemed to intuit her anxiety, because he got to his feet and watched her, wagging his tail whenever she looked at him—as if in encouragement.

"No," she said.

There was a long silence. Then he said, "Are you kidding?"

"I'm afraid not."

"Why won't you come over?"

Because she had to have more self-respect. She shouldn't have continued seeing him after that morning on the beach, when he'd admitted he didn't love her. Everything since then had been a sellout, and that was why continuing the relationship, at least on a romantic level, made her feel so…cheap. "I can't."

"Tomorrow then?"

She squeezed her eyes shut. If she left it open-ended, allowed the possibility to exist, she'd give in—if not tomorrow, then the next day or the day after. "No. I won't be returning, Keith. Not the way I've been doing since you came home."

He lowered his voice as he said, "You can see this other guy after I'm gone, Nance."

She thought about that, saw the practicality behind it. Why not take advantage of the time they had? That was how she'd been thinking the past several days, why she'd allowed herself to succumb to the urge that kept driving her back. But she had to take control of her own destiny even if that was painful. Anything less damaged her self-esteem. "For my own sake, it's important I do it now, while I still have a choice."

There was another long pause. Then he said, "Fuck," and disconnected.

The next several days were some of the worst Keith could remember. Although he was relieved to hear that Lana was being extradited from Australia, he couldn't stop thinking about Nancy. He hoped she'd give in and see him again before he had to leave. He knew she loved him—she'd said as much. But while he delved into his mother's finances in an attempt to save what he could, Nancy remained resolute. Over the next four days, she didn't call him once, and she didn't return any of his calls, either.

It wasn't until he left a message saying he needed to speak to her about Love's in Bloom that he heard back. Selling the business to someone else, someone who could purchase it outright, would've made what he was trying to do much easier; bailing out his mother's estate was taking all his available cash and then some, meaning he'd have significant debt. And yet he *wanted* Nancy to have the store. But when he made an appointment for Wednesday to talk about it with her, she wouldn't even meet him at the house. She suggested they get together at the store instead, and when he arrived, she wouldn't really look at him. She glanced away as soon as he began to search her face for any of the tenderness and concern that had been there before.

Keith tried to make the purchase contract as favorable to her as he could. He hadn't made a very positive impact on her life, and figured he owed her that much.

But she wouldn't allow him to go too far. She insisted on paying a higher price than he told her he'd accept, and although he'd offered to let her go three years without making her first payment, she'd insisted that payments would start as soon as they signed the contract.

"I can make this work," she said when they finally came to an agreement on all the terms.

"I know you can."

Her eyes met his without shifting away. "I'm grateful to you. I realize you've made a lot of concessions here. Another owner probably wouldn't have given me this opportunity. I want you to know how much I appreciate it."

He took her hand and was gratified when she didn't pull away. "I care about you, Nancy. I want you to have whatever you want, to be happy."

"I believe that."

"If you get into trouble on the payments, don't worry. We'll work out a new schedule, if necessary. You're taking on a lot. I'd hate for it to be too much."

"I've done my homework. If the store produces the way it has in the past two years, I'll be fine. And I'm planning to *increase* sales, not go the other way."

"You'll do great."

She stepped closer. "What's going to happen to Cold-iron House?"

"We'll keep it in the family."

"But leave it empty?"

"Rocki will probably move here with the two younger kids."

"Without Landon?"

"It doesn't sound like they're going to make it."

Because she'd always liked Landon, she found that disappointing. "I'm sorry to hear it."

"So am I. I think he truly hates himself for what he's done, but…it would be a difficult thing to overcome, so I can't blame Rocki if she chooses not to try."

"No, of course not. No one could blame her."

"I've managed to save almost everything else," he said. "Once I'm in California and back at work, I should be able to pay off the loan my mother took out on the bungalows. Eventually, everyone will get the inheritance they deserve."

She let her fingers curl through his. He liked that, but it was hard not to pull her even closer, to kiss her. He wanted that, wanted to feel her against him, as passionate as she'd always been.

"That's really something, Keith," she said. "Did you ever dream that *you'd* be the one to save the whole Coldiron estate? That your sisters would only inherit because of you?"

He shook his head. "Never."

"You've made good. You should be proud of yourself."

She'd always been in his corner—no matter what. "Thanks for sticking by me when I had no one else, Nance. Somehow you managed to believe in me, even when I was at my worst."

"And I was right about you," she said, releasing his hand. "I knew the great things you were capable of."

There was nothing left to say, but Keith hated to leave. The fact that he didn't feel free to touch Nancy the way he'd been touching her until recently, to kiss her and hold her, just felt…wrong. "Okay. I guess I'll see you at the funeral tomorrow?"

"I'll be there."

He turned to go, then hesitated at the door. "Did you ever take back that lingerie?"

She smiled when he looked over his shoulder at her, but it was the firm kind of smile that let him know she wouldn't be changing her mind. This time, her refusal was permanent. Unless he could give her more, she didn't want anything.

"You're going to make some man very happy someday," he told her.

"If not, I'll make myself happy," she said and that was when he realized he wasn't the only one who'd changed. These days Nancy knew who she was and what she wanted; she'd gained the confidence she'd lacked when he was with her before.

As much as his mother's funeral signaled the end of what'd happened on Fairham, Keith dreaded the service. Even as he dressed for it in an expensive black suit he'd purchased in Charleston, he knew the next few hours would be painful. Beyond the fact that he and his siblings were saying a permanent goodbye to their mother and would be coping with all the attendant emotions, Hugh Pointer had left Keith a message saying he'd be there to pay his respects.

Fortunately, he wouldn't be bringing his wife. Lana was already in the process of being extradited. Hugh had even more to grieve than Keith did—he'd lost his wife *and* his lover. But Hugh's presence would be uncomfortable even without Lana. It bothered Keith that he'd returned to the island in an attempt to cover up his wife's crime. That proved he placed Lana above Josephine. Although Keith could understand why he'd try to protect the mother of his children, especially once Josephine was gone, Keith couldn't help feeling defensive of his own mother, who'd died at the hands of Hugh's jealous wife.

As if having Hugh there wasn't bad enough, Rocki and her family were not only in town, they were getting ready for the funeral in the other wing. Keith couldn't imagine how heartbreaking it would be for her to stand over their mother's casket with Landon by her side, knowing he'd slept with Josephine less than two months ago. Keith considered it a miracle that they'd shown up, but she'd confided in him that she'd come for the kids' sake. Even Brooklyn had left college to be there. Regardless of how it had happened, they'd lost a grandmother. She felt she should give them the opportunity to say goodbye.

Then there was Nancy. Keith could easily guess how seeing her again would make him feel. He'd felt like shit when he saw her yesterday.

Bottom line, he needed to get back to California and get on with his life. His escape from Fairham was what had rescued him before; he assumed it would do the same now. The debt he'd created in order to save his mother's estate would mean he'd have to work extra hard and extra smart, probably for several years, but he didn't mind. He was actually looking forward to the challenge. It would keep him absorbed, interested in his work, actively pushing forward every day instead of sliding back and allowing himself to crave cocaine or Nancy or Fairham or anything else.

His phone buzzed, signaling a new text. He finished putting on his cuff links before picking it up.

The message came from Dahlia, who was far more determined and resilient in her pursuit of him than he'd expected.

Hey, gorgeous. You home yet?

No, he wrote back, but I'll be there on Tuesday.

Will you call me as soon as you get in? I miss you.

He felt resistant to the idea of seeing her again, but he attributed that to everything he was going through. She was a beautiful woman. Nice, too. There was no reason he shouldn't give her another chance.

Sure. See you soon.

30

Rocki felt as if she'd been moving through a dream world. Had she been told a few months ago that Landon would *ever* have an affair, she would've scoffed. Cheating on her with her own mother was…beyond belief. And yet the truth, the reality of what he'd done, wouldn't retreat. The knowledge lurked in the corners of her mind, hovered there, waiting to come roaring back just when it began to feel as though their lives could or should return to normal.

Her kids, especially Brooklyn, knew *something* was wrong. Fortunately, they were attributing most of her distress to the loss of Josephine. She'd been able to smooth everything over by claiming their marital problems revolved around the lie Landon had first told her—that he'd gone to Fairham while he was supposed to be in Las Vegas to borrow money from her mother without including her in the decision. Eventually she'd used the same lie to explain why the police had searched their house. Brooklyn was old enough to understand that the police wouldn't search unless there was more of a connection than simply being related—which had pacified the younger kids—allowing Rocki to keep the worst of Landon's actions to herself. The problem was, maintaining her silence made what he'd done harder to expel from her own soul. The betrayal just sat there—and festered.

Landon had offered to move out. When, after several more days, she couldn't allow him to return to her bed, he'd said he felt he should go. He couldn't bear the pain of seeing what he'd done to her in her eyes every time she looked at him.

But the thought of letting him leave hurt, too. She wasn't sure what to do. She was in her early forties, with three children who were quickly growing up. She'd never expected to be alone, couldn't imagine being divorced.

Was she wrong for hanging on? Was she only dragging them through more emotional turmoil?

Maybe she should let go. But that would break up their family—and she feared she'd regret that more than anything.

He'd suggested counseling. Would that help?

She didn't realize she'd stopped getting ready for the funeral, that she was simply staring at herself in the mirror, until Landon came up behind her.

"Are you going to be okay?"

She shifted her gaze to meet his eyes. "I don't know."

"We shouldn't be here," he said. "We could've told the kids something. That we didn't have the money. That they couldn't miss school. As far as I'm concerned, this is rubbing salt in the wound."

Since she'd learned about the affair, she'd only let him see her fully clothed. She was standing there, in front of the bathroom mirror, in a lacy bra and panty set, but would've covered up now if her robe had been handy. He'd left her room several minutes ago to make sure the kids had everything they needed to get ready, and she hadn't expected him to come back. The robe she'd been using was on the bed. She'd bought the lingerie for herself just yesterday because she'd needed something to make her feel sexy again after feeling so... overlooked and unappreciated. "You may be right," she said. "But we're here now. I'd like to get through it—for Maisey's and Keith's sake, if not for any other reason."

"It's only making you hate me more. I can feel it."

"I wish I *could* hate you," she said. "But I'll get there. I'm trying."

He closed his eyes, and when he opened them again, she saw the torment there. "I've told you how sorry I am. I tell you every day."

"If you'd cheated with *anyone else*, maybe I could forgive you."

His Adam's apple moved as he swallowed. "Right. I understand. And I don't blame you."

He hung his head as he turned to go, but in that instant, Rocki missed his hands on her body more than she'd missed anything else in her life. She turned, too, and caught his arm.

He seemed startled that she'd stopped him. A look of uncertainty crossed his face—one that suggested he was afraid to hope her actions really meant anything.

He was hurting as badly as she was. She'd understood that for several days. They were *both* in hell. And only she possessed the power to let them out.

But could she do it? Could she forgive something so heinous? Would forgiveness be enough? Or would the insecurities and fear this had caused destroy their marriage in spite of any attempt she made to save it?

They stared at each other for several long seconds.

Then his hand moved to her waist, and she could feel, even though he was tentative about touching her, that he was trembling. "I can't bear the thought of living without you," he said, his voice choked with emotion. "I've always planned on spending the rest of my life with you."

When she didn't withdraw, as she had at every other attempt he'd made to be tender with her, he rested his forehead against hers. "If you leave me, at least know that this is *all* on me. You never did anything wrong, never left me wanting, never looked unappealing to me or seemed boring. You've been the best wife any man could ever have. I just…got frustrated and dissatisfied with other parts of my life—with our constant financial problems. And I let myself get distracted, took you for granted. It's that simple."

"Simple?" she repeated. None of it seemed simple to her.

"My fault," he clarified. "*All* my fault. I was drunk that night, which didn't help. But please don't ever wonder if you somehow fell short and that's what caused me to…to screw up. Because that's not the case. You didn't deserve what I did. It was me."

But…most people could make a mistake, get tripped up by the wrong emotions or become confused about what they really wanted, couldn't they? What if *she'd* been the one? What if she'd met someone who dazzled her, caused her to forget everyday problems or created just enough of an ego trip to make her lose track of what was truly important? How would she want *him* to react?

He was accepting all the blame. Even in his mind, she would be justified to cut him out of her life.

But wouldn't a little forgiveness and mercy make them *both* happier?

"What would you do if it were me?" she whispered. "Is there someone else you'd like to sleep with?"

He sounded so hopeful she was almost tempted to laugh. "Maybe," she lied.

"Fine. Sleep with two or three guys. Do whatever makes you feel better. I'll take you back afterward. I'll take you back no matter what."

Of the two of them, he'd always been the more forgiving. There'd never been any big indiscretions like this, but he'd given her the benefit of the doubt on so many little things, had always been patient and kind even when she didn't deserve it. She supposed that was why she believed him.

Smiling, she wiped the tears that were glistening on his eyelashes. Then she slipped her arms around his neck and felt a huge and terrible weight disappear from her heart as they broke down and sobbed together. What he'd done was terrible. But he was more than that one mistake. Hadn't he proved who he really was during all the years they'd known each other?

Besides, she loved him—in spite of everything.

As Landon waited for his family to finish getting ready for the funeral, he wished he could load them all in the car and drive them straight back to the airport. He didn't want to attend Josephine's funeral; he couldn't think of her without feeling ill. He hated knowing how badly he'd hurt Rocki and vowed that he was going to make it up to her. They just had to get through this trip to Fairham. Then maybe they could put Josephine behind them and begin to rebuild their relationship.

Before that could happen, however, he needed to apologize to the other people in his life. Maisey's family had to feel even angrier toward him.

As soon as Keith descended the stairs, Landon asked if he could have a minute. At first, Keith looked as if he'd rather beg off, which would be understandable. They already had too much going on today. But to Landon's relief, he nodded and followed Landon into the drawing room, where he could have the privacy to apologize.

Landon expected Keith to give him hell. But that didn't happen. Keith listened quietly. Then he said, "With the mistakes I've made, I can't condemn anyone else. If you two can patch this up and stay together, I'll be glad. And I think Maisey feels the same."

"Really?" Landon's shock must've been evident in his voice, because Keith chuckled as he gave him an embrace that included a solid thump on the back.

"Just don't ever do anything like that in the future," he warned.

"I won't. I still can't explain how I did it the first time."

"Sometimes in life we make a wrong turn. Doesn't mean we can't find our way back."

That was such a generous response that Landon didn't know how to thank him. "I can't... I can't begin to tell you how much that means to me. I don't deserve your forgiveness. But I'm grateful for it. I'll take better care of Rocki. I swear it."

"I know you will," he said. "I'm heading out. I'll see you at the funeral home."

Nancy hung out with Jade around the periphery of the viewing area, as far from the casket as possible. Maisey had done a beautiful job with her mother's makeup, and Josephine's hairdresser had done Josephine's hair. Even in death, Keith's mother looked lovely—although not nearly as lovely as she'd been in life. Part of her appeal had been her unrivaled confidence.

Still, she was beautiful. And yet, when Nancy had gone by to pay her respects, she'd stared down at Keith's mother with a mild sort of aversion. Death, no matter how well packaged, was never an easy thing to face. So, after pausing briefly, she and Jade had slipped away. Now they were just waiting for the service itself—and wishing it was already over. Although she had her sister with her, which helped, Nancy still had a difficult time seeing Keith and not wanting to be with him. She would've given in and gone back to him—had almost done so a thousand times since he'd stopped by the store yesterday—but she now had a clearer understanding of what such a one-sided relationship was doing to her. His inability to love her in return took a small piece of her pride and self-esteem every day. She *couldn't* give in, not if she wanted to be the person she knew she could be. Why devote everything she had to him only to be discarded like an old sweater when he left?

"Don't turn around now, but he's looking over here again."

Her sister had been regaling her with news of Keith's every move—and every glance—since they'd arrived.

"Stop it," Nancy said for the third or fourth time. "It doesn't matter."

"Of course it matters," Jade insisted. "It's so obvious. He loves you. He just doesn't know it yet. And I have half a mind to tell him."

"Don't!" Nancy shook her head. "If he loved me, he'd say so."

Jade grimaced. "I'm not so sure. Since he's never been in love before, he probably figures that sick feeling he gets when he thinks about leaving you behind is indigestion. Men can be stupid that way."

"Keith is anything *but* stupid. Trust me, he knows what he wants, and it isn't me." She'd given him plenty of chances to change his mind.

"If you say so. But I'm not stupid, either. I can tell that dress is driving him wild."

She was wearing her Herve Leger off-the-shoulder bandage dress. And she, too, could tell that Keith liked it. She'd seen the way his eyes had skimmed over her when she first walked in, how they returned to her again and again.

"He can eat his heart out," she said, as if she was that indifferent.

Jade's eyebrows flew up almost to her hairline. "Whoa! You're playing hardball."

"When it comes to Keith, or any other man, I'm done settling. I don't want just a part of him. I'm finally at the point where it's all or nothing."

Before Jade could respond, a distinguished gentleman, his black hair sporting a touch of silver at the temples, walked into the room wearing a tailored black suit. He was with a young woman who had to be six feet tall. The definition in her arms and legs, and the way she carried herself, suggested she was an athlete—maybe a softball player? When the entire room went quiet and everyone turned to stare, Nancy realized this had to be Hugh Pointer and his daughter. She looked just like him.

Curious as to how Keith would react, she quickly

searched for him. His eyes narrowed and his mouth tightened when he saw that his mother's lover had come, but he made his way over and shook Hugh's hand.

Nancy was proud of him for being so gracious. Hard as this was for Keith, she couldn't imagine that coming here could be any easier for Hugh. He had to be blaming himself for Josephine's death and his wife's incarceration. That he'd made the effort to show his face, in spite of how he was likely to be viewed, suggested he'd sincerely cared about Josephine and felt bad about her death, even though he'd admitted to Chief Underwood that he'd tried to cover up his wife's actions.

Hugh seemed somber but friendly as he spoke with Keith. Nancy was too far away to hear what they said. She was more interested in his daughter, anyway. The girl's mother had just been charged with murder, and yet…she didn't appear to be upset.

"What's up with *her*?" Jade asked.

The girl had a strange look on her face, one that made her seem almost…pleased. But she was only eighteen. Nancy didn't really want to catalog her emotions as inappropriate. She lowered her voice. "People react to sadness in various ways."

"You think she's *sad*?" Jade said. "I'm getting the impression she only came here to flip everyone off."

As Nancy started to respond, she heard a gasp and turned to find Rocki nearby, with Landon and the kids. The blood had drained from her face, and she was clutching Landon's arm as if she was staring at a ghost.

"What is it?" Nancy heard Landon ask.

"I've seen her before," Rocki replied.

He seemed as confused as Nancy was. Wasn't Hugh's daughter from Australia? *"Where?"* he pressed.

"On the ferry. She came across with me the night Josephine was killed. Her hair was a lot darker, but I definitely remember her. I remember thinking how tall and pretty she was."

Landon leaned closer. "Did you say her *hair* was a lot darker?"

"Oh, my God!" Rocki murmured, and a chill shivered down Nancy's spine as she watched Landon move to the edge of the room and eventually pull Chief Underwood to one side.

31

Keith paced in the drawing room of Coldiron House while Chief Underwood sat on the couch, watching him. It'd been four days since they'd buried Josephine beneath the moss-draped tree in the family cemetery— long enough for the police chief to find a clerk in a wig shop in Charleston who remembered Marliss Pointer. Although they had the connection they'd been missing, Keith was still reeling at the knowledge that his mother had been killed by an eighteen-year-old girl. "But why would Marliss attend the funeral?" he asked. If she hadn't done that, she probably wouldn't have been caught…

"She was sure she'd won," Chief Underwood explained. "It was her way of taunting us, taunting *you* and your sisters, with the fact that she got the last laugh, that she'd taken something precious from you, too."

He'd been meeting with various lenders on his mother's properties, so he was wearing a business suit. He'd loosened his tie on the ferry, but the damn thing still felt like it was choking him. Taking it off, he tossed it onto the closest chair. "I get that part. She didn't know we'd found the wig, didn't even know she'd left behind that fiber. She felt she was above suspicion, as if she was so young we'd never dream she could be responsible."

"Exactly. She thought there was nothing to tie her to the crime," Underwood added. "She enjoyed parading through the funeral service with that smug expression on her face."

"Okay, but what I don't understand is why Hugh would agree to bring her."

"Why wouldn't he?" Underwood asked. "If she wanted to come? He thought she felt bad about what her mother had done. He didn't know *she* was the one who killed Josephine. Lana had taken the blame with him, too."

"But her mother was going to prison because of her! Didn't she feel any sadness or remorse?"

"She didn't blame herself for what was happening to her mother. She blamed Hugh for having the affair in the first place. She was proud that she stood up for her mother and did something about it."

"That's twisted."

"Yes, but that's the mind of a murderer. She's been seriously troubled for years, Keith. The Pointers have had her in and out of various psychiatric centers, spent a fortune on shrinks and medication. She's set fire to their house on three different occasions, once while they were sleeping!"

He rested his arm on the fireplace mantel. "Is she crazy?"

Chief Underwood frowned as she considered the question. "Not crazy, no. Just spoiled, willful, vengeful and extremely narcissistic. With her track record, Hugh probably didn't dare leave her behind. He told me he thought she'd be better off with him, in the States, where he could at least take her to visit her mother. He was planning to keep her here in South Carolina until she could adjust to what's happened."

"He never considered that it might have been her?"

"Why would he, when his wife was claiming she did it—and she had every reason to?"

"True…" Keith used his foot to smooth the thick nap of the carpet. "Her mother should never have let her know about the affair."

"I agree, but Lana probably wasn't thinking clearly herself. As far as she knew, Hugh had never been a man to stray. She was shocked to learn that not only was he having an extramarital affair, he'd been doing so for years. The fact that he *loved* another woman would be the biggest blow. I'm sure she was hurt, maybe so hurt she couldn't hold it in. And she spent a great deal of time with her daughter, who wasn't that great at making friends. I'm guessing she needed her daughter's empathy and support. They probably discussed the problem constantly from the moment she found out, especially when they were in Europe together, and Lana was so worried Hugh would see Josephine during her absence. While they were on their trip, Marliss helped Lana hack into one of his bank accounts she hadn't had access to. They saw that he'd given Josephine even more money than he'd admitted, and that he'd purchased her ticket to Australia."

"When you put it that way, are you sure Lana wasn't a party to the murder?"

"No. I believe she confronted your mother, just like she said, and your mother insisted she leave. Marliss was waiting for that moment and came in after her."

"They didn't see each other?"

"They claim they didn't. Marliss took a cab to the ferry from the Charleston motel and then rode across on foot, being careful not to let her mother, who was in the rental car, catch a glimpse of her."

"Fortunately, Rocki was on that same ferry and saw her at the railing."

"Or Marliss probably would've gotten away with murder," Underwood said, "since she had a mother who was willing to go to prison for her."

Keith rolled up his sleeves, since it was warm in the house. "So when did Lana find out what Marliss had done?"

"Not until Marliss returned to the hotel the next morning."

"It was cold that night—and it had started to storm by morning. Where did she sleep?"

Chief Underwood gestured around them. "Right here in the house. She said she stayed until five or so, then made her way down to the wharf on foot. She knew her mother would be taking the same ferry—again. And again, she was careful not to be seen."

"It's hard to believe her mother could miss her *twice*."

"There was the rainy weather, remember? And she was wearing a costume. She's the one who had on that wig, at least on the first trip—before she tossed it in the ocean."

He followed the chain of events in his mind. "If Lana was trying to take the blame for my mother's death, why didn't she tell you *she* wore the wig? Sure, it goes a long way toward proving premeditation, but why did she leave that detail dangling out there when it could get her daughter caught?"

"For just that reason—*because* it could get her

daughter caught," Underwood replied. "She knew that if she said she wore the wig, we'd want to know where she got it, and we'd double-check and learn it was a lie. It was safer to say the wig had nothing to do with the crime, that she had no idea how a fiber had ended up in the tub or how the wig that fiber came from showed up on the beach. Everything else fit so perfectly, she assumed we'd overlook that, and it certainly seemed to be working."

That day on the beach, when Simba ran back with the wig in his mouth, had been a good one, for more than one reason. But Keith pulled his thoughts away from Nancy and the way they'd made love that morning. "Thank God Simba found it," he said.

She nodded. "Otherwise, all we'd have is Rocki's testimony that she saw Marliss on the ferry—and that's not enough to convict her of murder. We had to place her at the scene. The wig does that."

Keith walked over to join her on the couch. "What I don't understand is why Marliss ever told her mother what she'd done."

"Lana got to the motel first and demanded to know where she'd been, and Marliss was so proud of herself that she confessed. She felt her mother would be glad, maybe even proud of her. She'd gotten rid of her mother's nemesis, once and for all."

Keith shook his head as he imagined how a mother might react to *that* conversation. "I wonder if she did feel a small amount of relief."

"Because someone would go that far to defend her? It probably made her feel loved. And she'd never have to worry about her rival again. But knowing her child was a murderer? I'm sure that made the situation worse rather than better."

"That couldn't be easy to hear. So how did she decide so quickly that she'd take the blame?"

"She probably couldn't bear to tell Hugh that she'd let Marliss get that involved. And she was hoping *no one* would have to take the blame. That's why she called him immediately after. No doubt she was in a panic. He claims he calmed her down, had her send Marliss home and flew here to help clean up, and I've got flight records to prove the travel part. They were hoping to find those letters, if not the wig that'd been thrown into the ocean by Marliss, not that Hugh would know Marliss was the one who did that. If they could destroy any incriminating evidence, they felt they'd be fine. They all had alibis that would've held up without closer inspection."

"But then I got in the way."

"Yes. When they couldn't clean up as they'd hoped, Lana realized something else would have to be done. So she decided to sacrifice herself, which fit with what she'd told Hugh, anyway."

"That's a big sacrifice."

"I get the logic," Underwood said. "Lana told me she's lived sixty-five years. She didn't want her daughter's life to effectively end at eighteen."

"Hugh never knew it was Marliss? You're sure?"

"I'm positive," she replied, "or he wouldn't have brought her to the funeral."

"That makes sense. So where is Marliss now?"

"She's in custody. We went to their hotel in Charleston this morning and arrested her. I would've held her the day of the funeral if I could, but it wasn't until Rocki recognized her that I went back to the wig shops with her picture instead of Lana's. And that was when I found the clerk who identified her."

Keith chuckled without mirth. "Hugh's got to be kicking himself for bringing her to the funeral."

"He's got to be kicking himself for getting involved with your mother in the first place," she responded. "He's lost his lover, his wife, who'll probably leave him, and his daughter. But your mother didn't exactly get off easy. She had a helluva last day."

Keith felt he'd dwelled on that enough. "It's a lot easier to believe that the athletic-looking girl I saw at the funeral overpowered my mother than her smaller, frailer and much older mother."

"I got busy yesterday and forgot to tell you that the toxicology report came back. It shows that Josephine had taken a sleeping pill, so even Lana could have done it." Underwood came to her feet. "So…are you going back to California now that all of this is over?"

"Yeah. I fly out tomorrow."

She scowled as he stood, too. "You're going to leave this beautiful home?"

He'd thought Rocki would move into Coldiron House with her kids, but now that she was staying with Landon, and they were going to work on saving their marriage and their businesses, it'd be empty. "Pippa and Tyrone will take care of it. And I'll visit when I can."

"What about Nancy?"

He tried to pretend he didn't feel a twinge of remorse at the mention of Nancy's name. He missed her already. "What about her?"

"It'd be a mistake to leave her, Keith."

"How do you know?" he asked.

She gave him a confident smile. "Because you love her."

* * *

She owned the flower shop. Nancy stood in the center of Love's in Bloom and twirled around, trying to console herself with the fulfillment of that dream. At least she was moving ahead with her life. She still had her family and her friends. And Simba, of course. Somehow she'd live without Keith—although she couldn't begin to guess how long it would take her heart to stop aching this time. It'd been a long haul five years ago. She hoped, now that she was older and more experienced with love and loss, she could bounce back more quickly. That remained to be seen.

He'd called to say goodbye, asked her to drive him to the airport since they'd returned his rental car when they were still seeing each other, but he had Tyrone to take him. He didn't need her. She told herself she'd be smarter to keep her distance—with her luck she'd break down and cling to him—and, for a change, she listened to her own advice.

The bell rang over the door, and she turned to see Jade. "What are you doing here?"

"I just came over to take a look at your new shop."

"But you've seen it hundreds of times."

"Not since it became yours."

Nancy smiled at her. If there was also a bit of melancholy in that smile, she couldn't help it. "Nice, isn't it?"

"Gorgeous! Classy. It's going to make you a lot of money."

"We'll see. For now, I'm just hoping I can meet my payments."

She held up a white paper sack. "I brought you a doughnut."

"What for?"

"Because," she said, and then she did something very uncharacteristic—she pulled Nancy into a hug. "You're going to be okay," she whispered. "I'm here for you and so is everyone else on Fairham."

The lump that swelled in Nancy's throat almost choked her. She couldn't speak, but Jade didn't seem to mind.

"Call me if you need anything," she said as she drew back.

"Thanks," Nancy murmured, but by then her sister was gone.

Keith loved being back at the helm of his company. He loved being in California, too. "There's no beating LA," he said aloud as he drove to work. It was February, still winter almost everywhere else, and he didn't even need a coat. No dark clouds or rain hung over the horizon, only endless sunshine.

He sang along to Hozier's latest album as he got on the freeway. But a few minutes later, he ran into traffic, which seemed to be snarled for miles and miles, and all of the enthusiasm he'd forced since his return began to wilt as he inched along behind the bumper of the vehicle in front of him. So what if LA was sunny most of the time? There was no smog and very little traffic on Fairham. He could easily get wherever he wanted to go. And Nancy was there…

With a curse, he jerked his mind away from the woman who seemed to consume more and more of his thoughts. He wasn't going to dwell on Nancy. She wanted more than he could give, and if she couldn't be happy with what he had to offer, there was nothing he could do to change that.

He'd moved on fine the last time he'd left Fairham, hadn't he? He'd just do the same thing.

Turning up the music, he sang even louder. Then he used Bluetooth to call Dahlia. Although he'd promised to text or call the minute he got back, he hadn't yet mustered the enthusiasm to talk to her. But he was desperate to distract himself in some way, so he had to override his reluctance to see other women, get swept up in the usual flow. With a little effort, hopefully he could stop craving the woman whose smile felt like sunshine regardless of the weather.

"Hey, gorgeous," Dahlia said.

He grimaced. The breathy quality of her voice seemed so contrived. "Hey."

"You finally home?"

"Yeah. Got back a couple of weeks ago."

"I've been waiting. It's been so long I thought you were never going to call."

The pouting seemed contrived, too. Or was it him? He hadn't been himself lately, hadn't even been working out. Just moving listlessly through each day required all his energy. "I've been busy. But I was thinking we could get together for dinner tonight."

"At your place?"

He knew what would happen if she came over. He almost suggested a restaurant so he wouldn't feel obliged to take things quite that far.

On the other hand, maybe sex with another woman was exactly what he needed... "Sure."

"What time?"

"Eight?"

"See you then," she said, but instead of looking forward to their date, he dreaded the moment she'd knock on his door. And even after she arrived and they'd eaten—and she started removing his clothes, he had to stop her.

He felt no desire for her whatsoever; he just wasn't interested.

After she left, he wanted to call Nancy, but he texted Maisey instead. How's Nancy doing with the flower shop?

His sister didn't respond. It was three hours later on the East Coast. He figured she'd get his message in the morning and he'd hear from her then. A few minutes later, however, his phone pinged.

Keith, it's the middle of the night.

Sorry. I was just worried about her.

You should be sleeping.

He couldn't sleep. Is she getting by?

Who?

Quit playing stupid!

While I appreciate everything you've done, big brother, and I love you dearly, I'm not giving you any information on Nancy.

I didn't ask about Nancy. I asked about the business.

Sure you did. It's only been two weeks. Nothing's changed with the business.

Thanks for nothing, he wrote back and went to bed, but it was several hours before he fell asleep.

"How are things going with that dating site?" Maisey asked.

Nancy glanced up from the "get well soon" arrangement she'd started. She'd told Maisey that as much as she loved working with her, she couldn't pay her to stay on. She was trying to cut costs so she could cover her own salary, the rent and all the rest of the overhead *and* make her first payment to Keith on schedule, which she was determined to do. Although she was trying to maintain the status quo, it was going to be hard enough just to keep Marlene on. But Maisey had insisted on coming in to help, anyway. She said she enjoyed it, needed her "girlfriend" time.

"It's fine," Nancy said.

"Any interesting men on there?"

Nancy thought of the pharmacist she'd gone out with twice. In the beginning, she'd felt optimistic about him. She still liked him, but their relationship hadn't taken off the way she'd hoped. After they went to the movies, he'd asked her out on a third date, but she'd turned him down. She couldn't feel any attraction to him when she was in love with someone else. She'd left her profile up, but she wasn't currently active on the site. "A few."

"No one in particular?" Maisey pressed.

"Not yet. But I have very little time for dating, anyway. If I want to succeed with this shop, I need to stay focused. One slow month could put me under. Heaven forbid I have two in a row."

"You're going to be fine."

"I hope so. But it's February. Thanks to Valentine's Day, February's a good month. What about March?"

"March will be a good month, too."

Nancy wasn't so sure. Josephine had real talent when it came to creating arrangements people wanted. Even after working at Love's in Bloom for seven years, Nancy feared she wouldn't be able to duplicate that "something special" Josephine brought to any endeavor.

Maisey reached across her for some greenery to add to her own arrangement. "So you're not hearing from that lawyer anymore?"

"Tom? No. I broke that off—" she was about to say "when Keith was here," but she didn't want to bring up Maisey's brother "—a while ago."

Maisey made a clicking sound with her tongue. "I'm sorry it didn't work out."

"I'm fine with being alone," she said, but she'd never felt more isolated or bereft in her life. Any moment she wasn't working she spent moping around her house, thinking of Keith. She told herself she should still be dating, searching for a mate if she hoped to have a family. The only way to put an end to the loneliness was to do something about it. But losing Keith a second time had created what felt like a physical ache that'd settled deep in her bones and wouldn't ease up. She wanted to start a family, wanted a baby—but she wanted it to be *his* baby.

On Valentine's Day, she'd sent him a text to say she hoped he was doing well. He'd texted her back immediately to tell her he missed her. He'd even tried to call, but she hadn't picked up. She wasn't going to give in and accept less than she wanted; she'd just wanted him to know that she wished him the best.

"You'll find the right guy eventually," Maisey said.

The bell rang, signaling a customer. Nancy was going to answer, but Maisey beat her to it. She wiped her hands and disappeared out front. A second later, she called back, "Nance? I think this is for you."

Nancy was expecting a delivery of new vases from a manufacturer she'd found online. Although she'd told the driver to come around the back, she figured this must be him, that he hadn't listened—so her jaw dropped when she saw Keith standing in the store holding a dozen long-stemmed red roses he'd obviously purchased somewhere else.

"What are you doing here?" she cried. She'd thought he might return eventually—to see his family and take care of his holdings—but she'd never dreamed she'd see him again so soon.

"I came back for you," he said simply.

She looked at Maisey, whose smile widened slowly. "Did you know about this?" she asked.

"No," she replied, laughing. "But it's about damn time."

"I'm sorry," Keith said, but he wasn't talking to his sister. He was talking to her. "I hope you'll take me back."

Nancy accepted the flowers he thrust at her. "Take you back? What exactly does that mean?"

Keith chuckled softly as he stepped close and pulled her into his arms. "It means I've been miserable since you stopped seeing me. It means I can't get you out of my mind." He pressed his forehead to hers and lowered his voice. "It means I can't live without you, Nance."

Maisey must've taken the flowers, because the next thing Nancy knew, she had her arms around Keith's neck and was kissing him with all the feelings she'd kept bottled up for the past few weeks. "I could kill you for what you've put me through," she whispered when she could speak.

"I'm sorry. But you know me." He offered her a sheepish grin. "I have to do everything the hard way."

She still wasn't sure how this translated to their lives. "So…are you moving home?"

"Yes. I'm moving into Coldiron House, where I belong," he said. "And you're moving there with me."

Nancy's heart nearly stopped as he took a velvet box from his pocket. "Oh, my God," she murmured.

"Will you marry me?"

Inside was the most beautiful ring she'd ever seen. "Are you sure?" She studied him, trying to read the strength of his commitment. "I don't want you to do anything you might later regret."

"After what I've been through the past few weeks without you? I couldn't be *more* sure," he said and slipped the ring on her finger. "Maybe it took me a while to meet you halfway, Nance. But I didn't make this decision lightly."

"What about your business?"

"I can run my business from here, eventually move more of my holdings to the east coast. I'm not going to leave you now."

EPILOGUE

Hugh Pointer sat in his office, staring at his phone. Six months had passed since his daughter was indicted for murder. Sitting through her trial, watching her go to prison, had been excruciating, especially since he blamed himself. If he'd never met Josephine, never fallen in love with her, none of this would have happened. But he couldn't change the past, and who knew what Marliss might've done in the future? She'd never been quite right. As much as it pained him to admit it, that was the truth.

"Are you going to do it?"

He glanced up to see his wife standing at the entrance to the room, watching him. After Marliss was arrested, they'd separated for a few months, but then they'd gotten back together. That was why he hadn't made this call sooner. He'd been determined to put Lana first, to win her back and be the husband she deserved. But the desire to reach out had been there all along. Part of him felt he owed it to Josephine, as well as Keith. It was just that after everything he'd put Lana through, he wasn't sure he had the right to fulfill that desire, even now that so much of the truth was already out.

"I'd like to," he told her. "Are you sure you're okay with it?"

She frowned. "I won't pretend it's easy for me."

"If I didn't love you and our kids, I would've left you for Josephine years ago, Lana."

"I know that. And Keith is as innocent in all of this as I am. But...it's still hard." She stared at the carpet for several seconds, then she lifted her gaze. "Go ahead," she said and left the room.

He listened to her steps fade down the hall before picking up the phone.

When Keith answered, he sounded surprised—which was nothing more than Hugh had expected. They hadn't spoken to each other since the funeral. "Hello?"

"Keith, it's Hugh."

"I figured as much. I don't get many calls from Australia. How are you?"

"Recovering somewhat. You?"

"I'm better than ever, actually—about to be married."

Hugh couldn't help smiling. "It's about time," he teased. "Who's the lucky lady?"

"Nancy Dellinger. You might've met her at Mom's funeral."

"I admit I wasn't paying much attention to the guests that day."

"Completely understandable." An awkward silence ensued, during which Hugh cast around for the best way to approach what he had to say. Keith eventually prompted him by asking, "What can I do for you?"

He almost chickened out, then cleared his throat. "I have something to tell you, Keith. Something that might be rather...upsetting—although I hope it won't be too terribly bad, given your age and the fact that you've already lost both parents."

"I'm listening," Keith said, but there was some re-serve in those words, some caution.

"I admit it's something I've wanted to address for quite a while."

Silence.

"Are you there?"

"Yeah, I'm here."

He fidgeted with the stamp dispenser on his desk. "Your mom and I—we were together a long time. I mean, it was in fits and starts but...we could never fully walk away from each other."

"How long?" he asked. "Pippa told me it was more than fifteen years."

"It was forty-two years, to be exact," he said. "I met her the same year I married Lana."

When Keith didn't respond right away, Hugh got the impression he was starting to catch on. "That's most of your life—and all of mine," Keith eventually said.

"Yes."

"Is there any significance in that?"

Unsure of how he might react, Hugh tightened his grip on the phone. "Yes," he said again.

"Are you saying that...that Malcolm wasn't my fa-ther?"

"*He* thought he was."

"I guess that's a no."

"There've never been any tests. We can do that if... if proving it matters to you. It isn't necessary for me."

He didn't respond.

"I'm sorry if this disappoints you, but... I was hoping you'd rather have a father who's alive, and who wants a relationship with you, than one who died so long ago."

Nothing.

"Malcolm was a good man," he went on. "I'm not trying to replace him. I'd just like to get to know you. But I'll completely understand if…if you're not interested."

When he still didn't get an answer, he figured that *was* his answer. "Okay, well, I'll be here if you change your mind," he said and was about to hang up when Keith finally spoke.

"The wedding's June 30. I'll send you an invitation."

Hugh got to his feet. "You'd like me to come?"

"Yeah. I'd like you to come."

Keith's voice had conviction in it, and that made Hugh feel the invitation was sincere. "Okay. Thank you. I'll be there," he said, and for almost the first time since he'd met Josephine, he felt he had his life back.

* * * * *

AUTHOR'S NOTE

If you've read any of my other books, you'll know I enjoy working with flawed characters. I think it's because I love a good "come from behind" win. The bigger the challenge, the sweeter the victory, and that's often how it goes in my stories. People figure out how to get on top of their lives, how to beat back their demons—let's face it, we all have them—and thrive. Nothing is more encouraging to me, so I hope you will enjoy this story about a man with a checkered past who finally comes to terms with his difficult upbringing and controlling mother—and finds love.

If you like this book, look for *The Secret Sister*, which is another Fairham Island story. And if you've already read that, maybe you'd enjoy a novel from my popular Whiskey Creek series, which focuses on a group of friends who've grown up together in a small town in California's Gold Country, not far from where I live.

I love to hear from my readers—and I always respond. Feel free to get in touch with me via my website at www.brendanovak.com. Enter my monthly drawing while you're there, and sign up for my mailing list so that I can send you an email whenever I have a new title out. You can also download a PDF of my entire book list, which, with more than fifty books in my backlist, is getting quite extensive.

I hope you enjoy your visit to Fairham Island!

Brenda Novak

QUESTIONS FOR DISCUSSION

1. One of the main themes of this novel is forgiveness. What would you say each character has to forgive? And do you feel that being able to forgive will improve their lives? In what ways?

2. Some people handle adversity better than others. Why do you think that's the case? What makes the difference? How can one person thrive in spite of their difficulties while others get crushed beneath them?

3. At times, we suffer from the bad decisions of those we love. It often doesn't seem fair and can cause quite a bit of resentment. What are the dangers of harboring resentment? What's one way you believe we can overcome resentment?

4. Most people believe that, to a greater or lesser degree, forgiveness should be part of everyone's life experience. But is there a line beyond which we are justified in holding a grudge? Do you feel that certain characters in this story crossed that line? If

so, which one(s)? Would you be able to forgive that person if you were in the same situation?

5. After reading *The Secrets She Kept*, do you feel any empathy for the person Josephine was? Why or why not?

6. Which character in this story did you empathize with most? Why?

7. Keith possesses some spectacular character traits—but those same traits can often become a stumbling block for him. Which traits would you say serve him well in some applications but trip him up in others?

8. They say "time heals all wounds." Arguably, the same could be said for love. Do you believe that's true? Why?